W9-AXO-413

Magic at the Gate

"The action-packed fifth Allie Beckstrom novel amps up the magical mayhem.... Allie's adventures are gripping and engrossing, with an even, clever mix of humor, love, and brutality." —*Publishers Weekly*

"Devon Monk takes her story to places I couldn't have dreamed of. Each twist and turn was completely surprising for me. *Magic at the Gate* truly stands out." —Reading on the Dark Side

"A spellbinding story that will keep readers on the edge of their seats." —Romance Reviews Today

Magic on the Storm

"The latest Allie Beckstrom urban fantasy is a terrific entry.... This is a strong tale." —Genre Go Round Reviews

"First-rate urban fantasy entertainment." —Lurv a la Mode

Magic in the Shadows

"Snappy dialogue, a brisk pace, and plenty of magic keep the pages turning to the end. Allie's relationships with Zayvion, her friend Nola, and the other Hounds add credible depth to this gritty, original urban fantasy that packs a punch." —Monsters and Critics

"This is a wonderful read full of different types of magic, fascinating characters, [and] an intriguing plot.... Devon Monk is an excellent storyteller.... This book will keep everyone turning the pages to see what happens next and salivating for more." —Fresh Fiction

continued ...

Magic to the Bone

"Brilliantly and tightly written . . . will surprise, amuse, amaze, and absorb readers." —*Publishers Weekly* (starred review)

"Loved it. Fiendishly original and a stay-up-all-night read. We're going to be hearing a lot more of Devon Monk."
— Patricia Briggs, *New York Times* bestselling author of *River Marked*

"Highly original and compulsively readable. Don't pick this one up before going to bed unless you want to be up all night!" —Jenna Black, author of *Sirensong*

"Gritty setting, compelling, fully realized characters, and a frightening system of magic-with-a-price that left me awed. Devon Monk's writing is addictive, and the only cure is more, more, more!"
— Rachel Vincent, *New York Times* bestselling author of *My Soul to Steal*

"An exciting new addition to the urban fantasy genre. It's got a truly fresh take on magic and Allie Beckstrom is one kick-ass protagonist!"
— Jeanne C. Stein, national bestselling author of *Crossroads*

"The prose is gritty and urban, the characters mysterious and marvelous, and Monk creates a fantastic and original magic system that intrigues and excites. A promising beginning to a new series. I'm looking forward to more!"
— Nina Kiriki Hoffman, Bram Stoker Award–winning author of *Meeting*

"Monk's reimagined Portland is at once recognizable and exotic, suffused with her special take on magic, and her characters are vividly rendered. The plot pulled me in for a very enjoyable ride!"
— Lynn Flewelling, author of *Glimpses*

Books by Devon Monk

The Allie Beckstrom Series
Magic to the Bone
Magic in the Blood
Magic in the Shadows
Magic on the Storm
Magic at the Gate
Magic on the Hunt
Magic on the Line

The Age of Steam
Dead Iron

Magic
on the
Line

An Allie Beckstrom Novel

Devon Monk

A ROC BOOK

ROC

Published by New American Library, a division of
Penguin Group (USA) Inc., 375 Hudson Street,
New York, New York 10014, USA

Penguin Group (Canada), 90 Eglinton Avenue East, Suite 700, Toronto,
Ontario M4P 2Y3, Canada (a division of Pearson Penguin Canada Inc.)
Penguin Books Ltd., 80 Strand, London WC2R 0RL, England
Penguin Ireland, 25 St. Stephen's Green, Dublin 2,
Ireland (a division of Penguin Books Ltd.)
Penguin Group (Australia), 250 Camberwell Road, Camberwell, Victoria 3124,
Australia (a division of Pearson Australia Group Pty. Ltd.)
Penguin Books India Pvt. Ltd., 11 Community Centre, Panchsheel Park,
New Delhi - 110 017, India
Penguin Group (NZ), 67 Apollo Drive, Rosedale, Auckland 0632,
New Zealand (a division of Pearson New Zealand Ltd.)
Penguin Books (South Africa) (Pty.) Ltd., 24 Sturdee Avenue,
Rosebank, Johannesburg 2196, South Africa

Penguin Books Ltd., Registered Offices:
80 Strand, London WC2R 0RL, England

First published by Roc, an imprint of New American Library,
a division of Penguin Group (USA) Inc.

First Printing, November 2011
10 9 8 7 6 5 4 3 2 1

For my family

Acknowledgments

Without the many people who have contributed time and energy along the way, this book would not have come to fruition. I'd like to give a much-deserved thank-you to my agent, Miriam Kriss, and my editor, Anne Sowards, two consummate professionals and all-around awesome people who make my job easy.

My love and endless gratitude go out to my fantastic first readers and brainstormers, Dean Woods and Dejsha Knight, whose loving support and brilliant insights not only make the story stronger, but also make me a better writer. Thank you also to my family, one and all, who have been there for me every step of the way offering unfailing encouragement and sharing in the joy. To my husband, Russ, and sons, Kameron and Konner, if I haven't said it lately, thank you for believing in me. You are the very best part of my life. I love you.

Lastly, but certainly not leastly, thank you, dear readers, for letting me share this story, these people, and this world with you.

Chapter One

It had taken Bartholomew Wray, the overseer of Portland's Authority, who was apparently my new boss, exactly forty-eight hours to contact me for a standard-procedure meet and greet.

By "contact," I mean he sent to my door two goons who asked me if my name was Allison Beckstrom, if I was the daughter of Daniel Beckstrom, and if my civilian job was Hounding. I said yes to all three, which scored me the grand prize of a meet and greet. And by meet and greet, I mean small room, bright light, two-way glass, and interrogative Truth spells that would be illegal if anyone knew about them.

The room itself wasn't too bad—a conference area on the sixth floor, tucked away behind the very real attorney's office in smack-center downtown Portland. A redwood and marble table took up the middle of the room, while bookshelves on three of the walls bulged with gold-embossed leather volumes that I bet no one had touched since they'd been shelved. The other wall held two tall windows, blinds closed tight.

The carpet was burgundy with whorls of gold at the edges. It gave the whole room a gilded-picture-frame feel, and it was so thick, I felt like I was wading through loose sand when I walked across it.

I had been escorted by the goons, who were both taller and wider than me and had opted for the twinsy look in matching black suits, white shirts, and black ties, topped off with the standard secret-bodyguard accessory: reflective sunglasses. The heavier, darker-featured goon on my left smelled of garlic and pepperoni, while the blond, acne-scarred goon on my right smelled like brown sugar and pork.

My escorts walked with me down the length of the redwood table to an unassuming little black walnut desk in the corner.

Goon Two waved a hand toward the plain leather chair, and I sat. I'd tried conversation in the car, tried conversation during the six flights of stairs (no, I had not let them talk me into riding an elevator). By the second floor, it was pretty clear they were paid to keep the chit-chat to a minimum.

I leaned back and didn't ask questions while the goons positioned themselves at each end of the room. One stood next to the door we'd entered through; the other took the door directly opposite.

And then they started casting magic—something in the Privacy spell category. It was aimed at the room in general, not me specifically, which was good. If they tried to work a spell on me, they'd be in for a helping of hurt.

That they were casting a spell wasn't all that unusual. That they were working it *together* piqued my interest. They started the spell small, and when the magic they cast sizzled like a cheap sparkler, Goon One canceled his spell and adjusted what he was tracing to make it more closely match Goon Two's spell.

They were Contrasts. I hadn't seen a lot of magic users cast magic together—well, except for a few Soul Complements, me and Zayvion Jones included. Zay's best friend, Shamus Flynn, and I were Contrasts, which meant that sometimes we could make spells a hell of a lot stronger if we worked together, and sometimes magic backfired and blew things up.

But the goons had it down to a routine. All through the cast, and it seemed to be a long and complicated spell, Goon One kept an eye out for things going wrong—like all the oxygen getting burned out of the room—and negated it before it became a full-force killer.

And then they were done weaving the spell between themselves and throughout the room. They both said a word, a single syllable, and my ears were stuffed with cotton. I swallowed hard, tasted the chemical sting of the combined magic—like they'd just drenched the room in antiseptic—didn't like it much, and tried to get my ears to clear.

Should have packed some magical chewing gum.

"So now no one can hear us, see us, or probably remember us coming into the room," I said with all the boredom I felt at their theatrics. "Do we get to have our little chat now? And if we do, would one of you like to fill me in on why Mr. Bartholomew Wray wanted me to meet him here today?"

I didn't add "alone." And no, I hadn't told Zay or anyone else that I was coming here. One, it hadn't seemed like that big of a deal. The first time I'd gone to meet my teacher, Maeve Flynn, I hadn't alerted the search and rescue or anything. I figured the new boss of the Authority would be following the same rules he expected the rest of us in the Authority to follow.

And if he wasn't, I could more than handle myself.

I was no slouch with magic or a blade.

Also, I wasn't as alone as most people. My dead father had been possessing a corner of my brain for months—ever since a magic user had tried to raise him from the dead. He'd been pretty quiet lately, but I knew he was always there, listening.

The goons still weren't talking. "Listen," I said, "I wasn't the one who called this little barbecue. If he wants to talk to me, he knows where I live."

I stood.

Just as the door across the room opened.

In strolled Bartholomew Wray. I'd never met him, but that punch-in-the-stomach kick of recognition from my dad, who was still curled up and possessing a part of my brain, told me he knew the man.

Wray was about my dad's age, maybe a couple inches shorter than me, and dressed in a nice jacket and slacks, button-down shirt but no tie, collar undone. His receding hairline and the pompadour comb-back, which crested in a six-inch wave, only made the top of his head look too wide and his cheekbones too sharp above his narrow, pointed chin.

Eyes: watery blue. Lips: thin enough I was pretty sure they'd break under the weight of a smile.

"Ms. Beckstrom." He wasn't looking at me. He was reading the report in his hand. "Thank you for coming today. Please, sit—" This was when he glanced up.

And stopped dead in his tracks.

Shock, surprise, and then an uncomfortable half smile that he managed to prop up with a stiff sneer. "You certainly resemble your father."

Ah. Well, now I could assume they had not been friends. I wondered whether he held grudges.

"So I've been told," I said.

He adjusted one sleeve, catching at the cuff links there as if they were worry stones, and then motioned at the chair behind me. "Please, have a seat so we can begin."

I sat. "What are we beginning?"

He took the chair on the opposite side of the desk and one of the goons came over with two glasses of water, placing them on the coasters near each of us.

"Didn't they inform you?" He raised silver eyebrows and glanced at each of the goons in turn.

"They said it was a standard-procedure meeting of some kind," I said. "And I have no idea what that means."

He glanced back down at the report in his hands. "I'm not surprised. No one has been following procedure during the past five years, apparently. And no one has reported the lapse in discipline."

"Isn't that your job?"

He flicked a look at me.

"Supervising?" I said. "Which means working with the ground troops and maybe checking in every once in a while so you know when something isn't going right?"

"I have a large region to cover, Ms. Beckstrom," he said. "I can only focus on a specific problem, such as Portland, if it is brought to my attention. No one called me."

"And you haven't stopped by in the past five years."

He held my gaze for a long moment. I suddenly knew he and I would never be friends either.

"No one followed procedure and contacted me until things were in this sorry state of disarray." He sniffed and pulled a pen out of his breast pocket, clicking it three times and then poising it over the report.

"I'll need you to sign this form." He spun it in my direction and held out the pen for me.

I slipped the form off the desk and sat back to read it all the way down to the fine print. It gave him permission to work a Blood magic Truth spell on me. The fine print was all about how I wouldn't fight him, sue him, or complain if I found out he had me Closed for what I revealed while I was under its influence.

"No." I spun it back around in front of him.

His eyebrows notched up. "Do you understand that this form protects us both, and leaves a trail for other people to follow if anything goes wrong?"

"Yes. That's why I'm not signing it."

"I'm not certain you are aware of your position here, Ms. Beckstrom."

"Listen," I said. "I know you want to work a Truth on me. You want to know what happened out at the prison, and the Life well. You want to know what part I had in the fight and deaths at both places. Fine. I'll tell you. But I will not sign anything that connects me in writing to the Authority."

"That seems a strange stance to take since you are so very involved in the Authority, Ms. Beckstrom. As was your father."

"My father's dead. I'm sure he signed a lot of papers too, and some of those might have made a nice easy trail for the people who killed him. I Hound for a living, Mr. Wray. When you're in the business of tracking old spells—often illegal spells—back to the people who cast them, you don't want anyone to know where you've been, what other cases you're working, or who you let get stabby with Blood magic Truth. I won't leave a trail that would tie me to you."

"Very well, then." He reached down and opened a drawer in the desk. He shuffled past several files and finally pulled out a new form and began writing on it. "This indicates that the unnamed member of the Authority refused to sign but is willing to be questioned." He paused, while each of the goons in turn left his post and initialed the form; then he handed the form to me.

"Please read it."

I did so. More of the same legal mumbo jumbo, with the exact same small-print clause as the other form. I nodded.

"I'll initial that the unnamed read it and that it was witnessed by Mr. Harrison"—he nodded toward Goon One—"and Mr. Ladd"—he nodded toward Goon Two.

Well, at least I had their names now.

He initialed the paper, slipped it back into the file

folder on top of his desk along with the other unsigned form, and, after squaring the edge of the paper to properly align with the folder, sat back.

"Mr. Ladd," he said, "please inform Ms. Whit we are ready for her."

Goon Two turned and cast your basic Unlock, then opened the door behind him. The door's angle blocked my view, but in a minute a woman strolled in.

She was tall and big-boned, her sandy hair cut short and messy around her face, which seemed to be dominated by wide lips and a strong jaw, lending her a tomboy look, even though she must have been in her thirties. She had on a cardigan over a tank top and slacks, and running shoes. She wore very little makeup, and smiled appreciatively when she caught sight of me.

"I've been looking forward to meeting you," she said, striding over with her hand out to shake.

I stood. I was right. We were about the same height. Her hands were calloused enough that I noticed the rough ridges running like rings down her fingers and along her palm. I tried to think of what would make those kinds of wear marks. Came up blank.

"The famous Daniel Beckstrom's daughter," she said with a gold-star voice.

"Allie," I said. "Just Allie."

"Melissa," she said. "Whit." She searched my gaze for recognition, but I had none to give her. Not even Dad flinched at her name. No, he was being suspiciously quiet.

I just nodded.

"Well," she said, dropping my hand like I'd gone dead. "Are we ready?" She pulled a slick, thin Blood magic blade out of the hip sheath hidden by her sweater.

"Ms. Beckstrom has read the papers and signed off," Bartholomew said. "You may begin the Truth spell."

I'd wondered what she had to do with all this.

She glanced around the room, then rolled a chair from next to the table over to my side, positioning herself like a nurse about to take my blood pressure.

"Do you want me to use physical restraints?" she asked.

"What? No. Why would I want that?"

She glanced over at Bartholomew. He shrugged. "It's within her rights to refuse them."

"You're just casting Truth, right?" I asked.

"Yes. But it's a very . . . detailed spell," she said. "I wouldn't think anyone here would have used it. It's difficult," she said just in case I wasn't catching on. "But don't worry. I do this all the time. Haven't lost anyone yet. Well, not on accident." A smile stretched her lips just a smidgen too wide for the sane kind of happy.

I opened my mouth to tell her that maybe she could just hold off on the creepy Blood magic user shtick and let me get my own set of witnesses in the room to make sure nothing went horribly wrong. But with the first stroke of her knife through the empty air in front of me, she caught up the edge of the goons' spell that was still lying like a heavy cloak over the room and so, too, she caught up my ability to speak.

Another Contrast? The place was just crawling with them.

Then she slashed the knife across her hand, a straight line through the meat of all four fingers—that's what the calluses were from—and the blood blade drank down her offering of blood, mixing it into the spell she traced. A spell that locked me into the chair as surely as if she'd buckled me in and set a whale on my lap.

Her eyes were glassy, her lips forming the words of the spell even though she didn't so much as whisper.

She didn't have to. Magic followed each stroke of her blade, formed to the rhythm of her unspoken words. She closed the spell and Truth took hold like a vise on my head that squeezed at my temples.

Lovely.

"Set," she said. "Ask her anything you want. She'll tell the truth."

I heard the chair squeak as Bartholomew got up and sat on the corner of the desk. He moved my glass of water aside and brushed the condensation off his fingertips and onto his slacks.

"Tell me your name," he said.

"Allison Angel Beckstrom," I said.

"Yes." That was from Melissa.

Huh. So it wasn't just Truth. She was acting as a lie detector too. I'd never seen the spell used this way before—didn't know you could use Truth on someone without using at least a drop of their blood, and I had most certainly not let her cut me.

I wondered if Dad knew how this spell worked.

From the uncomfortable shifting of his thoughts in my head—some of which I caught—he did, and he thought it was oversanitized and outdated. A failed attempt to adapt a spell outside a specific discipline, which resulted in an inferior spell with an even higher pain price.

Terrific he had an opinion about it. Less terrific an inferior spell with a higher pain price was currently attached to my head.

"Were you involved in the battle at the Life well a few days ago?"

"Yes."

Melissa nodded.

Bartholomew rubbed at his cuff links again. Note to self: get into a high-stakes poker game with him. His tells were so loud I needed earplugs just to be in the same room with him.

"Tell me who was there."

"Everyone?" I asked. The vise on my head was starting to get uncomfortable. Inferior spell, wrong discipline meant the price of pain leaked to me. Faster would be better.

"Yes," he said.

So much for fast. This was going to take some time.

"Me, Zayvion Jones, Shamus Flynn, Terric Conley." That covered the current members of the Authority. Now to sum up the ex-members who were there. "Sedra Miller, Dane Lanister, some of Dane's men, and Roman Grimshaw. Also, there were some dead people there: Mikhail, Isabelle, Leander, and my dad."

"Your father?" Bartholomew asked.

Out of that entire list, the last four people were Veiled—ghosts of dead magic users who had been possessing the living. And of those four people—Mikhail, who had died years ago and was once the head of the Authority; Isabelle and Leander, who were the most powerful magic users in history, along with being two very sick and twisted souls bent on killing anyone in the way of their plans for ruling magic; and my father, who was a successful businessman—my dad, the most recently dead, was the only one who sparked Bartholomew's curiosity?

"Yes." Short, sweet, let's get this the hell over with.

"Where was your father?"

"Possessing me."

That got me a long, doubtful stare.

"Is he currently possessing you?"

"Yes." I was starting to sweat. The pain from the spell was growing stronger, sending out licking tendrils to burn down my neck.

"Let me speak to him."

"No." Hey, it was a Truth spell. I had to answer his questions truthfully. I didn't have to do what he told me to do. If he stacked Influence on top of this little bundle of fun, then things would be different.

But I hadn't signed up for anything except Truth. At so much as one Influency wiggle of his fingers, I would be so out of here.

"Why won't you let me speak to him?"

"Because I don't want to."

"Why?" The word pressed like he'd just put the heel of his palm against my forehead.

Ouch.

"Because I don't like him." Or you. Somehow I managed to shut my mouth before that last came out.

"If I forced the issue?" he asked.

"Do you have a form for that?"

The corner of his lips twitched, but it did not produce a smile. "Yes."

"I won't sign it."

"Perhaps another day," he said. "Tell me what happened at the well of Life."

I paused, trying to gather my thoughts. So much had happened that led up to the fight at the well, I wasn't even sure where to start. Jingo Jingo, one of Portland's powerful Death magic users, kidnapped the head of the Authority, Sedra Miller. Sedra had been possessed for years (though we hadn't known it) by Isabelle, who was waiting for Leander to return to life. Probably me stepping through the gates into death to save Zayvion's soul had done something to let Leander into this world. Not that we'd figured that out before we'd ended up having to buddy up with Roman Grimshaw, the ex-con Guardian of the gates, whom we'd accidentally helped escape from prison, and Mikhail, Sedra's long-dead lover, who was hell-bent on killing Isabelle and saving Sedra's soul even if that meant possessing and nearly killing Shame.

Brevity. I needed it.

"When we walked into the room above the well, I

saw Sedra Miller and her bodyguard, Dane Lanister. Several of Dane's men were already dead. Sacrificed, I think, for the spells they were casting so that Leander and Isabelle could both possess Sedra at the same time."

"Who was with you?"

"I just told you that."

"Who among you was possessed?"

He had to have heard this before. At least three times, from Shame, Terric, and Zay. I was the last of the people directly involved in the fight to be called in. And they'd all told me they'd gone over the exact same story with him. No surprises were going to come to light from this. We were all telling the truth, under the geis of a Truth spell. Even though it was a crappily constructed spell, it still did the job.

"My dad possessed me," I said. "Mikhail possessed Shame Flynn, and Leander and Isabelle possessed Sedra Miller."

"Yes," Melissa said.

"Continue, and do speak up." He fingered the cuff links. What? Did he have a recording device hooked up to them? "What happened after you walked into the chamber?"

"Sedra Miller—who was possessed by Isabelle—said she was going to kill us all, and especially Mikhail, whom she knew was possessing Shame. She said that she and Leander were going to rule all magic."

I swallowed, and took my time to inhale and exhale a couple times. The pain was getting worse, skittering out along my shoulders, but I was good at handling pain. Hounds almost always Proxied the pain of their own spells, unlike most magic users I'd met in the Authority, who hired out for Proxy.

I glanced at Melissa. She was sweating, smiling. I could smell the pain on her and knew she was carrying at least some cost of this spell. It didn't seem to bother

her. As a matter of fact, from the way she licked her lips, and from how dilated her pupils were, it looked like she was enjoying the pain.

Masochist. Probably cast the crappy pain-leaking spell on purpose.

"And what did you do?" Bartholomew asked.

"We fought them, Zayvion, Roman, Terric, Shame-Mikhail, and I. We used magic and our weapons and it almost wasn't enough. They almost killed us. All of us. Zayvion and Roman were able to take care of the Veiled who Leander and Isabelle dragged out of the well. Shame-Mikhail and Terric fought Sedra-Isabelle and Leander. They were able to force Leander to exit Sedra's body. He then attacked me. I was already a little busy dealing with Dane, who had brought a gun to the fight along with magic. Leander somehow pulled me out of my body. I almost died."

I swallowed, tasting the acrid burn of that memory on the back of my throat as if I were still standing in that underground room, filled with magic, the dead and dying, and trying to decide if I should return to my own body or join with Zayvion and be with him forever as one.

"Things got a little blurry for a bit," I said. "But I know Shame-Mikhail eventually forced Isabelle out of Sedra's body. That's how Sedra died. I think Mikhail crossed over into death with her soul. I didn't see how Roman got away. But I know Leander and Isabelle didn't just walk into death. I think they might still be loose. Here. Maybe in the city."

"Yes," Melissa said again.

"How did Dane Lanister die?"

"I didn't see it." That was true. But I knew how he died. Zayvion shot him through the head because Leander had possessed Dane and was using him to remove my soul from my body.

He considered that answer. And I waited for the big questions: why did we let Leander and Isabelle slip through our fingers? Why did we break into the prison filled with magical criminals and not only ended up with ex–Authority members Greyson and Chase dead but also set the spirit of Leander and the ex–Guardian of the gates, Roman, free? Why did we join up with Mikhail—the dead, exiled ex–head of the Authority—and Roman, both of whom were considered enemies to the Authority?

But all he said was, "Very well. Just one more question, Ms. Beckstrom. How long have you been possessed by your father?"

It took me a second to count back. "Six months or more."

"But your father died eight months ago."

"Yes."

"Tell me, how is it he possessed you?"

"How do you not know this? Maeve sent you reports on me, even before I started training with her."

"If I wanted Maeve Flynn's information, I would have asked her here and put her under a Truth spell." He didn't say it like he was angry, or concerned. Which was what bothered me. This man was above us, all of us here in the Authority. He could, and from that statement would, do anything he wanted to us. And there was nothing we could do about it.

"Tell me how your father possessed you," he repeated.

The pain kicked up a notch or twelve as it snapped along my ribs. I breathed through it. In through the nose, out through the nose.

"I don't know how he did it." Calm, clear. Like I wasn't hurting enough to scream. Go, me.

"Surely you must have some memory of when and how it happened," he pressed. "I understand you keep notes. In a notebook, I believe."

"Dad's dead body was on a slab. Frank Gordon, who was a member of the Authority at the time, was using magic, light, dark, Life, Death, and I don't know what else. I didn't know it then, and I don't know now what he was trying to do. Maybe he was trying to bring my dad back to life. Maybe not. I was there trying to save some girls who had been kidnapped and were being used as Proxy victims.

"Dad stepped into my head. I don't know how. He's never told me."

Bartholomew narrowed his eyes, then shifted his look to Melissa.

"Yes," she said, sounding a little surprised.

Right. Mr. Wray needed a second opinion on whether I was telling the truth. For a man who had risen in power and status over people I considered wickedly deadly with magic, it was a real disconnect to see him needing a second opinion on anything magical.

Maybe he wasn't good at Truth spells. Or maybe he sucked at magic. I wondered if someone could brown-nose his way up the Authority's ladder.

"Thank you, Ms. Beckstrom. That will be all for today." He stood and I looked over at Melissa.

She was practically glossy with sweat, her cheeks hot red. And she was smiling all the way back to her molars.

"How'd you like it?" she asked.

"I didn't," I replied, well, truthfully.

"I'm so sorry," she said with no remorse. "This might sting a little."

She slashed her knife through the air, breaking the Truth spell. The spell backlashed so hard, a hot line of pain whipped across my chest.

I hissed.

She faked a little surprise. "Oh, I'm so sorry. I didn't know it would kick like that."

Lying bitch.

The weight of the spell took a couple seconds to lift, but finally my head, my body were mine to move again. I stood and brushed my hair back behind one ear while I reached for my backpack.

I turned and headed to the door. Goons or no goons, I was not staying here a second longer.

"Ms. Beckstrom," Bartholomew said.

I paused in front of the goon who was blocking the door. Clenched my hand to keep from throwing magic at him, and turned to look at Bartholomew.

"I want you to know that I am going to do everything in my power to clean up the mess you and the other members of Portland's Authority have made. And if you cooperate, I am confident we will find a place for you and your skills within the organization."

Sounded like a threat to me. "And if I don't cooperate?"

His eyebrows hitched up, stacking wrinkles up to his hairline. "If you don't cooperate, you will expedite procedures that will put your file and service on review. And with the current state of things, I do not think the results of your continued . . . service would be favorable."

"Good to know," I said.

He gestured at Goon Two to open the door for me, which he did.

I stormed out of there and through the attorney's office, not caring whether it would blow Bartholomew's cover. My head was pounding and I was shaking from after-pain sweats—that I-want-to-crawl-into-bed-and-not-come-out-for-a-week kind of feeling. The backlash in the middle of my chest from the spell still burned hot—it was either blistering or would soon—from my belly up between my breasts to my collarbone. She'd broken that spell with the intent to make me hurt.

And on top of all that I was angry. Angry at myself for going there alone. I'd watched my father in enough business negotiations to know you should always, *always* bring a witness into any contentious situation. And I was angry at Bartholomew for being a dick.

Zayvion had said as much, though in a politically correct sort of way. I should have paid attention. I should have had him come in with me.

"Beckstrom!"

I stopped. I was on the street outside the lawyer's office. Somehow got down all six flights of stairs without paying a damn bit of attention. That kind of detail tracking would get me killed.

Could this day get worse?

I glanced at the people walking the streets, then over at the cars.

"Hey!" The voice called out again. And then I spotted him.

Anthony Bell, the kid who wanted to be a Hound. The kid who had been involved with Frank Gordon, kidnapping and killing those girls to try to raise my dad from the dead. The kid who my friend Martin Pike had tried to help out—and instead had died for—was walking my way, smiling.

He had on jeans, a white T-shirt, and a dark hoodie. Walking next to him was a woman who looked enough like him that I figured she was his mom.

"Allie," he said. "I was gonna stop by and talk to you. This is my mother. Mom, this is Allie. Beckstrom."

"Marta," she said, leaning forward to shake my hand. I shook. Her hand was warm around my icy palm.

"Nice to meet you," I said, trying to get my social norms in line.

"Anthony told me you were considering letting him job-shadow a Hound," she said.

"Really?" I leveled a look at Ant.

"No, Mom," he said. "I told you I was gonna ask her for a job shadow."

"Listen," I said to both of them. "We've talked about this. I don't think Hounding is a first-choice career move. And I told Anthony that I wouldn't even consider his Hounding with my—" What did I call us? Group? Union? Pack? "With me and the other Hounds until he got out of high school."

Marta was nodding and nodding, and beaming with pride. "And he did!" she said. "My boy finally got tired of acting out, got cleaned up, and finished his school. Look." She dug in the massive purse hanging off her shoulder and pulled out a cell phone.

"Just last week. Isn't he handsome?"

"Mom," Anthony moaned.

I glanced down at the cell phone. A photo of Anthony in graduation robe and cap smiled back at me.

"He's been looking forward to talking to you about the job shadow," she continued.

"I don't—," I started.

"I know it's a lot to ask. After everything that has happened." She didn't look away from my gaze, which I respected. Her son carried a big share of the blame for why Pike was killed. But he wasn't the only reason for it. Pike had confronted the killer alone with no one to back him up.

Hounds are stupid like that.

"It would mean so much to him, and to me," she said, "if you would give him this chance. Just a trial run for a month or so."

I shook my head. "I still don't think Hounding is a long-term line of work."

"I just need a start," Ant said. "A few weeks' training. I just want a few weeks' training. Enough so I know."

"So you know what?" I asked.

"If I can do it like Pike said I could."

Shit. I could make it easy on him and on me and just

tell him he couldn't. But Pike had told me Anthony was good, and might even be a really good Hound if he could get his life together.

Taking on another responsibility was the last thing I needed. There was no chance in hell I was going to let him follow me around. And I couldn't leave him alone in a room with the Hound who usually followed me around, Davy Silvers. Davy had idolized Pike and blamed Ant for his death. He'd throw Ant out a window first chance he got.

I supposed there were other Hounds I could buddy him up with. Sid Westerly was pretty even-headed. He could probably take Ant in for a few weeks and show him the ropes. And Sid did some kind of computer programming on the side. Maybe he could push Ant toward a better sort of career and get him out of my hair for good.

"Fine," I said. "Call me before you come by the den. I'll talk to a couple people and see who's up for a shadow. Nice meeting you," I said to his mother.

"You too," she said. "Thank you, Ms. Beckstrom. Martin always spoke so highly of you and now I know why."

I smiled and tried not to let my real feelings show. I didn't think she understood how dangerous it was to be a Hound. Was pretty sure she didn't know the suicide rate, or the burnout that drove anyone with any sense out of the business. No, from her genuine smile, I could tell she saw this as a chance for her son to follow his dreams and make something out of his life.

Considering the road he had been headed down—magical crime, jail time, probably death—Hounding looked positively civilized.

"Thank you," I said. "Remember, Bell—call. If you show up unannounced, I will not be responsible for how you are greeted."

He nodded. He knew Davy hated him. Knew the other Hounds probably didn't like him much either. "Got your number. I'll call."

I strode down the street toward the MAX stop. The wind, warmer now that May was almost done, picked up and brought with it the smell of the bakery on the corner. My stomach cramped at the buttery toasted smell of bread and I considered stopping to get something to eat. It was almost noon, and I hadn't had anything but coffee today. But I'd promised Zayvion I'd meet him for lunch at the Works.

No time to go home and change out of my sweaty clothes, I caught the next train and hoped Zay wouldn't notice just how sick I looked and felt.

But by the time the MAX dropped me off half a block from the restaurant, I was feeling even worse. Fever must have set in from that crappy magic spell. Plus, the burn down my chest was making it painful to move my arms. I don't know how that bitch Melissa managed to make me bear so much of the cost of that damn Truth spell. I didn't like it. If that's the way the new management was going to run things, I wanted no part of it.

I tucked my hands deeper into my jacket pockets and put my head down against the wind that seemed colder than it had just a few minutes ago.

I was in a bad mood and going downhill fast.

I didn't even see the guy striding toward me. Didn't expect him to hit me in the gut. I stumbled back, one arm thrown over the echoing agony in my stomach and chest. Managed not to go to my knees, but was slow on the recovery. He was fast, came in close. Close enough I got a lungful of the rotted smell of death and body odor that stank so bad my eyes watered.

Close enough I could see the weird green glow of

magic flash in his eyes. A green glow I'd only ever seen from the Veiled.

He grabbed my backpack and took off running. I turned and traced a Tracking spell, but as soon as I called on magic my arm went numb. Too damn much pain in too short of a time. I botched the spell, swore, tried again, and still didn't get it right.

Finally nailed it on the third time. But by then he had disappeared, leaving me nothing, and no one to track.

Chapter Two

There wasn't anything except my sweaty gym clothes and a couple oranges in the backpack. My phone, money, and journal were all in my jacket pocket, where I always kept them.

But in all my life living in Portland, I had never had anyone steal my purse or backpack.

I guess it was that, or the fever, that left me more confused than angry as I walked, a little more carefully, and with one arm protectively across my stomach, down to the restaurant.

The Works was a nice little sandwich shop squished between two larger businesses. On good days, like today, they put two tables out front so people could take in the nice weather. The tables were out, and one was occupied, but not by Zayvion.

So I took myself inside.

Inside was larger than it looked, owing mostly to the high ceiling with skylights and slowly spinning fans. Soft music of a slightly Celtic origin played, and somewhere to the side a fountain poured water over stones.

It had been a couple years since I'd come here. I was suddenly really glad Zayvion had suggested it.

Zayvion sat across the room to the left, near the fountain and, as was his habit, where he could see the door and out the windows. He had on a green T-shirt that looked good against his dark skin and was tight enough to show he was in excellent shape. His ratty blue coat was hooked over the back of his chair.

He and I had been lovers and more—Soul Complements—for long enough, it was hard for me to imagine my life without him. He'd been there when I'd channeled a wild magic storm, lost most my memories of him, of us, and knocked myself into a coma. I'd convinced him we were worth a second chance, and he'd agreed, even though being with him, and knowing who he really was—Guardian of the gates, the Authority's go-to enforcer of law and order—meant I'd gotten mixed up with all the secret magic user Authority stuff too.

Not that I would have been able to avoid getting mixed up in it all. I was a Beckstrom. We seemed destined to attract trouble.

I lifted a hand in a wave as I walked over to him.

His smile faded to a frown, then a scowl. He stood.

I'm a tall woman. Zay still had an inch or two on me. And when it came to sheer intimidating width of shoulders and don't-fuck-with-me bouncer vibe, he had me beat flat.

"What happened?" he asked as he pulled a chair out for me.

Have I mentioned those old-fashioned manners of his? So cute.

"Bartholomew called me in today."

"Allie . . . ," he began.

"You don't have to tell me what an idiot I am." There was a cup of coffee, black, and a glass of water on the table in front of me. Zay had drinks on his side of the table, so I guessed he had ordered for me. I lifted the water. Drank a sip to see if I was going to be able to keep it down. My stomach hurt. Inside and outside.

"You went alone." He wasn't asking.

"Yes. You didn't tell me how bad it would hurt."

He tipped his head a little like he hadn't heard me right. "It hurt?"

Oh, wow. He was going to snap the coffee cup in half, one-handed.

"Yes. And it's over. But my chest still hurts. Zay, put the cup down. You're going to crush the nice china."

He put the cup down. "And?"

"And some guy on the street stole my backpack."

"And?"

"And he hit me."

"Bartholomew?"

"No, the guy on the street. Oh, don't look like that. It was a slug in the stomach. If I wasn't already sore, I wouldn't have lost my breath." If I wasn't already sore and sick from the Truth spell, I probably would have seen him coming and could have blocked him before he got close enough to touch me.

Those were the things I didn't say. See? I still had some sense in my head.

"Did you recognize him?" he asked in a very reasonable voice considering the anger I could feel wafting off him like steam. That was one thing about being a Soul Complement—you could feel the other person's emotions. And sometimes, when Zayvion and I touched, we could each hear what the other was thinking.

"No."

"Could you identify him in a morgue?"

"Funny. I'll file a police report later. There was nothing valuable in my bag. Right now I just want to hold still for a couple minutes."

He leaned both elbows on the table and folded two fingers over his mouth. He didn't say anything, just watched while I picked up my coffee cup, took a tiny sip, and then put it back down. For once, coffee wasn't making everything better.

I glanced at Zay, who was still staring at me, and then

tried my water. Cool, clean, it seemed to go down a little better than the coffee. I closed my eyes, savoring the momentary peace, letting the soft music and gurgle of the fountain take my day away.

One of Zay's hands rested gently on my shoulder, the other on my elbow. "Let's go."

I hadn't heard him get up. He's quiet, yes. But I should have heard his chair slide back. I might have drifted off for a second.

"We haven't had lunch," I complained.

"I'll order in."

And then he was helping me out of the chair and across the room, two things I hated to admit I needed.

"Almost there," he said after we'd been walking for a while. He had parked around the corner, and it didn't take long to get to his car. He opened the car door for me. I eased into the seat with a grateful sigh and closed my eyes again.

"Tired," I said, or thought I said.

I woke up when the engine turned off. Zay was talking on his cell phone. Apparently someone was going to meet us somewhere.

"What's up?" I asked. The sleep had helped with the pain and cleared my head enough for me to know I had really checked out there for a while. Whatever had been laced in that Truth spell was a hell that just kept on giving.

"Dr. Fisher is going to take a look at you." He pocketed his cell phone. "Think you can walk?"

"I'm sore, I'm not dead."

He just gave me a steady look.

"What?" I asked.

He reached over and gently drew his fingers across my forehead and tucked my hair behind my ear. I loved it when he did that. It was sweet, intimate. But his fingers felt like ice. Zay never had cold fingers.

So, that would be an affirmative on the fever.

Lovely.

"You done arguing?" he asked. "'Cause I can wait until you get it all out."

I thought it over. He wasn't joking, and since I had a good hour or three worth of complaints, I gave in. "Fine," I said with a sigh.

Zay got out of the car and a rush of air stabbed in like an arctic breeze. I knew it wasn't really that cold out there. The fever made every stray breeze hurt. I zipped my jacket all the way up to my chin and put my hood over my head.

Stupid air.

I reached over to open the door, but Zay was already there, one hand reaching down for me.

I took his hand. Walking wasn't as bad as I'd expected, but my stomach and chest stretched in painful opposition with every step. It felt like my skin was going to rip open if I moved too fast.

"Did you use magic today?" he asked me once we had entered Dr. Fisher's office.

"Not really."

"So, yes?"

"I tried to Track the guy who grabbed my backpack but didn't get it right in time. I didn't use the Truth spell. They used it on me, but since I paid the price for it, I guess that sort of counts."

"More than sort of," he said.

Dr. Fisher's office was on the ground level, surprisingly warm with dark red accent walls and burnt orange, creams, and brown. Plants took up the rest of the decor and made the space feel less like a doctor's office. There was no one waiting in the lobby.

Zay walked with me up to the receptionist, who was behind a counter.

"Allison Beckstrom to see Dr. Fisher," Zay said.

She checked her computer and nodded. "Go right in. Last door at the end of the hall."

We headed off that way. About two steps into it, Zay wrapped his arm around me and I slipped my hand into his back pocket.

Nice. He was warm, smelled of pine and coffee. I could feel his anger radiating through his calm exterior.

"I'm fine," I said.

"Mmm." He opened the door at the end of the hall. The room looked like most of the other doctor's rooms I'd been in except this was painted a warm taupe and the windows, set high where the wall met the ceiling, were curtained. Also, it was large enough I didn't immediately feel the tickle of claustrophobia down my throat.

An examination table stretched in the middle of the room, and a small desk and two chairs took the other corner. I eyed the examination table, and instead took one of the chairs by the desk.

Zay paced around the room, restless as a tiger in a cage.

"What did they ask you?" he said quietly while studying a chart that mapped the three basic Syphon spells and the circulatory system.

"What happened at the wells." I kept my voice low. Dr. Fisher worked for the Authority, so it was a pretty safe bet her room wasn't bugged by the police. Still, the majority of her patients were not a part of and didn't know about the secret group of magic users—or how those people could use magic. It was worth staying cautious.

"Anything specific?" he asked.

"Who was there. How Dane and Sedra died. A lot about my dad—how he possessed me, if he still possessed me. That kind of thing." I ran my hand back through my hair, pulling it up off my neck, then letting it fall again. I was tired of hurting.

"Did he ask about Leander and Isabelle?"

"Not much. That's weird, isn't it?" Leander and Isabelle seemed to me to be the biggest danger, and the biggest problem we were dealing with right now. Not my dad.

Zay stopped staring at the chart and leaned against an open space on the wall. "I don't think he's convinced that Leander and Isabelle are really loose in this world."

"Excuse me? He doesn't believe you? Or Victor?" I said. "What about Terric or, hell, Shame? We've all told him the same thing—the truth."

Zay frowned. "He hasn't said he believes any of us."

"Hello? Truth spells. How could we lie?"

"His job isn't to believe us—even under Truth. It's to stop the hemorrhaging of deaths, to end the magic battles, join the factions, and make this branch of the Authority strong again. He wants to do that before someone above him notices the problems and before the public is harmed or finds out about us."

"We're on his side. We want all that too," I said.

He shrugged. "He's the Watch, Allie. They see things differently."

There was a soft knock on the door and Dr. Fisher walked into the room. She looked tired but she smiled, her strong, yet motherly face falling quickly into concern.

The door shut behind her and I smelled the slight metallic spark of magical wards and locks activating.

"Who has been casting magic on you?" No preamble. I liked that about her.

"Melissa Whit."

"Missy knows better than this." Dr. Fisher sat in the other chair across from me and dug something out of a locked desk drawer. It was a chain of beads, separated by gold, copper, and silver links. The beads were either crystal or glass, round and flat and the size of her thumbnail.

Each bead was etched with what looked like glyphs.

"Hold this in your right hand, curled in your palm," she said.

I took the necklace and swirled it onto my palm. It was heavier than it looked, and warm.

"I'm going to cast an Activation spell," she said. "You shouldn't feel anything at all. If you do, let me know immediately."

She inhaled, paused—probably to set the Disbursement of what price she'd pay or to make sure she knew how she was going to Proxy the pain of the spell—then drew a fluid, clean-lined spell in the air between us.

The beads in my hand went individually warmer or colder, which was weird but not extreme. And then three beads glowed neon blue.

"It's glowing," I said, kind of amazed. I'd never seen a necklace react to a spell like this.

"That's what I was hoping for." She leaned forward, studied the beads but did not touch my hand, or even exhale.

She sat back, cast another spell, and the beads stopped glowing. "Let me have that."

I gave her the necklace and rubbed my palm over my jeans. It hadn't hurt, it just felt heavy with untapped magic. Made me a little itchy.

"Zayvion, would you please stand behind her, and Ground if needed?"

"What are you going to do?" I asked. Sure, I trusted her, but this was magic we were talking about, and my latest brush with it—well, before the beads—hadn't gone so great.

"I'm going to set a Dispel to get the residue of that spell off you."

"Like a Syphon?"

"Yes, but more gentle."

Gentle sounded good. I nodded.

Zayvion placed his palm on my right shoulder. He wasn't Grounding me yet, so I didn't feel mint from his touch.

Dr. Fisher pulled magic from the networks surrounding the building as if she were selecting a book from a shelf, and cast Dispel.

I braced for the sensation of magic surrounding me, but instead felt a light breeze wrap from my feet up to my head and then pull away, taking the ache with it.

I was covered in sweat, my T-shirt soaked through. The fever had broken.

"How's that feel?" she asked.

"Really good," I said. "Even my chest feels better."

"Your chest is bothering you?" she asked. "In what way?"

"The spell hurt the most there. When Melissa broke it—the spell, not my chest—it burned."

Zay's hand tightened on my shoulder.

"Let me take a look." She stood. "I can get you a gown to change into."

"No, that's fine. I have a bra on. Zay, you're going to have to let go of my shoulder so I can get my shirt off."

He removed his hand. Didn't say anything. But I'd learned a long time ago that when that man went silent, someone was going to turn up dead.

I got my arms out of my coat and left it in the chair behind me. My shoulders didn't hurt to move. That was something, right? I pulled my shirt up and off over my head and looked down at my chest for the first time since the Truth spell. "Well, shit."

A wide red welt plunged from the top of my right shoulder between my breasts and down to the edge of my jeans.

"Let's get you on the table so I can look at that a little closer," Dr. Fisher said.

Zay had paced around from behind me and taken a look at my injury.

Man was not happy. Man looked like he was going to break someone.

"It's fine," I said, trying to pull my shirt back over my head and doing a poor job of it. "I'm fine. It's going to be fine." My brain finally caught up with my mouth and I realized I'd said the same thing three times. I was babbling. Worried and feeling exposed. I didn't like people seeing my wounds. Didn't like showing the pain that magic put me through.

"Allie," Zayvion said so softly it was no more than a breath. He held out his hand and nodded at the table. Didn't say anything else, but I saw the sparks of gold in his eyes.

I'd probably have had to knock him down to get out of the room. Dr. Fisher was already standing and talking about it not looking to be too bad of a wound, but she just wanted to check it out to make sure.

For the record, I didn't know who she was talking to because I hadn't heard her, and I was pretty sure Zay didn't believe her.

I was certain neither of them would let me go without her finishing the exam. I took Zay's hand and stood. He walked with me over to the table like he was delivering me down the aisle at a shotgun wedding.

"For cripes' sake," I said, climbing up on the table and lying back. "It's a burn. I've been burned by magic lots of times."

"Never hurts to be careful," Dr. Fisher said. She put on a pair of latex gloves and stood at the side of the bed farthest from the door. She leaned over a bit and studied the burn.

"Does it hurt?"

"Not as much. It was burning a lot when it happened. And afterward for a while."

She pressed one finger gently on the mark. "Does this make it worse?"

"It kind of stings. Listen," I said, looking from her to Zayvion and back. "It's not bad. It feels like the burns I've gotten from the Veiled, only bigger. Those always go away in a week. I'm sure it's fine."

Dr. Fisher nodded. "I'm going to press along the entire burn. Let me know if the pain gets more severe anywhere, or if you are unable to feel my touch."

She did so, working from my shoulder down to my hip.

"Do the muscles hurt when you bend or breathe?"

"Not anymore."

"And what changed that?"

"The Dispel you cast."

"Is there any area that's more tender?"

"No," I said. "It's all sore."

"All right." She took off her gloves and threw them away, then washed her hands at the sink in the corner. "I'm going to give you some burn cream. Non-magic. It should help you heal faster. You," she said, pulling a sample box out of the cupboard, "will call me if you feel any worse than you do at this moment."

"Sure." I sat up and pulled my shirt back over my head. Zay, who hadn't said a word, handed me my coat.

I put it on and gave him a look. "You okay?"

He smiled. There was nothing but anger in his eyes. "All good."

Dr. Fisher glanced over at him, but didn't say anything. Zay was usually good at hiding his emotions. Not right now.

"So, will you both be attending the funeral tonight?" she asked as she walked over to me with the sample cream.

At that, Zayvion completely closed down. No more

anger in his eyes. No pain, no sorrow. Which was a lie. The funeral was for Chase. She had been killed because of all the crap going on with the Authority. Chose the wrong side of the fight. Since her lover and Soul Complement, Greyson, was on the side she had chosen, I couldn't really blame her. When Leander decided that possessing Greyson was his best option, he'd killed Chase with her lover's own hands.

Chase used to be a Closer, trained beside Zayvion, was his lover before she dumped him for Greyson. He used to love her. Maybe part of him still did.

"We'll be there," I said. "Are we done?" I held up the cream.

"That should be it," Dr. Fisher said.

"Thank you."

I got off the table. My stomach and chest didn't hurt as much as before, but the fever had left me weak, hungry, and tired. I'd take any one of those over the pain. As far as I was concerned I'd come out on the sunny side of this situation. I had a feeling Zayvion didn't share my opinion.

He didn't say anything as we walked down the hall, but from the pressure of his arm around my back, fingers hooked into the belt loop of my jeans, he was full into angry and protective mode, heading straight for furious and overbearing.

Three people sat at a distance from one another in the waiting room, two reading magazines, one talking on her cell phone. None of them looked up at us as we walked through.

I shifted a little away from Zay's grip as we reached the street, but he pulled me in closer and silently walked the half block or so—I didn't remember walking that far when we got here—to his car.

He opened the door, and stood there, holding it and watching me as I got in the car, like he expected me to fly into bits at any moment. It was sweet. And annoying.

"I'm fine, Jones," I said. "Let it go."

He opened his mouth and took a breath, then looked up like he'd heard a sudden noise. He scanned the street and buildings around us, looked back at me, flat, expressionless. Except for the chips of gold glinting in his eyes.

Man had a choke hold on anger. "Let it go" was not in his repertoire at the moment.

He strode around the front of the car, got in, and started the engine.

"Where would you like to go?" he asked.

"Home." I opened the glove box, which contained a neat stack of paper, a pen, and was otherwise clean and dust free. I was starving. I had an orange in my backpack, but that was long gone now. "Got anything to eat in here?"

"No. What do you want?"

"A burger. Anything."

He took the next turn and headed away from the general direction of my apartment but toward the general direction of fast food.

"So are you going to smolder or are you going to talk about it?" I asked.

"About what?"

"Whatever you are so damn angry about." I could usually get a good read on him—hell, we could usually hear each other's thoughts if we were touching—but he had closed down so tight that it was uncomfortable, bordering on claustrophobic, to be in this small space with him and his anger.

"No."

"Fine." He wasn't the only one in a bad mood. I was too hungry, too tired, and too damn cranky to pry anything out of him.

He pulled onto Hawthorne and into a Burgerville drive-through.

"What do you want?"

"Pepper bacon cheeseburger, Coke, large fries."

He ordered that and nothing else.

"Hunger strike?" I was pretty sure he hadn't had lunch—we were supposed to meet for that, and there wasn't time for more than a sip of coffee before he whisked me off to the doctor.

"Not much of an appetite. I'll eat . . . later."

"That pause something I should worry about?"

He turned and gave me a smile. "Of course not."

And that said it all. There was more than a pause to worry about. That man had the look of vengeance.

"Holy crap, Zay, can't you just drop this? I got hurt by magic. Whoop-de-doo. I always get hurt by magic. That's how magic *works*."

"Truth spells," he said, a little too loudly.

I raised an eyebrow, and he inhaled, his nostrils flaring.

"Truth spells," he repeated in a slightly quieter tone, "should not leave burns."

Well, he had me there.

Whatever snappy reply I was fishing for slipped away as the girl behind the window handed the food to Zay in exchange for cash. Exact change. Yes, he was like that.

Zay gave me the bag, and I wouldn't have cared if the city suddenly fell under zombie attack. Nothing was getting between me and that burger.

I was so hungry my hands were shaking, but that didn't keep me from practically inhaling the food. Burger, fries, gone.

I belatedly noticed the Coke Zay had set in the cup holder. I picked it up and took a few drinks, feeling more human than I had for hours.

Before the Truth spell. Before the punch in the stomach. Before my backpack had been stolen.

The food was doing a good job of clearing my head, and we were just pulling into the parking area behind my apartment.

"You know what I really want right now?" I said as Zay turned off the car. "A shower. And a nap."

"Are you going to report your backpack stolen?" he asked.

I thought about it for a second. The way my life was going, I was pretty sure it hadn't been a random crime. But if it was for nefarious reasons, I had no idea how my sweaty gym socks could be used for evil.

"No, I don't think so. There wasn't anything in it except my gym clothes and a couple oranges. I'll just get a new bag." I opened the door. Got one foot out when I realized Zay was not moving.

"You coming in?"

"I have some things to take care of."

"Do I want to know about it?"

His brown eyes flashed with chips of gold. "I doubt it."

"Don't get killed, okay? We have plans tonight." I put my other foot on the concrete.

"I'll be home in a couple hours."

I stood and, despite myself, smiled. I didn't think he'd noticed it, but he'd started referring to my apartment as "home." I didn't think he'd even stopped by his own place for months. I hadn't asked him to move in. It had just sort of happened, slowly, naturally. I liked it.

He drove off and I headed to the door. A familiar shadow shifted from the corner of the building and stepped into the sunlight.

Davy Silvers grinned, and I wondered once again how old the kid was. If I had to guess, he was old enough to be in college, but shouldn't be drinking.

"Hey, boss. How's it?"

I shrugged. "It's been worse. What are you doing here?"

"Just keeping an eye on my favorite employer."

"What do you want?"

He feigned an innocent expression. "Nothing."

"Did Zayvion call you?"

"That would be telling."

I opened the door to the building, stepped in. Davy was quick. He caught the door and stepped in right after me.

"Davy, I'm in a bad mood. Do you really want to find out if it's bad enough for me to dock your paycheck?"

"He told me to stick around until he came back."

I thought back on it. It was possible Zay had called Davy while I was eating the hamburger. I had been hypnotized by the cheesy beef goodness. "He called you?"

"Text."

Well, that made more sense.

"I don't need you hanging around. Zayvion's just being sensitive today."

"Today?"

Okay, that made me smile. "He is a little overprotective, isn't he?" I said.

"Like condoms at a retirement home."

I laughed. "Go home, Davy. I don't need one man, much less two, looking after me."

"I was going to stop by anyway," he said.

I was at the bottom of the stairs, and paused to look back at him. "Why?"

"Drew the short straw. The Hounds have been talking."

I rolled my eyes. "No, we cannot upgrade the electronics in the den. If they want to play online all day, let them pay for it themselves."

"Not that."

"No personal chef, no sick-day pay—no pay,

period—no living there permanently, no roof parties, and no, I will not ask Violet to invent a holodeck."

"Who wanted a roof party?"

"Bea."

Davy smiled. "You have to admit, it would be fun."

"No." I started up the stairs. "Have I covered their demands?"

"I didn't say there were demands."

"So?"

"I'd rather talk in private," he said.

We clomped up the three fights of stairs, and I paused outside my apartment door. I leaned in without touching it because that Ward Zay had slapped across my threshold didn't like it if you stayed in contact with it for too long.

No sounds from inside. Stone, my pet gargoyle, hadn't been around since he'd revealed himself to my best friend, Nola, and the young man she was fostering, Cody. I figured he was hanging out with Cody, since Stone and Cody got along like two long-lost pals, or maybe he'd found a nice cozy rooftop where he could nest.

I missed the dumb rock, but I had to admit it was nice not having to constantly unstack everything in my house. Stone was all about the stacking.

I inserted the key, which canceled the Ward, and walked into my apartment.

"Make yourself comfortable," I said as I shrugged out of my coat and hung it on a hook by the door. "I'll make coffee."

Davy strolled past me into the living room. "So, it appears you and Mr. Jones are a going thing," he said.

"It appears," I said. "You been seeing Sunny lately?"

Sunny was a Blood magic user and part of the Authority. She'd taken a shine to Davy when we'd ended up at the den, recovering from a fight.

I pressed the button on the coffeemaker and walked into the living room.

Davy had slouched down on my couch and was looking through something—one of Zayvion's IKEA catalogs. "She's nice," he said.

"Just nice?"

He smiled, though he didn't look away from the magazine. "What I do on my off hours isn't any of your damn business," he said. Then, "Boss."

"Don't care if it's my business. Are you dating?"

He finally looked up. "Yes. And that's all I'm saying."

I sat at the table and put one foot up on the extra chair. "So what did you want to talk about?"

"We've decided you need a guard."

"We? We who?"

"The Hounds."

"Be specific, Davy. I'd hate to kick the wrong asses."

"Me, Jamar, Jack, Bea, Sid, Theresa. We'll be taking shifts looking out for you."

"Shifts? Guarding me? Are you crazy? I don't need to be guarded. I don't need anyone looking out for me."

"Okay, then don't think of it as us looking out for you. We'll just make sure you stop doing stupid things. Alone. I mean, you can continue to do stupid things, but not by yourself."

"No. Absolutely not," I said. "Vetoed. Next."

Davy draped one arm over the back of the couch and grinned. "I told them you wouldn't like it."

"You were right. Now you can go back and tell them I said no."

"Mm-hmm."

"Davy, tell them no."

"Sure. I will."

"And tell them that if I catch so much as a hair from any of them in my footsteps, I will kick their asses."

"See," he said, sitting forward, "that's where your plan sort of falls apart. You can't really do anything about this, boss. If we want to guard you, we will. And we know how to stay out of sight and one step ahead of you so you'll never catch us at it. Until we save your life, that is."

I opened my mouth, closed it, and chose to glare at him instead.

He was right. I didn't have any real leverage over the Hounds—hell, I didn't want any leverage over them. The only things I could do to stop them would be to shut down the den, or what? Revoke their kitchen rights? The Hounds drifted in and out of that place like leaves in the autumn wind—and I had planned it that way. It was a place to hold meetings, nurse headaches from using magic or other dangerous substances, and that was it.

They weren't my employees or my family, and most of them weren't even my friends. And because of that, I didn't have a hammer to swing in this fight.

"Fine," I finally said. "I'll explain to them just how I will make each of their lives a living hell if they guard me."

"That sounds like fun. Gonna give me a hint?"

"I am rich, Davy Silvers," I said airily. "There is no evil I can't finance."

"Well," he said, pushing up and heading to my kitchen, "you are rich. We like that about you. But you are also involved in things that will likely kill you." I heard the gurgle of coffee pouring into mugs.

"And we can't have that," he said. He walked out of the kitchen holding both cups. "You, Allie Beckstrom, are our golden goose. And there isn't anyone in this town we're going to let hurt you."

I took the coffee he offered. "It's a good thing I like you, Davy," I said. "I've knocked people's teeth out for telling me they want to use me."

"Not use." He took a sip, and when he looked back at me, he was very, very serious. "Not that at all. But, Allie, we've suspected for some time that you are mixed up in things that are very dangerous—even Pike knew it. And"—he held up one finger at my protest—"we know you aren't going to tell us exactly what those things are. No problem with that. None at all. But we are . . . grateful." He shrugged. "For what you've done. Hounds always have one another's backs. That's Pike's rule, and that's the way we're running things."

"I thought I was running things," I grumbled.

"Not this. We're going to look out for you. Whether you want us to or not."

I put my coffee cup down and stared out at the street for a while. Davy took his place back on the couch again. He didn't say anything for a bit, which was good. I needed some time to think this through.

I liked the Hounds, especially Davy and his overprotective cohorts. But the Authority was filled with nasty people who used magic in nasty, illegal, secret ways. To open the Hounds up to the possibility of sitting across from Bartholomew while Melissa whipped them with Truth spells wasn't my idea of me having their back.

But if I let them in on what was really going on in this town, they'd be in it up to their necks, and just as likely would be killed for that knowledge.

"It will kill you, you know," Davy said.

"What will kill me?"

"Worrying all the time."

"Who says I'm worrying?"

"You get this weird frown and hold your mouth crooked when you worry," he said.

"I do not."

He just took another drink of his coffee. "You remember what I do for a living, right?"

"What you should do is track down illegal spells. What you always seem to be doing is being a pain in my butt."

He flashed me a quick grin. "I'm a multitasker."

"Nothing I can do to talk you out of this stupidity?" I finally asked.

"Nope."

I took a deep breath and let it out. "Don't expect me to make it easy on you. If there's any way, any time I can shake you off my trail—the whole lot of you—I will."

"I was sort of hoping you'd see it that way. Wouldn't be any fun if it was easy."

I stood. "I'm going to take a shower, then probably nap for a half hour. You're welcome to my kitchen and TV. You are not welcome to my computer, or any of my journals. You are the very most welcome to my front door. As in opening it. And leaving through it."

"TV sounds good," he said.

"Fine."

"Fine."

I stomped off toward my shower, wondering why I'd ever thought having friends and so damn many people in my life was a good idea.

Chapter Three

The half-hour nap was really more like forty-five minutes of me tossing and turning and punching Zayvion's pillow. I was tired, yes, but more than that I was frustrated. Davy thought he and the rest of the Hounds could just follow me around, and Zayvion was all in my business to the point that he couldn't handle my going up against magic and coming out with scraped knees.

I was being smothered by good intentions. And I had no idea what to do about it.

Punching the pillow went only so far, and really, it just made me tired.

So instead I rolled over, decided I should apply some of the burn cream, and did that. Then I pulled a blank journal out of my night table and wrote down everything that had happened lately. I may have resorted to grade-school name-calling when mentioning Zayvion and Davy's stupid-boy stupid-headed-overprotectiveness cooties.

When I heard Zayvion come in and Davy leave, I put the journal away.

Zay walked into the bedroom, pausing in the doorway. I heard the front door click shut behind Davy.

"You done upholding my honor?" I asked.

He frowned. "Didn't have anything to do with your honor."

"You did go yell at Bartholomew, didn't you? About slap-happy Melissa and her Truth spell of pain?"

"I . . . spoke to him."

"And?"

"He said you were the only one who complained that the spell was painful. He suggested you are oversensitive."

I smiled. Not in a happy, friendly kind of way. "Isn't that sweet?"

Zay had been walking toward the bed, but stopped. "I've never heard that tone of voice," he said. "I'll take it you disagree with him?"

I tugged down the collar of my T-shirt, revealing the red slash. "You can take it I think he can fuck a fence for all I care."

Zayvion nodded. "Pretty much what I think too."

That caught me by surprise. "You don't like him? He's your boss, Zay. Your boss's boss's boss, as a matter of fact."

"I can work with him. I can work for him. I can also not like him." He sat on the edge of the bed. "The funeral is in a couple hours," he said quietly.

Oh. I had forgotten. The Authority—well, really Maeve—had set up a graveside service for Chase. I didn't know much about who would be there—didn't know if Chase had parents or if maybe those services had already been held and now the Authority was going to gather in private to honor one of its own.

"Want some sleep before?" I asked, trying to push my anger away and be a sensitive partner instead.

"What I want is to punch someone in the face. That didn't work out."

"Who were you going to punch?"

"Melissa Whit."

"Zay," I said. "A girl?"

He gave me a bland look. "She knew exactly what she

was doing when she cast that spell on you. She made it hurt because she didn't think there would be any repercussions. I told her if she ever touched you again like that, I'd empty out her brain and Close her so damn hard she wouldn't remember how to feed herself."

"Did that make you feel better?"

"No."

"You could hit Davy. He's been a pain."

"What's Davy done?" Zay looked over at the bedroom door, his hands curled into fists. I leaned across the bed and put my hand on his arm.

"It's a joke. Well, half a joke. He is a pain. But I don't want his face pounded in. Yet. He and the Hounds have decided they need to be my personal bodyguards. They're going to take shifts." I rolled my eyes.

"Which Hounds?"

"The usuals: Bea, Davy, Jack, Jamar, Sid, and Theresa."

"And you said yes?"

"I very much did not say yes. No one listens to me," I grumped.

That got a small smile out of him. "They're your Hounds. If you don't want them following you, keep them busy doing something else."

"I hate micromanaging."

"I could take away their memory of you."

"Tempting, but no thanks. One person with holes in her head is enough."

He shifted and put his arm around me. "I could keep them busy putting out other fires," he murmured into my hair. "Fake up some illegal spells."

"I'd rather you spent that kind of time and . . . creative attention on me."

"I thought you wanted some space. Said I was overreacting."

"You were. But right now, this is nice."

He held me, quiet. We didn't have to say much for our real feelings to be known to each other. I could feel the sorrow in him, the pain of loss. Going to his ex-girlfriend's funeral was probably one of the last things I wanted to do today, but I knew Zay needed it. Needed the time to give his grief space, ritual, and form.

"Want to talk about it?" I finally asked.

"No."

He let go of me and then walked over to the closet.

"Want to tell me what to expect?" I scooted back so my spine was pressed against the headboard of the bed, my knees tucked up.

"From what?"

"The service. Who's going to be there? What kind of an event? Will it be like when we reburied Dad?"

He pushed hangers aside one at a time—mostly my sweaters and the three dresses I owned. I don't think he was paying any attention to the clothes.

"Not a reburial, but yes, only members of the Authority will be there. Her parents are dead, but she had an aunt, lives out of state, who signed off on her burial. Chase had that all set up, the money put aside for it."

"So she was buried with no one to witness?" I asked.

"There was a priest—she saw to that too. Some friends from when she was in school, a previous employer. People were there."

"Were you there?" I tried to think if he'd had an hour or two away from me when he would have slipped off to stand by her grave. Realized, yes, he very much could have.

"No."

He stopped mincing through the clothes and just shoved them to one side and found a pair of slacks and a sweater.

"It's not formal," he said. "It won't last long. Anyone who wants to say their good-byes will be there."

"Only from Portland?"

"I don't know if Maeve called in other members of the Authority. I don't know if Bartholomew let her."

He shrugged out of his T-shirt and walked off to the bathroom.

I got out of bed. Thought about putting on a dress, decided on black slacks and a gray cashmere sweater instead, got dressed and put on my boots. I didn't bother with makeup, but did brush my hair back and clip it. It was getting longer now, falling just below my shoulders, and the streaks of white showed no signs of fading. After a moment of considering myself in the mirror, I decided to put on a little mascara and lip gloss.

Good enough.

There was a knock at the door.

"Someone's at the door," I called to Zay. Ever since Dane Lanister had walked in and waved a gun around, Zay and I checked with each other before opening the door.

The shower turned off. "It might be Shame," he said.

I picked up Zay's blood blade, tucked it in my left hand, and walked to the front door.

It wasn't that I lived in a particularly rough kind of town—it was just that particularly rough kinds of people seemed to make a point of coming to my apartment.

I traced the glyph for Impact with my right hand and held it with no magic. Then I looked through the peep-hole.

Shame stood there, hands in his peacoat pockets, sunglasses on, a black knit beanie tight over his head. It was May and the temperatures were mild—mostly short-sleeves-and-no-jacket weather. But I hadn't seen Shame in less than three layers since Mikhail had possessed and nearly killed him.

Frankly, I was surprised Terric wasn't with him.

I shook off the Impact and opened the door.

"Hey," I said. "What are you doing here?"

He tipped his sunglasses down with one finger. "I brought the booze, of course."

I looked down at his empty hands. "Uh-huh. Come on in." I stepped back and held the door open as Shame walked in. He was still moving slowly, as if the bottoms of his feet hurt or his bones were hinged together wrong. I checked down the hallway. No Terric, no booze.

"So," I said, shutting the door. "Booze?"

"It's in the car." Shame eased down onto my couch and took off his sunglasses, squinting against the light coming through the window. "Thought Jones could use the exercise. Lifting, hauling. Like a manly man."

Shame looked tired. No, more than that, he looked pale and a little sick, the bones of his face cutting too sharply beneath his skin.

"You come here alone?" I asked.

He nodded. "Why?"

"I just thought Terric would be with you."

"God no. Can't get rid of that wanker lately. It's killing me. Ducked out when he was in a meeting with Bartholomew."

Zayvion walked into the living room. "Who's in a meeting with Bartholomew?"

"Terric. Mum too."

"What's the meeting about?" Zay asked.

"Dunno. Wasn't invited. Wouldn't have gone if I were."

"I thought Terric was going to help you with the drinks," Zay said.

"Listen," Shame said, "I get that you all think Terric is my personal nursemaid or some such. But let me reiterate, slowly and clearly: I don't like being around him. He bothers me. I don't care what Bartholomew wants with him. I'm just glad I got some damn breathing room."

Zay sat in the chair by my window. "I thought we said we'd do the wake at the den."

Shame frowned, then nodded. "That's right. Well, the hooch is in the car. It can stay there until after the service."

"Hold on," I said. "What 'we' said we were doing anything at the den?"

Zay shrugged. "We thought we'd get together after the service. Just, you know, friends for a beer or two in memory. Didn't I tell you that?"

"No."

"I'm sure I did. You must have forgotten."

I shook my head and stomped off to go get my journal. I opened it, flipped through the pages. A lot of short handwritten notes—my life, all of it I dared not forget—written here. "There is nothing in here about you using the den. If it's not written down, you didn't ask me."

"She's got you there, Jones," Shame said. "You've been out-anal-retentived."

Zay raised one eyebrow at Shame. "So," he said to me, "you won't mind if I invite a few friends to the den tonight?"

"There might be Hounds there."

He shrugged. "So?"

"Is Bartholomew going to be there?"

"I said friends." When I held his gaze, he said, "No."

"Fine," I said. "I don't see why not. And next time ask before you plan." I pointed at Shame. "Both of you."

"Yes, dear," Zayvion said.

I glared at him. "Is there anything else you haven't told me that you plan to do with the things I own and you don't?"

He paused and then slowly looked me up and down, undressing me with his gaze. "A few things. I'm sure Shame won't mind if I go over them again."

Shame held up one hand. "Save it. I've already heard all the lovey-dovey out of you I can stand. We get it. You like her hot smokin' bod. Some of us don't have a girl-friend, you know."

"Whose fault is that?" I asked.

"What are you insinuating, Beckstrom?"

"Nothing. How about we start driving?"

Zay stood. "She's insinuating that if you were ninety percent less annoying, you might get a date once in a while."

"It's called character, Zayvion. Women prefer it over that silent-stalker trick you use to pick up chicks."

"I don't stalk women."

"Oh?" Shame shifted on the couch, putting his arm up over the back so he could turn to face me. It looked like it hurt him to move that fast. Still, he grinned and propped his chin on the back of his hand. "Let's find out. Allie, I never did hear the story of how you and Zayvion met. Do tell."

"No," I said as I walked into the kitchen.

"Aw, c'mon. I'm sure it's romantic. A story your kids will want to hear someday." He batted his lashes at me.

"First," I said, coming out of the kitchen with a bag of potato chips, "our kids won't want to hear it because we're not going to have kids. Second, no."

"We're not going to have kids?" Zayvion interrupted. He sounded genuinely surprised. "Were we going to talk about it before we made that decision?"

I was surprised he was surprised. "I didn't think you wanted children. I mean, the lives we live—the stuff we do. Hard to change diapers in the middle of a firefight, and then there's braces and school and . . . kids are messy."

"So you decided no children." He was keeping his ex-pression carefully neutral.

Had I? No, I guess I hadn't decided. I'd just assumed

he wouldn't be interested. "I didn't really think it through," I said. "Do you want children?"

He paused long enough for me to realize my heart was beating a little faster. This was more important to me than I'd let myself think about. It was a commitment, a possibility, a future for us I hadn't really thought was an option. Maybe I wanted children.

But I didn't know if we'd ever have room in our lives for that maybe to become a reality.

"I want us to talk about it," Zayvion finally said. "To decide. Together."

"So you like kids?" I asked.

"Always have," he said softly.

"Oh." I didn't know what to say. There was something about his expression, a promise there that I'd never expected.

"Hello?" Shame said. "Can we get back to more important things. He was stalking you, wasn't he?"

I stared up at the ceiling and blew out a breath of air. "Zayvion. Make him stop."

"I wasn't stalking her," Zay said. "I was following her. And besides, that's not the first time we met."

"What?" I looked over at Zay. He was pulling his jacket off the back of the chair and shrugging into it.

"I first met you out in St. Johns," I said. "In Mama's neighborhood."

He zipped his coat. Didn't say anything.

"Zay," I tried again. "I know I met you in St. Johns. You were following me. You were working for my dad."

"That wasn't the first time we met."

"See?" Shame piped up. "A good stalker won't be seen for weeks, maybe even years."

"Months," Zayvion said.

"When?" I asked. "Where?"

"I was on a job. Undercover in Lon Tragger's blood den."

I frowned. "The job I Hounded for Pike? For his

granddaughter? You were there? I don't remember seeing you."

"I couldn't forget seeing you. Covered in blood, carrying a gun and saving that girl. Wild. Fierce."

Shame put his beanie on and gave me a smile. "Very sexy."

"Oh," I said. Lame, but when he looked at me like that, all I had left was lame.

"And how long did you stalk her?" Shame asked like a schoolteacher encouraging a child to show and tell.

"I didn't stalk her." He said it to Shame, but he was still looking at me.

"How long?" I asked.

"I couldn't get you out of my head," he said quietly. "I tried. Tried not to look for your apartment, tried not to trail you on Hounding jobs, tried not to think of you. Constantly."

"How long?" I asked, quieter. I took a step forward and placed my hands on his chest. I could feel his heart beating through the padding of his old coat.

"Months," he said. "Until I was assigned by your father to follow you. Until I couldn't stand it any longer. Until I had to ask you out. Until I knew I'd keep asking you out until you said yes. All my life, if that's what it took."

"Oh," I said again.

He leaned down and I lifted my head just the slight difference between us. His lips were hot, soft, and found mine with loving intensity, with sweet, warm familiarity. And I suddenly realized we'd been together long enough now that I knew exactly what he was saying with that kiss. How much he loved me, how much he had fallen in love with me at that very first meeting. And how even if magic or death stood in our way, he'd find a way back to me. Even if it took all his life to do it.

"Sweet stalker love," Shame said. "Maybe I have been doing it wrong, Jones."

I pulled away, looked into Zayvion's eyes. "I'm glad you followed me."

Shame sighed. "Jesus. I need to get laid."

Zay and I looked over at him at the same time. Shame was staring out the window. In the late-afternoon light he looked so pale his skin was almost translucent. I felt the shock of concern run between Zay and me. I didn't know if I was feeling it or if Zay was. Probably both. Shame was a thin ghost of his usually dark, vibrant self. Like he was fading away from us even as we watched.

"What?" He turned and studied first my expression, then Zay's. Then he scowled.

Zayvion let go of me and walked over to pick up his car keys from the bookshelf.

"Go on with it. Get it out of your system," Shame said. "Because I am not driving the entire way with that pity crap from the two of you."

"It's not pity," I said. "We're just worried about you. Friends worry."

"I'm fine."

"Think you're really up for this?" Zay asked, like he was discussing what kind of pizza Shame wanted for lunch.

"I swear, if one more person asks me if I'm okay, I am going to break their legs," Shame said.

Zay nodded. "Good to know. We'll take my car."

"Mine's full of booze."

"Which is why we're taking my car," Zay repeated.

Shame, in a very un-Shame way, didn't put up a fight at all.

"Where is the service being held?" I asked as I pulled my coat off the hook and made sure I had keys, my journal, and my wallet. No backpack for me. Getting mugged sucked.

"Graveside," Shame said. "She's at the Pioneer Cemetery, right, Z?"

Zayvion nodded.

"Which Pioneer Cemetery? Hillsboro?"

"No," Zay said. "Down in Salem."

"So we have an hour's drive?" I asked.

Shame nodded, and tugged on the beanie he was wearing. Then he put a lot of effort into making it look like it didn't take any effort to stand up from the couch and stride across the floor.

"Not if I were driving," he said. He gave me a quick grin as he passed me and walked out the door, but I could smell the pain on him, a sour scent mixed with his usual clove and cigarette smell.

Zay walked out next, his finger running across the back of my hand, his concern and his comfort transferring to me more quickly and thoroughly than words.

Right. All we could do was keep an eye on Shame and hope he didn't let his stubbornness get in the way of his good sense.

Oh, who was I kidding? This was Shame I was worried about. He didn't even have sense, much less good sense.

I locked the door and the Ward kicked in like a snap of electricity that poured out a solid liquid wave of hurt.

Zay and Shame had paused at the top of the stairs. Shame had his arms crossed over his chest and was glowering at Zayvion. Zayvion had his hands tucked in the pockets of his coat, and from his body language I'd say he was doing that to keep from strangling Shame.

"What's up?" I asked as I walked over to them.

"We're taking the elevator," Zay said. "Aren't we, Allie?"

Shame shifted his glower from Zayvion to me.

"Legs. I break them," he said.

"Oh, sweet hells. Get in the damn elevator." I stabbed the button. The door immediately opened with a happy little bell tone.

I held my breath and strode all the way to the back wall, then turned. Zay and Shame were both standing outside the door, with the same expression on their faces—shock.

"Get in the damn elevator," I said. "Before *I* start breaking legs."

Zay stepped in, and Shame followed behind him. Zay pushed the button for the lobby and the door closed.

I shut my eyes and counted down from one hundred, trying to go as slowly as possible. I hit minus two hundred and the bell dinged. Zayvion and Shame were smart enough to get out of the elevator and get out of it quick. Good thing, because I would have just run them over. I kept walking across the lobby and shook my hands, trying to get the smallness, the closeness, the suffocationness of the elevator off me.

It did not matter how many times I forced myself into an elevator, it still freaked me out. I shuddered, and pushed out the door to the back parking lot, where Zay always parked his car.

The boys followed me more slowly. So slowly, in fact, that I had time to lean against the passenger's side door of Zay's car and watch them.

They were talking, both looking straight forward at me, both with their hands in their pockets, walking shoulder to shoulder, close enough that they almost brushed arms.

Zay hadn't had a great time of it lately. The coma, death, the magical fight, getting pounded on by Dane Lanister's men, and the escaped prisoners. He was a little on the thin side, a little on the hard-and-angry side, which just made him look like he was sculpted entirely out of bone and muscle and attitude.

Shame, however, seemed frail. He was wearing the sunglasses again, the peacoat collar flipped up, the beanie covering his dark hair. Even so, he had a hunch to his shoulders that made it look like his chest hurt and that even walking against the wind was a chore.

What I needed to do was find out exactly what was wrong with him—well, I knew what had hurt him: being possessed by Mikhail's spirit. But I hadn't heard about the physical damage it had left behind, or what his prognosis of recovery was. Just so I wouldn't forget, I pulled out my journal and jotted down a note: ask Dr. Fisher about Shame's health.

Zay strode up beside me and unlocked the doors. I got in the front and Shame got in the back.

Zay turned on the radio, the volume low. Classical. I'd never seen Zayvion use his radio. He always drove with it off when I was in the car. I glanced over at him, but he just flicked a glance at the rearview mirror.

Okay, so he had turned the radio on for Shame. I still didn't know why. We had barely made it out of Portland's city center before I heard the soft snoring from the backseat.

Shame was shrugged up against the window, fast asleep, the beanie in his hand tucked between his face and the window. His hair bristled at odd angles. He'd recently cut it pretty short all over except for his bangs, which still brushed the edges of his eyebrows.

Zay stretched his hand out and took mine. I could feel his worry. For Shame. For me, I supposed, and for saying good-bye to Chase one last time.

We didn't say anything, not wanting to wake Shame. I finally closed my eyes and drifted off for a few miles.

I woke up as Zayvion was decelerating for the exit. It'd been a while since I'd driven down to Salem. The outer edges of the city had built up some, and businesses had done their usual swapping out so that where once there was a pizza joint, now there was a chain Chinese restaurant, a shoe store, a bank, but otherwise not much had changed in Oregon's capital city.

"Do you know the way?" I asked Zayvion softly.

"I've been here before." He navigated through the city center, then left the main roads for a neighborhood in the hills.

Shame stirred and stopped snoring. He shifted enough that I knew he was awake.

"We there yet?" he asked.

"Almost," Zay said. "How was your nap?"

"Fucking awesome. I'm thinking of going into napping as a career. I hear there's a lot of future in it."

I glanced back. Shame was smiling, but the hard light in his eyes betrayed how annoyed he was that he had had no choice but to nap.

"So what did Dr. Fisher say your recovery time would be?" I asked. When in doubt, be blunt.

Shame swallowed, and looked out the window, as if there was an answer the passing trees and houses could give him. "She doesn't know. One day at a time is all we can do for now."

"Is the crystal still in your chest?" I asked.

He nodded. "It's there. I'd show you, but it's too damn cold in this car."

It wasn't cold at all in the car, but I was nice enough not to point that out.

"This is it," Zay said.

He drove between the brick columns of the gate and then up to a mortuary at the top of a hill. He parked between the other cars already there.

"We have to walk?" Shame whined.

"Yes." Zay got out and so did I. Shame followed a moment or two later. Zay opened the trunk of the car and reached into it for something.

The graveyard was beautiful in its own way, trees and bushes bursting with leaves, flowering cherry trees fluffy and pink above marble gravestones and concrete crypts. Birch trees, maples, massive oaks and cedars and cinnamon-barked madronas stood at attention among the crooked headstones.

The cemetery was built on rolling hills with just enough height to give a view of the blue horizon and the western hills that eventually lead to the Coast Range.

Zay closed the trunk. He started walking down a concrete path toward the north side of the graveyard, carrying a handful of daffodils tied with a red velvet ribbon. Shame paused next to me and just stared at Zayvion's back. "You okay?" he asked me.

Funny, I'd been thinking I should ask him the same thing. I shrugged. "I think so. Just worried about him. And you."

"That's one of the things I like so much about you, Beckstrom. You worry about everyone."

"Trust me," I said, "I don't." We started walking and I set my pace to Shame's. His nap seemed to have done him some good, and we made respectable progress, keeping up with Zayvion. The road narrowed to a single-file path for a bit and Shame walked to my left over the edge of well-tended grass. With each step, the grass beneath Shame's feet lost its vibrant spring green and withered as if it had been burned, or suddenly died.

Was he pulling that much life energy out of the things around him? Or maybe he was drawing that much energy out of living things as a side effect of being possessed by a dead and very powerful Death magic user. I didn't have a chance to ask him.

The path opened up again and Shame joined me on it.

"So does the Authority always gather like this?" I asked. "I don't remember a ceremony for Liddy."

"It depends. Chase had her burial all set up—most of us do. But I think Zayvion's the one who called for this."

"Really?" I peered at Zayvion's back. He hadn't told me he was behind this get-together. As a matter of fact, he'd told me Maeve set it up.

"Didn't tell you, did he?" Shame was quiet for a bit. "If he hasn't said it, her death really tore him up."

"I know," I said. And I did. What I didn't know was why he wouldn't have talked to me about it. I would have helped, would have at least been there to talk over the details.

Zayvion had been pulling away. I'd just passed it off as him needing time to think, or time to deal with the new boss in town. But he'd been coming home late most nights, and though we'd certainly been together, I'd known for a while that he was holding a part of himself separate from me.

"Did he tell you anything else?" I asked.

"Zayvion doesn't usually talk about these things," Shame said softly, like he was afraid he would hear us. "He's private. I thought he might have talked to you about it. But you know how it is." He shrugged as if that was all that needed saying.

I didn't know what else to say, so we strolled along. Shame held his breath for a moment, like he'd just caught sight of something surprising. Then he let it out slowly. Pretty soon I heard footsteps behind us. I glanced back.

Terric was striding toward us, his white hair a flash of moonlight in the middle of the sunny spring day. He wore a tailored gray trench coat, slacks, and shiny shoes. I glimpsed a tie at his collar. In his hand was a small bouquet of bright orange tiger lilies.

Very slick and stylish.

I suddenly felt completely underdressed.

"Afternoon," Terric said, catching up.

"Hey," I said.

Shame grunted. But I could tell from the ease of his shoulders, from the subtle relaxing of his gait and posture, that Terric being near him seemed to lessen the pain, or at least give him some strength. He even took a nice deep breath, which was good to see since all he'd been doing was breathing off the top of his lungs.

"How'd it go today?" I asked Terric.

"What do you mean?"

"With Bartholomew."

Terric made a sour face. "I don't know that his objectives and mine are in alignment."

Shame snorted.

"What are his objectives?" I asked.

"To reorganize the entire Portland Authority."

"What?" Shame said. "Why in God's balls is he talking to you about that? You don't even live here."

"That's why."

We rounded a bend in the path. The grave was clearly marked by the small crowd of people who surrounded it.

"He can kiss my ass," Shame said quietly, "if he thinks he's going to tell me what to do and who to follow."

Terric pulled a pair of sunglasses out of his pocket and nodded toward the grave. "Later, Flynn. Let's handle one tragedy at a time."

The people gathered were all members of the Authority. I recognized most of them, though I was surprised to see at least a dozen unfamiliar faces.

"Who are the extras?" I asked.

Shame finally stopped glaring at Terric and looked around. "Lots of people from the business side of things, civilian interface jobs."

I frowned.

"Teachers, doctors, accountants, plumbers," Terric provided. "Just because you run around with people who get into magical fights all the time doesn't mean that the majority of the Authority is on the defense side of the organization."

"Oh." I hadn't thought about that, but it made sense. The Authority was more than just a handful of people who chased down creatures that slipped through gates or took people's memories away. The Authority was the defining and far-reaching mediator between the unknown magics and the average magic-using citizen.

I suddenly realized it was a lot larger organization than I'd been thinking.

We walked toward the grave, still out of hearing range. "How many people are under the Authority's employ?" I asked.

"In the Portland area?" Terric asked. "I don't know. Shame?"

"Maybe a hundred thousand."

Correction. I had vastly underestimated how large the organization was.

I scanned the faces, doing what I could to remember them. Dad, who was still in my head and still active, though the binding Shame and Victor had cast on him made him less likely to take over my body, had been quiet for days now. I didn't know if he was exhausted from fighting Leander and Isabelle, or if he was secretly planning to take over the world.

Probably the latter.

Even here, seeing people he must have known, people he must have liked or disliked, he said nothing. It was, frankly, not like him to leave me alone, but I had to admit I liked it.

The people I knew were Shame's mom, Maeve; the Closer and her boyfriend, Hayden; Zayvion's mentor, Victor; the goth-punk Blood magic user Sunny; the twins, Carl and La. Joshua had gone back to his family in Seattle, and Nick also wasn't here. I didn't see Bartholomew, Melissa, or the goons. That was nice. I preferred this to be a private affair with people I didn't have a reason to hate.

Chase's gravestone was classic, pretty even: a lovely white marble with a blue ribbon running beneath her name, set in the ground. Beneath her name and birth and death dates was carved FRIEND, WARRIOR, LOVER.

Zayvion walked over to stand near the head of her grave, and the people who had gathered moved aside to give him room. He stared down at the headstone, the daffodils forgotten in his hand. The soft May breeze stirred across the grounds and a robin sang out while chickadees chittered in the nearby rosebushes.

It was a beautiful day.

I glanced up, away from Zayvion, away from the silence of those gathered, and scanned the horizon. At a distance, I saw a figure watching us. I knew that man—Davy Silvers. He didn't come any closer, wasn't near enough to hear us speak even with his keen Hound ears.

I couldn't believe he'd followed me here. And then I caught the slight movement on the other side of the tall grave markers near Davy. Sid Westerly, another of my Hounds. Not far from him was Jack Quinn.

What. The. Hell.

"Didn't know you invited your friends," Terric said quietly.

"I didn't."

I had no idea why they were here. Maybe to Hound this, but why? Who cared about us grieving Chase? Who were they working for? Detective Paul Stotts tended to use Hounds when dealing with magical crime in the city, but I didn't think he knew Chase, and as far as I knew, no one here was on his suspicious list. So I didn't think he'd send one Hound, much less three. Maybe the Hounds needed something from me. An emergency I had to handle.

I stuck my hand in my pocket and checked my phone. Nothing. No messages, no reason for the Hounds to be here on this nice sunny May day.

They didn't come any closer. Didn't motion me to come to them.

Then it hit me. Davy had said they took a vote and decided they were now my bodyguards.

Oh, hells no.

But I was not about to storm away from this to tell them off. Chase deserved at least that much respect from me.

After the long silence, Victor finally spoke.

"She had a wonderful laugh," he said quietly. "I remember many days during training when she'd get some sort of joke or something she'd seen stuck in her head, and she'd giggle half the day away. Even when she was training very, very hard. I will miss her." He placed a purple orchid on her gravestone.

Maeve was next. "She loved romance novels but didn't want anyone to know." There was a slight chuckle among the crowd. "She thought people wouldn't believe she was tough if they found out she was always hoping for a happily-ever-after. Blessings to you, dear heart." Maeve placed a sprig of heather on the stone.

Terric cleared his throat. "Chase broke my arm. Twice. And she always ate all the popcorn at movies. But she was a really good listener. Kind. She always had time for me when things were confusing. I'm going to miss her very much." He bent and set the tiger lilies among the other flowers.

Other people stepped up, spoke a word or two about her, spoke a memory or two. I felt like I was listening in on a life and meeting a person I had never known. And I regretted I hadn't had the time to know her like the other people gathered had.

Zayvion finally spoke. "I loved her," he said quietly. "I always will." He placed the entire bouquet on her headstone.

I just stood there, sad, my face hot and prickling. I wasn't sure if I should cry, comfort Zayvion, or leave him alone. I knew he loved her. I'd known that from the beginning. But I couldn't help but wonder if her death had brought into sharp focus how much he still loved her. If maybe there wasn't as much room in his heart for me now.

I took a step backward, needing space, needing air away from the grief that all these people felt. I wanted to cry, but not for the same reasons as them.

Shame, beside me, reached out and caught my hand.

I looked over at him. He didn't look at me, but squeezed my hand once and didn't let go.

It seemed like everyone had done their share of saying something, and all the people who had flowers in their hands had already laid them down on the grave.

"Well," Shame said, "one thing I remember about Chase was the girl knew how to party." A couple people chuckled. "Therefore, in her loving memory, we are going to get wasted. Anyone who wants to join us, come on over to Beckstrom's place next to Get Mugged. Second floor. We'll be there until the booze gives out."

He let go of my hand and nestled a bottle of Irish whiskey among the flowers. "I'll miss ya, lass."

And then Shame turned and started off toward the car. Other people eventually did the same, trickling away in ones or twos. I thought for sure Terric would follow Shame, but he instead moved to stand next to Zayvion.

Zayvion hadn't moved. Not since he placed the flowers on her headstone. I wasn't sure if he even saw any of us.

I looked up and watched Victor and Maeve exchange a concerned look. Then Maeve spoke. "We'll see you soon, then, Zayvion."

Zay still didn't move.

Victor glanced over at me. "If you need help"—he nodded toward Zay—"let me know. There are resources available."

I didn't know if he meant resources like grief counseling, or resources like taking away Zayvion's memory of her. I wondered if they would do that—Close someone to take away pain.

No, that didn't seem likely. As far as I could tell, everyone in the Authority had to bear their share of hurt.

"Thank you," I said.

Zay looked up, looked toward me, but I was pretty sure he didn't see me. His eyes were red-rimmed.

I tried to smile, didn't quite make it. "Hey," I said. "How about we go make sure Shame isn't vandalizing your car?"

He didn't say anything. Victor and Maeve had already headed down the path, leaving no one by Chase's grave but Zay, Terric, and me.

"Time to go," Terric said. He put his hand on Zayvion's shoulder, then shifted slightly toward the cars. "Zayvion. It's time."

Zayvion finally seemed to come out of his daze. He took a step or two, his gaze on me alone. I held out my hand, but he wrapped his arms around me.

A shock of pain, loneliness, and raw sorrow whipped through me at that touch. But behind it, within it, was an overwhelming love and gratitude that I was here, beside him. Alive.

We stood there for a while. Until Terric once again put his hand on Zay's shoulder. Then we walked back toward the car, slower than we had come. I don't think Zayvion was paying attention to much of anything and was glad Terric had decided to pace along with us.

Shame was waiting at the car, smoking, not vandalizing. He saw us coming but stayed where he was.

"Z's got the keys," he said when we were close enough.

"Zay?" I said. "Give me the keys to the car."

Zay pulled them out of his front pocket and handed them to me.

"You got him?" Terric asked. "Them?"

I nodded. "I'll drive. Unless you want to take Shame?"

"He does not want to take Shame," Shame said. "Shame's going to be just fine in the backseat taking himself."

"Nasty." Terric grinned.

Shame scowled, but couldn't quite smother his smile. "Shove it, Terric."

I unlocked the doors and Shame got out of the way and opened the front door for Zayvion. Zay got in without a word and closed his eyes. Shame shut the door, then got in the back.

"See you there," Terric said. "I assume your shadows are coming too?"

I looked behind me. Davy and Sid were walking this way. They weren't trying to hide. They were Hounds. If they wanted to hide, they could disappear in an empty room.

"I guess. I'll let you know." I stormed over to them, and they stopped so that our conversation wouldn't be heard.

"Why are you here?" I asked.

Davy tipped his head and gave me a curious frown. "You do remember me telling you we were going to be your bodyguards, right?"

"At a graveside service an hour away from Portland?"

"Even in your shower if we can figure a way."

"Don't," I said. "I appreciate your concern, but trust me on this. I don't want guards, I don't need guards, and having guards—even thickheaded, well-meaning ones, will make my life more difficult."

Sid coughed. "At least you'll be alive to complain about it. What's the deal with going back to the den?"

I rubbed at my face with my left hand. I swear, I

simply could not keep track of all the lives I was supposed to be grateful to complain about. It would be easier if I just blurted it all out and told them about the Authority.

But despite the fact that they were seriously pissing me off right now, I liked them.

Enough. Well, enough that I didn't want to see them dead.

"These people—friends of Zay's, friends of Chase's—want to get together for some drinks. They needed space, so I offered the den. You got a problem with that, you are welcome not to come."

"There's free booze?" Davy asked. "Best thing I've heard all day."

I glared at him.

"See you there, boss." He strolled off to his car, Sid rumbling along beside him.

Fabulous. Just.

I got in the driver's side of the car and slammed the door shut. Zay still had his eyes closed and didn't even twitch at the sound. I knew he wasn't asleep. He was just turning inward, blocking out the world again. I reached over and put my hand on his leg. The sorrow was still there, but it felt like his other emotions and his thoughts were at a far distance. I could still feel him, but with a world of sorrow between us, I wasn't sure that I could reach him.

I pulled my hand away and started the car. I liked driving Zay's car. It was powerful, a little tight on the gas and brakes—like Zay—and it reminded me of the sense of freedom and space I always felt when I got behind the wheel.

It was something I'd been doing for too long now. Always taking the passenger's seat when I should be the one driving.

"What about the booze?" I asked Shame.

"I'll get it. Just take me to my car and I'll haul it over to the den."

"Think you should be driving?" I asked.

I caught his grin in the rearview mirror. "Oh, probably not, but where's the fun in being reasonable?"

"Shame."

"I'm fine. Sleeping helped. I should be able to navigate a few streets between your apartment and the den. You can even follow me if you want."

"I plan on it," I said.

"I knew you would."

"Why?"

"'Cause you worry all the damn time. Anyone ever tell you that?"

"Yes," I said. "All the damn time."

Chapter Four

I dropped Shame off at his car, then followed him to the den. Zay still hadn't opened his eyes, not even when Shame had made a big noisy show of getting out of the car.

Shame parked in the one spot open in front of the den (lucky bastard) and I went around the block and found parking down two blocks or so.

I turned off the engine. "Zay?" I said quietly as the cooling engine clicked and snapped.

He didn't open his eyes.

I reached over. Shook his shoulder. "Zayvion?"

He jolted forward, and since he hadn't latched his seat belt, slammed his hand against the dash, stopping himself from hitting the window.

"Hey, hey," I said. "It's okay. We're in the car."

He shot a look at me. His eyes were dark, almost completely black.

"Zayvion?" I said calmly. "You need to wake up."

He blinked hard, shaking whatever that darkness was from his eyes. Maybe he'd been asleep, maybe he'd just shoved himself so far back into that pain that it was a long road back to reality.

"You with me?" I asked. "We're at the den. For Chase."

Those words seemed to sink in.

He exhaled and sat back. "I thought . . ." He stared out the window. "We're at the den?"

"Yes."

He looked over his shoulder. "Where's Shame?"

"In his car. Or probably up in the den finding someone to unload the hooch."

"Zay," I said, "are you—"

"Let's go," he said. He opened the door and stepped out into the late-afternoon light.

I squeezed the steering wheel and tried not to hit something. I hated being cut off, brushed off, pushed aside.

He was mourning. Grieving, I reminded myself. He deserved a little time and space. I'd do my best to give both to him.

Today.

Tomorrow was a different story.

I got out of the car, locked it. Zay waited for me on the sidewalk. I stepped over to him. "Let's get going."

He started walking, and it was like watching someone rebuild a kicked-down sand castle. With each step, he pulled his shoulders back, relaxed his body language, and moderated his breathing, settling his face into a pleasant neutral expression.

No red in his eyes. No sorrow caught in the corners of his lips, in the shallowness of his breath. The Zayvion that opened the door for me when we walked into the lobby of the building was not the same man who had been sitting next to me in the car. And I didn't think this Zayvion was anything more than a well-practiced disguise.

Maybe I did need a drink.

We walked across the lobby and up the stairs. The sound of people talking greeted us before we reached the second floor.

That was a new thing. Hounds tended to make a point

of being quiet. But it wasn't the Hounds gathered here. Or rather, wasn't just the Hounds.

I walked up to the doors and let myself in.

Maybe three dozen people were standing, or lounging on the couches and chairs, talking. Someone had had the foresight to take all the files off my desk in the corner, and, I hoped, lock them in my desk. The wine, beer, and hard liquor were set up by category in the kitchen, and a pot of something that smelled like tomatoes and basil and garlic was simmering on the stove. Platters of finger food were set around in easy-access places.

Zay paused, for just half a second, then fastened a smile into place and strolled out into the crowd.

I watched him work the room, shaking hands, patting shoulders. Finally shook my head. If he wanted to act like everything was both peachy and keen—all the power to him. I wanted a glass of wine.

I walked into the open kitchen area, where Davy was hanging out, eating and talking to Sunny. They both had a beer in their hands, but I didn't think they'd looked away from each other long enough to actually take a drink. Davy had a soft, almost goofy smile on his face that I'd never seen before, and Sunny's eyes were bright as she excitedly told him about a band that was coming to town that she really wanted to see, but tickets were so hard to get.

I could tell Davy was already working out who he'd have to blackmail to get her tickets to that show.

Ah. Young love.

I glanced at the wine, chose a red, and poured myself half a glass. I figured I was going to be the driver tonight. Even if Zayvion didn't drink, I didn't trust his decision-making skills at the moment.

The wine was bitter and went down hot. I mooched around the kitchen until I found rolls and cold cuts, then made myself a sandwich.

I ate that and watched the people gathered. Zay talked quietly to Victor, who had taken him off to one corner of the room where they could both lean on the windowsills and look out at the city. Zay had somehow scored a beer, and from the angle he tipped it to drink, it was already almost empty.

I could read their lips just enough to know they were talking about Closing, and Bartholomew. Victor seemed to be calmly explaining something to Zayvion that involved "your duty" and "Guardian" and "Authority" and "superior." Zayvion seemed to be in an arguing mood, and more than once said "no" and "not you" and "it's not right."

Shame had commandeered the lion's share of the couch, one arm across the back, one leg up on the coffee table. To my surprise, he had a can of Coke—not a glass of whiskey—in his hand and was pouring on the smile and charm to a pretty blonde I'd never met.

Terric strode into the kitchen. He'd taken off his coat and sunglasses, but still cut a sharp figure in slacks, shirt, and tie.

"Allie," he said.

"Terric." He walked past me and straight to the tequila. He poured a shot, and winced as the blonde on the couch laughed. Shame's chuckle followed hers, low and naughty. Terric set his shoulders and took the shot back in one gulp.

Interesting. "So who is she?" I asked.

"Tiffany Lowe." He poured another shot. "She's in marketing."

"The Authority has a marketing department?"

Terric half turned and gave me a look.

"Okay, okay. I just have a hard time wrapping my head around the idea of the entire thing being run like a corporation."

"Believe me, it is." He swigged the second shot, then replaced the shot glass on the counter and pushed it away with his fingertips, his fingers still stretched out, but not touching it. He stood and stared at the empty shot glass while Shame and Tiffany laughed again.

I moved over so I could lean against the counter. Not because I'd have a better chance to stop him from pouring the entire bottle down his throat.

Okay, mostly for that.

"You don't like her?"

"She is a perfectly lovely person," he said through his teeth.

"Oh?"

He rolled one shoulder and took a deep breath. Then he picked up the tequila bottle.

"Might want to slow it down, Terric. You've got all night to get hammered."

He poured, but filled the shot glass only halfway. "Isn't that the damn truth?" he said. He picked up the glass, but did not drink out of it. He did, however, turn and look at Shame.

Shame glanced up, as if someone had called his name. He caught Terric looking at him and raised an eyebrow. Terric just lifted his glass in a toast. Shame frowned but lifted his Coke.

"So she really is a perfectly lovely person?" I asked.

"No," Terric said. "Not when I knew her. She was the kind of person who would do anything—and anyone—to get what she wanted. And she wanted to be the head of the Authority, a Voice at the very least."

"So why's she flirting with Shame?"

"I can't imagine. He is just the only son of the last member of our local branch who is a Voice—Blood magic too. If she's harboring a discreet habit of blood and drugs—highly possible considering her past—she just might want to get on Maeve's good side." He paused, sipped the tequila. "Or, you know, maybe she wants Shame to get her on Maeve's good side."

"And we're not interfering because . . . ?"

"He knows what he's getting into."

"Then why are you angry?"

He glanced over me, maybe a little surprise in his eyes.

"Jealous?" I asked. I suddenly realized I'd never come out and asked Terric if he was gay. It just hadn't crossed my mind that it mattered. But maybe it mattered very much to Shame. Maybe that was part of why Shame didn't want to be around Terric.

The surprise faded away to annoyance. "I'm not jealous." That was a lie, but I could tell he couldn't admit it. "I'm glad he's happy—my God, I haven't heard him laugh in weeks. He's barely smiled. . . ."

Shame chuckled again and leaned in toward Tiffany, as if whispering a secret. Terric swallowed another mouthful of tequila, his gaze burning with heat, fixed on Shame.

"I just want . . . it's not like I'm asking for his undying devotion," he said. "But it'd be nice if he didn't make me feel like I was a dirty inconvenience."

"He asked Mikhail to heal you," I said. "When he thought he was going to die if Mikhail possessed him, he only thought about you, Terric. That doesn't sound like an inconvenience to me."

"You think he did that for me?" Terric gave me a wry smile. "He did that for himself. For his guilt, his failure. He wasn't thinking about me. When Mikhail touched me, it marked me. Changed how I can use magic. I can handle some of the"—he paused, realizing that talking in a normal tone was practically shouting when you were around Hounds—"other spells that used to make me sick. But it's not like it made it so I could take over for Zayvion."

He meant take the job as Guardian of the gates and use both light and dark magic, something Terric had once trained for.

"The real good that seemed to come out of it is when I'm around Shame, I think it eases his pain. He won't admit it. Since being around him also makes me feel better, he won't have it. And now he can sleep easy knowing he sacrificed his own health so I could be repaired from him attacking me all those damn years ago." Terric knocked back the rest of the drink. "There is no talking sense with him. No getting a straight answer, an honest feeling, a logical agreement. It is maddening."

The door opened and I glanced up. Grant, the owner of Get Mugged, came strolling through the door, two platters of food in one hand. So that's who Zay hired to cater this.

He caught my eye and strolled over. "Hey there, Allie. Quite the shindig you're throwing. I assume my invitation was lost in the mail?" He grinned and placed the platters of bite-sized quiches and fancy desserts on the counter.

Normally, I'd have tried to find some excuse for Grant not to be here. These people were part of the Authority, and I did not want him getting mixed up with them. But hell, I figured he'd been here when we'd all come licking our wounds from the fight with the Veiled at Maeve's inn, so he might as well be here with us now.

Plus, he cooked like a frickin' angel.

"I just found out about the party a couple hours ago," I said. "Otherwise, of course I would have invited you."

"No harm done. So—" He gave Terric, who was still staring at Shame, a nice long look, glanced over at Shame, then back to me. "Want to introduce me to your friend here?"

"Oh, sorry. Terric Conley, this is Grant Rhine. Grant

owns Get Mugged, and Terric is a graphic designer and friend of Zay's from Seattle."

Terric snapped back into focus and finally noticed Grant.

"Pleased to meet you." Grant extended his hand and Terric took it and shook.

"Nice to meet you," Terric said.

Shame's laugh cut off suddenly and I looked over at him. He was glaring at Terric. Terric didn't look at Shame. He didn't have to look at Shame. Instead, Terric grinned at Grant, warm, a little sexy, a little drunk.

"It is *very* nice to meet you," he amended, holding Grant's hand just a bit too long. "So what delicious treats have you brought with you tonight?"

Grant smiled. He knew what Terric was doing. Must know that there was some sort of bad blood between him and Shame. Didn't look like he cared. "Quiche and marionberry key lime tarts," he said. "So good they're a class five sin."

"Class five, eh? Can't wait to get my mouth on that." Terric walked past him to get a look at the food, and loosened his tie with one hand.

Grant, his back to Terric, waved one hand in front of his chest, fanning himself and mouthed the word "hot" to me. He tapped the ring finger of his left hand and raised his eyebrow in question.

I shrugged one shoulder. As far as romantic relationships went, Terric was available.

But when I looked over, Shame was still glaring at Terric.

"I don't know what to try first," Terric continued. "What goes best with tequila?"

"Besides me?" Grant gave me a wink and turned to Terric. "Anything on that platter should be a nice chaser."

Terric picked up a quiche and popped the whole

thing in his mouth. He chewed, and his eyes widened. "That's really good."

"Thank you," Grant said. "You should try the tart." He reached past Terric, angling so they stood shoulder to shoulder, and chose a tart for him. He handed it to Terric.

Terric took a bite out of it and smiled at Grant.

"You're amazing," Terric said.

"And that's just my cooking," Grant replied.

Tiffany, next to Shame, let out a giggle. Shame had scooted over and put his arm around her, his head tipped in toward her, his finger tracing down her chin to the neckline of her blouse.

It was like a game of who could out-jealous whom.

Sweet hells. This was so none of my business. The last thing I needed to deal with was two boys playing underhanded games with each other's feelings.

I walked away, leaving Shame and Terric to their little flirt fight. Zay was still engrossed in his conversation with Victor. Although I'd classify the conversation as an argument at this point. Zay was holding a very subtle Mute spell between the thumb and finger of his right hand. I could hear them talking, but none of the words were clear. He must have modified the spell with a Distraction to help avert curious eyes without being obvious about it.

Nice piece of magic, that. Especially for an angry man who'd had a couple drinks.

Maeve was sitting down to a poker game with Jack, Hayden, Sunny, and a couple people I didn't recognize.

Davy had managed to detach himself from Sunny and was instead over by the TV talking with Sid.

I went that way.

"Hey," I said when I was close enough.

They both nodded and made room so I could stand next to them.

"What I want to know," I said, "is how much it's going to cost me to buy my way out of your bodyguard services."

"Not open to negotiation," Davy said.

"Oh, I'll listen," Sid said amicably. "How much do you think it would take?"

"I'd offer you each a thousand. And an extra five hundred each if you talk the other Hounds into giving it up too."

"Last time you offered us money it was five times that much," Sid said.

"I can't believe I'm having to pay to get rid of protection services," I said, irritated. "You should be happy I don't file a restraining order on the lot of you and have you arrested if you're found in the same city with me."

"What do you think, Davy?" Sid said. "Fast money."

"Nope." Davy tipped up his beer, gave me a hard look. "We are your guards. End of conversation."

"Sid?" I said. "Tell me you have the sense to realize that if I don't want to be followed, I will make your trying to do so a miserable experience."

"I do have that sense."

"So?"

He pushed his glasses back up his nose. "I'm with Davy on this," he said cheerfully. "These people you're involved with? I've done some checking up on them."

I rolled my eyes. This was exactly what I was worried he would do. "And you don't like what you've found?"

"No. Everything I've tracked back to these individuals pans out. Looks legal, legit, common. But my gut tells me there's something more. On paper, these people are fine. They don't stand out in any appreciable way. But when you meet them in person, or when you get a bunch of them together all in the same room . . . Well, look at them. They don't add up. They're hiding something."

"Everyone's hiding something," I groused. "I don't

know why you suddenly have to get all protective about me."

"We like you," Davy said.

"And your money," Sid said.

"Which I'd be happy to give to you if you'd stop following me around."

The phone on my desk rang and Jamar answered it. He looked over at me, said "yes," and hung up. Wondered who was checking in on me.

"Going to tell us who died?" Davy asked, changing the subject.

"Will it get you off my back?"

"No."

I glared at him. He took another drink of beer, unconcerned.

"Her name was Chase. She was a friend of Zayvion and Shame and Terric. I guess she knew all these other people too, except for the Hounds, of course. Or, at least I don't think you knew her, did you?"

Davy and Sid both shook their heads.

I shrugged. "I don't know why they didn't hold the memorial somewhere else."

"You don't?" Davy gave me a pitying smile. "It's because they knew you wouldn't say no. You never say no when someone needs something."

I raised one eyebrow. "You think so, huh?"

"Not that it's a bad thing," Sid amended quickly. "We appreciate the place, and we especially appreciate you didn't say no to the food and booze."

"Free booze," Davy added.

"The best kind," Sid said.

"Enjoy it, boys," I said, " 'cause this is the last free booze you'll see here in a long, long time."

For all my grumpiness, everything did seem to be going just fine. People were clumped up in small groups talking, Hounds and members of the Authority mixed and blended as if they'd been gathering like this for years. No one appeared to be fishing for secrets, crossing lines, getting their memories taken away.

Maybe we'd get through the next couple hours without anything bad happening.

A girl could dream anyway.

Then the door opened and Anthony Bell walked in. He paused just inside the doorway as if expecting to be immediately thrown out.

"Fuck me," Davy growled.

"I invited him to come by," I said. "Not tonight, and he was supposed to call, but I did invite him, Davy. He wants to be a Hound. And as long as the rules of the den are followed—Pike's rules—he can have his chance."

"Aren't you done defending him?" Davy asked. "He's a loser, Allie. He's a nothing."

"He's a Hound," I said in my boss voice. "That means he's a part of us until he does something to make us kick him out."

"Killing Pike wasn't enough?"

I ignored that. Davy and I had rehashed Pike's death plenty of times. And while I didn't expect Davy to forgive Anthony, it wasn't only Anthony's fault that Pike died. Pike had gone into a dangerous situation without any backup—breaking one of his own rules he set for the Hounds—and had done so even though he'd agreed he would take the police with him.

"I ran into him and his mother this morning," I said. "She's nice, Davy. Pike liked her and took Anthony on because he cared about her. She cares about her son. I owe Ant a second chance. And he's getting one. You don't have to be around when he's here. You don't have to be a part of it."

"I hate everything about this," he mumbled over the neck of his beer bottle as he took another drink.

"Noted," I said. "Leave him alone, okay? I don't want to see you two within twenty feet of each other."

"I go where you go."

"We'll see. Stay out of my way tonight. This is a pretty open floor plan, and everyone here is a friend. You've got good eyes and ears. Use them."

I walked over toward Anthony, who, once he realized he wasn't getting kicked out, had helped himself to a Red Bull and some chips.

"Didn't think you'd show up tonight," I said.

"Saw Zay's car outside and figured you'd be here. I called. Jamar said you were here."

"Next time call me. My cell," I said.

"All right." He shrugged. "What's the party for?"

"Friend of Zayvion's who died."

"Who?"

"Her name was Chase."

He shook his head. "Didn't know her."

"She was nice."

The last word didn't come out quite as convincing as I'd hoped.

"But you didn't like her, eh?"

"She was also Zayvion's ex-girlfriend." And that pretty much explained it all.

Anthony looked across the room, spotted Zay, who was staring out the window. Victor was still standing next to him, also looking out the window. Neither of them was talking. It didn't look like either of them had won the argument, but Zay had dropped the Mute and Distraction.

"Ex," Anthony said. "Right." He turned back to me. "This a private thing? Want me to go?"

I wanted to say yes, but I was done trying to keep all the parts of my life from colliding. "Don't go anywhere near Davy. He'll kick your ass."

"Got it." Anthony's voice was a little quieter, and more serious than I'd heard before. Maybe there was a chance he had learned a thing or two. "Anything else I should know about the people here?"

"Nothing I can think of."

"Then I'm gonna get some food, okay?"

"That's what it's here for. The next Hound meeting—the next real one where we work out who's covering which part of town and who they're partnered with—will be Monday morning, seven o'clock. Got that?"

"I'll be there."

He finished off his drink and strolled to the stove, where he ladled a bowl full of the soup.

I thought about telling him he should also keep his hands off Sunny, since Davy and she seemed to have a thing going, but hell, he'd figure it out.

I snagged a beer out of the refrigerator and wandered across the room, saying my hellos to a few people while I took a winding route to Zayvion.

I was pretty sure he didn't see me coming, was pretty sure he didn't hear me.

Still, before I was close enough that both he and Victor should sense me, Zayvion shifted and gave me a smile over his shoulder. "Hey."

Victor stirred and turned. "Thank you for offering this place, Allie," he said, leaning his hip against the windowsill. "It's . . . refreshing."

I hadn't had a chance to talk to Victor since he'd been fired from being a Voice of the Authority for Faith magic.

He didn't look like he was taking the news too badly. As a matter of fact, he looked more relaxed than I'd ever seen him. Instead of the perpetual suit and tie, he was wearing a button-down shirt and jeans. I'd never seen him in jeans. He didn't look like he'd gotten any sleep, but the wary edge he carried in his eyes and body language had softened slightly. Maybe getting fired was a good thing for him.

"No problem," I said. "How are you doing?"

He raised his eyebrows. "Fine, in the long term. In short-term matters, I have ... concerns over the direction Bartholomew is taking things, but nothing so great I think I should call foul."

"They fired you." I said.

He shrugged. "They had to put the blame on someone they could discipline. That someone was me."

"And you're okay with that?"

"No." He looked at me, his eyes hard with anger. "I am very much not okay with that."

"They're idiots for what they've done," Zayvion said, pretty much voicing my opinion. "I don't know how I can follow that man. He doesn't even understand what he's doing, much less how to use magic—"

"Your job," Victor said. "Following him means you are doing your job. And your superior's capabilities aren't yours to question, Zayvion. You might not like him, but you will do as he says. No matter what he asks you to do." Here he gave Zay a hard look. This was obviously a point of contention between them. "That is your duty. To follow orders."

Zay scowled.

Victor didn't seem to care. "It's important we get things back on an even keel. This is no time to be questioning our jobs, our duty, or the methods of those who are in charge. This is the time to make sure all the loose ends get tied up and things go back to normal."

"He fired you," Zay said quietly. "If you're not a part of ... it," he said, to avoid saying "the Authority," "it will never be back to normal."

Victor pressed his lips together in a hard line. This had all the earmarks of the argument they'd gone over many times.

"Making hasty and uninformed decisions won't help anything, Zayvion," Victor said, though he was looking at me. "You getting angry does none of us any good and it certainly won't serve your ability to perform your duties."

"So how about another beer?" I handed Zay the beer and he took it. He was carefully reconstructing his mask of calm again, though I could feel his annoyance. "What's up with Anthony?" he asked.

"I told him he could come by if he called. He called. He came by. He has lousy timing."

Zay checked to see where Davy was in the room— still next to Sid, though Sunny had left the poker game to join them. She took Davy's hand and wandered off to the far side of the room with him. She walked until his back was against the wall, then took the beer bottle away from him. Davy was smiling now.

Sunny stood on her tiptoes and kissed him. Thoroughly.

Well, looked like things were working out for those two.

"Zayvion tells me you had your backpack stolen," Victor said, in a very nice small-talk segue.

I looked away from the lovebirds. "Nothing in there but my gym clothes, so they didn't get anything. Stupid and annoying, though."

"Did you track him?"

"What?"

"Did you use magic to track him?"

"I tried. Blew the spell. I wasn't feeling very well after my meeting with the new boss."

Zayvion slouched so his hip was propped against the windowsill.

"Have you been using magic much, Allie?" Victor asked.

"As much as always, I guess. Why?"

"I was curious. I heard you had a strong reaction to

magic when you saw Bartholomew. Dr. Fisher told me," he said to answer my unspoken question. "And Zayvion also brought it to my attention."

That was interesting. Victor wasn't a Voice anymore, which should mean he didn't have any sway in the Authority. Or at least no more than any other person. And yet both Zay and Dr. Fisher had gone to him with concerns about me. For Zay it made sense, I guess. Victor had been his teacher, mentor, and boss for years. But I didn't expect Dr. Fisher to go to him about me.

"We've all used more magic than normal lately," he said. "I wondered if it contributed to your discomfort."

"Could have." I walked up closer to Zayvion and looked out the window. "Or it might have been because his right-hand chick is a bitch and took her time to make sure that Truth cut deep."

"Oh?"

"She put pain in it, Victor. On purpose. And she enjoyed it."

"Hmm," he said.

Zay didn't glance at him, but I could tell this was another part of the argument they'd been having.

I didn't know what good arguing with Victor would do. He had no more power than the rest of us now.

"Has he assigned someone to your place?" I asked.

"Not yet," Victor said. "Though I suggested a few people I thought would be well suited to the position."

"Who?"

He shook his head. "Let's see what he does, who he chooses." He drank the last of his scotch. "It will say a lot about him." He gave me a steady look, glanced at Zay, who had gone back to staring at the city beyond the window, and said, "If you'll excuse me, I need to refresh my drink." Victor placed his hand kindly on Zayvion's arm, then strolled off to the kitchen.

I leaned my shoulder against Zay and felt the heat of

his anger, mixed with frustration and sadness. And, almost like a top note on too many deep scents, his relief that I was there, next to him.

"And everyone says I worry too much," I mumbled as I slipped my arm around his waist, hooking my finger in the belt loop of his jeans.

He shifted his beer to his left hand and draped his arm around me. "You do," he said.

"So do you," I said.

"I hide it better."

That was true. I stared out at the street, content in his arms, content in this moment, content that he was sharing some of his sorrow with me, holding me instead of pushing me away.

Evening was coming on, the day not yet ready to give up to dusk, but the sunlight gone a deep tangerine orange and gold, cutting yellow edges over the buildings and casting blue shadows below. A few people walked the street, many of them headed to Get Mugged or coming out of it, and I realized once again that Grant had set up a very successful business that seemed only to be getting more popular.

I wondered if he would ever give it up, sell out, turn it into a franchise. I heard him laugh, and Terric chuckle. Things were certainly changing. All of us were changing. It was strange to suddenly notice that I, and my friends, wouldn't be this way forever. That we might choose paths that took us far away. That we might take paths that meant we'd never see each other again.

Zayvion's arm tightened for a moment. He might not be able to tell exactly what I was thinking, but he could probably feel my melancholy. I leaned my head on his shoulder and watched the people walking on the street below.

A flash of green caught my eye. I focused on the source, hoping it was nothing more than an odd reflection off a store window, a car windshield, or maybe a camera flash.

But it was a man, wearing a brown sweater and a green scarf and a painter's cap. He was walking up the block, keeping pace with the rest of the crowd. The green flashed again. He paused, slowed his steps, and pressed his hand against his chest.

"What's wrong with him?" I asked Zay.

Zay glanced down. "Asthma attack?"

"He flashed green." I used my right hand to draw a very small Sight spell, set my Disbursement—muscle aches—and set magic into the glyph. Magic poured up into me and down my arm in a sticky, nauseating wave.

I held my breath to keep from throwing up my lunch and calmly focused on the Sight. A man-shaped, watercolor shadow stepped out of the guy on the street, stretching out of his chest, head, then legs one at a time, and last, his arms and hands. It was almost as if the watercolor shadow had been stuck inside and had grown too large. Like a crab shucking its shell, the shadow—the Veiled—pulled completely free and walked down the sidewalk, not exactly solid, but less insubstantial than before.

"Do you see that?" I asked.

Zay had also cast a quick Sight spell. "It doesn't look solid."

"It's not just a ghost either."

The Veiled strode up the block, then paused. It turned, looked straight at the den—straight up at Zayvion and me. And then it started toward us.

It got halfway across the street before it faded from sight, both magical and mundane.

"Um," I started.

Zay pulled away and strode across the room. A few people looked up as he passed. He walked out the door and I was on his heels. He took the stairs—faster than the elevator—and so did I. Within a second or two I heard more footsteps. Davy, for sure. After a floor, someone else.

Zay took the lobby in a few strides. I jogged to keep up. Once we hit the sidewalk, Zay poured magic in a very precise Sight spell.

I paused beside him. I wasn't feeling very well. That Sight I'd cast made me feel like I had a horrible case of motion sickness. And pounding down the stairs hadn't helped any. I was going to lose it. I jogged to the bushes and weeds on the corner and retched.

Good-bye, wine. Good-bye, lunch.

The breeze pulled over the back of my neck and across my bare arms. I sucked down lungfuls of it, trying to get the cold to settle my stomach. My right arm itched. It felt like hot oil was trickling down every line of magic there, scratching me bloody and leaving behind a hot, uncomfortable, cramping sensation.

To sum up, I was feeling fresh as a tulip, thank you.

"Need some water?" That was Davy.

"Napkin?" I asked. He produced one from somewhere, and I used it to wipe my mouth with shaking hands. I felt like I'd just been kicked in the gut by the worst and fastest flu ever. As I straightened, I was no longer nauseous. Even the pain in my arm was already easing.

Weird. Really weird.

I blew my nose and wadded the napkin up in my fist. Then I stepped back and looked around.

Zayvion was up on the corner past Get Mugged. He seemed to be smoking a cigarette. He didn't smoke. So, that was an Illusion. I was surprised to see Anthony across the street, where we'd last seen the Veiled, and walking up to the next block. What was he doing out here?

"You do know we have a bathroom," Davy said.

"What?"

"You could have puked there." He shoved his hands in his pockets and glanced at Zay, avoiding, I noticed, looking at Anthony. "What's up?"

"I don't know. I thought I saw something out here. Zay decided to check it out. Let's go see what he says."

"What sort of something?" Davy asked as we walked. He paced himself to my stride, close enough he could catch me if I stumbled, but far enough away that his shoes wouldn't get dirty if I got sick again. He was a pretty smart young man.

"I don't know. A flash of magic I've never seen before."

"Maybe a new ad?" Davy didn't pull Sight, but he took a closer look at the buildings around us. "Art? They're doing those magic art walk shows all the time now."

"Maybe." We passed in front of Get Mugged and I peered through the window, looking for flashes of green. Nothing.

I inhaled the deep burnt-chocolate scent of coffee and it didn't bother my stomach at all. Other than the lingering heat radiating off my arm, it was almost as if I hadn't been sick.

I stopped next to Zayvion. "Hey."

He threw down his cigarette and rubbed it out with the toe of his boot. That motion was mostly just to cover him letting go of the Sight and Illusion and whatever other spells he'd cast that he didn't want people to see. Worked pretty well. I don't think anyone on the street would look his way twice, though I knew Davy saw right through it.

Zay turned, his eyes filled with the gold fire of magic use, and put his arm around me, tipping his head in close. We started back toward the den. "You feeling okay?" he asked.

I nodded. "I'm okay now. Well?"

Zay kissed my temple gently. In that touch, that intimate contact, I could tell he hadn't found anything, hadn't felt anything, hadn't seen the Veiled.

Didn't mean it wasn't there, couldn't maybe still be there on the street. The Veiled were the leftover bits of dead magic users. Ghosts who wandered the city, and usually weren't any problem. But recently, they'd become more than a problem. Leander had crossed over into life, and then he had found a way to use the experimental technology my father had made—disks that could hold magic and let the user access that magic without a price—to make the Veiled solid. And when dead fragments of powerful magic users came back to life, they tended to be angry. The last batch had tried to kill me, and my friends.

Luckily, there was a swift way to deal with them— remove the disks from their necks and drain the disks of magic. Disks weren't easy to recharge, and as far as I knew, Leander didn't know what spells it took to do that. Without the disks, the Veiled were insubstantial ghosts.

But the Veiled I had seen just a few minutes ago didn't seem to have a disk in its neck. It had stepped out of a man. That was something new.

Davy lingered a moment, looking up the street after Anthony. Then he shook his head and followed behind us.

"So?" Davy asked. "You see anything, Zay?"

"Not really." That was mostly the truth.

"I'm getting pretty tired of you two keeping secrets from me," Davy said. "How many times do I have to tell you I'm on your side?"

"What side are we on?" I asked.

Davy shrugged. "Don't care. Just can't keep an eye out for you or for danger if you don't tell me what I'm supposed to be looking for."

"Beer," Zayvion suggested. "You should be looking for beer. Because that's all I want right now."

We started up the stairs, and Davy did not take the elevator, which meant Zay and I had no chance to talk.

Once we reached the second floor, the sound of everyone talking and laughing washed out into the hall, and I decided I didn't care. So I'd seen a Veiled. They were all over the city. Yes, it had appeared to be inside someone, but we saw no sign of a dead body, or the man actually being harmed in any way. Maybe it was just one of those things where the living and the dead were accidentally occupying the same space at the same time, and somehow, temporarily, merged.

Whatever. I wanted some tea to settle my stomach.

We walked back into the room. The party had gotten a little louder. The poker game had gathered a few onlookers, and the pile of cash in the middle of the table was respectable. Only three people were still in for that hand—Jack, Jamar, and Maeve.

Victor was sitting with some people I didn't know. He had refilled his glass, and looked comfortable.

Shame stood behind his mother and was dividing his time between watching the poker game, with his arm around Tiffany's waist, and glancing over at Terric.

Terric must have had another shot. Okay, maybe two. His tie was off, tucked into Grant's back pocket and his shirt was unbuttoned, revealing glimpses of his very toned chest and stomach. Grant and he were across the room from the poker game, near my desk, both standing, though Terric leaned against the wall, probably for support. Grant had a beer. Terric was grinning and describing something using a lot of hand motions to get his point across. Whatever he was talking about, it looked dirty.

I glanced at Shame again, and he didn't look angry.

No, when he looked at Terric there was concern and a kind of compassion I hadn't ever seen in his eyes before.

He caught me staring and just held eye contact with me, not explaining, not ignoring. There was a sort of pained reluctance to that look, as if he were trying to make a decision and having a very hard time of it. Then he turned his attention back to the poker action.

Terric laughed. Shame shook his head and slid a smile his way. Terric had the kind of laugh that was contagious, and I found myself smiling too.

Maybe the two of them, Shame particularly, would get it through his thick head that they were both pretty good guys who could have a decent friendship, if they'd just forget about the Soul Complement angst.

"Stop babysitting." Zayvion pressed a cup of tea into my hands.

Aw, I hadn't even asked for tea. I took a sip. Peppermint. Even though I am a coffee drinker, my stomach probably couldn't have handled much more than this. "Thank you," I said.

He nodded once toward the poker game. "I'm gonna get in on the next hand. You want to play?"

I shook my head. "You bring home the money, baby. I'm going to drink my tea."

Zay hesitated a second and took in the whole of the room as if just now realizing it was filled with people. His gaze held a moment on Terric, and then he looked at Shame, who was convincingly entranced by the cards.

Zay walked over to Terric.

Oh, I was not going to miss this. I walked that way too, hoping to catch whatever Zay was going to say to Terric.

Unfortunately, Zay just said hi to Grant and exchanged small talk about the great job he did catering the event.

I found a comfy spot on one of the oversized leather

chairs and drank my tea. Zay, having finished his sudden need to be social, with no more than a "How's the te-quila?" to Terric, and likely had also satisfied his curiosity of what was going on between Terric and Grant, strode over to the poker table.

Tension was high as the last hand was called.

A cheer roared out from the crowd. Maeve stood and bowed. Shame was quick to help her gather the spoils of her win, and pocketed a wad of it before she slapped his hands away. Then the six chairs around the table filled up with new players, Zayvion among them.

With a room full of Authority members and Hounds and civilians, I did something I never thought I could do. I sat there, relaxed, and didn't worry about a damn thing.

Chapter Five

The gathering started breaking up about midnight. I made Davy call cabs for anyone who'd been drinking, including Victor, and, wonder of wonders, no one argued with me about it.

Grant had left just before midnight. He didn't need a cab because he lived below Get Mugged next door. To my great surprise, Terric had not gone home with him. Terric had, however, shed his shirt, his shoes, his socks, and his belt in that order over the last three hours or so. He'd spent most of the evening barefooted, wearing nothing but his black slacks.

Not that the women in the room had seemed to mind.

Let me put it this way: it wasn't the clothes that made that man.

Pretty soon it was down to Zayvion, me, Davy, Shame, Terric, and a few of the other Hounds—Jack and Bea, who were snugged up and sleeping on one of the bunks along the far wall, and Sunny, who was sitting cross-legged on a top bunk, unbraiding her hair and watching every move Davy made.

"You staying?" I asked Davy.

He looked around the room, his gaze resting on Sunny. "Don't feel like driving."

I gave him a look.

"I mean," he amended, "I wouldn't dream of driving

since I drank one whole beer four whole frickin' hours ago. You?"

"Think I'll drag Zayvion home." I glanced at Terric, who was standing in front of the windows that overlooked Get Mugged. He had a beer in his hand and was drinking it while humming to himself. There was no way he was sober.

"Let me see what I can do with Terric," I said.

"Go get him, Mom."

"Shove it, Silvers."

I walked over to Terric. He must have seen my reflection against the dark window.

"Hello, Allie," he said quietly. "Whatever are you up to?"

"I'm offering to take you back to my place, where you can sleep on a couch. Or I'm offering to leave you here, where you can sleep on a couch."

"Lot of couches in those offers." He took a drink of beer.

"I can call you a cab."

"Mmm." His eyes, in the dark reflection of the glass, shifted. And I knew why. Shamus was walking this way.

I turned. Was going to say something, but Shame spoke first.

"I got him," Shame said. He was sober. I didn't think I'd seen Shame take so much as a sip of beer. "So, Ter, you gonna stare out at the empty all night?" He put his hand on Terric's shoulder. "Or you going to put your shirt on, for all that's decent, man?"

"I'm not wearing a shirt?" Terric sounded surprised.

"Nope." Shame handed him his shirt. "It's right here."

"How do you do that? Find my shirt like that? You always know. When I need stuff."

"Yes. I always know you need a shirt." Shame gave me a tolerant look. He apparently had done this with Terric more than once. "If you'd stop shedding your clothes every time you drink, I wouldn't have to try to keep you from getting arrested for indecent exposure."

"Mmm," Terric said. "True. Don't want to do that again." He worked on getting his arms into his shirt's sleeves.

"No, three times is enough," Shame drawled. "I'm done bailing your naked ass out of jail."

Terric got into the shirt and buttoned most of the buttons. "False arrest. I wasn't naked."

"Socks don't count, Ter."

"You want me to call you guys a cab?" I asked. "Unless . . . is Tiffany still here?"

"No," Shame said, "she is not. We don't need a cab. Ter's gonna sleep it off on the floor."

I hesitated. Terric had finished buttoning his shirt, and put his beer down, carefully, on the windowsill.

"What happened to all the couches?" he asked.

"Fine," Shame said. "You can sleep on the couch."

"I'm not tired."

"Maybe not," Shame said, taking Terric's elbow and guiding him over to the couch. "But we are tired of you."

Terric nodded. "Sensible."

Shame steered Terric until he was sitting on the couch. "There you go. I'll find you a blanket and a barf bucket."

"No." Terric reached out for Shame and somehow caught the sleeve of Shame's hoodie. "Tiffany's okay," he said. "You don't need my opinion, but I don't care. Happy for you and all whatever. But just . . . Could you stop with the anger? It's not my fault we can use magic. It's not my fault we work so good together. And I really . . ." He looked up at Shame, searching for something in his face. "I really want us to be . . . something."

Shame rubbed his fingers over his head, as if trying to wipe away Terric's words. "We are something, Terric,"

Shame said quietly. "You are drunk and I am tired. Go to sleep."

Terric laid back on the couch and propped his arm over his eyes. "You know what I mean, Shamus," he said in a soft voice. "You want it too. Friends. Us. You know I'm right."

"So full of shit." Shame walked away to the bunks against the far wall, apparently having forgotten he had promised Terric a blanket.

I walked in the opposite direction and pulled out a spare blanket from the shelf. I draped it over Terric, who had already passed out, and took a look at the rest of the room. Davy had claimed the top bunk with Sunny and they were whispering to each other. Shame settled into one of the reclining chairs that faced the windows and stretched his legs out.

Everyone else was asleep, including Zayvion, who was sprawled across the largest couch, which he had folded back to double the sleeping space.

Looked like my choices were to wake Zay up, drag him out into the cold and drive him home, then up the three flights of stairs to my house, or just walk a few feet and curl up beside him.

I chose easy, and settled down on the couch next to him. Zay shifted so I could put my head on his chest and my leg over his.

"Everyone done?" he mumbled, only half awake.

"Yes," I said. "Everyone is very done."

Even though there were plenty of people snoring, and thoughts about Shame and Terric, and Zay, and even the Veiled kept circling in my head, I slept a lot better than I expected. When I dreamed, all I saw were flashes of green light and the Veiled walking through bodies.

Sometime in the middle of the night, when it felt as if I'd only been asleep long enough to begin dreaming,

I heard a soft knock at the door. Feet hit the carpeted hardwood, and from the pace, I knew it was Davy shuffling to the door. He probably hadn't even gone to sleep yet.

I wondered who was at the door. Someone must have left something behind, or maybe Grant was back to try to convince Terric to go home with him.

Davy held his breath briefly while he looked out through the peephole. Then I heard him slide the chains and bolts.

"Thought you fucking went home," Davy said. "Everyone's asleep. Party's over. Go away."

There was a pause. A whisper I couldn't quite catch. I rolled onto my side so I could see what was going on. The light from the hall threw the person in the doorway in shadows. I wasn't sure who Davy was talking to, couldn't catch his voice, couldn't see his face.

Then Davy stepped back, walking away from the door, and the person followed him into the room. It took a second for my eyes to adjust, but I could finally make out who it was–Anthony.

Well, no wonder Davy was upset.

I shifted to go back to sleep when I realized something wasn't right. Anthony was following Davy, and I mean close on his heels. I guess Davy was tired enough not to notice. But Anthony didn't look right.

Then I saw it—a spark of green light.

"Davy?" I sat.

Davy stopped and Anthony ran into him.

Davy yelled.

Anthony hadn't just run into him, he had bit him on the shoulder.

Davy spun away and slammed a fist into Anthony's face. Anthony reeled back. He turned and ran, holding his hand over his bloody nose.

Davy was shaking. The room filled with people startled awake and ready to kick ass. But none of us were fast enough to stop Ant before he ran out the door.

I ran, rushing past Davy, who was swearing, out into the hall, barefoot, breathing hard. Footsteps pounded from the room behind me, the faintest hush of shoes on the stairs ahead of me leading down.

Down.

I hit the stairs at a dead run. Heard the front door bang closed before I'd even made it down a flight. Didn't care. Just kept going.

Made it to the bottom floor, bare feet slapping hard on the cold marble. I pushed out the front door, looked up and down the dark street. Didn't see anyone on the street at all.

I took a deep breath, shivered at the icy cold, set a Disbursement—headache this time—and drew a Sight spell. I pulled magic into it. The world broke into shades of old magic among vibrant new spells, bright neon dripping down buildings, pastels drifting along the empty street.

Didn't see Anthony, and couldn't hold the spell any longer.

Magic burned, sticky and painful, down my arm to my fingertips. I clenched my teeth to keep from throwing up. What was wrong with me?

I canceled the spell and stood there, shaking, barefoot in the night, trying not to lose the peppermint tea I'd drunk a few hours ago. I swallowed hard against the bile rising in my throat and blinked back pain tears.

My arm felt swollen and hot and heavy. Something was really wrong.

It took me a minute—not a good sign—to notice there were people around me. Zay, Shame, Davy, Bea, Sunny, Jack. It took me more than that minute to realize they were talking, making some kind of plan to hunt Anthony down.

" . . . take the east blocks," Zayvion said. "Got that?"

Everyone agreed and split up, Zay and Shame jogging off to his car, Sunny and Bea headed down the street, and Davy and Jack standing there staring at me.

"You want to go get your shoes or what?" Jack finally said.

"Right." I walked back into the building and took the stairs as quickly as I could. The sticky pain in my arm was easing and I didn't feel quite as sick.

So, that was good news.

I found my shoes and made it back downstairs in no time. I was feeling better, though still moving a little like I was walking against a hard wind.

Jack threw his cigarette down, crushed it, and tipped his head. "You okay?"

"Sure. Why?"

"You haven't said anything about the plan, and you generally make a point to tell us it's wrong and boss us around."

We started walking toward Davy's car.

"I missed the plan."

They both paused. "You sick again?" Davy asked.

"I'm fine."

"When you cast magic—did it make you sick?" he persisted.

"It's been a long damn day," I said.

"So, yes."

"Yes."

He glanced at Jack. "Ever heard of that?"

"What?" Jack said. "That magic hurts? Gee, no, Silvers. That's headline news."

"Ass," Davy said. "You setting Disbursements?"

"Davy," I said, "drop it, okay? I'm fine. What's the plan?"

Davy keyed the locks on his car. Jack took the backseat, which I hadn't really expected. I took the front and shut the door.

The door hadn't even latched before Davy did a very illegal U-turn, rolled the wrong way down a one-way street for half a block, then turned west.

"Is it only when you use Sight?" Davy asked.

"The plan," Jack said over my response, "is to hunt that little pecker."

"You throwing first?" I asked.

Jack shrugged. "That's fine." He took in a breath, held it, clearing his mind and focusing on the glyph he drew, then pulled magic into it.

It was a form of Sight, not the same one I used, but both our spells were subclasses of Sight. It didn't seem to make him sick. Figured.

"You okay?" I asked Davy. "Did he bite you?"

Davy's jaw clenched and so did his knuckles on the steering wheel.

"I think so. Haven't had a chance to see how deep it is, but so help me God, if he drew blood, I'm going to break his jaw. I'm serious, Allie. I don't care how much you think he can redeem himself. He's an ass. Even Pike would have given up on him by now."

I rubbed my eyes with my left hand, my fingers icy cold, even though my right arm still burned hot. "I can't think of anything to excuse this," I said.

Well, unless maybe that green spark I'd seen was caused by a Veiled. I didn't think Davy would take that reason as an excuse for getting bit. I'd just have to find another way to help Anthony once we got this straightened out. Maybe Sid would take him on as a private student and make sure he stayed far, far away from Davy.

"Hounds don't harm Hounds," I said. "Not at the den. He knows that. I'll tell him it's off-limits and try to hook him up with someone else."

"Finally, there's sense coming out of your mouth." He glanced in the rearview. "Anything?"

"Nope," Jack said. "Keep driving."

Jack canceled the spell, and drew another. I didn't know how far out he was casting, and I didn't feel like drawing on magic to find out. If I had to guess, I'd say he was looking in maybe a three-block radius, which would be a more detailed view than throwing Sight any wider.

"Your right shoulder?" I asked Davy.

He nodded.

"Want me to look?"

"Sure."

I unlatched my seat belt and turned on the overhead light. I glanced back at Jack, but he was looking out the window and didn't seem to care about the light. Looking through Sight, electric light wouldn't make that much of a dent in what he could see. Spells, especially new ones, outshone regular light. Any Hound worth a paycheck knew how to see the older, ashy spells through the glare. Since we were looking for Anthony, we were looking for new spells—things he would use to hide or conceal himself.

Davy wore a T-shirt, and I was pretty sure he had been wearing that when Anthony came in the room.

I pulled his sleeve up.

"Ow!" he said. "Too hot and too cold. What are you using? A lighter and an ice cube?"

"My fingers."

"Your fingers hurt."

I touched my fingers to my face. Hot and cold, yes, but not enough that I'd yelp about it.

"Don't be a baby." I pulled his sleeve up to reveal the top curve of his shoulder. He hissed.

I didn't see any marks, but his skin was bruised. From the yellow of the light and the slide of traffic lights rolling through the windows, I couldn't tell how bad it really was.

"Does it hurt?"

"Your fingers hurt."

"Does your shoulder hurt?" I asked.

"Higher up is more sore. Maybe he just stabbed me."

"Maybe." I dropped the edge of his sleeve and plucked at the material of his shirt so I wouldn't brush his skin.

I tugged the neck of his shirt back enough that I could see higher on his shoulder, at the base of his neck. "You're bruised," I said. "It's a weird black-green. But I think that's just the edge of it. I can't tell if it's bleeding or not. There's no blood on your shirt, though."

"Did you have to choke me just to tell me it's hurt?"

"I didn't choke you," I said settling back into my seat.

"You made it worse."

"It hurts more?"

He sat forward so as little of his back as possible touched the seat. "I told you it hurt. You had to stab at it."

"Davy, I barely touched you," I said gently.

"Don't barely touch me again."

That didn't sound like Davy. Even when he felt like hell, he never lashed out like that. Something was wrong.

"Got him!" Jack pointed at the window, his finger thumping into the glass. "He's down that alley and throwing magic like a son of a bitch. Stop the car, Davy."

Davy just kept driving.

"Davy," Jack said. "Stop the damn car."

Davy slammed on the brake and Jack bolted out the door.

"You stay here, okay?" I said to Davy. I did not need him killing Anthony. And from the anger rolling off him, I was pretty sure that's just what sort of mood he was in.

He didn't answer, just stared straight ahead, breathing a little hard. I got out of the car and Davy started coughing. Maybe he wasn't feeling well. Why hadn't I noticed that before?

Still dark, still cold, I shoved my hands in my pockets to keep from casting a spell. Right now, I was going to be backup and let Jack handle point. If Anthony threw something at either of us, I'd reconsider my position.

The alley stank of stale water and restaurant garbage, something with a curry overtone coming up out of the sewer grate. Jack walked straight down the alley like he was strolling through broad daylight. And since he had drawn another Sight spell, I assumed he could see everything as clearly as if the sun were out.

I just kept my eyes, ears, and nose sharp, and looked for any sign of Anthony.

That's when my phone rang.

Jack threw a Mute at me, and I didn't bother blocking the spell. I pulled out my phone and glanced at it. Zay.

"What?" I asked as I navigated over a pile of wet paper and something that looked like a tangle of panty-hose, or a gutted octopus.

"Bartholomew called us in. Shame and I. You find Anthony?"

"Jack has a line on him but no visual. We're still looking."

Zay paused, probably trying to figure out how to be next to me and how to follow his boss's orders at the same time.

"I'll see you back at the den after you're done," I said. And then I hung up.

There we go. Problem solved. He could go see what the almighty Mr. Wray wanted him and Shame to do, and I'd corner Ant and shake him until his brains poured out his ears.

The Mute Jack had thrown wore off slowly, little things coming to my attention. First the sound of traffic, then the whistle of a far-off train, and finally the sound of Jack, being very quiet as he took off running.

I was right on Jack's heels. I didn't see Anthony.

We booked it to the end of the alleyway. And then Jack stopped. Fast. So fast, he threw both hands out to keep me from taking another step, just like someone would do if they were standing at the edge of a sudden cliff.

Or what they would do if they were standing next to a dead body.

Chapter Six

I had fast enough reflexes to stop in time. Still, once I glanced down at the dead body, I felt like a Mack truck had just run me over.

It was Anthony.

He was dead.

Jack wasn't casting anything. He was just standing there, very, very still. He finally fished a cigarette out of his pocket and lit it. Then he took two steps backward.

"Found him," he exhaled with smoke.

I knelt, careful to keep my shoes far enough away that they wouldn't get bloody. But even without magic I knew there was no blood. Anthony wasn't breathing, that was obvious, but I didn't know what had killed him.

"Did he fall?" I asked. I reached out to touch the back of his head—he was lying sort of sideways—and Jack held out a pair of latex gloves for me.

"I'm assuming yes," Jack said. "He was on his feet running last I could tell, magic pouring out of him like a fucking sieve. I've never seen that. It was ... like he was bleeding magic."

I got the gloves on and felt his neck—no pulse—checked for injuries on the back of his head, his chest. Nothing.

He wasn't wearing the hoodie I'd last seen him in. Just a T-shirt. I pulled it up to see if there were any injuries on his stomach.

"Holy shit," I breathed.

Jack leaned in closer.

Black and blue lines ran from his hip and across his stomach like a tentacle creature lay just beneath the surface of his skin. The lines wrapped up the left side of his chest and wove together over his shoulder.

"What the hell is that?" Jack asked.

I just shook my head and rolled Ant enough that I could get a good look at his shoulder. Well, as good a look as I could in a dark alley. "You have a flashlight?"

There was a snick, and then Jack held his lighter closer to Ant's skin.

I pressed against the lines, bruises, whatever they were. What they weren't was a vein—not raised enough—or a tattoo—not flat enough. The mark was harder than his unmarked skin. I checked to see whether it ran down the back of his shoulder, and it did, tendrils reaching out to hook around his spine.

"Have you ever seen that?"

Jack shook his head.

I let go of Anthony, then pulled off the gloves and took a deep, calming breath. I needed to Hound this. To see if some kind of magic was the cause of this. The last few times I'd called on magic, it had made me sick.

So I stood and took a step or two back. Jack gave me a curious frown.

"You might want to move in case I barf," I said. I calmed my mind and set a Disbursement for muscle aches, then drew the beginning of Sight, Smell, Sound. I wanted one good hard look at this, at whether there was any foul play behind it.

Jack, wisely, backed off to stand behind me. He didn't draw on magic—which was good. I didn't know if he and I could throw at the same time and not have disastrous results.

I drew magic up out of the network lines and poured

it out through my fingers. My stomach clenched again, and I took a couple steps to one side and puked up the tea I'd drunk. I didn't let go of the spells, didn't lose focus.

Because I'm that good.

I wiped the back of my left hand over my mouth and tried hard to ignore my stomach. Magic hurt when I used it—I mean immediately hurt, not Disbursement hurt. I felt like I was standing under a too-hot sun, burning and swelling.

Ignore. I needed magic to show me what had happened to Ant.

Spells at either end of the alley lit up bright blue and soothing green and rose, but other than that, there weren't any spells—which was pretty much what I expected from an alley. People walked through alleys but very few permanent spells were used in them. There weren't even lingering spells from clandestine activities—Hush for drug deals, Illusions for stalkers, that sort of thing.

No, what was in the alley was me; Jack, who had tendrils of magic clinging to him like a slight haze of sunrise-colored cigarette smoke—that would be the Track he'd been using to hunt Ant; and Anthony, who did not look like Anthony.

Where Anthony Bell should be was a black man-shaped lump. Through the eyes of Sight, it was as if not magic but tar covered him from head to toe. As if something had sucked all the . . . the everything out of him, leaving a burnt husk behind.

I canceled the spells. I was breathing heavily, lightheaded and sick.

"Jack, tell me what you see. Use Sight on him."

Jack didn't argue, but cast a nice tight Sight. "Burned out?" he asked. "Fucking hell, Allie. I've never seen that done to a person."

I looked over at Anthony with just my eyes. "It's only when you see him with magic. Physically he's not burned—well, unless that's what those marks on his skin are. But he's mostly not burned. It could be a spell."

It could be Blood magic, Death magic, dark magic, something I had little training in and Jack wouldn't even know about. But I knew enough about Blood magic to know it wasn't that—no sweet smell of cherries. It didn't look like any Death magic I'd ever seen, though Shame would be able to tell me whether I was right. And as far as dark magic went—hells if I knew what it could and couldn't do.

"No spell I've ever seen," Jack said. "You want me to clean up so it doesn't look like we've been here?"

"No," I said, not because I wanted to be mixed up in Anthony's death, but because I'd met his mother. I'd looked into her eyes and told her that I would let her boy be one of my Hounds. And I wasn't going to leave one of my Hounds dead in the street. Even if he had hurt Davy.

"I'm going to call the cops," I said. "If you want to take off, that's fine."

Jack threw his cigarette down and didn't bother stamping it out in the wet alley.

"We said you don't go anywhere alone. None of us goes anywhere alone. I'll wait."

I had already pulled out my phone and dialed.

"Detective Stotts," a familiar voice said.

"Paul, this is Allie. I have a dead body on my hands. Anthony Bell."

"Where? Are you safe?"

"I'm fine. I don't even know how he died. We were following him. We're . . ." I looked at Jack. Jack told me which street we were on and I relayed that to Stotts.

"Who's with you?" Stotts asked.

"Jack Quinn. We'll stay here until you arrive."

"Give me ten minutes."

I hung up, and Jack sniffed, then found a relatively slime-free part of the wall to lean against. He lit another cigarette.

"So I guess you're pretty good friends with him now," he said.

"Who? Detective Stotts?"

He nodded.

"Not really. He's dating my best friend. And he's been . . . nice to me. But it's still just business between us." And I intended to keep it that way. The less Stotts was in my life, personal or magical, the better for him, and Nola.

"And him?" He tipped his chin toward Anthony.

I rubbed my left hand through my hair and suddenly realized I'd forgotten my coat. It was spring in Oregon. That meant it was cold. I crossed my arms over my chest and looked at Ant's still body.

"I ran into him and his mom this morning. They showed me his graduation pictures. He wanted to be a Hound. She asked me, they both asked me, if he could join us. I said yes."

"So he died the way he wanted to," Jack said. "A Hound can't expect any more than that. If it's not one thing that kills you, it's another."

I supposed that was his idea of a comforting remark. It just made me feel worse.

I heard footsteps. Jack did too, because he flicked his cigarette to the ground and scrubbed out the ember. The footsteps were coming from behind us. Not Stotts. No, it sounded a lot like Davy's pace.

I glanced over my shoulder. Sure enough, Davy was striding down the alley, like he was out to start a brawl.

"Settle down, Davy," I said. "He's dead."

Davy didn't slow. I put one hand out to stop him from storming past me and stepping on Anthony.

Davy grabbed my wrist and pulled me toward him.

"Hey," Jack warned.

I stumbled on the slick concrete. Which may have been the only thing that saved me.

Davy started coughing. And a flash of green sparked in the center of his chest. Even coughing, he was inhumanly strong and dragged me toward him, toward his mouth.

That was not Davy in those eyes. There was nothing but black—no whites at all—just black and tiny sparks of green swimming in the inky depth. I'd seen eyes like that. On the Veiled.

Jack threw a spell at Davy, and even without Sight I could see the magic sink into him. Just like I could see the magic—no, the Veiled—pulling out of him.

A pastel, foggy hand reached out of Davy's hand that was around my wrist and pointed at my head.

Oh, hell no.

I pushed at the foggy hand with my free hand. Nothing. I pulled as far away as I could, trying to keep from tripping over dead Anthony. A pastel person seemed to be taking shape between me and Davy, as if trying to get free of one body and into the other.

And by other, I meant mine.

Jack was swearing.

I finally realized he was swearing at me. "Would you just fucking duck?"

I ducked as far as I could with Davy's hand still twisting my wrist.

Something hit Davy from behind.

Davy fell, dragging me with him. I scrabbled to get away from him, my left hand landing square in the middle of Anthony's chest.

There was a pastel flash.

And I could have sworn Anthony inhaled.

"Shit!" I pushed away from him. Davy was on his

hands and knees, coughing like he was going to lose a lung.

"Anthony's moving!" I yelled.

Jack cast another spell—Impact, I think—and threw it at Anthony. No, not Impact. Freeze.

Anthony was no longer moving. But I didn't know if that was because of his deadness or because of Jack's spell.

Davy pushed back to sit on his heels, his hand on his thighs. He was no longer coughing. "Fucking Christ," he whispered. "What the fuck?"

Took the words right out of my mouth.

Jack looked over at me. For an explanation.

"Davy, I think you were occupying the same space as a dead person—a ghost. Shut up, Jack."

Jack hadn't said anything. He just held up his hands to indicate he didn't care how crazy the answer was, he was just looking for an answer.

Typical Hound.

"I think it—the dead person, ghost thing—is gone now," I said. "That's why you were coughing. I think it went into Anthony."

We all looked down at Anthony, who was still not moving, though his blank, glassy eyes stared wide.

Davy was sitting no more than a few inches away from Ant and seemed to notice that. He pushed up onto his feet and staggered a couple steps before he caught his balance. Neither Jack nor I reached out to help him stay steady.

With unknown magics, and an unexplained dead, un-dead, maybe re-dead body at our feet, neither one of us was dumb enough to touch Davy, who may have just had too much deadness in him.

"You okay, Silvers?" I asked him.

He rubbed at his face, then his neck, rolling the shoulder Anthony had bit.

Oh. No.

"Davy, do me a favor, okay?" I said calmly. "Pull your shirt off so I can see your shoulder again."

He stood there, breathing a little hard, his hair messed up, and his skin that flulike pasty green-white color. "Really?"

"Yes."

He pulled off his shirt, wincing when he had to roll his shoulder to get it over his head.

"Turn around and let me see your shoulder and back," I said.

He turned. A bruise, not nearly as dark as the marks on Anthony, was spreading out from the very noticeable bite mark on the back of his shoulder. The edges of the bruise had a few ragged lines starting off it, like a storm cloud just beginning to drop streamers of rain. I had no doubt those streamers were going to turn into lines. Just like the lines on Anthony.

"You've been bit, Davy," I said. "Anthony bit you."

He turned his head to try to see over his shoulder, but didn't have the right angle on it. "Does it look bad?" he asked.

I glanced at Jack, who still had one hand up, his pointer and thumb pressed together as if he held a spell there. Which he probably did. He caught my look. There was no mercy in his eyes.

"Yes, it looks bad. But I know a doctor who might be able to help you. Dr. Fisher. I think you've met her before."

"Can I turn back around and put on my shirt? I'm fucking freezing."

"Go ahead."

"The spell on Ant is about to wear off," Jack said. "You ready?"

"Davy," I said, "I want you to step on the other side of Anthony. I need to keep you in my sight, and keep you out of the range of fire. Over there by the wall should work."

He looked at Jack, looked at me. "Christ," he whispered. But he did as I said, and stepped around Anthony, careful not to touch him. He tucked his hands into his armpits and stood with his back against the brick wall.

"Don't use magic," I said to him. "We don't know what effect that will have on you right now."

He swallowed, nodded.

"Okay, Jack. Let's see if he has a pulse."

Jack canceled the Freeze spell with his left hand.

Anthony didn't move, didn't breathe.

We waited. No exhale, no inhale, no heat radiating off him. No movement at all. If Ant was alive, he was faking death incredibly well.

"He doesn't look alive," I said. "But we're not going to risk anything. Jack, I want you to take Davy back to the den. Keep an eye on him. Davy, you're basically under house arrest until I get you a doctor."

"Like hell—"

"And Jack is going to make sure you stay put at the den until Dr. Fisher shows up. Got that?"

"Who's going to guard you?" Davy asked, all the fire gone out of him. He had closed his eyes. If his knees hadn't been locked, I didn't think he'd be standing.

"Detective Stotts is on his way here now. I'll be fine."

Jack let go of the spell he'd been holding and instead pulled out a Bowie knife and a set of handcuffs. Man wasn't messing around. "Let's drive, Silvers. Walk."

I opened my mouth to tell Jack to stash the knife, but decided he was right. Maybe having a weapon in his hand would discourage Davy from trying to grab him like he grabbed me. Or maybe the Veiled that had possessed him was gone now, leaving Davy exhausted and used.

"He's still one of us," I said as Davy pushed away

from the wall and walked, dazed, down the alley toward the car. "Don't hurt him."

"I got it," Jack said.

I grabbed his arm before he passed me. "I mean it, Jack. He's like a little brother to me. Don't hurt him."

Jack just looked down at my hand on his arm, then gave me a steady gaze. I let go of his coat, and he strode down the alley to where Davy was waiting on the sidewalk.

I inhaled and blinked back sudden tears, then pulled out my phone. Things were going to hell. Ant was dead. I'd just looked into his mom's proud, hopeful eyes and told her I'd do what I could to look after her boy. That I'd take him in and help him on his way to the dream he most wanted to achieve.

Didn't matter that I'd also told her how dangerous it was. First day on the job—hell not even that, he wasn't on a job—and he wound up facedown in a dirty alley.

On top of that, Davy was hurt, Jack might be a little trigger-happy, and every time I pulled on magic I felt like it turned me inside out. I crossed my arm over my chest where the burn from yesterday morning still stung, and rubbed my arm to try to stay warm. Davy was right—my left hand was very cold and my right was fevered.

Dad? I thought, just to see if he was still there, just to see if everything between him and me was the same.

No reply. Which didn't mean he wasn't there, but wasn't exactly reassuring either.

I cleared my throat and dialed Dr. Fisher.

"Dr. Fisher," she said, a little huskily.

I didn't think I'd ever been so grateful to hear her voice.

"Hi, this is Allie," I said, even though I probably didn't have to because she had caller ID. "Davy Silvers was hurt. By magic. Can you come see him?"

She paused. "Where are you?"

And that's when I realized it was the middle of the damn night.

"I'm waiting for Detective Stotts to come by. I'm Hounding tonight. But Davy was with me and he's hurt."

"Davy's one of the Hounds?" she asked.

"Yes. You met him a while ago at the den. He's young—under twenty maybe—thin, blond, always following me around."

"How is he injured?"

"Magically, otherwise I wouldn't have called you. I mean I wouldn't have disturbed you in the middle of the night."

She paused again. "Allie, I think it might be better if you took him to the hospital. Call 911 if you need an emergency transport."

I stopped pacing. "Is it because he's a Hound?" It sounded like I was accusing her of betraying her Hippocratic Oath. I knew I could take him to any one of the hospitals to have him looked at by normal doctors who knew how to treat normal magical injuries.

But one, this was no normal magical injury I'd ever seen before, and two, Dr. Fisher had never once turned me away when I was in trouble.

What had changed?

"Yes," she said. "Partly it's because he's a Hound. Allie, you know I have been very busy. Bartholomew has me . . ." She paused for an extra-long moment, then sighed. "I have a very specialized list of clients and patients I've been tending. I simply cannot bring anything else into my practice right now."

I heard a car brake and an engine turn off. Stotts. Or so I hoped.

"Bartholomew told you not to help me, didn't he?" I asked.

"This is nothing I want to discuss on the phone," she said.

Which meant two things—yes, it was Bartholomew, and her phone was tapped—or at the very least her house calls were being monitored. Possibly by Bartholomew.

He was either paranoid or an ass.

"I'm disappointed," I said. "Good-bye."

I hung up. I wasn't going to throw a snit about it. I just needed a way to help Davy before Stotts showed up and got his nose mixed up in my business. Yes, I wanted him to figure out what to do with Ant, but I wasn't sure I wanted him to help me with Davy.

Hell, I didn't even know if Davy needed anything more than a good night's sleep.

Who could I call?

Collins.

I jumped. I had not expected my dad's voice so loud in my head.

Who? I asked.

Eli Collins. A colleague of mine. Very good with magic, and with medicine. Not a part of the Authority. Not anymore.

He's a doctor? I asked.

He's an expert in magical injury.

That was not quite a yes. *He's trustworthy?*

I trusted him when I was alive.

And that wasn't quite a yes either. But really, what choice did I have? *Do you remember his number?*

He did, and I dialed. A cheerful voice with a slight English accent answered. "Good morning, this is Collins."

It was what? Three a.m.? No one in his right mind should be that happy at three a.m.

"Hello, my name is Allie Beckstrom," I began.

"Allison. I've wondered if I'd ever hear from you. My deepest condolences on your father's death."

"Thank you. I understand you're a doctor?"

"Is that what he told you?"

I heard a car door slam and the hard-soled footsteps of someone headed my way. I paused long enough to listen to the pace. It sounded like Stotts. I thought it was Stotts. But whether it was or wasn't, I needed to wrap up this call quick so I could deal with whoever was approaching.

"He told me you could help a friend of mine who's been hurt by magic."

"I certainly can try. Where would I meet this friend of yours?"

"He's at the old warehouse next to Get Mugged. Do you know where that is?"

"Get Mugged, the coffee place?" he asked.

"That's it."

"Do I need to know anything else before I arrive? Or will this be clean?"

"Clean?"

"Will I need to arm myself?" He sounded amused.

"I wouldn't. The place is occupied by Hounds and most of them have some sort of weapon on them and are twitchy about strangers. He's a Hound and he's hurt. I'm trying to get him medical care."

"Of course. I shall proceed with the utmost discretion. And you will guarantee payment?"

"Yes."

"Very well. Pleasure doing business with the Beckstroms again."

"Right," I said, not paying all that much attention. "Good-bye." A figure was walking toward me—and from his build, his walk, and the trench coat and long scarf he was wearing, I knew it was Paul Stotts.

"Hi, Paul," I said. "I need to make a quick call. Anthony's right here." I pointed at where Ant lay, but didn't have the heart to look at his still, still body again.

I dialed Jack's phone.

"Quinn," he said.

"I'm sending a doctor over. His name's Eli Collins. I'll pick up the tab."

"Got it. Stotts there?"

"Just showed up. How is he?"

"Same."

"Be there soon." We both hung up. I turned to Stotts. He handed me a cup of coffee, and I almost wept out of gratitude. I was freezing, sick. Worried about Davy, angry and sad about Anthony. Coatless and tired.

The smell of regular, plain old normal coffee filled my senses and did what it alone could do to ground me in reality. Told me the world was still moving forward, regular people were working regular jobs, coffee was being brewed, all was well somewhere out there.

I took a grateful sip.

"Thank you," I said.

"So tell me what happened." Didn't ask me why I was out, coatless on a cold night, in the middle of an alley with a dead guy at my feet. Of course in my line of work—Hounding—this was just a normal day on the job.

"Anthony came by the den tonight. We were having a sort of . . . memorial for a friend of ours who died."

"Who?"

"Her name was Chase. She was Zayvion's ex-girlfriend."

"How'd she die?" he asked.

"Overdose," I said without hesitation. It was the lie the Authority had circulated, and the one they expected us to stick to. I think I managed that one word pretty well. And besides, if he checked the records of her death—not that I thought Stotts would suddenly become curious about a stranger's death when he had a fresh dead person on his hands—he'd see all her stints in and out of rehab. He could probably even shake down a couple dealers and they'd tell him she'd bought from them.

Even though she hadn't. Even though she didn't use drugs. Even though it most certainly was an insane magic user from the other side of death who had killed her—quite horribly—with Death magic.

He'd find the cause of death overdose. Because that's what the Authority said it was. And that's what they wanted him, and everyone else, to find. The Authority, all those record and paper-pushing people like Tiffany Lowe back at the party, were very thorough about covering the Authority's tracks.

"So then what happened?" Stotts asked. He knelt next to Anthony's body, but didn't touch him.

"He attacked Davy Silvers. They have history."

"Pike?" Stotts asked.

"Yes. I think Anthony bit Davy—not in a fight. He just walked up behind him and bit him on the shoulder. I don't know why. Davy hit him. Then Anthony ran out the door. There were a lot of us there. Some who had been drinking. But enough of us heard it and ran out after Anthony to try to stop him."

"And you happened to find him?"

"Jack Quinn was with me. So was Davy. Jack was using Sight. Thought he spotted Anthony down this alley, using magic. So we got out to follow him. And this is what we found."

Stotts straightened and looked down the alley and back out at the street.

There was just enough light that the sky had gone from black to a bruised blue. Nowhere near morning, but time was passing. I wondered how long I'd stood here.

"And so you called me. Why me, Allie?"

I took another drink of the coffee. "Could be because you bring me coffee," I said.

"Or?"

"I think magic was involved. Something . . ." I stared at his profile, strong, handsome. A good man who did his part to keep magical crime off the street. I could lie, tell him Anthony had been mixed up in illegal magic—and that had been true at one point, but I was pretty sure he really had done his best to clean up his life and move away from that sort of thing.

"Allie?" Stotts looked over at me.

I decided to tell him the truth. "There was something really strange about him, Paul. He bit Davy—and he'd told me over and over that he was planning to stay out of his way, just as long as I accepted him back into the Hounds."

"Did you?"

I nodded. "I saw him and his mother this morning—well, yesterday morning. He finished high school. His mother was so proud of him—" I swallowed hard against tears again. This was killing me. I inhaled and pushed all my emotion away. People died every day. I'd seen it. And right now, my job was to hand this over to Stotts to see if he had any idea about the marks on Anthony. Then I'd go back home, or maybe to the den, check on Davy and get another four hours of sleep.

"She asked me if I'd let him back in to the Hounding group. I told them yes. So he came by earlier in the evening, left, and then he came back. What time is it?" I asked.

"Four o'clock."

"So almost two hours ago, he showed up, bit Davy, and ran off."

"And how was magic involved?" he asked.

"Jack said he was using magic like he was leaking it."

"Jack said. What did you see?"

"I didn't cast."

He raised his eyebrows and took a drink of coffee. "Want to tell me why not?"

No. But I would anyway.

"It's making me sick—immediately ill. I don't know if I'm completely screwing my Disbursements or what, but every time I use it, I feel like I'm going to hurl. So I let Jack hunt him."

Stotts nodded. "Hold my coffee and step back a bit."

I did so. He inhaled, exhaled, twisted the ring on his left hand—his wedding ring he still wore even though his wife had died. I noted it was now on his pinky. Maybe it had been there for a while. Maybe it had been there since my friend Nola had been in town.

Interesting.

He cast a nice, clean Sight and held his hand spread wide as he directed the Sight down the alley, back up the alley past me. He frowned.

"You sure you're feeling okay?" he asked me.

"I'm fine. Cold. Can you hurry?"

He turned back to face Anthony and cast another spell—this one much more complicated. I was once again impressed with his training. For some reason I had this idea that only members of the Authority or Hounds were any good at casting magic. But Stotts could stand shoulder to shoulder with either and more than hold his own.

I couldn't quite catch the motions since I was standing behind and to the side of him, but it seemed to be a variation on Sight. He didn't move, didn't really even seem to breathe. He simply stood there and looked at Anthony. I knew he was looking through magic, seeing things I wished I could see.

"Well?" I asked.

He didn't answer me, but dropped the spell and pulled out his phone. He thumbed a key. "This is Stotts.

I want the van down here. Full containment. And a stretcher. Third grid seven. That's it." He put his phone in his pocket and stepped back to me.

"Did you Hound him at all?" he asked.

"Yes."

"What did you see, Allie?"

"He looked burned out, burned up. Or like tar or something covered him. Smothered him."

He nodded. "Can you tell the signature of whoever would have thrown a spell like that?"

"No." A chill washed over my skin. That's what seemed so weird about it—I mean, yes, it was weird anyway, but there was no signature. It wasn't like someone had thrown that smothering magic at Anthony. It was more like magic had consumed him without any hand to guide it.

"Allie?" Stotts asked. "Are you going to be sick?"

"No." I was already sick. But I refused to give in to it. "I need to walk. Is it okay if I go, or do you need me?"

He glanced up at the sky, then at the street. Even though it was only four in the morning, the city was stirring, the sounds of cars and traffic scratching to life, distant, but rising.

"I don't want you out alone. I'll call you a cab."

I considered fighting him on that, but really I didn't expect him to give in. "I got it." I dialed, got a cab company. By the time I hung up, a familiar white van pulled up and blocked the alleyway. Stotts' crew.

"See you around, Stotts," I said.

Paul was still staring down at Anthony, his coffee untouched in his hand. I didn't know if he heard me. But by the time I'd gotten to the sidewalk, he finally said. "Be careful, Allie. This is . . . something else."

He didn't know how right he was.

Chapter Seven

The cab got there just as Stotts' crew were getting out of the van. I didn't stay and say my hellos to the police officers. All I wanted was a long shower and a change of clothes. I didn't have a change of clothes at the den, so I asked the driver to take me home first.

I kept my phone in my hand, waiting for a call from Jack or Zay or, hell, Stotts. But no one called. I asked the driver to wait and jogged into my apartment building. I stopped outside my door, like I always did, and listened for any sounds. Nothing. Not even the rustle or snuffle of Stone in there messing around.

I was beginning to wonder where Stone was. I hadn't seen him for a couple days now, and even if I didn't happen to be in the apartment when he was, he always left evidence of his visit—usually in the form of stacking up something I'd sworn was unstackable, like spoonfuls of Jell-O. That had been fun to clean up.

I let myself in, grabbed a clean shirt, tank top, sweater, jeans, socks, and underwear and wondered where my gym bag was. Stolen. Right. So I stuffed my clothes in a shopping bag and jogged back down the stairs. Eventually I realized my phone was ringing.

By the time I dug it out of my pocket, it had stopped. The caller ID belonged to Jack. I dialed him back.

"Quinn," he said.

"Hey, Jack. How's it going?"

"You know this Eli Collins?"

"Never met him. Was recommended to me, though. Why? He legit?"

I got back into the cab and gave the driver the address for the den.

"Too good to be true," Jack said.

Hounds are suspicious. Collins might just actually be that good and be true. He was my father's contact, after all, and my father never settled for second best. "Think he's dangerous?"

"Everyone's dangerous for the right price," he said.

"Well, I'm paying him not to be dangerous. He help Davy any?"

"That's the thing. Said he won't start without talking to you first."

"So put him on," I said.

"Not on the phone. Here. He wants you here."

"I'm on my way. Anyone else still there?"

"Just us Hounds. All your other friends took off."

I thought about who of the Authority had stayed the night. Terric, Shame, and Zay. Zay and Shame had gone out hunting Ant and then been called away by Bartholomew, so I knew they were gone. Terric must have gone home, or maybe Zay and Shame had taken him to see Bartholomew. I just hoped he hadn't driven. Boy was probably still a long way from sober.

Sunny had stayed too. But everyone else—Victor, Maeve, Hayden, and all the people whose names I hadn't memorized—had left around midnight.

They'd probably all gotten lots of sleep. Probably hadn't had someone bite their friend. Probably hadn't had to chase someone through the night down a dirty alley. Probably hadn't had to deal with a dead body, a dead kid.

Lucky bastards.

"Allie?"

I still had the phone to my ear and the silence had stretched out. "I'll be there. Tell Collins to wait a minute."

I hung up. The morning was nice. Blue sky with just a string of clouds pulled across it, and not even cold enough for me to see my breath. I just wished I felt as sunny and upbeat as the weather.

It didn't take long to get to the den. I didn't see Zay's car, or Shame's for that matter. I paid the driver with the credit card in my jean pocket and stepped into the building, listening. Low voices to the right—that would be the paranormal investigators who rented out the office space on this floor. No sound from above. Hounds made it their job to be quiet. Always.

I headed up.

By the time I reached the top of the stairs, I decided it was stupid not to get something to eat at home or on the way. I'd lost everything I'd tried to keep down, and I was tired. My knees were doing that weird low-blood-sugar quiver.

But I pulled my shoulders back and stepped into the room like nothing was wrong.

"Morning," I said. "Someone better be brewing coffee."

"All set," Bea said from the kitchen space. "And there's scones."

I knew where the scones came from. Grant.

I took in the room as I headed for a cup of coffee. Sid was still here, snoring in the easy chair by my desk. Someone had done a good job of cleaning up the place so it didn't look like a party had happened. I had to guess that was Bea. Jamar and Theresa weren't anywhere to be seen.

Jack stood near the windows over by the bunk, and on the bottom bunk lay Davy. Standing next to Davy, and directly across from Jack like a gunfighter in an old western duel, must be Eli Collins.

"So good of you to come by," I said as I put the pot back on the burner and picked up a scone. I took a bite, chewed and swallowed. Maple hazelnut. Delicious melt-in-your-mouth Grantness. "I'm Allie Beckstrom."

Jack flicked a gaze my way, and Eli Collins turned.

"Very pleased to meet you, Allison." He extended his hand. He was younger than I'd expected, maybe in his early thirties. Thick sandy brown hair cut just a little short, wire-rim glasses, a suit vest over a white shirt with rolled-up sleeves, and slacks. His face was long, friendly, and handsome. Except for his eyes. A little too bright, a little too happy. Just this side of madness, if I had to make the call, and since I'd invited him over here, I had to.

I shook his hand. "Nice to meet you too." His handshake was gentle, not soggy, reassuring. Maybe he knew he projected a "mostly mad" vibe and made up for it with a nice firm handshake. The handshake felt sane.

"So are you a doctor?"

"I am not currently practicing, though I specialize in magical wounds. I've forgone that for years, to instead pursue research and development."

Jack gave me another look. The one that said, *Can I throw this clown down the elevator shaft now?*

"Jack tells me you wanted to talk to me before treating Davy?" Enough time had been wasted. I was tired, hungry, and in no mood for polite conversation.

"In private, if you don't mind."

"Come on out of the room then." I turned and picked up the rest of the scone and popped it in my mouth, washing it down with coffee before I reached the door. I headed up the stairs and Mr. Collins followed without a word. In the back of my mind, I realized he could be trying to get me out of sight so he could murder me or something.

He's not going to kill me, is he? I asked Dad.

I don't think so.

Well, not complete confidence, but enough. Plus, those weapons-training and self-defense classes hadn't gone to waste. I could handle myself.

I unlocked the door and held it open for him to walk in first. He stepped in past me, his shoes making a pleasant thump across the beautiful original hardwood floor. I flipped on the light—not that I had to. Morning poured long rectangles of light across the room, giving it a soft burnish. The mattress on the floor in the far corner with my spare quilt and extra blankets was hidden in shadow, leaving the room looking as if it was empty, untouched.

"Very nice property," he mused in that pleasant accent of his. "Is it yours?"

"I lease. So what did you want to talk to me about?"

"This friend of yours, the young Mr. Silvers?" Good lord, he made it sound like the first act of a stage play. "Do you understand how, exactly, he has been injured?"

"No." Honesty. The only way to fly.

He paced toward the high windows, his hands behind his back, right hand clasping left wrist. "Let me be very clear as to the injuries I see upon him then." He paused in front of a window as if gathering his thoughts, then turned and stood in front of the wall between the windows.

So he was a cautious man who didn't like to give people a clear shot at him through windows, if people were watching. That indicated a shady past. Of course the very fact that he knew my father indicated a shady past.

"He has been infected." He stopped as if that explained it all and watched my reaction.

"By what?"

"Ah," he said finally catching on that I wasn't trying to play dumb. It came naturally.

"First off, I believe he was involved in Blood magic rites. You are acquainted with the Authority, are you not?"

Okay, now I was fully awake. I held his gaze, trying to read the reasons behind that question, trying to read anything behind those smiling, too bright eyes.

"Yes."

"Good, that will simplify my explanation. He's been used for dark Blood magic. Not recently, but within the last year. It has left a mark on him. Changed how he uses magic, I'd think, though it may have been gradual enough that he didn't notice it."

He was right. Davy had been put in the hospital because his ex-girlfriend Tomi had gotten mixed up with Greyson, who had been using dark magic and Blood magic to release the Hungers through the gates of death into life.

Davy hadn't ever quite been the same since. For one thing, he could feel when other Hounds were hurt, especially if they were hurt by magic.

His medical records wouldn't be difficult for someone like Collins to find. So I was not impressed. "And?" I asked.

"And that is why I believe the infection is spreading so quickly in him."

"What infection?"

"He's been bitten by a Veiled."

We stood there a moment, just staring at each other. Outside, the train whistled and a car or two drove by. He didn't flinch, didn't twitch, didn't change his stance on what he'd just said.

"He was bitten by a kid," I said. "Another Hound."

"Really? Who?"

And I suddenly did not trust this man with any information at all. Dad said he was once aligned with the Authority. He might still be, might be on his own, or might be aligned with someone or something else.

"Another Hound," I repeated. "Can you treat the infection?"

"I can treat it. I am uncertain that I can cure it. It isn't like a cold or some other common malady, Allison. Your friend Davy is being poisoned." He paused to see how that news sank in. When I gave no outward indication that it surprised me, he added, "By magic. Magic is poisoning him. And unless we can stop the spread of magic inside him, I am afraid there won't be any chance to cure him at all."

"You're telling me he's going to die?"

"Yes," he said, a little too excitedly for my taste. "But that isn't the crux of it. The heart of the matter is that magic is poisoning him. I've never seen this before. It is almost as if the magic itself is tainted. I can't know, of course, unless I run some tests."

He paused again, watching me. Finally, "That's what I wanted to ask you about. Since he is fevered and barely coherent, I couldn't very well have him sign permission. I wondered if you knew of a parent, a spouse?"

"No. We're Hounds. We don't talk about our private lives."

"That puts us at loggerheads, then. Unless you have any legal say for his health care while he's under your employ?"

"Tell me what kind of tests you're going to run. In detail. Then I'll sign your papers."

He clapped his hands together. "Wonderful! All the preliminary tests will be done with the least amount of discomfort to Mr. Silvers. I'll need to draw blood, a urine sample. I'll want to set a very low-level Syphon on him to see if we can draw the toxins out via conventional magical techniques." He raised his eyebrows, and I nodded.

"I take it you'll want me to run these tests here?" he asked.

"Can you be discreet?"

He took in a short breath as if he were going to say

something, but instead he just smiled. It was a comforting kind of smile, even though his eyes, his body language told me he was at his core a man who had killed other men. And enjoyed it.

"Very."

"Then here is fine. This floor. We can bring a bed up." I looked around the room. Not much to work with. Just the mattress and the kitchen that was stocked, but not for more than a few days.

"This will work very well," Collins said. "Perhaps we can borrow some of the furniture from downstairs?"

"Yes."

"Perfect," he said. "I shall unpack my things. I left my bag in the car."

"You'll have a Hound with you at all times," I said as we walked toward the hall.

"Yes, of course. I'd like to examine you also, Allison," he said once we were in the hall.

"Me? Why?"

"I believe magic might have changed you."

"Old news," I said, shoving my magic-marked right hand into the pocket of my jeans. I didn't want Collins to touch me, or magic around me. The last doctor who'd gotten all interested in how magic had changed me had tried to kill me to raise my dad from the grave. And right now, I needed to stay clearheaded so I could keep an eye on what he was going to do to Davy.

One sicko at a time.

We started down the stairs. "If you reconsider," he said, "for science."

"I'll let you know."

It took about an hour to get one of the bed frames broken down and taken up the elevator to the second floor. We also transferred a couple chairs and a long folding table. Sid and Jack helped me move things, while Bea stayed with Davy.

Mr. Collins whistled his way happily out to his car, and then hummed to himself as he set up equipment that would have made a mad scientist drool. I didn't recognize half of the things he spread out on the table, but I could feel the magic worked into them. Most of his medical equipment reminded me of my dad's storm rods, or the disks that held magic.

It was like he had a trunk full of my dad's experimental magic-tech equipment.

Much of it is, Dad said quietly. *We worked very closely together before I met Violet. He helped develop much of the medical applications of my products.*

So Dad had known him for years. I wondered if he and I had ever met.

"Are you ready for us to bring Davy?" I asked.

Collins glanced over his shoulder. "Yes."

"Should we take any precautions?"

He stopped fiddling with the buttons on some kind of monitor screen and looked up at the rafters. "You say someone bit him?"

"Yes."

He looked back down at the table and started messing with things again. "We have no indications, but just to be on the safe side, you might want to gag him."

"No."

"Then a piece of tape over his mouth would work." He turned. "Maybe a surgical mask. Something to keep him from accidentally biting someone."

"He's barely conscious. He's not going to go around biting people."

His bright eyes flicked over my face as if he couldn't decide which part of my features interested him most. He finally settled on my lips. "We don't know how this magical infection spreads. It might be simply from touch, though I'm assuming many people have touched him and up to this point no one is feeling any ill effects?"

I nodded. I didn't feel any crappier than I usually felt.

"It could be an airborne pathogen, fluid, blood, magic. We don't know. Not yet. But if we want to stay safe, we must consider gagging Mr. Silvers." He pressed his lips together with a short nod and turned back to his work.

I wasn't going to gag my friend. I walked out of the room, leaving Jack behind to keep an eye on Collins, who was humming again. I was suddenly glad Jack kept a big knife on him.

I took the stairs down to the main room. Bea had pulled an easy chair over by the bunk where Davy was sleeping.

"Ready for him?" she asked without looking up. Hounds. Good ears.

"Has he moved?"

"No. He mumbled some, like he was having a dream, but otherwise he's been pretty quiet. Still running a fever, though."

"Let's see if we can wake him," I said. "If not, we're going to have to figure out how to carry him upstairs."

Bea hit the MUTE button on the TV remote and stood. "I can wake him."

"No magic."

"Really? Why not?"

I shrugged one shoulder. I could make up a lie, but I didn't see why I should. "Mr. Collins thinks it might be some kind of infection from using magic. If we use more magic on him, I don't know if it will make it worse."

I walked over to the bottom bunk. Davy was pale, sticky green where the shadows lay across his face and just the lightest shade of blue around his lips and eyes. I wondered if the mark on his shoulder had gotten worse. Wondered if it had spread like the tentacle mark on Anthony. Didn't bother looking now. I was sure Collins would do a thorough check once we got him upstairs.

"Davy," I said in a moderate voice, "time to get up." I

put my hand on his forearm and shook him a little. Nothing.

"Davy," I said louder. Then, "Silvers. Wake up." I didn't put Influence behind it, even though I wanted to. Instead I shook him. Hard.

He exhaled a low, drawn-out moan, his eyes flickering.

"Wake up, Davy. We gotta move you. Come on, you can do it."

His eyelids pulled up, and then closed again, harder, as if he were trying to clear the dream from behind his eyes.

"Al?" he breathed.

"Gotta move, Davy. I'm going to help you up. Can you stand?"

He swallowed. It looked like it hurt. "Yes."

That was my boy. Bea and I helped him sit, then both got our arms around him, his arms over our shoulders. It was a little awkward since Bea was almost a foot shorter than me, but we got him standing.

"Got your legs under you?" I asked him.

Davy was shaking and sweating. He worked on putting weight on his feet.

"Here," Sid said as he came into the room. "Let me get on the other side of him."

Bea and Sid switched places and Sid and I got Davy, who amazingly managed to put one foot in front of the other, into the elevator.

I think my heart was beating harder and I was sweating more than Davy by the time that damn door opened.

"Almost there," Sid said calmly, to me, not Davy. Davy wasn't doing anything but leaning on us. If I hadn't known any better, I'd have guessed he had passed out.

"Come on, Silvers," I said. "Let's get you in bed."

Davy mumbled something, but it was so slurred I couldn't make it out. Sid and I got him across the hall to the room, and then Mr. Collins hurried over and helped us pick him up and carry him the rest of the way to the bed that we'd set up.

It didn't take any time to get him settled.

"All right," Collins said, as if he were looking over a grocery list. "Let's see. I think we should get him out of his shirt and into more comfortable pants. Those sweats you brought up should work."

He pulled Davy's T-shirt carefully off over his head. And sucked in a breath. "Hello, what do we have here?" He folded Davy's shirt and placed it on the chair next to the bed. Then he bent and peered at Davy's chest.

Well, not just his chest. At the tentacle lines snaking across his shoulder and down his collarbone toward his sternum.

"Is this new?" he asked me.

"It's not a tattoo," I said. "I saw something like that on the person who bit him."

He gave me a sidelong glance. "I'd like to meet this person who bit him. Take a look at his marks too."

"He's dead."

Collins nodded. "Easier to set up a meeting, then, as I'm assuming his schedule will be clear."

Ass.

"Was it identical?" he asked as I handed him the sweatpants and we pulled away the blanket. We both paused. Davy was wearing jeans. Collins looked at me, wondering if I was going to take part in this declothing operation.

Fine. I figured Davy would rather I undress him than some stranger. Let's just hope he was wearing shorts.

I unbuttoned his jeans, slid the zipper down. Hallelujah, we had shorts!

Davy didn't move at all but I could feel the heat coming off the skin of his flat stomach and chest. Boy was burning up.

"Are you going to put him on an IV?" I asked.

"I plan to. Careful."

He didn't have to tell me. I pulled Davy's jeans off as quickly as I could, but tried not to pull too hard. His legs were just as hot as the rest of him. By the time I had his jeans off over his feet, he was shivering hard enough to shake the bed.

Collins tucked the sheet and my heavy quilt back over him, leaving only his head, shoulders, and left arm out of the covers.

He opened a new needle package, set it on the table, got out everything else, and set a shunt in his arm. He was quick with the needle, steady-handed and sure. He hummed quietly, nodding to himself every once in a while as if he were constantly going over a checklist in his head. He hooked the IV bag on a hat rack we'd brought up from downstairs.

Then he pulled out a thin steel plate about the size of his palm and broke the seal on its edge with his thumbnail.

He exhaled. As he inhaled, he drew a spell with his left hand, holding the round steel plate in his right. He finished the spell, and held it pinched between his thumb and pinky. He flipped open the top part of the steel plate, revealing a golden glyph nestled like lacework inside.

No, I shouldn't have been able to see magic without using Sight. I blinked, and couldn't see the golden spell—though I could've sworn I'd seen it.

With a deft twist of his wrist, Collins flicked the spell he'd cast across the plate. I knew the two spells would mingle, join, and become something very different and tricky to cast—Syphon, a spell that was usually used in medical care. He guided the spell as if it hovered like a helium balloon over the plate in his hand, and then gently placed the plate on Davy's chest.

He waited a moment, then cast several quick spells in a row, pausing to touch his fingertip to Davy's chest, to his shoulder where the bite and darkness spread, then to the IV line, and finally he flourished his fingers over the hat rack like he was getting rid of spiderweb strands.

The Syphon was set. It would slowly drain the magic from Davy.

"How's it working?" I asked.

Collins studied his handiwork. "As well as to be expected, I think." He pulled on a pair of latex gloves. "A few seconds into it is a bit early to give a final determination, however. Are you staying?"

I thought about it. I'd gotten almost zero sleep. It was midmorning, and I hadn't heard anything from Zayvion or the rest of them, so I could only assume they didn't need me. That was fine. I was not up to seeing Bartholomew or his pet torturer, Melissa, right now.

Jack had found a chair and was texting on his cell. Sid was unloading some groceries in the kitchen area.

"For a while," I said.

I'd only had a scone to eat today. I was starved. I gave Davy one last look. He appeared to be sleeping. "Did you give him painkillers?"

"A mild sedative in his IV to help him sleep. Nothing fancy." He flashed me a smile. "Yet. I'm going to draw some blood first."

I glanced over at the kitchen again, and my stomach rumbled.

He looked at me. "Go ahead. I'll narrate."

I didn't like being told what to do by this man, but I was starving.

Since he was paying no more attention to me, but instead getting the vials and needle ready, I walked over to the kitchen. "Who's paying for all the food?" I asked.

Sid shrugged. "Took it out of petty cash."

"We have petty cash?"

"Yes. You. You're our petty cash."

"In that case, I want food."

"What can I get you?" He opened a cupboard showing soups, cans, and boxed goods.

"Anything I don't have to chew through tin to get at would work. Though I'll eat tin, if that's all we've got."

Sid pursed his lips and shut the cupboard. He opened the refrigerator. "How about a deli sandwich or salad?"

"Yes."

He pulled out a wrapped deli sandwich from the local market down the street and handed it to me. It weighed as much as a newborn baby.

"I think I love you, Sid."

He chuckled. "Still want the salad?"

I leaned my elbows on the countertop, unwrapped the sandwich, and dug in. Sweet hells, I was hungry. "This should do," I mumbled.

"So do you know what's wrong with Davy?" He put a tall glass of orange juice in front of me and I swallowed down half of it. I'd taken out a third of the sandwich already, but my hands were still shaking from hunger.

From across the room, I heard Collins say, "I'm going to draw his blood now. Three vials."

What did you know? He really was narrating.

"That's what he's supposed to tell us," I said.

"And?"

"So far he thinks it's an infection. A magical infection."

"Any reason why we aren't taking him to a hospital?"

I took another big bite and chewed. "I don't think it's something a regular doctor would know how to handle."

"Think? Didn't know you had a medical degree, Allie."

Okay, I got it. He was worried about Davy. I was too. "This guy used to work with my dad on medical technology, Sid. He has all the equipment the hospitals would have. Probably more. We can take Davy in if you want to, but I don't know how much moving him will help."

Sid glanced over at Collins.

"There now," Collins said. "That's the last of the blood. I'm setting these aside and taking his vitals again."

"He's odd," Sid said.

"Most people who are good at magic are," I said.

"Mind if I look him up?" Sid finally asked.

"Shocked you haven't already."

"Give me a bit."

I finished my sandwich, then wandered back over to check on Davy. Collins was still humming, making notes on his handheld.

"How's he doing?" I asked.

Collins scratched at his eyebrow, then looked up from his notes and over at Davy as if just noticing he was there. "Stable. I think the Syphon might be helping." He glanced at me. "This is going to take some time, Allison. More than an hour or two. More than a day or two."

"How long?" I turned and stared out the window. Normal life was moving along out there, people going about their daily rituals, hurrying to get to normal jobs, normal lunches, normal meetings with normal people. Yes, death and disease happened out there on those sunny streets too. But from here, it all looked simpler, easier, nicer on the other side of the glass.

"If the Syphon continues to retard the spread of the infection, and the tests give me results of what exact kind of infection we're dealing with, then I think we'll be able to calibrate the medication and spells and see a change in the next three days."

"Three days," I repeated. Maybe we should take him to a hospital. "Would you be willing to see him at a hospital?" I asked.

He set the handheld down. "I could," he began slowly. "Many of my ... techniques would not be accepted there. He would receive care, I'm sure, but I don't know that any of the hospitals in the area have the ... technology to find an answer for him. He has been poisoned. By magic."

"You make it sound like that's never happened before," I said distractedly.

"It hasn't."

I turned away from the window. "What?"

Collins was carefully lining up all the items on the table, things that looked like blood pressure cuffs and monitors and metal and glass sticks etched with spells and more of those flat plates that contained Syphon, and other medical spells.

"I don't want to make assumptions until I see the results of the tests."

"But?" I encouraged.

He turned to face me and folded his hands. "It might be a spell someone cast on him. It might be a spell he cast that went terribly wrong. Even so, those outcomes, to my knowledge, do not result in poisoning or infection."

I just shook my head. I was tired, had been pretty sick myself just lately, and probably wasn't thinking straight.

"Something has poisoned magic, Allison. Or at least, that is my assumption. The tests will prove or disprove my theories."

"You can't poison magic," I said. "It's not like you can just walk up to a lake of magic and pour poison in it."

He gave me a look of droll tolerance. "No. I am sure," he said with thinly veiled sarcasm, "that there is no conceivable way to poison a resource that can be funneled and directed through networks, streams, and collected in cisterns."

And wells. That's what he wasn't saying. The magic in the wells could be affected—there had been a lot of fights around the wells, and whatever Leander and Isabelle had done at the Life well, sacrificing, killing people, fighting us with magic, could have also poisoned the magic in the well.

"Oh shit," I whispered.

He smiled, watching my lips again, too much bright sunshine for such a horrendous realization. "I would like to run some tests on you, Allison. To make sure you aren't suffering any effects from the marks you carry."

"No," I said, a little creeped out. Was he coming on to me? Some kind of "hey, let's play doctor" pickup line?

"Absolutely not," I added. "Take care of Davy. That's what I'm paying you for."

"Speaking of payment," he said, turning back to the items on the table. "I don't believe we've gone over the details." He picked up something that looked like a scalpel, considered it in the sunlight, and smiled softly before placing it gently back down on the table.

"I'll pay you what my dad paid you."

"Very well. Very generous, in fact. Now, if you'll excuse me, I'll begin running tests on his blood." He clacked and clicked around with things on the table, and I walked over to one of the comfortable easy chairs we had dragged up to the room. I dropped down in the chair, and sat in it sideways, pulling my feet up onto the seat next to me. Hells, I was tired.

Jack was pacing now, Sid sitting in the other chair closer to the door, working on his handheld, probably looking up Collin's background.

Collins was humming, a soft song, something classical that teased at the edges of my memory.

Chopin, Dad said.

That was right. One of the pieces Dad loved. I closed my eyes, just for a minute, listening to the men in the room: Jack's footsteps, Sid tapping on his keyboard, Collins humming as he handled glass and metal, and Davy's solid, restful breathing.

And I fell asleep.

Chapter Eight

I dreamed of Zayvion. He was smiling. We were walking on the beach. I felt sand, soft beneath my feet, and his hand in my hand, his fingers wide and warm between mine. Birds flew overhead, so many that they blocked the sun.

And Zayvion turned to me, pulled me hard against him, and kissed me until heat pooled in my belly and every inch of my skin felt tight and hot.

The ocean lapped around our feet, ice cold, and when the wind pushed past us, it was cold too. I pulled back enough to look up at Zay.

Only it wasn't Zay holding me. It was Eli Collins. He smiled, his eyes slipping from my eyes to my lips. He leaned down, and I couldn't push him away, didn't want to push him away.

Instead of kissing me, he whispered my name against my lips.

"Allison."

The ocean at my feet picked up his words, echoed my name back to me: "Allison, Allison, Allison."

And then he said, "Remember me? Remember us?"

I pushed away from him, but I didn't have to. Collins was gone. Zayvion stood there. "I love you," he said. "I always will." He turned and jogged down the beach, his stride sure, powerful. Running away from me, to a horizon that was on fire, his sword in his hand.

And then my phone rang.

I fumbled for it, worried I'd drop it in the water. "Hello?"

But the voice on the other end was garbled, filled with static.

"Hello?"

Someone on the other end was calling my name.

"Allison. Allie."

"Allie," Jack said.

I woke with a start. Jack Quinn stood far enough away from me I couldn't hit him. Smart. I was still curled in the easy chair on the upper floor of the den. And my phone was ringing.

I dug for it in my pocket. I was stiff from being bent in half. I swung my legs the right way over the chair seat.

I flipped my hair out of the way and cleared my throat. "Beckstrom."

"You have an appointment with Bartholomew Wray," the male voice I did not recognize said. "Please come alone."

"Where?" I asked.

"The same meeting room as before."

And then he hung up. I looked at the caller ID and there was nothing but a row of dashes. No numbers, no symbols. I was pretty sure the voice belonged to one of Bartholomew's goons, but I hated going on nothing but pretty sure.

"Who's Wray?" Jack asked.

Hounds have good ears. It was a useful trait until it was my business they were listening in on.

I noted Collins had stopped humming as soon as Jack asked about Bartholomew. Jack, and probably Sid, wherever he was in the room, noticed that too.

"A guy I've done some jobs for. Bigwig of some corporation. Very hush-hush, cryptic shit." I held up the phone as if in example. "But not a big deal."

Collins was working again, but he wasn't humming any longer.

I stood and winced at how stiff my legs and neck were. Sleeping in chairs was hell on my muscles. I stretched, then walked over toward Davy.

He looked the same, still resting, still like he was in pain, still unconscious.

"Any change?"

"Other than this?" Collin pulled the blanket away from Davy's chest. The mark was growing. Black tendrils reached all the way from one shoulder to the other and had snaked down his right biceps. The lines were dark, twisted and knotted back on themselves.

I caught the slight stink of tar and infection.

"Is he still running a fever?" I asked.

He nodded. "He's stable, though. No changes. For the better. Or the worse. Well, except for that." He pointed at the mark before pulling the cover back up over his chest.

"So this appointment," he said casually, "how long exactly do you think you'll be gone?"

"I don't know. He didn't say."

"In that case I would like a deposit on my services before you leave."

"What?"

He stopped fiddling with the dial on the side of a small metal tube on the table. "In case your appointment lasts . . . much longer than you expect."

He knows something, Dad said.

"Walk with me and we'll talk over the details." I grabbed my coat from the back of the chair, and strode across the room. Jack was on my heels. I spun.

"Give me some room, Quinn. This is a private matter."

He sized me up, weighed my mood, and took a step back. "I'll follow you to wherever your meeting is."

"I know. But I want someone here with Davy and

Collins, twenty-four seven." I glanced at Sid. "You got that?"

"I've put together a rotation," Sid said absently. "I'll take first shift overnight. Jamar said he'd come by tomorrow."

"Thanks," I said. "Coming, Collins?"

"Of course. After you." He motioned to the door.

I opened it, walked out into the hall as far away from the echoing stairwell and elevator as I could get.

"Listen," I said. "I don't have my checkbook on me, but I'd be happy to pay you as soon as I get back."

He leaned against the wall and pressed his fingers straight down into his front pockets. With his white shirt rolled up to his elbows, and his vest still buttoned, he looked a little too formal for this place.

"I've had very few dealings with Bartholomew Wray," he said in an unaffected tone. "None of them have been pleasant."

"I can handle him. I've handled him before," I said.

"How long will this appointment last, Allison?"

"Why do you keep asking me that?"

"Because if you don't arrive back here within the specified day, or week, or month, then I will assume you have had your memories wiped, and that will make collection of your debt . . . difficult."

I stood there, frozen. I'd always known it was a possibility to be Closed by the Authority. But to Collins, it sounded more like it was a probability.

"Well," I said, swallowing until my voice was strong and even again. "We can't have you going forward without some kind of guarantee of payment. What do you want?"

He pulled a piece of paper out of his vest pocket and held it out to me. "I'd like you to very clearly state what you owe me payment for. And the amount, if you'd be so kind."

I peered at his face, trying to read what the hell he was doing this for.

"If you forget our arrangement, this will be a beginning again, for us both," he said.

"An IOU?"

"A way for us to remember just what sort of business we are conducting. Never hurts to be safe instead of sorry, does it? So neither of us does anything to overstep our understanding." He was looking at my lips again.

I didn't know why it made me blush. Creepy magical doctor guys were not my type. I so didn't like him looking at me like I was a fruit that needed picking.

"Do you know me?" I asked.

That caught him by surprise. "What?"

"Have you known me in the past? Have we been introduced? Did we . . . have something?"

The smile was back, the crazy glint in his eyes. He looked away from my lips. "It has been my utmost pleasure to meet you for the first time, today, Allison."

I couldn't tell whether he was lying. Which bothered me. I was usually pretty good at that sort of thing. We could have known each other. In the dream I certainly seemed more than happy to kiss him. The memories from my years of college were practically wiped out of my head. It was possible we had crossed paths.

I would know if we had ever dated. Wouldn't I?

I snatched the paper out of his hand and pulled my notebook out of my coat pocket and used it as a hard surface to write on.

I made myself a note, something simple and straightforward that said I owed Collins for medical services for Davy Silvers. I signed my name, and then coded the note in the corner with the symbols I used in my book. The one for I-don't-know-how-much-to-trust-this-guy and the one for he-knows-about-the-Authority.

I handed it back to him. "Good-bye, Collins. My money's good. And I expect your care for Davy to be worth every damn penny."

"I shall spare no expense."

I took the stairs, not bothering to worry about Jack following me. I knew he'd tail me. Davy and the rest of them had made it very clear they weren't letting me get into any situation alone. The best I could hope for was that by the time we hit the building, I could talk Jack into staying outside. Because if I couldn't, I was pretty sure Bartholomew's goons would take over the negotiations. With their fists.

Once outside, I inhaled the clean, open air. It was going to be one of those almost-summer days, with just enough wind out of the gorge to keep it from being too hot. So nice. Nice enough to walk, but I didn't have the energy to trod uphill for a couple miles. I could call a cab, could take the MAX light rail.

One thing I would not do was let Jack drive me. The phone goon had said I was to arrive alone. I didn't want to make Jack, or any of the Hounds, more of a target than they already were.

Why didn't I own a car? My dad's business, really mine now even though Violet was running it, had plenty of money set aside for my "expenses." It was how I was paying my rent, it was what paid for my food, especially since I'd gotten involved with the Authority and wasn't working steady Hounding jobs—not even for Stotts, who had basically hired me for contract work.

For that matter, the business probably had cars in its fleet they would have been happy to give me. I so didn't know how to rock the rich-girl benefits.

Well, maybe it was time to start. But first, I had to get to Bartholomew's. Cab would be easiest.

Even though there was a lot of this block that was still undeveloped, Get Mugged pulled in enough business that I was sure a cab would be cruising for custom-

ers. I only had to wait about two minutes. A cab was
down one block and I leaned out and flagged him.

The cab stopped in front of me and I got in the back.

"Can you take me downtown?"

"Sure thing," the driver said.

He didn't make small talk, had the radio playing quietly on a talk show or a news station. I wasn't paying a
lot of attention. I was thinking about why Bartholomew
wanted to see me, and figured it had to have something
to do with how he was going to run the Authority now
that he'd fired Victor from being the Voice of Faith
magic. Or something about how Jingo Jingo was to
stand trial for kidnapping Sedra and attacking other
members of the Authority. Indirectly, Jingo Jingo was
also responsible for Liddy's death, Shame having a crystal stuck in his chest, and Zay almost dying.

To say I didn't like the man was a gross understatement.

I hoped I would have my chance on the witness stand.

Maybe Bartholomew was going to hold the trial. I
thought back on what I'd heard, and didn't recall anyone telling me there was going to be a trial today. Just to
be sure, I pulled the notebook out of my pocket and
thumbed through the pages. Nothing. No notes about
the trial at all.

And no notes about Collins, though I didn't really expect any. If we had . . . history, it would have happened
several notebooks ago and those were back in my apartment. I'd check when I had the chance.

But for now I made notes. Caught up about Chase's
memorial, about Davy, the Veiled, my backpack being
stolen. Put some notes in there about Collins and the
tension between Zayvion and Victor. Even mentioned
Terric hitting on Grant, or maybe it was the other way
around, but that they hadn't spent the night together as
far as I could tell.

By the time I was done, we were pulling up beside the building.

"Thanks," I said, handing him the twenty in my pocket. "Keep the change."

I got out and watched as Jack drove past. Probably finding a decent place for his stakeout. Or just a decent place to park. Either way, it was good knowing he was only a phone call away. I strode into the building. The smell in the lobby, a slightly soapy odor of whatever it was they used to polish the marble floors, hit me, and my hands started sweating. That scent meant only one thing to me now—danger and pain.

That's one of the problems of being tortured somewhere. When you go back to that place your body, your subconscious, remembers the pain, and no matter how reasonable you think you are, fight-or-flight instincts kick in.

I didn't bother with the woman perched behind a marble counter, I didn't stop at the elevators. I took the stairs up and found a sort of meditative pace in the steady fall of stairs beneath me. I could deal with whatever Bartholomew threw at me. And if his pet, Melissa, put so much as a finger on me, I'd break her arms.

No Truth spell for me today. Or ever again.

By the time I reached the sixth floor, I was in an ass-kicking frame of mind. Whatever this little meeting was about, I was ready to deal with it.

Goon One and Goon Two were standing on either side of the door at the top of the stairs. This wasn't the same room where I'd met Bartholomew. Looked like they were waiting for me, though.

They didn't say anything, but even with the dark glasses on, I knew they were watching me, my hands, checking to see if I was carrying any obvious weapons.

Not obvious weapons, no.

Goon Two, the shorter of the pair, opened the door

for me. Still didn't say anything, just stood aside as I walked past. I stepped into a high-ceilinged room with a wood floor that looked original to the building, and two walls of windows. The lights were heavy chandeliers dripping with crystal, and all lit.

The room wasn't empty. A long table had been set up on the stage that took the bulk of the windowless wall to my left. Bartholomew Wray sat behind that table. Behind him stood three more goons, each larger than the last, all wearing dark matchy suits and glasses.

Chairs and tables created neat rows down the center of the room. At those tables and chairs sat at least fifty people. I recognized some of the faces, the twins, Carl and La. My dad's accountant, Ethan Katz, was in the mix, and I was pretty sure some of the people who had been at Chase's memorial last night. Who I did not see was Zayvion. Or Shame. But I finally spotted Terric sitting near the back. He glanced over at me and nodded. Since there were a couple empty seats beside him, I headed that way.

It was strange not to see Victor or Maeve or Hayden or some of the Seattle crew in the crowd. I had a bad feeling about this.

No one looked at me as I walked in. Bartholomew was reading through some papers, and the quiet murmur of voices covered my footsteps. I sat next to Terric.

"What's up?" I asked.

Terric shrugged. "I've been in questioning all day," he said, his voice hoarse.

I glanced at him. He looked like hell. He needed a shave, his hair was a mess, and he was wearing the same clothes I'd last seen him in, sans tie, which I think Grant still had. His eyes were glossy and red. And while some of that might be because of the hangover I could only imagine he was sporting, a lot more of it was from fatigue and the very real sense of pain that was radiating from him.

"Questioning?"

"In a room, alone. Being tediously grilled over whether Shame and I are Soul Complements. I got so tired of them trying to make me say we weren't that I told them to get Shame and give us the fucking test. They left. I thought I'd see Shame walk in. But instead one of Bartholomew's men came back and told me there was a meeting I needed to attend. I came in about ten minutes ago. Nothing's happened."

"What do you think this is about?" I asked.

Terric shook his head. "God only knows. I can't think straight after last night." He gave me a rueful smile. "I might have overindulged just a bit."

I smiled back at him. "Oh, you most certainly did."

He rubbed his face and tried to smooth his hair. "Was I a complete ass?"

"Not complete, no. But you and Grant seemed to hit it off pretty well."

"Mmm," he said. "Have you seen him today?"

"No. I've been busy."

"With what?"

"Davy's been hurt." I thought about telling him more, but wasn't sure how many people were listening in and decided to just leave it at that.

"You take care of that?" he asked.

I nodded. "A doctor's looking in on him."

Not Dr. Fisher. No, she walked into the room from the door to one side of the stage.

I liked Dr. Fisher. She had always been nice to me, and had some of the best treatments for magical injuries and wounds I'd experienced. She was practical and almost always in a fairly calm, pleasant mood, even when things were going to hell and blood was everywhere.

Which was why it was such a shock to see her now. Her cheeks were red and her skin was too pale. She did not make eye contact as she walked to one of the chairs set to one side of the stage—not actually on the stage but at the head of the room and facing toward the audience.

She sat, folded her hands in her lap, and looked straight ahead, chin tipped up.

Bartholomew stacked his papers and looked out across the room. He adjusted his gaze to flick over each of us as if counting a tally. When he saw me, he scowled.

"Ladies and gentlemen," he began. "Members of the Authority. Welcome here today. You have been invited to witness a historic day in Portland's magic community. Today I will be announcing the new Voices who, along with myself, will help guide the city of Portland, and all within it, to easier, more prosperous times. This infighting will stop today, and from here forward, I will see to it that magic is handled correctly, and that peace will rule among the members of the Authority again."

You could have heard dust collide. Everyone was hanging on his every word.

"I have gone over the allegations and weighed the information and testimonies of the people involved in the most recent crisis and conflicts."

I looked around the room. All the body language was tense. Dr. Fisher still wasn't making eye contact, though her hands were clenched together instead of resting easily in her lap.

Otherwise, you'd think she wasn't really here, or was trying very hard not to be.

"There will be, of course, consequences to bear for the situations that have been allowed to progress over the last few months. As has always been the way of justice in the Authority, those who lead will take the highest responsibility of blame for the current situation."

I didn't know what he was getting at. Those who had led, those who had at least tried to keep magic safe and the city safe from people like Greyson and Frank Gordon, and Leander and Isabelle, weren't even in the room.

My stomach suddenly clenched. What if they weren't here because he'd locked them up? The thought of Maeve or Victor or maybe even Zayvion locked away in one of those cells where only magical criminals were kept made me break out in a cold sweat. Oh, this was bad. Very bad.

Bartholomew lifted a sheet of paper and read: "For failing in his task of upholding the tenets of the Authority, and for inciting war, failing to protect magic and putting the innocent at magic's mercy, and for treason against the Authority's laws, Victor Forsythe has been Closed."

It was like a punch to the gut. Terric, next to me, hissed.

"That can't be right," I whispered beneath notice with everyone else muttering in surprise.

"Dr. Fisher," Bartholomew continued, "can you verify for the record that Victor Forsythe has been Closed?"

"Yes."

"And can you verify at what level he has been Closed?"

"Eight."

"What's eight?" I asked Terric.

"It means he still remembers the Authority, and how to do magic, but not his time spent being a Voice of the Authority."

"How many years has he been a Voice?" Terric didn't answer me, so I tapped his leg. "How many years?" I whispered since the noise in the room was quieting.

"At least fifteen."

Holy shit. They'd just taken fifteen years of his life away. My stomach rolled again and nightmarish dread spread through me. This wasn't right. This couldn't be right.

Bartholomew waited until the room settled down. He

leveled a disapproving stare at the few people still whispering. Once everyone was quiet, he began again.

"For failure to protect the Blood magic well from attack, and acts of unsanctioned magic use, and obstruction of critical information regarding the Authority and Authority business, Maeve Flynn has been Closed."

I put my hand over my mouth and looked around the room for Shame. He was nowhere to be seen. Which was no surprise. I expected he was with his mom. Or maybe gagged and tied up somewhere so he didn't kill anyone.

I glanced at Terric. His face was very, very calm. It was like he hadn't heard a thing Bartholomew said. It was like nothing could bother him. But his hand nearest me was clenched so hard around the base of his chair seat, I could see the bones of his fingers.

He was furious.

And very Zen.

One of the marks of having Victor as a teacher.

"Dr. Fisher," Bartholomew said, "can you confirm for the record that Maeve Flynn has been Closed?"

"Yes."

"And can you verify at what level she has been Closed?"

"Five."

Okay, I was done being shocked. Now I was just mad as hell. They couldn't do this. That man—Bartholomew Wray—couldn't just swoop in here and hurt my friends.

Yes, he can, Dad said from somewhere in the middle of my brain. *He has done it before in the past, he has done much worse in the past, and he will continue to do such things today. Especially here.*

Why especially here? I asked.

He has a long history with the Authority and the people of the Authority in Portland. A bad history.

I was going to ask him to fill me in on that, but Bartholomew was talking again. I missed some of it, but heard him say that Mike Barham, who I didn't like, and who had turned on us during the wild magic storm, had been Closed. Dr. Fisher said it was a level one.

Fuck him. Mike Barham was a jerk who had sided with Jingo Jingo and Chase and Greyson and tried to kill us all. People had been hurt from what he did. People had died. And he was skating out on a level one Closing?

Someone had to stop this. I made a move to stand. Terric's hand shot out and wrapped around my wrist so hard it hurt. I looked over at him.

"Not now," he said without looking at me. And then he added, so quiet I almost couldn't hear him, "Not yet."

It took everything I had to sit back down. I wasn't the only one in the room upset by this turn of events. I couldn't be the only one who was angry that Bartholomew was acting as judge and jury and taking away people's memories, people's lives.

But no one else moved to stop him. No one spoke up. No one seemed willing to argue with him.

Terric had said that the Authority wasn't composed of people who only closed gates to death, and fought the magic-stealing Hungers, and tracked down Veiled who went around biting people. He'd told me at the party last night that the majority of magic users in the Authority were regular people, businesspeople putting in their forty-hour workweek to keep the big business of the Authority running.

And Bartholomew was the vice president of that company. If they wanted to keep their jobs—hell, if they wanted to keep their memories—they had best stay quiet, nod at everything he said, and not cause trouble.

Problem was, I had never made a good business-person.

Wait, Dad said. *Wait until you have all the information.*

I don't need all the information, I thought.

I do.

Okay, that bothered me too. I didn't know what Dad thought he could get out of this situation and I wasn't sure I wanted to find out.

I'm not trying to get anything, Allison, he said. *Bartholomew and I go a long way back. He never does anything without hedging his bets.*

Sounds like someone you'd be friends with, I thought sourly.

I didn't say we were friends. No, quite the opposite. He and I were always at odds. On everything.

Great. Was the guy who was screwing with my friends and maybe even permanently hurting them the opposite of my father? And since my father had been a heartless, unforgiving bastard with an angle on every deal, what did that make Bartholomew? A sweet, reasonable man?

He Closed Victor.

He Closed Maeve.

And, as I tuned back in and listened to him finish reading the list, I learned he had also had Mike Barham Closed—though not enough for my tastes—and the nice family man Joshua Romero from Seattle, and the gorgeous Nik Pavloski. Of the people from Seattle who had stayed here in the Portland area to help us out when the shit hit the fan, all of them had been Closed. Except Terric and Hayden.

It made no sense. It made me furious.

He has a reason, Dad said. *He always has a reason.*

Fuck him and his reason, I thought. *There's no reason good enough for me to stand aside and let my friends be hurt.*

I couldn't agree with you more, Dad said with something suspiciously like admiration. *But if you wait, we will know which reason he is publicly claiming. Once we*

*know that, we can begin to guess the true motives he
won't admit to.*

"With that attended to," Bartholomew said, shuffling
papers to one side, "I will now reassign the positions that
have been recently vacated."

Terric's breath came in short, shallow gasps. I didn't
know if he was dealing with Shame's anger or pain or
something like that, or if he was furious, or if he was
going to throw up from the hangover.

But when I looked at him, his gaze was riveted on
Bartholomew like he was watching a nightmare unfold.

"We have the unprecedented opportunity before us
to assign the Voice positions for the disciplines of the
following magics: Faith, Blood, Death, Flux."

It was like listening to a death row roll call. Each of
those disciplines had been held by people close to me:
Victor, Maeve, Liddy, Dad.

"I will of course take the position of Life magic, and
Head of Portland's Authority until the region shows the
appropriate improvement," Bartholomew said.

Terric stopped breathing for a second. I looked over.
His Zen mask was shattered by something that looked a
lot more like fear.

"The position of the Voice of Faith magic, I grant to
Terric Conley."

What?

He was giving it to Terric? Terric didn't even live in
Portland. Couldn't he find someone else skilled in the
discipline who was a part of this Authority and ask him
to hold it?

People clapped politely like Terric had just won a
church raffle for a leaf-sweeping service instead of one
of the highest-ranking positions for a magic user to at-
tain.

I could tell Terric was shocked because he'd just broken out in a sweat. But I only knew the fear and anger

running through him because I was sitting so close to him. To anyone else, Terric seemed to take it well, managing a tight smile and nodding once to acknowledge the applause.

But he was furious. Even angrier than he had been. I wondered if he could turn the position down.

No, Dad said. *It is an "honor" you cannot refuse.*

"The position of Blood magic, I give to Melissa Whit."

That masochistic bitch? Bartholomew's little Truth spell pet stood, and looked surprised, even managing a blush.

She's one of his people, Dad said. *She's been his underling since before he climbed to the Watch position.*

Okay, so I could assume she'd march in lockstep with his rules and regs. It made sense that he'd put her in that position.

"For the other two positions of Death magic and Flux magic, I have weighed every possibility and all the candidates. You will all keep in mind that who I choose for these positions are the people I believe are the best to help restore this branch of the Authority to stability and strength. I have very carefully considered every outcome of my choices and am certain that my decisions are sound.

"The position of Death magic will be granted to Jingo Jingo."

The entire room went dead silent. Except me.

"Oh, hells no."

And then Jingo Jingo walked into the room.

Chapter Nine

J ingo Jingo should have been unconscious in a hospital, or at the very least, in a wheelchair. He'd barely survived Sedra's attack when she'd broken out of the cage he'd stuffed her in. I didn't know how he was even walking. He shuffled in slowly, the cane he gripped in one hand looking like a toothpick beneath his huge bulk.

Half his face was bruised and so swollen he couldn't open one eye. He had a bandage across the bridge of his nose, a line of stitches tracking across his shaved skull, and a brace on his neck. His hands were wrapped in bandages, and he wore loose pants and a long coat with only one arm through the sleeve. The other arm was in a sling.

And each of the things holding him together—bandages, stitches, brace, and sling—had the very subtle signature of Dr. Fisher's handiwork.

No wonder she didn't have any time for Davy. She'd been trying to stitch this monster back together.

I glanced over at her. She was staring straight ahead, making no eye contact.

Jingo Jingo was followed by two goons who helped him ease down into a chair set to the side at the back of the stage in shadows.

Screw this.

Terric tugged on my wrist again, but I pulled my hand away from him and stood. "Jingo Jingo betrayed the Authority, was part of the mechanism that kidnapped Sedra, and made treasonous deals with Mikhail and my father."

"Sit down," Bartholomew commanded. "This is not open for discussion."

"I don't care." I walked down the empty line of chairs and started toward him. "Jingo Jingo is a child molester and should be locked up."

"Can you prove that accusation?"

No, I couldn't. All I had was my dad's word on it and the ghosts of dead children I always saw around him when he cast magic.

"Yes," I bluffed.

Bartholomew narrowed his eyes. "In times of great need, a person's past cannot be seen as more important than his present. You have no proof of a crime being committed. Jingo Jingo is the best Death magic user in Portland."

"You're wrong. Shamus Flynn is the best Death magic user in Portland."

He blinked once slowly, then sat back in the chair, a look of complete dismissal on his face. "I disagree. Shamus Flynn had uneven talent and a poor attitude."

"Did you Close him?" I was below the stage, looking up at him, but close enough I could smell his cologne. Something with heavy spice overtones. It mixed with his sweat and turned sour.

"That hasn't been necessary. Yet. If you continue to disrupt this proceeding, Allison Beckstrom, we will, however, consider Closing you."

"Allie." Terric stepped up behind me and took my arm. "Sit down. You're embarrassing yourself."

I turned to tell him exactly how much I cared if I was embarrassing myself.

Listen to him, Dad said. *You need information right now. Getting thrown out of this meeting won't help you, and it won't help Shame or Victor or Maeve.*

Terric's face was schooled in a calm, pleasant mask. But I could see the fire in his eyes. Looked like he was thinking along the same lines as my dad.

The goons left Jingo Jingo and walked over to me. They stank of him—formaldehyde and licorice.

One of the goons motioned to the audience. The other just waited to see if I'd go back to my seat or stay and cause more trouble. His fingers were spread to cast a spell, probably something that would knock me out.

Hells.

I turned and walked with Terric back to my seat, every eye in the room on me.

Bartholomew waited until both Terric and I were seated. I noted one of the goons made his way up past Terric and me and stood at the back of the room.

"There is one last position open," Bartholomew continued. "The Voice of Flux magic. This is a very new discipline. It has been proposed that blending magic with technology is not a true discipline. Furthermore, it has been argued that joining magic with technology is a violation of the true purpose of magic, and possibly creates more problems with magic than using it in its natural state."

Lies, Dad said. *Misdirections. Ever since man discovered magic, he's been finding new and better ways to use it. Our adaptation is our strength.*

I got the feeling Dad didn't think Bartholomew would grant a person the position of Voice of Flux magic. I got the feeling Dad thought Bartholomew wanted to end any mention or legitimacy of the Flux discipline.

He would. If it suited his purpose.

What's his purpose? I asked. *To piss us all off?*

I don't know yet.

It was kind of strange. I'd gotten used to my dad having a handle on everything that was happening inside the Authority. Even though I hated him in my mind using my body like some kind of parasite, I had to admit his information—what he would share—had come in handy.

Yes, I knew he was playing his own angles, just like Bartholomew. He wanted magic in the right hands, and dark and light magic joined together. He'd told me that often enough.

It bothered me that he didn't know what Bartholomew might be planning.

I have been dead for several months, my dad said in a droll tone. *I am a little out of touch with certain details.*

Bartholomew was talking again. "But I am willing to give this discipline another chance. Now that it is no longer under the stranglehold of Daniel Beckstrom, I believe Flux magic can take magic to new and useful horizons. And the Voice of Flux magic will help us to solve our current unrest and recover those things which have fallen into the wrong hands.

"I grant the position of the Voice of Flux magic to Violet Beckstrom."

I felt the shock and anger roll through my body like a wave of heat. Some of that emotion was mine. I liked Violet. She was nice, smart, and had just had my one and only sibling. I did not want to see her mixed up in the Authority, especially not when this ass was running the show.

And the rest of the anger, well, that was my dad. He went white-hot in the middle of my head. Supernova. I literally had to close my eyes and take in a deep breath to cool my brain, then exhale to keep control. If he'd had his own body, I was pretty sure he'd be yelling. I'd only ever seen my dad yell once. That hadn't gone well for the target of his scorn.

When I opened my eyes again, Bartholomew was still onstage, papers neatly stacked between his fingers, staring at me. Daring me to stand up and tell him to shove it. Daring me to make a commotion so he could Close me.

I refused to let him play me.

So I smiled.

It took everything I had, but I did it.

He frowned. That, apparently, was not the reaction he was looking for.

The door opened and Violet walked in. She wore a nice jacket and blouse and slacks, her red hair pulled back in a chignon. Her ruby wire glasses seemed to set her eyes on fire. She looked professional, put together, and ready to take charge.

Only she had no idea what she was walking into.

Kevin Cooper, her bodyguard, who was very much a part of the Authority, walked behind her, just as he was always behind her. He scanned the room. He did not look pleased. No, he looked tense.

Kevin knew exactly what they were walking into.

Bartholomew glanced over at Violet and smiled and nodded to her. Dad, in my head, went very, very still. My head turned—but not of my own volition—to stare at Bartholomew. Only it wasn't me who was looking at him, it was Dad.

And then the white-hot anger in my mind snuffed out. Leaving behind a cold, hard, dark resolve.

What? I thought to Dad.

He had let go of my head, had stopped looking through my eyes, had retreated back to the cocoon place Victor and Shame had made in my mind to help control him. And then he pulled away even further, digging in deeper, fading until I couldn't even sense a trace of him.

What the hell? One, I didn't like that he could hide in my own head that well, and two, I didn't like that he had suddenly decided to do it.

Bartholomew watched me, and could not hide his

flicker of interest, of hunger, as he watched what I would do now that Violet was walking into the room.

What I did was sit back and give him a fuck-you glare.

Violet chose a chair on the outer edge of a row, and Kevin sat in the row behind her. She must not have spotted me in the crowd.

"These appointments begin immediately," Bartholomew said. "I will meet with the Voices in my chamber in a half hour. Thank you all for your time. The Authority is grateful for your service."

He stood and, taking the papers, walked down off the stage and out of the room through the door at that end. I was pretty sure it didn't lead back out into the hall, but into a second room—the one Jingo Jingo had come out of. The one in which he and Melissa had worked the Truth on me.

Two goons took their places on either side of the door.

He'd need more than a few goons to keep himself safe.

I turned to Terric. "Did you know about this? Any of this?"

He shook his head. "I'm just as surprised as you are."

"He can't do this, Terric. I won't let him do this."

People were getting up, talking, excited. Several were headed our way to talk to Terric.

He leaned toward me, a smile on his face, and gave me a hug, like I'd just congratulated him. "Don't talk like that. He'll have you Closed. We'll talk later. Find Shame."

And that was all the time he had because then people were there, patting him on the back, excited, smiling. He stood and shook hands, and looked every inch the happy, surprised, humble recipient of a great new position.

I knew that wasn't how he felt about it. I'd felt his fury. But he knew how to put on the act, put on the face.

He stepped out away from his chair, and a small, congratulatory crowd gathered around him.

There was no way he was breaking free from them anytime soon. So I got up and walked over to Violet. She was still sitting and talking to a woman in the chair beside her, but she hadn't drawn the crowd of fans that Terric had pulled in. Violet was only tangentially involved with the Authority. Dad had worked hard to keep it that way, and to make sure she could develop her technologies, which eventually became his technologies, without the Authority's oversight.

It had worked well for her. She'd developed the disks that could carry magic in them and gave the user the access to that magic cost- and pain-free. She had been working on developing other technologies before Dad was murdered.

I wasn't sure what she was currently working on.

It must be something Bartholomew thought was very valuable, if he wanted to keep her under the Authority's thumb.

Kevin looked up as I came over, and the cool disinterest on his face faded for a moment to reveal a spark of anger before he coughed politely into his fist and put his don't-give-a-damn back into place.

This was the first time I'd seen Kevin at any of the Authority's meetings, fights, or get-togethers. He hadn't even been at Chase's graveside memorial, come to think of it. Kevin had been flying pretty low, staying under the radar, not taking sides, instead putting his bodyguarding duties for Violet as his top priority. Even over the Authority's wishes.

I was pretty sure he was in love with Violet. I still didn't think she knew.

"Hi, Violet," I said in my best chipper voice.

"Allie, it's good to see you." She stood and I gave her a hug, and the woman next to us got up and found someone more interesting to talk to. I had the distinct feeling people were going out of their way not to be seen near me.

Smart of them.

"It's good to see you too," I said. "Can we talk? About the business?"

"Sure." She started toward the door, and Kevin fell into place behind her. "Is something wrong?"

"No, I just have a couple questions."

We made it to the door and into the hall, Kevin following at a polite distance. I was right. People moved aside as we approached.

I strolled the opposite way of Bartholomew's retreat. I figured the place was littered with spy spells, and actual people spying on us. Throwing a Mute wouldn't do much good. It'd just look even more suspicious and gather even more attention. So instead, I just walked a little way, then asked, "Do you understand what position they are giving you?"

"Kevin and I have had long talks. I have a fair understanding of what will be required from me. And," she added, "the costs involved if I don't meet those requirements."

"It's dangerous," I said.

"Your father held this position for years."

"And then it got him killed."

She stopped walking and turned toward me. "What do you know about his death?"

"Not enough to take it to the police, but enough that I am sure the motives point back to people involved in the Authority."

"James Hoskil was convicted of killing him," she said.

"Won't be the first time the courts have gotten it wrong."

She frowned.

"Especially if there is a powerful organization, or

people, or person who want the courts to get it wrong," I added.

"Is this accusation enough for me to turn down the position? You have no proof, Allie, and if I align my work more firmly with the Authority, I will have more access to the other disciplines of magic use. Think of what that will mean for developing new technologies. And you'll benefit from it as well. Beckstrom Enterprises has invested in several of the patents I'm developing to bring to market."

"I don't care about the money." A man walked brusquely past us and headed down the stairs. I waited until he was gone before continuing. "I don't care about it. What I care about is you and my baby brother. I've just watched the Authority make two of my friends pay the price for failing to meet Bartholomew's requirements."

She was quiet a moment. "I understand you're worried," she said evenly. "And I really appreciate your talking to me about it. But the access to their magical knowledge, new magical knowledge that might be the key for me pressing forward with my designs—" She shook her head.

"I can't turn it down, Allie. I can't walk away from that kind of knowledge. But Kevin had his concerns too and I've written up a contract that Mr. Wray signed. It specifies what information they can remove if I am ever to be Closed. My memories of working with the Authority and the people of the Authority will be taken, but my research with magic and technology integration will not be. It's the chance of a lifetime."

I couldn't believe that she was calmly weighing the risks and then writing up contracts to outline how exactly someone should give her a lobotomy. That kind of practical, logical, unemotional decision making was beyond me.

"There's nothing I can say to change your mind?" I asked.

"I can't see how the risk outweighs the benefits of knowledge." She took my hand. "And I might just step down after a month or two. But I am going to do this, Allie. Even if it's just for a short time. I want to."

"Things weren't as bad before Bartholomew came into town," I said trying to give her something. And while that was true, it was also true that things hadn't been good for the Authority for as long as I'd been involved. "I do not agree with his methods or his decisions. I don't trust him. At all."

I wanted to say more, to tell her everything that had happened, that had been happening. But some of what had happened involved my dead dad's support and help. Violet was a very smart woman. It wouldn't take her long to start asking me questions, poking holes in the sequence of events. It wouldn't take her long to begin wondering if my dad was still alive.

And I did not want to put her through that pain again. He was dead-ish. But she had loved him very much. If she knew his soul or whatever, still resided in my head, would she start developing tech to try to house the undead? And what would the Authority do with that kind of technology?

"I will proceed as cautiously as I can." She smiled. "And really? I don't think my life will be that much different. I'll go down to the lab during the day, and spend the rest of my time raising little Daniel." She started walking. "That's pretty much how it would be even if I weren't working with the Authority. It's all good."

"I hope it will be," I said as we walked back toward the meeting room. But I knew, with every stitch of my being, that it wouldn't.

Violet strolled into the room. I paused in the doorway. As Kevin walked past me, he whispered, "I'll watch her. You and I need to talk."

He didn't pause, just kept walking. I was pretty sure no one would have seen him speaking to me.

A few people headed over to talk with Violet. Terric was still surrounded by a crowd, as was Melissa Whit. Jingo Jingo wasn't there. I wondered if I could look up where he was staying. Maybe I could go solve the problem that was Jingo Jingo on my own.

I turned and started down the stairs. Maybe Violet and Terric were handling this the right way. Staying calm, being logical. Playing the game Bartholomew wanted to play.

Bartholomew wasn't a permanent fixture in Portland. He was the Watch for the entire region, so it made sense that someone somewhere would need his attention soon. It was possible Violet was right to think of this as a one- or two-month gig.

My gut told me different. My gut told me this was just the beginning of a very bad thing.

Chapter Ten

I strode across the lobby and pushed open the door. The snap of fresh air felt good, the rumble of traffic rolling past, the distant drumbeat of a car radio, all filling me with that decidedly elusive feeling of normal. It might also help that I could not feel one tiny bit of my father's awareness in my head.

It wasn't much, but, hey, any silver lining in a head full of clouds.

Jack was probably on the sidewalk somewhere, or the street, watching me. I just stood there for a second thinking things through. I couldn't talk to Terric until he got away from the crowds. Violet didn't want to listen to me. Kevin said he'd talk to me later.

So who did that leave?

I could go try to find Victor or Maeve.

Or Shame. He had to be spitting mad about his mom.

Unless he'd been Closed and Bartholomew was just lying to me.

I started walking, my hands in my pockets. No, Terric would know if Shame had been Closed—they were tied tight both from being Soul Complements and whatever that crystal in Shame's chest had done to bring them closer. Terric would sense it if Shame had had part of his memories removed.

So where was Zayvion during all this?

Maybe keeping Shame from trying to kill someone?

I pulled out my phone, dialed Zay's number. It rang. No one picked up. That was odd, but not unheard of. I'd seen him turn his phone off before.

Okay, Shame. I dialed. It went straight to voice mail. So not helpful.

"Want a ride?" a familiar voice asked.

I looked over. Jack was leaning against the corner of the building.

"Where are you going?" I asked.

"Wherever you are."

He put his cell phone in his pocket and started walking up the street away from me. I caught up to him.

"So, how'd the meeting go?" he asked.

"We are not going to speak about it."

"That so?"

"It's confidential, Jack. The kind of confidential that costs lives."

He smiled. "Still think we can't handle your big problems, don't you? There's nothing you can get mixed up in that I haven't seen, Beckstrom."

"I'm just quirky that way," I said. Let him think it wasn't a big deal. So long as he didn't get too involved in my business and the Authority, he might live long enough to keep that I've-seen-everything talk going.

His car was down a side street. We waited for a break in traffic to cross the road.

A flash of green caught my eye. At first I thought it was a reflection of traffic in the store window across the street, but then I saw it again, a little more to the left of the window.

A woman stood there. She was coughing, her arm curved over her mouth to keep from spreading germs. With each cough, sparks of green flecked around her, like maybe a dozen bees wove through the air.

And then I saw the hazy watercolor form of a Veiled pulling itself up and out of her, like someone trying to shed a tight coat. First the chest, then the head, then finally, the arms and legs, hands and feet. All the while the woman coughed.

When the Veiled stepped fully out of her, it seemed solid, or at least more solid than it should be. The woman clutched at her chest, and bent over, taking in huge deep breaths. The Veiled started walking down the street.

"Do you see that?" I asked.

Jack scanned the street. "What?"

"The . . . that . . . hells." If he could have seen it, his reaction wouldn't have been "what?"—it would have been "what the fuck?"

"Tell that woman"—I pointed—"I need to talk to her."

I jogged across the street, headed for the Veiled. I managed not to get hit, though three cars laid on the horns and brakes.

The woman was going in the opposite direction from the Veiled. Even without Sight, I could see it—him—walking down the street. It moved a little faster than a normal walk, as if each step were on ice, gliding it forward more than a normal step would. He did not look back at me, did not seem bothered by the people around him.

I calmed my thoughts and set a Disbursement. I wanted to stop him, and find out if he was solid like the Veiled whom Leander had commanded, or if he was something else. Any kind of Veiled could be dangerous. I wasn't going to take any chances of facing one down alone, nor was I going to let him walk the city and hurt someone.

I drew the glyph for Hold, easy, basic, should work, even at a distance, even on a Veiled. Then I drew the magic from beneath the ground. It was hot, painful, burning, licking. I gasped, froze in my tracks. My vision clouded, the edges buzzing with black, closing down. I couldn't see the Veiled anymore. Couldn't see the buildings around me.

Allie, my dad said. *Don't!*

And then I was pretty sure I didn't. Because I passed out.

I woke up staring at an elderly woman's face. She had the most amazing manicure, with little bunnies painted onto the space of each peach-lacquered fingernail. Spring colors, I supposed, all wrapped around her tiny bright green cell phone. She was talking on the cell, answering a lot of yes and no questions, and giving a street address.

Strange.

"Oh, she's awake now. Are you all right?" she asked.

What I was, was lying on the sidewalk, a handful of people gathered around looking down at me. There was something soft under my head that shushed like a nylon jacket when I nodded.

"I'm good. I'm fine." I worked on sitting and all the faces blurred a bit, then settled back into focus.

"You really shouldn't move," the nice lady said.

"No, I'm fine." I touched the back of my head. It was bleeding. "Seizures," I lied. "I'll be fine."

One of the men in the crowd suffered a sudden attack of chivalry and helped me up onto my feet. The lady on the phone told whoever was on the other line, 911 I'd guess, that I was fine, mobile, and didn't need an ambulance.

Which was all good and well, but didn't change the fact that I'd totally lost track of the Veiled. What had hit me?

Magic, Dad said. *You channeled it, and it knocked you out.*

Okay. That wasn't good. What had I been pulling on magic for? I'd been following the Veiled, right? I looked around and didn't see him. What I did see was magic—

spells hung on the sides of buildings, personal spells clinging like ribbony spiderwebs around people. Soft neon-colored glyphs, jagged, flowing, pulsing with magic. Rigid Refresh spells in deep golds, silver, and copper attached to walls, street meters, cars, as if they were riveted there. I should not be able to see magic without casting Sight. I should not be seeing it right now at all.

Am I using magic? I asked my dad.

He did a strange sidestep thing in my head, paused for a moment, then said, *No.*

Can you see what I see? I asked.

A different sort of sidestep, and then I felt his presence next to me, as if he were standing over my shoulder and leaning down to say something in my ear.

You can see magic? You shouldn't be able to see it with your bare eyes.

I know that. Maybe a side effect from hitting my head? I tentatively probed the back of my head with my fingers. My hair felt like a bloody, tangled mess. There was a knuckle-sized lump there, and everything around it hurt. Yuck. I needed to have someone look at it. Maybe see a doctor. At least take a pain pill.

I think a doctor is a very good idea, Dad said in a calm, encouraging tone.

Why are you being so helpful? I asked.

Allison, you have a head wound. I live in your head.

True. But I didn't want to see a doctor. I wanted to go find that Veiled, or maybe get a cab and go home and take a nap.

I looked around for Jack. He was striding my way, no spells clinging to him, though a sort of dark shadow surrounded him, like someone had outlined his entire body in charcoal.

"Come this way," he said. And then he did something Hounds simply do not do. He touched me. He took my arm and led me away from the last few people who had lingered to see if I was okay, and walked with me briskly down the block and across the street.

"You okay?" he asked, still not letting go of my arm.

"Hit my head. It's bleeding."

We were across the street now and Jack's car was there. "Get in."

He let go of me and walked around to the driver's side of the car. I pulled on the door handle and happened to glance at my arm. A black charcoal stain covered my arm in a handprint-sized area. The same charcoal that had been surrounding Jack.

I knew Hounds didn't like touching people because Hounds didn't like leaving their scent on someone to track them by. But this was more than scent. Wasn't it?

I got in the car and sniffed my sleeve. It smelled like whiskey and smoke—Jack's smells—but only faintly. I rubbed at my sleeve to see if I could wipe the charcoal mark off. No luck. But that mark didn't cling to my fingertips or otherwise smear or travel.

It didn't seem tangible. It seemed more like magic. Or the residue of magic that had been on his hands.

"Did you cast magic on me?" I asked. I looked over at Jack.

He was watching me like someone watches a wild animal. With extreme caution. "No. Let me see your head, all right?"

I turned my head and tucked my chin. "Right on the crown," I said. "But you might want gloves. I think I'm still bleeding."

I heard a click of a flashlight button depressing, and then he moved my hair out of the way with something that was not his fingers. A comb maybe.

"Looks to be just a lump and a cut. Not too deep. Not worth stitches, I don't think. But it is not bleeding, it's gushing." The flashlight clicked again and Jack unzipped his jacket pocket. "Here, press this on it."

I turned back around and took the clean dark blue handkerchief he offered me and pressed it to the back of my head.

"Where to next?" he asked. "Hospital?"

I thought about it. Bed sounded good. But I needed to find Shame. Terric had asked me to, and I didn't know if that meant Shame was hurt or needed help.

"Let me call someone," I said. I pulled out my phone, dialed.

"What?" Shame asked. Oh, he was not happy. Not happy at all.

"Where are you?"

"Home. Why, Bartholomew sending you out to drag me in?"

"No. I need to see you. For my own reasons."

"Fine." He hung up.

Well, he was in a cheery mood. "Can you take me out to Maeve Flynn's inn?" I asked.

Jack started the car and pulled out into traffic. "You want to tell me why your head's bleeding?"

"Did you find that woman?"

"Yes. But she refused to wait until my unconscious friend could talk to her."

Nice. Sarcasm. The perfect side order with my headache. "Did you get her name?"

"No. But I could find her if I had to."

Hounds. Loved their attention to detail.

"Your head?" he asked.

"I passed out."

"Why?"

"I used magic and it kicked my butt."

"Did you set a Disbursement?"

"Yes. I did everything the way I normally cast magic. And I blacked out."

"What were you casting? Why were you casting it?"

"I could tell you it's none of your business."

"You could." He didn't say anything else.

"Do you see anything strange about the city?"

He chuckled. "You're going to have to be a hell of a lot more specific."

"Do you see magic?"

"The results, the effects, yes. Illusions, that sort of thing."

"No. I mean, can you see the spells? Right now, without Sight, can you see . . ." I glanced at the road we were traveling down, noted a big fat Attraction spell hugging a storefront. "Can you see that Attraction over there? How it's sort of gray blue with sparks of gold at the center?"

He looked. Looked at me, then looked back at the store. "No."

I didn't say anything. Then he said, "Can you?"

I nodded, which hurt my head, but didn't change the fact that I could still see magic.

"Have you always seen magic like this?" he asked.

"Not without Sight."

"Want to go back over what kind of magic you were casting before you hit your head and why?" he asked.

"Want to risk having my words pulled, painfully, out of your brain by people who don't want you to know this stuff?"

"Those people in the car with us?"

"Not as far as I know."

"Then talk," he said.

"I was casting a Hold."

"At who?"

"Do you believe in ghosts?"

"What, like Davy talking to Pike?"

"Sure," I said, looking over at him and trying to get a read on whether he believed. "Like that."

"Davy thinks he saw him," Jack said. "Heard him. More than once. I wouldn't believe in ghosts unless I saw them with my own eyes."

"Then you won't believe what I'm saying, but I saw a ghost step out of that woman I told you to follow."

"Like in the alley with Davy?"

"Yes."

He drove for a bit, silent.

"Why Hold?" he finally asked.

"I wanted to stop it so I could get a better look."

"Does magic work on ghosts?"

"Not always. Sometimes."

"And a ghost stepping out of someone is unusual behavior?" he asked.

See, this was what I liked about Hounds. They could take the impossible, the improbable, the outrageous, bend their minds enough to entertain an acceptance of the possibility, and then ask what the indicators, habits, and behaviors of the thing were—all necessary bits of information for having to track something down, or track a spell back to it.

"She was coughing," I said. "And then the ghost stepped out of her and went walking down the street."

"Why worry about a ghost?"

"I thought it might use magic."

He laughed. "You really did hit your head."

"I thought it might use magic before I hit my head."

He glanced over at me with the smile still on his face. "You're serious?"

"Very."

He just shook his head and watched the road. "I knew you were crazy, Beckstrom, but I didn't think you were certifiable."

"I don't care if you believe me, Jack," I said closing my eyes. "As a matter of fact, I don't recommend it. For your own good."

"So ghosts can use magic," he finally said.

"Some of them."

Jack just made a *hm* sound, thinking about that.

I didn't fall asleep during the drive. My head hurt too much for me to rest. But I kept my eyes closed. Seeing all the spells, seeing that much magic covering everything, running like leaves tiptoeing over power lines, snaking up buildings, wrapping like rope around people, plants, cars, made me a little sick to my stomach.

Well, that or the fact that I was very likely concussed.

Pretty soon I heard the hum of the tires over the bridge, and not long after that the access road and gravel of Maeve's parking lot.

"Allie?"

I opened my eyes.

"Looks like the inn's still closed," he said.

"It probably is. But I'm here to see Maeve, not to get a cup of coffee. Thanks, Jack. See you."

"Not letting you in there alone," he said.

I dug in my pocket. I had two twenties and a ten on me. "Fifty bucks, and you stay out here instead of following me into my friend's house and getting in the way of my personal conversation."

He nodded and took the money. "Done."

I got out of the car and winced at the pounding in my head. The wind felt a lot colder here by the water. I walked to the front door. It was strange to see the porch light off, and the sign turned to CLOSED. Next to the sign a piece of paper said the restaurant and inn was going through renovations and would be open in a month.

I guess renovations sounded better than saying that the Veiled tried to kill us here and we had to lock the place down so they couldn't get to the magic well beneath the inn that no one knew about.

I tried the door. It didn't open. So I rang the doorbell. Nothing for a bit. Jack was still in his car, the engine idling. I folded my arms over my chest, and really wished I'd asked Jack if he had an aspirin, or maybe a few cc's of morphine stashed in his glove box.

Finally, I heard the muted tread of footsteps approaching the door.

I did not expect to see Hayden looking through the high glass.

The locks clacked, and I got a whiff of the fresh-cut-grass smell of a Ward being canceled. Then he opened the door.

"Allie."

Hayden was tall, a good six or more inches over my six feet. He was also wide-shouldered and had that Northwestern lumberjack look. Magic flickered black and red around him, in thick bands that crisscrossed his chest, then split to wrap down his arms like bracers, and finally pooled in his hands.

He'd come down from Alaska to help the Authority after my dad died, and had rekindled a relationship with Shame's mom, Maeve.

"Hey. Is Shame here?"

He looked out past me at Jack's car.

"The Hounds won't let me go anywhere alone," I said. "I paid him to sit out here so I could have some privacy."

"Anyone else with you?"

"No. Well, you know, my dad." I lifted my hand and pointed at my head.

His eyes narrowed suddenly. "Come on in," he said. He stepped aside and I stepped in. It was only when I lowered my hand that I realized my fingers were covered in blood.

"Where are you hurt?" he asked.

"I passed out and hit the back of my head. It's just a bump and a cut. And a headache and a dizzy."

"I'll get Maeve." He started across the room to the side of the inn that led to her home.

"No, that's okay. I just came to check on Shame."

"Not listening," Hayden said. "Have a seat. Pour yourself a drink."

And then the door closed behind him and all the polite yelling in the world wouldn't have done me any good.

I looked around the room. It didn't appear that we'd had a life-or-death magic battle here. The burnt walls and ceiling were repaired, the tables all solid, each with a folded white tablecloth in the center of it, chairs pulled up tight as if any minute Maeve's employees would come in and set things up for hungry patrons.

But even though the room looked normal, the smells that I associated with the place were gone. No deep, buttery scents of bread and pastries, no heavy onion and meat and herb aromas, no sweet pies, coffee, wines. The inn felt like a hollow shell of itself, as if it too were a ghost of what it had once been.

"What are you doing here?"

I turned. Shame was standing in the hallway opposite to where Hayden had exited. I knew that behind Shame were meeting rooms, rooms I had trained in when I was first learning the different disciplines of magic, and stairs that led up to lodging where Zayvion had recovered from his coma, and down those same stairs eventually, to the Blood magic well.

Shame was a slice of darkness against the shadows behind him, only his pale, pale face catching any light. Magic surrounded him, just like it surrounded the door, and, now I noticed, faintly strung across the doorway he stood within.

The magic around Shame wasn't a charcoal outline like it was around Jack or black and red bands like around Hayden. It was moving, a constantly drifting stream, like sunset-colored smoke lifting up off things—off living things: the plant in the corner, and farther away, off the plants outside the windows, streaming a faded fire into him, into the crystal embedded in his chest.

But that crystal wasn't just sucking in life energy. It was also consuming Shame. I could see it radiating outward, a soft pink glow, chewing away at the hard, clean blackness of him, leaving behind nothing but his bones.

Holy shit. The crystal was eating him alive. No wonder he'd been so frail since Mikhail had possessed him. Whatever Mikhail had cast on that crystal to allow him to use Shame's body must have changed it.

I suddenly realized Shame was dying.

"I'm . . . Shame . . . God. I really need to talk to you." It came out stilted, breathy. I felt like someone had just knocked all the air out of my lungs. I didn't want Shame to die. I was losing everyone. Everyone I loved. But all I could do was stand there, frozen, as everyone died around me.

Shame tipped his head down, his bangs falling to cover his eyes. "What?"

I shook my head. "I don't want to lose you."

Shame held his breath and was very, very still. "Who sent you?"

"No one. Nobody. Well, Terric . . ."

"Fuck him. Did he tell you to take me back to him? Like a dog to beg for Bartholomew's favor?"

"What? No. He was worried—"

"Turn around and leave, Allie. And when you and Terric and Bartholomew all get together to decide just how to put me down, tell them I will be more than happy to show them just how good of a Death magic user I really am."

Okay, something about this conversation had gone

terribly wrong. Between the head wound and the emotional shock of knowing Maeve had been Closed, Victor had been Closed, Violet was in danger, and Davy and Shame might both be dying, I just could not track why Shame was so angry at me.

He thinks you're working for Bartholomew, Dad said, being helpful again. *He thinks you're here to haul him in to Bartholomew. Which probably means he is not on speaking terms with Bartholomew, or that he is not doing what Bartholomew wants him to be doing.*

"Shame, listen. I don't give a damn what Bartholomew wants. I don't think I like him and I'm damn sure I don't like how he's running the Authority right now. I came here to see if you're okay, to see if your mom's okay. And to get a bandage for my head."

I walked over to the nearest chair and sat down because my legs were starting to shake. Yes, my back was toward the door, but right now I wasn't going to be much good in a fight if a fight came through that door. Right now I needed an aspirin. Or maybe just a nice skip down Unconsciousness Lane.

Shame walked out of the shadows and into the room.

Boy was too damn thin. The black peacoat Terric had loaned him looked too big on him, and his cheekbones cut a hard line, his cheeks hollowed into shadows. His eyes were green, rimmed by black.

He moved like he wasn't in pain—I couldn't tell whether that was true—but even that small acknowledgment of health made me feel better.

"What did you do to your head?" he asked.

"I was Hounding a Veiled and I passed out and hit my head on the sidewalk." I felt like I'd said that story so many times that the reality of that statement didn't even bother me anymore.

"That's not like you." He had stopped across the table, and rested his hands, in black fingerless gloves, on top of the chair back. He wasn't coming closer to me. He wasn't sitting down. Shame was being cautious. Distrustful.

Well, he was always those things. He was just being more so than usual.

"Magic isn't working right for me, Shame," I said. "Every time I use it, I get sick. Or pass out."

He studied me a second. "Have you seen Bartholomew?"

"Just that once when he had Melissa work those Truth spells. Well, and today in the meeting where he reassigned the Authority Voice positions."

"Did he now? How efficient of him." Shame smiled. I'd never see so much hatred.

I suddenly wondered if maybe I should be doing a little judicious mistrusting myself. Shame was not acting like Shame.

"Do tell," he said sweetly.

"Sit down," I said. "I'm tired of looking up at you. The lights are killing me."

"Did you really hit your head?"

I held up my bloody hand. "Yes."

"For Christ's sake, Allie, why didn't you say you were bleeding?"

"Oh, I don't know. Maybe because I hit my head?"

That got a tight smile out of him. "You take any meds?"

"No. Jack gave me this." I put the bloody cloth on the table. "I swear, if this room doesn't stop spinning, I'm going to puke."

I pressed my right hand—then thought better of it since it was hot and painful and pressed my left hand against my forehead. At least my left hand was cool. I shifted so that my fingers were over my eyes. And just sat there for a minute, eyes closed, no magic to see, no spinning room to see, no dying angry Shame to see.

"Here, love," Shame said from right next to me. "A drink will do you good."

"Can't."

"It's water."

I opened my eyes, squinted against the light. Shame sat in the chair next to me. I hadn't even heard him move. Had I fallen asleep? "I don't remember you moving," I said.

"You hit your head. Mum's on the way. I was being a dick. Now you're all caught up. Here's the water. Here's the pain pills. Shut up and take both."

I took the water, sipped. Cool, clean. I felt like I hadn't drunk anything in days. Shame dropped the pain pills, two, in my hand. I did what I always did when I was hurting and someone gave me medicine. I took a good hard look at it.

"Codeine," Shame said. "I thought about giving you the ones Dr. Fisher usually prescribes for magical injuries, but you hit your head—even the most unmagical idiot can do that—and you told me magic was making you sick." He leaned back in his chair. "Those are straight up chemicals with no magical contamination."

I hadn't even thought about that. If magic was making me sick and I took a pill laced with magic, I wasn't going to be doing myself much good. "At least one of us is still thinking," I mumbled.

Shame just gave me a catlike stare through half-lidded eyes.

I took the pills and drank the rest of the water.

"Room still spinning?" he asked.

"Not so much."

"That's good. So Terric told you to come get me?"

"Find you. He was worried. Angry. And he couldn't get away."

Shame's hands clenched into fists. It was the only outward indication that what I said bothered him. Still was looking at me with catlike boredom.

"Why couldn't Terric get away?" he asked.

"Because everyone was congratulating him." I gave Shame a steady gaze. "Bartholomew named him the Voice of Faith magic, Shame. He took Victor's position."

The wave of anger that rolled off Shame was palpable. And with my screwed-up vision, it was also visible. A white-hot wave, like the shock ahead of a blast. The crystal, the magic coming into him, all snuffed out under the force of his anger.

"He didn't want it," I said. "You know that."

"Do I?"

I glared at him. "Yes. You do. Be angry at him for something else, Shame. Terric didn't tell Bartholomew to give him Victor's job. He was just as mad about it as you are."

He blinked, slowly, and the anger went down a notch, that white-hot wave thinning, though it was not gone. "So he's celebrating now."

"No. He's pretty much trapped by a crowd of well-wishers, and then he and the other Voices have to go to a meeting with Bartholomew. They're probably there now."

"Who are the other Voices? Who did Wray set up in our places?" he asked.

The door across the room opened, and I heard the three-step rhythm of Maeve walking in with her cane. She still hadn't recovered from the magical battle in St. Johns during the wild magic storm. Hells, none of us had recovered since then. And some of us had gotten worse.

"Allie," Maeve said. "It's good to see you. Hayden says you hit your head?"

"Fell," I said.

Magic made Maeve look taller and filled her with a silver-green light that reminded me of frost on spring blooms. It certainly made her look stronger than her current physical condition.

I wasn't sure what to say to her now that I knew she'd been Closed. I was usually the person in the room with missing memories. It was odd to wonder how much of me she remembered, how much of the things we had done together, been through together she would know.

"Mum," Shame mumbled. "Want a seat?"

"I've got it." She tugged on one of the empty chairs and dragged it over next to mine. "So, I hear you've had a hard time of it lately," she said.

Hayden set a first-aid kit down on the table and just gave me a steady look.

"It's been interesting," I said. "How are you doing?"

"Well, I can't remember much of what happened." She opened the first-aid kit and pulled out packages of clean gauze, scissors, and wipes.

"Since the wild magic storm," Hayden said.

"Yes," she agreed. "And I'm not at all happy that I've been relieved of my position in the Authority. But it's very nice of Bartholomew to let us keep our home and business here."

Shame swore, and pushed up to his feet. "Nice? That bastard took everything we had—everything you have worked hard years for, Mum. He took—"

"Shame," Hayden cut in. "Enough. Your mother's tired. Don't make this miserable for us all."

Okay, so I could guess she didn't know she had been Closed. So we what? Tried not to point out the things she didn't know?

There was no chance in hell I would be able to keep track of all that. Especially not with a hit to the head.

"Maeve?" I said.

"Yes, dear?"

"Do you know they Closed you?"

Shame threw both hands in the air and started swearing again, pacing, and digging in his pocket for a cigarette.

Hayden just sighed. "I should report you for that, Beckstrom," he said.

"Are you going to?"

He lowered himself into the remaining chair and rubbed his palm over his forehead, eyes, then beard. He laced his fingers together and leaned his arms on the table. "Not yet."

Maeve was still unpacking supplies. "I'd wondered." She gave me a wan smile. "Can't be in this business without wondering not if but when you'll be Closed. Was there a strong reason why?"

"Bartholomew thought it was a good idea," I said.

"Do any of you agree?" She looked from my face to Hayden's haggard expression, to the back of Shame, because he was still pacing and smoking. Maeve didn't even tell him to take the smoking outside.

After none of us responded, she raised her eyebrows. "I see. How long ago?"

"Today," I said.

Hayden nodded. "I'm not keen on what Wray has been doing," he said, "but there isn't a lot of recourse to fight him at this point. We could take it up with the Ward."

"No, Closing members is a local problem, and falls squarely on Wray's shoulders to solve," she said. "I've known many people who have been Closed and have continued on comfortably with that knowledge. I knew what I was in for when I accepted the job."

"Now, enough brooding. Allie," she said in her brisk, motherly tone. "I want to see your head. Shamus, for the love of heaven, smoke outside if you must smoke. Hayden, if you'd bring up the lights a bit?"

Hayden left the table to do so, and Shame followed his mother's request by walking to the other end of the room and crushing his cigarette out in the bar sink there.

"Turn so I can see your head," Maeve instructed. I did. She put on a pair of gloves and then gently probed the area, eventually employing wet wipes. "You did a number on yourself. Quite the lump. But the cut isn't too deep. I don't think you need stitches. Are you nauseous?"

"The room was spinning when I first came in, but I'd been walking. Also, I'm having weird visual distortions."

"Distortions?"

"I can see magic. Even without casting Sight."

Hayden whistled low. "That's a new one."

"That," Maeve said, "sounds like symptoms severe enough to call in a doctor. Hayden, would you see if Dr. Fisher is available to come out here, or for us to bring Allie to her office?"

"Be right back." The big man got up and walked off down the hall a bit and pulled a cell out of his pocket. He dialed a number and paced slowly as he waited for someone on the other end to pick up.

"Have you taken any pain medication?" she asked as she picked up a chemical ice pack and shook it to activate the cooling properties.

"Shame gave me a couple codeine. I think they're starting to kick in."

"Good."

"Can I . . . can I help you, Maeve?" I asked. "I know—well, I understand what it's like to lose memories, bits of yourself, your life."

"I'm not sure if it's memories they've taken or my abilities and understanding of magic. And"—she handed me the ice pack—"I'm not ready to deal with any of that just yet. Shamus?" she called. "Come back here now and join us."

Maeve wasn't looking at him, but I was. He was leaning against the bar, his arms crossed over his chest, staring at the floor, dark, hot, angry. I didn't think he'd do what his mother said, but then he tipped his head up. His eyes through the heavy fall of his bangs were green, bright, and feral.

He untucked his arms and walked over to us, silent, hands in fists at his sides, looking like someone who was about to wade into the middle of a fight.

She looked up as he stood next to the table. "Are you all right then?" she asked.

Shame sniffed. "Why wouldn't I be?"

"I'm asking if you've been Closed too."

"No." He looked over at me, raised an eyebrow. "Have I?"

"Not that I know of, not that Bartholomew said."

Maeve just leaned back in her chair and chuckled. "I never thought I'd see the day where I was considered more of a risk to the Authority than you, Shamus."

Shame opened his mouth and scoffed. "How can you say something like that to your only son?"

But he smiled, probably the first real, Shame-like smile I'd seen on him since I came in the room.

"I'll want both of you to be as clear and honest with me as you can be," she said. "I know I'm missing things, but I'm not senile. If I don't understand something you're saying, and if you don't think it will cross Bartholomew's boundaries of what he doesn't want me knowing, I'd appreciate it if you'd fill in the details."

"Bartholomew Wray can fuck off for all I care," Shame said.

"Shamus," she said sternly, "like it or not, he is the Watch of this region. He is your superior. You will do as he tells you to."

"Of course I will," he said.

"Shamus," she warned.

"Promise and cross my heart."

They glared at each other for a moment but Shame was not backing down. Maeve finally sighed. "Where did I go so wrong with you?"

"You didn't," Shame said. "You went right with me. I went wrong all by myself."

"Well," Hayden said, walking back to us. "Dr. Fisher will not be making house visits any longer. Neither will she be treating anyone in the Authority in emergency situations."

"What?" Maeve frowned. "Why ever not? She's been doing that for the past fifteen years."

"Wray's orders," Hayden said.

We were all silent for a moment. Maybe it was just sinking in how total, how complete, his rule was going to be.

"Fucker," Shame muttered.

"I want you seen by someone, Allie," Maeve said, undeterred. "A doctor who knows the ways of the Authority."

I thought about it. "I know a guy," I said. "He seems to be up on the magical tech/medical interface. And he used to be a part of the Authority, I think."

"What's his name?" Hayden asked.

"Eli Collins."

"Collins the Cutter?" Shame asked.

"What?" I said, startled.

"He was a brilliant up-and-coming surgeon on the Authority's rosters," Hayden said. "Did one too many unapproved experimental procedures and got Closed, and Closed hard. I thought the best he'd be able to do with his future was relearn to tie his shoelaces."

"How did you come across him?" Maeve asked.

"He, uh, knew my dad."

They all stared at me.

"Was he working for your dad?" Maeve asked.

"I don't know. Maybe. Yes."

"Huh," Hayden said. "Maybe he had more connections in the Authority than I've given him credit for. Fell into the Beckstrom safety net."

"I don't know," I said. "Did he hurt anyone with his experiments?"

"Oh, most definitely," Shame said. "Wicked bugger. Hurt a lot of people."

"When he was practicing magic," I said. "But he's a medical expert, right?"

"As much as any torturer is," Shame said.

"Enough, Shamus," Maeve said. "Why do you think he'd help us now?"

"Because I hired him. To help a friend of mine, a Hound, Davy. Who was . . . hurt."

"Hurt how?" Shame asked.

"He was bit, but I think he was bit by a Veiled."

Maeve frowned. "Has that been a problem lately?"

I couldn't help it; I laughed. "No. Or I don't think so. Yesterday was the first time I've seen it happen. Though I think—" I shook my head and regretted it. "Ow," I said. "I think I've seen more Veiled on the street. And, um . . . inside people."

"Ick," Shame said.

Maeve just took a deep breath and let it out. "I didn't realize how very annoying it would be to have gaps in my memories. I don't know how you put up with it, Allie. So tell me what Mr. Collins is doing with your friend."

"He's trying to treat the infection the bite caused. With what appears to be normal medical intervention, and also with magic, and magic tech."

"And," she said, "you think he'd be willing to look at your head, and maybe hazard a guess as to why you are seeing magic. Were you bit by a Veiled?"

"Not that I know of."

"Take off your clothes," Shame said.

"What? No."

"If there's a bite, we'd see it. You saw the bite on Davy, didn't you?"

I couldn't help but notice that he was trying very hard to hold back a smile.

"Yes, I saw the bite."

"So we'd be able to see yours."

"I am not taking off my clothes."

"Do you remember being bit?" Maeve asked.

"No. I passed out the last time I used magic. But a lot of people were around. I think someone would have noticed if I were being bit."

"Without my memories of the full situation, I don't feel comfortable giving you advice, Allie," she said. "But you should have your head looked at by a doctor, and you should have a doctor see if your vision problem is of a physical or magical nature."

"I'll go see Collins." I figured I needed to check in on Davy anyway.

"If you think that's right," Maeve said.

"I, for one," Shame said, "still think you should take your clothes off."

"Not a chance, Flynn."

"Fine. Then let me drive you," he said.

"I have a ride. Jack Quinn's out there."

"I'll take you anyway."

I didn't know why he was being so insistent about it, but was too tired to fight him. "Fine." I turned to Maeve. "Thanks for the medicine and for everything."

"Ah, now," she said. "This isn't the last of things. Just because I'm not a Voice of Blood magic doesn't mean I'm done with the Authority. Despite what Bartholomew may or may not do, this is my home. And the Authority has always stood as the protector for all those who use magic. I'll fight for that cause until the day my bones are cold."

I stood. The room stayed in its current un-spinny mode, so I risked leaning down and giving Maeve a hug.

She hugged me back. Strong and warm and reassuring as if nothing at all had happened since the day I'd first met her.

I wanted to tell her that everything was going to be okay. That I was going to try to find a way to save Shame, to bring her memories back, to keep Bartholomew from making all the stupidest, most hurtful decisions possible.

But instead I just smiled and started toward the door.

Shame drifted up beside me, quiet, but burning hot.

"You going to tell me why you didn't want me to go to the den with Jack?" I asked as I opened the door.

"I don't have ulterior motives," he said. "But if we want to talk, really talk, we'll have the best chance in the car."

"Why couldn't we really talk back there?"

He pulled out a pack of cigarettes, tapped out a cig and lit it in his cupped hands. He exhaled smoke and tipped his chin toward the inn. "Do you really trust him?"

"Him who?" Yes, I'm an idiot. I turned around to see who he might be talking about.

Hayden was at the door, behind the glass, locking it behind us.

"Hayden?" I asked. "Oh, come on, Shame. Hayden's in love with your mother. And he's fought right along side us every step of the way. Why wouldn't I trust him?"

"He wasn't Closed."

"Neither were you," I said.

"Does that make sense?" he asked.

"Nothing Bartholomew is doing makes sense to me. Maybe he just doesn't see you as a threat."

Shame smiled. "Wouldn't that be grand?"

We were at his car now. I just waved at Jack, who didn't respond. Not that I'd expected him to. All I expected was that he'd follow us.

I got in Shame's car, and practically groaned at the soft seat and headrest. Shame threw his cigarette into the gravel, scanned the parking lot, then got in the car too. He made it look like he wasn't hurting, but the scent of pain on him told me otherwise.

"So are you?" I asked Shame.

"Am I what?" he said.

"A threat."

He started the car and drove down the access road. "He hurt my mother. I'm not a threat. I'm a promise."

Chapter Eleven

Shame drove like there wasn't another car on the road. Which was not true. My friendly little warnings and suggestions that he try not to double the speed limit fell on deaf ears. I decided I'd have fewer heart palpitations if I closed my eyes, so I did. With far less horn honking and screeching of brakes than I expected, we arrived at the den.

"You coming in with me?" I asked as Shame parallel-parked at about thirty miles an hour.

"Yes."

I was actually glad about that. If magic was knocking me out, I couldn't use it more than once to protect myself before I'd end up sucking pavement. I didn't have my sword or blood blade on me. Which didn't mean I couldn't defend myself, under normal circumstances. But medicated and with a possible concussion weren't exactly normal circumstances. I was not at my best.

Not that Shame was either. But he, at least, was in a killing mood. He probably wouldn't feel the pain of a fight for a week.

Shame and I got out of the car and strolled down past Get Mugged. He looked in the window and scowled. I had no idea what he was scowling at, so I looked in too.

All I saw in there were a few people sitting at tables, reading, drinking coffee, and Grant, by the counter, talking to a man and laughing.

"Shame?" I said.

"Shut up." He stormed off toward the den.

I glanced back in the shop, saw Grant lean a little closer to the man as he handed him back his change.

Oh. "You knew Grant was gay, didn't you?" I asked as I caught up with Shame.

"Not talking about it."

"Because I was sort of surprised when he and Terric hit it off back at the wake."

Shame said nothing.

"I mean, I knew Grant was gay, but no one told me Terric was."

"Terric is whatever Terric wants to be," Shame said. "What difference does it make?"

"Well, it would have explained some of your behavior toward him."

Shame spun. "That has nothing to do with him and me."

"Doesn't it?" I just looked at him. Offering no judgment, but accepting no bullshit.

I had to give it to him. He held my gaze for a full thirty seconds before he finally looked away.

"So none of your damn business," he said.

"Agreed. But Grant is my friend. And so is Terric. I probably would have introduced them to each other before, if I'd known."

"Terric doesn't need your help introducing himself to people." Shame had started walking again. "And I don't give a damn who he's with."

I followed, a little slower, puzzling out Shame's body language. I knew he wasn't gay—he'd told me so, and at this point I could only assume he was being truthful. Since he and Zay and Terric all used to hang out together, I could guess he'd found out Terric was gay a long time ago.

Shame opened the lobby door, and I was right behind him. "You just find out recently about him?" I asked.

"About who?"

"Terric."

Shame stopped before the bottom step. He didn't turn. He didn't face me. He just stared at the wall. "I've known he's gay since he told me and Zayvion back when we were still teenagers. I do not care if he's gay. I do not care if he dates men. I am not gay. Terric's known that since we were teenagers. None of that matters. None of that makes a difference. In what he and I—what we might have to be."

"Soul Complements?"

He winced as if even hearing it was painful.

"It's not like you have to sleep with him to cast magic with him, Shame."

He turned, just enough that I could see his face and all his sharp, dark edges in profile. "I am very aware of that, Allie. My objections to Terric don't have anything to do with his sexual orientation." He turned the rest of the way and leveled a look at me. "Got that yet?"

"Not really, no." His heartbeat was too high, and I could smell the discomfort, the fear on his skin. He could tell me, and tell himself that Terric being gay made no difference in their friendship, in their using magic together, but he was lying.

"If it's not that he's gay," I pressed, "then what is it?"

"I just . . ." He looked away from me, back at the wall. "Soul Complements. It's intimate. No, it doesn't have to be about sex. But it's about being in someone's life, hell, in their mind, forever. They know what you're thinking, know what you want, know your stupid jealousies and fears and desires. They know how much you're hurting, even if you lie."

He paused. Long enough I probably should have said something. But I didn't.

"It's about being committed to someone for the long run," he said so softly, I almost couldn't hear him. "And it's about being vulnerable. I'm no good at either of those things."

"I think you're wrong," I said.

"Thanks for the support," he said.

"I think," I said, brushing away his comment, "that you can commit to someone. You already have. You are Zayvion's best friend. You are my friend. And friendship means you're going to be there for the long run. It means you feel safe around the other person. No matter how vulnerable you are."

"They don't call it Soul Friendship, Beckstrom," he said.

"Maybe they should."

He finally looked over at me again. "Is that was it is between you and Jones? Friendship?"

"No. But Zay and I decide what we have between us. We define what being Soul Complements means *to us*. No matter what anyone else tells us it should be. No matter what magic wants us to do or be. We decide what we are."

"Magic doesn't work like that," he said. "There's always a price to pay."

"I didn't say it was easy."

He considered that for a moment. "You think it's worth it, don't you?"

"Yes."

"I—" He shook his head. Then, quietly: "I just don't know." He climbed the stairs, his boots making the most noise I'd heard out of him all day. He didn't look back, which was fine with me. I was holding on to the railing to keep my balance as I walked. My head didn't hurt— thank you, narcotics—but the only sport I was fit for right now was championship holding-very-still.

Stairs sucked.

As I slogged upward, I realized I still hadn't heard from Zayvion. I wondered where he was, wondered why he hadn't contacted me. I needed to call him again, but right this minute one-foot-up and one-foot-down was all I could handle.

I was happy to reach the second floor. I was also out of breath. Shame paused outside the door to the den and seemed to notice I was lagging behind. He frowned. "You look like hell."

I lifted my middle finger.

He laughed. It was good to hear.

I walked past him and leaned on the door until it opened.

Not a lot of people in the den. Sid was there, watching a game on TV. "Welcome back," he said without looking away from the TV. "Nice to have you by again, Shamus."

The way I was huffing and puffing, Sid had probably heard us coming a block away.

"Hey," I said, heading straight to the kitchen and pouring myself a glass of water, "anyone else around?"

"Bea's upstairs," he said.

With Davy, probably with Collins. "Is Collins still here?"

"Yes." He said that like maybe he wished the good doctor would pack it up and take off.

"Trouble?"

Sid turned the TV on mute and finally shifted so he could look at me. "Allie? Are you okay?"

"So good." I finished off my water, keeping one hand clenched on the edge of the countertop, my knees locked.

"She needs to see the doctor," Shame said. "Is he upstairs?"

"Yes. Let me help." He got up and then Sid and Shame were walking over to me with twin expressions of worry.

Fabulous.

"Oh, knock it off. I'm not in that bad of shape."

"The last person I saw who was as pale as you," Sid said, "had been dead for twenty-four hours."

"Who says I haven't?" I laughed. I thought it was funny. They weren't laughing. They were taking my arms and putting them over their shoulders. And then they were walking. I think I lost track of exactly where we were going. But when the elevator door dinged, I was awake like the damned sirens of Armageddon had just gone off.

"Don't," I said.

"Darlin', why don't you ever stay unconscious when I want you to?" Shame asked.

"Bet you say that to all the girls," I slurred. And then we were in the elevator and I closed my eyes. Between the weird stomach-pressing lurch of the elevator, my fear, and my general discomfort, I was pretty sure if I kept my eyes open I'd scream.

"Still with us?" Shame asked. We were walking again. I must have checked out. I checked back in.

"I'm fine," I said. Didn't even slur. Go me. "Let me walk, Shame. I got it."

"Fine. Show us what you got, hotshot." He let go of me. So did Sid. I brushed my hair back out of my eyes, my right hand too hot and trembling. Then I squared my shoulders and walked into the loft space.

The lighting here was soft, yellow, and much easier on my eyes than the fluorescents downstairs. Note to self: upgrade lighting. Even though there were plenty of floor-to-ceiling windows, someone had managed to carefully unroll the ancient shades and pull them down so that only the uppermost parts of the windows let light into the room, catching it up among the rafters, and filtering it down into the rest of the room.

Bea was indeed in the room—sitting sideways in the big easy chair I'd fallen asleep in, and doing a crossword puzzle in ink.

"Hey, guys," she said. "Here, Allie. Do you want to sit down?"

Her tone of voice must have broken the trance of whatever it was on the table filled with ever-growing numbers of contraptions that had held Collins so riveted.

"How's Davy?" I asked.

He gave me one long, slow look, from my feet all the way up to the top of my head. And then he totally ignored me and talked to Shame instead.

"It's been a long time, Flynn," he said.

"Wish it were longer," Shame said.

Collins bit down on a reply. "What happened to her?"

"She fell and hit her head."

"Is that your story too, Allison, or did Flynn help you make that up?"

"It's my story. But mine also has me trying to cast magic and passing out. Then hitting my head."

"That's quite a different story," he noted. "Let's see if you can lie down."

"Where?" We didn't have an extra bed up here. We didn't even have a couch.

"The chair should work."

I walked over to the easy chair. Bea, the sweetie, came to my side and put her arm around mine, helping to steady me.

"You are hot as fire, girl," she said. "Literally. I think she's running a fever," she said before I could get my reply together.

I sat in the easy chair but didn't lean back. Instead I cradled my face in my hands, and kept them there by propping my elbows on my knees.

"Took two pills," I said, figuring Collins would want to know.

"Mmm," he said, as he pulled a chair in front of me

and put a blood pressure cuff on my arm. "What sort of pills?"

"Shame said they were codeine."

"Were they, Shamus? Were they codeine?" Collins asked.

"Yes. They were. What's that?"

"A stethoscope," Collins said with droll emphasis. "You'll find them all the rage these days." He pressed the disk against my back, my chest, and listened. Then he brought a flashlight out of his vest pocket and examined the back of my head, then my eyes, and then he helped me lean back in the chair.

A blanket seemed to appear out of nowhere and wrap around me. Good blanket. Stay.

"Shame?" I said.

"What?"

"Don't let him get me naked."

Collins laughed, one hard bark that turned into a cough. Someone patted my shoulder, Shame, I was pretty sure. "Don't worry, love. He couldn't if he tried."

With that, I went to sleep. Deep, like diving from a cliff into tranquil dark waters.

It was wonderful. And ended much too quickly.

" . . . going to have to get a few supplies, and a change of clothes. She should wake up soon."

"She's awake now," I mumbled. I opened my eyes, stretched. Sweet hells, I felt good.

"How are you feeling?" Bea asked.

The light in the room had changed. It was early evening now. I must have gotten a couple hours of sleep.

"A lot better." I sat forward and my head didn't hurt. Also, I was still dressed. Bonus. "Really a lot better."

"Want something to drink?" Bea asked. "I made iced tea."

"Sure."

Bea went to the kitchen and it took me a minute to realize what was different. I could see the magic around her. The magic around Jack had been a charcoal haze. But Bea seemed to have a fuchsia aura. Very pretty, actually. She even left fuchsia footsteps on the floor that faded away almost instantly as she walked.

"So," Collins said as he unrolled his starched white sleeves. "You have a concussion. After talking to Jack Quinn, I'm surprised you didn't do worse damage. There might be a slight headache off and on for the next week or so. Otherwise, clean bill of heath there."

Collins didn't have magic surrounding him like Bea did. Yes, I was staring.

Instead, magic wrapped a thin wire garrote around his neck, so tight that it moved when he swallowed. Silver wires bound his wrists and both his thumbs, and when he turned to the table to pick up something there, the magic that lingered on the table drew away from his touch, like oil retreating from water.

Those wires, those bindings, repelled magic. I wondered how he could even get his hands on enough magic to complete spells, much less cast those delicate medical spells. It must have taken a hell of a lot of focus on his part.

Shame was sitting in one of the windowsills, the window cracked open. He had his knee up, his elbow propped on it. The cigarette in his hand was near the open part of the window, smoke drifting outside.

Magic made Shame look like a sleek, dark-edged fighter. It also bathed him in sunset-colored mist that streamed in from the windows—magic from trees and other living things feeding him, feeding the crystal burning in his chest.

Shame nodded at me. "The clunk to your noggin wasn't the worst of it."

"Okay." I stood. Felt more like me than I'd felt in a

long time. I stretched again, rocking up on the balls of my feet. "What was the worst of it?"

"You apparently cast a spell on yourself," Collins said. "But it was so tangled up, so compressed and impacted that it took some time to unwind."

"I threw magic at myself?"

"I said apparently," Collins repeated. "There are other theories."

"Such as?" Bea showed up with a glass of iced tea.

"Such as someone had a spell already cast on you and when you pulled on magic it triggered." He plucked his coat jacket off the back of the chair and shrugged into it. "Or you were pulling on magic and somehow never let go of it, leaving it to run rampant through you. Or about half a dozen other possibilities. Whatever it is that has caused magic to do this to you will not kill you now. The outcome—" He stopped buttoning his coat and tipped his head down, letting his eyes take me in again, from the bottom of my feet, slowly up the curves of my body, then finally to my face, where his gaze shifted from my lips to my eyes and settled there.

"The outcome of your treatment is very favorable," he murmured.

I gave him a look that said "Back off, creepy" though all I said out loud was, "Good. I like favorable."

He seemed to get the message and toned down the creepy stuff, though he smiled like it was all an old joke we had shared for years.

Had we shared anything for years? I didn't know. There was no memory of him, not even a niggle of knowing him in the past.

More likely he was just a slightly crazy magic user looking to push my buttons.

I so didn't have time for this.

I dragged my fingers back through my hair and

scrubbed at my scalp, avoiding the bump, then walked over to where Davy was sleeping.

"How's he doing?"

"His condition hasn't changed much. It hasn't gotten worse either. But it will take me more time to track down whatever it is he's afflicted with. And more equipment. Which is why I'm on my way out. I should be back in a few hours. Good eve. Allison. Flynn. Everyone."

Shame just held up one hand, and didn't even watch him leave. He was looking out the window, looking down at Get Mugged.

I took a drink of the iced tea and studied Davy. He was still pale, still asleep. His breathing was a little lighter, more even. He didn't look he was struggling for every breath.

And since I still had the weird magic vision, I could see the black lines of tainted magic spreading out under his skin, curling toward his organs, while the thin, impossibly delicate Syphon spell slowly absorbed the magic and drained it into an electronic device.

I could also see the other spells Collins had set up on Davy. One for Sleep, one for Ease, and one that I didn't know the name of, but that seemed to be attached to another little machine propped on the table and tied in to the Syphon spell.

Poor kid.

"He been down since last night?" Shame asked around an exhale of smoke.

"I think so. Bea, do you know if he woke up at all?"

"Nope. He's been resting. Dr. Collins hasn't left his side. Are you staying for a while, Allie?" she asked.

I shrugged. "I was thinking about going home." Or finding Zayvion. It suddenly hit me that I didn't know where he was. "Do you need a break?"

"I think Jamar was supposed to be here an hour ago to take the next shift. He's a no-show."

I nodded. "I can hang for a while. Who's on next?"

"Theresa should be coming in around midnight."

"That works for me," I said.

"Thanks!" she said, all dimples and smiles. "I'll see you tomorrow."

She pulled her stuff together, grabbed her purse and coat.

"Bea," I asked before she was out the door.

"Yes?"

"Do you know if Davy has family in the area?"

She shook her head. "He never said so. But we checked. Sid checked. We didn't find anyone."

"Thanks."

She walked out and shut the door quietly behind her. That left me, Shame, and a sleeping Davy.

It was quiet, the only sounds in the room the hush of traffic outside the window, and the flick and exhale of Shame's smoking. I stared at Davy for a long moment, then decided I wasn't doing him any good. I paced off to the kitchen to see if there was any food.

"You seen Zay today?" Shame asked.

"Not since we were out hunting for Anthony." I opened the refrigerator. Stared at the contents without really seeing any of it. "Have you?"

"Yes."

I waited, decided I couldn't handle anything that thrived in that much bright and cold, and shut the refrigerator door. I tried a cupboard instead. Crackers. Caramel corn. I grabbed the caramel corn.

I opened the box and walked back out into the room. Too restless to sit, too tired to stand, I paced instead, close to the windows, where I could watch night lower its veil on the world.

"And?" I asked. "Where was he?"

Shame sucked the last heat off the cigarette and tossed it out the window. He exhaled, then shifted on the sill so both his legs hung over the side. "Did he call you?"

"No."

"So you haven't spoken to him at all today."

"No." I wanted to tell him to stop stringing me along and just tell me, but at the same time I knew something was wrong. I wasn't sure if I wanted to add one more bad thing to my day. A hard suspicion was growing like a lump in my stomach and I knew that Shame was about to make it worse.

"You'll want to," he said. "Talk to him soon. He's probably at home."

"Why do I want to talk to him?"

Shame paused, and all the fire, all the anger, all the laughter drained out of him. He suddenly just looked tired, uncomfortable, and very, very human, even though the crystal in his chest spun tendrils of smoke into him.

"He probably doesn't want me to tell you—but I will." He rubbed his palms over the thighs of his jeans, as if wiping away an itch, or pain.

"Let's start here—you know Zay loves you, right?"

"Good lord, how bad can this news be? Of course I know he loves me. Spit it out, Shame."

"And I can only assume that you love him too, what with that moony-eyed look you get whenever he walks into the room."

I put the caramel corn box down and crossed my arms over my chest.

"So I want you to think about that," he said. "You love him. For whatever your reasons are—and some of those reasons probably have something to do with his personality, his morals, who he is. Unless maybe you're just into him for his fine bod?"

"Not just," I said.

"Zayvion's a good man," Shame continued. "He has better morals than I have, that's for damn sure."

"What did he do?" From the way Shame was hedging around the subject, a thousand very bad things were taking root in my imagination.

"He Closed them."

Oh shit. That was one bad thing I'd been afraid to think about.

"Who?" I needed to sit down; instead I paced.

"Victor," Shame said softly, "Mum, Joshua, Nick, Mike. All of them. He's the Guardian of the gates and one of the strongest Closers, especially since Victor, the head of Faith magic and therefore the head of Closing, was one of the people who got shut down."

I just kept pacing, trying to absorb the information, trying to think about it objectively even though my stomach was sick and my face was too hot, and all I could think of was Zayvion, not my lover but the Closer. Cold, blank, a mask of Zen taking memories, taking pieces of their lives away, leaving behind holes and pain.

I did not want to think of him like that. I did not want to think of him as someone who would coolly destroy the people he cared about because he was ordered to do it. Because he had a duty and a superior to follow.

But that was exactly what he had done.

"Where is he?" I asked.

"Don't know."

I glanced over at Shame. "You let him do this? You knew he was going to Close your mother?"

Shame rolled one shoulder and glanced down at the floor. "I wasn't there. They didn't tell me. He didn't tell me. Not until after. I don't think he knew what they were going to make him do. By then it was done. I can't undo it—only Zayvion can."

"And you didn't tell him to undo it?"

"If," he said, his voice a little louder, his elbows locked, arms straight against his thighs, "I told him to undo it, Bartholomew would just have someone else

Close her. Someone who might not be my friend. Someone who doesn't give a damn about my mother and would tear her mind to shreds just for fun."

"They can't do this," I said. "They can't do this, Shame."

"It's too late, Al," he said quietly. "They already did. Welcome to the nightmare."

I paced. There had to be a way to change this, to get Bartholomew to see that Victor and Maeve and everyone else had been working in the best interest of the Authority and had done everything possible to keep the city, the people, and magic safe. He had to see that they had been under almost constant attack, betrayal, and infighting. That the other people involved—Sedra, Isabelle, Leander, Jingo Jingo—had been working toward the goal of tearing the Authority apart for years.

It wasn't their fault they had been fighting a losing battle since day one. It wasn't their fault Leander and Isabelle had been planning their revenge for hundreds of years.

But I guess I had to see Bartholomew's point too. From the outside it looked as though Victor and Maeve had failed in keeping the Authority and magic safe. Closer examination of the facts would show that wasn't true, but I didn't think Bartholomew wanted to see the facts. He wanted a clean slate and a new set of shoulders to lay the weight upon, and people to blame if things went wrong.

It wasn't the way I would run things. I was pretty sure it wasn't the way Victor and Maeve would have run things if they were in his position. But it was the way it was.

And Zayvion had been an instrument, a brutal tool in his hands.

Shame hopped down from the windowsill and wandered off into the kitchen. I paced, making sure to look over at Davy every time I passed by his bed. Still sleeping. All the spells still pulsing, all the magic still trying to cleanse him of the taint, the poison, the toxic magic that spread through him.

I didn't say anything more. I didn't know what to say. My emotions were tying up in knots and I didn't know how to see Zayvion as innocent in this. He could have said no. He could have told Bartholomew he was wrong. Hells, he could have Closed Bartholomew.

But like Shame said, Bartholomew always had his men around him. Protection. Muscle. Plenty enough to make any kind of objection moot.

I didn't know when Shame turned on the TV. I didn't even know they'd brought a TV up here. But it was droning in the background and the light had drained away from the sky. It was late. Still not midnight, but that was probably only a couple hours off.

My feet hurt. I think I'd been pacing for hours.

"What are you watching?"

Shame jumped a little. "Jesus, Beckstrom. Nice to see you come back to earth. Next time send a warning beacon."

"Were you sleeping?"

"No." He rubbed his eyes and shifted in the easy chair. "Watching TV." He pointed the remote at it.

I decided to make some coffee. "News?"

"Yes. They're all fussing about some kind of flu going around the city."

"Like that's news?"

"They think so." He turned up the volume. "Pour me a cup, love?"

"You eat?"

"I think so."

I pulled a sandwich out of the fridge and split it onto two plates, then poured coffee for us. "No milk."

"I'll survive. Sugar?"

"Yes. Lucky you." I scooped sugar into his cup, then brought everything out and handed him the plate and cup.

Shame stood. "Take the chair—it gave me a knot in my back. Plus, I need to take a leak."

I didn't argue. Let him sit on the wooden stool. I dropped down into the chair, still warm from Shame. The remote stabbed at my thigh, so I picked it up and turned the volume down a little.

The newscaster was indeed talking about a flu. Only she called it an epidemic. She also said that hospitals were feeling the impact, and encouraged people to head down to an emergency room only if they were displaying all of the symptoms, but not if they had just one or two of them.

I guess it was a good thing we'd kept Davy here.

Shame came out of the bathroom and picked up his sandwich and coffee. He took the footstool.

"So how long are you staying here tonight?" he asked.

I shrugged. "Until Theresa shows up."

"What about Collins?"

"Don't trust him as far as I could shot-put him," I said.

"I like how your default mode is cynical and distrustful."

"I like to think of it as realistic and self-aware."

He chuckled but had to chew and swallow.

"Same thing," he mumbled. "You going to go see Zay?"

Was I? I didn't even know where he was. I didn't even know if he wanted to see me. Yes, I hadn't tried to call him more than once, but he hadn't called me either. The phone worked two ways.

"Do you know where he is?" I asked.

Shame frowned. "Like I said earlier. If I had to guess? His place."

"Think anyone is there with him?"

"Like who? You really are suspicious. What happened to all that 'we decide what we are together' trusty stuff? And to answer you—I have no idea. Why don't you call him?"

"Later." I finished my sandwich, paid scant attention to the TV until Shame took the remote and changed the channel to something with a lot of car crashes and explosions.

The door opened and I glanced back. Collins was walking in, a duffel in one hand, a bag from a Chinese restaurant in the other.

"Evening," he said.

"Don't you have somewhere else to be?" Shame asked.

"Nowhere else that's paying me an hourly wage." He strode over, dropped the duffel on the clear space on the tabletop, and shrugged out of his coat, folding it carefully and draping it on the chair next to Davy's bed. Then he got busy with the food, pulling a carton and a pair of chopsticks out of the bag.

"Where are the Hounds?" he asked.

"Shift change. I'm it."

"Excuse me?" he said.

"I'm the Hound on duty until Theresa shows up."

He laughed, a short, quiet sound.

"What's so funny about that?" I asked.

"You're not a Hound."

I got up and took my plate into the kitchen. "Yes, I am."

"But you're Daniel Beckstrom's daughter. He'd never stand for that."

"I don't care what my dad stands for. I'm a Hound. Have been for years."

"Stood for," he corrected me.

"What?"

"Your father. What he stood for, not what he stands for."

Oh, right. He didn't know my dad was still alive-ish. In my head. "Whatever. You get the things you needed for Davy?"

"I think so. Have you heard about the flu that's going around?"

"It's on the news," I said.

"And it is clogging up the medical community, slowing down prescriptions, and generally being a complete annoyance. Also, I don't think it's a flu."

"Really?" I asked. "How many patients have you examined to make that diagnosis, Doctor?"

He pointed the chopsticks at me. "None. But I don't have to. Do I, Shamus?"

"Don't drag me into your neurosis," Shame said. "I have enough of my own."

Collins grinned, then dug in the carton for a piece of meat. "I think it's a cover-up."

That got Shame's attention.

"You working for Bartholomew?" Shame asked.

"No, but I've seen the Authority from the outside for more years than I've seen it from the inside. This flu epidemic looks like someone's trying very hard to cover their tracks."

"How about we follow up on that with a Truth spell?" Shame said.

Collins laughed. "How about we don't?"

Shame stood up. "Not joking around. Now."

Collins raised his eyebrows and gave Shame a long look. Then he sucked in a short breath and went back to eating. "That's not going to work for me, Flynn. I don't want a Blood spell between us. I've sworn off that kind of magic. And I refuse to use it again."

"You don't have to use it," Shame said, advancing on him. "I will."

Collins sighed and put his food down, then brushed his hands together. "No Truth spells. Just look into my eyes, Flynn. I am not working for Bartholomew. I do not like Bartholomew. I wouldn't care if he jumped off a cliff, or died in a back alley somewhere. We do not have good history. I took my case to him, back in the day. He didn't lift a finger to help me."

Shame tipped his head a little. "Rather have a Truth spell."

"Not going to happen. And in the scheme of things, it doesn't matter. I'm here to help Allison with her friend and to collect a paycheck. Once Mr. Silvers is on his feet again, I will bother you no longer."

"I can only hope."

"And that hope will not be in vain." He went back to eating, but then walked over to look down at Davy. "Allison, are you still seeing magic?"

"Yes."

"Would you come here and tell me what you see?"

Might as well. I walked over, gave him the rundown. The spells he'd cast on him, the branching black tendrils digging into him, and the various streams and lines and webs of magic around the room.

He nodded and threw the empty carton into the wastebasket. "I'm going to see how accurate your vision is." He calmed his mind fast, like a rock falling to the bottom of a pool, set a Disbursement with a flick of his wrist that looked like it was going to add to a headache he'd been nursing for several days, then traced the glyph for Sight.

Collins cast in a sort of blocky, learned-by-rote manner, the wires of magic around his wrists, thumbs, and throat restricting his movement, which surprised me. It was like he'd been trying to learn how to hold a pencil all his life, but his handwriting was still so bad no one but he could read it. I wasn't sure magic would follow the lines he'd drawn. I wasn't even sure I could follow what he'd drawn.

But when he called on magic it was like listening to

someone with an unexpected, amazing voice sing. He must have been very, very good back before he'd been Closed. Magic pulled easy and strong out of the networks that surrounded the building and snaked out like a liquid ribbon at about waist height, to fill the glyph he held and to catch it on white fire with stark black edges.

It smelled weird. Hot and rotten. I covered my nose.

"Problem?" Collins asked as he brought his hand, and the spell along with it, up to his eyes so he could peer through it. The smell did not seem to affect him.

I breathed through my mouth. That didn't help. I could taste the stink. "Smells."

"Shame, do you agree?"

Shame sniffed the air. "What does it smell like?" he asked.

"Rotten meat. Dead people. Death."

"Not to me," Shame said.

Collins was done looking around the room through Sight. "I think you gave me a clear and fair assessment of the magic in the room." He unpinched his fingers, releasing the spell and breaking its lines.

I made a strangled sound and walked over to the window, opening it and sticking my head out far enough to breathe the clean air. Only it wasn't clean. I could smell the stink out here too, the faint whiff of sweetly decaying meat.

The air pressure changed as someone walked in through the other door.

"What's up?" Theresa asked.

I was glad she was here. I pulled my head back in and turned around.

Theresa looked like she always looked. Tough, no nonsense, thick black hair and strong features. She was wearing jeans and a hoodie, and of course jogging shoes. Theresa often Hounded for Nike, and dealt with the pain of casting magic by being a chronic fitness freak.

"Do you smell anything?" I asked.

"I smell a lot of things," she said with a completely straight face.

"Does magic smell weird to you? Right now, here, I mean."

She frowned and inhaled. "I hadn't noticed. A particular spell?"

"Collins just cast Sight. What does that smell like to you?"

She sniffed, then drew a glyph for Smell that hung in the air like a collection of raindrops. Nothing intricate like I'd use while Hounding a crime scene, but something plenty sensitive enough to catch what I had smelled.

"It's a little . . . I don't know," she said. "Sour?"

"Like rotting meat?" I suggested.

She inhaled, opened her mouth this time to get more of the scent on her palate, the raindrops glistening as they touched her lips. "I could go with rotten."

"But you only smell a hint of it?"

She nodded, and waved her hand to break the spell. The raindrops turned into mist that drifted lazily upward. "Why? It's not like magic doesn't stink up the place sometimes."

That was true. It just seemed like I was overly sensitive, or overly aware of it lately. "I just wanted a second opinion. That's all."

She nodded. "So I'll take watch with Mr. Collins. How's the kid doing?"

"He's doing well, or at least he's not losing any ground," Collins said. "Tomorrow should tell me more."

"What happens tomorrow?" I asked.

"I find out if the measures I've been taking are adequate. And I make some hard choices for how to adjust what I'm doing."

"No hard choices without me here," I said.

"If you're here," he agreed.

"No. Listen to me. No hard choices on Davy's care unless I sign off on them."

"I don't believe we agreed to that."

"Just now," I said with a smile. "We agreed to it just now. And Theresa heard us and will tell the other Hounds; she stood as witness to us sealing the deal."

He opened his mouth, then smiled back at me. "I do enjoy your interpretation of how one negotiates. So you just tell me how it's going to be with no room for any sort of compromise?"

"No compromise when it comes to him. Got that?"

"I understand what you're saying. But if there is something I can do to treat him and you are not here, nor are you available for comment or consultation, I will not guarantee that I will not take action."

"Was that your long about way of telling me no?"

"Yes."

I thought about it for a minute. It'd be easy to force him into my position, I was the one who was signing his paycheck. But he was right. It would be stupid for me to demand he wait to try to find me if it was a matter of life or death.

"If his life or recovery is drastically endangered, then yes, you can treat him without checking in with me," I said.

"Glad you see it my way."

"Oh, I still see it my way," I said as I walked across the room to get my coat. "Your way just fits in enough with what I want that I don't see a reason to argue with you. I'll be back in the morning." I walked out of the room, and Shame followed.

"Where am I taking you?" Shame asked.

"Zay's apartment."

Chapter Twelve

While Shame drove, I tried calling Zayvion. His phone went immediately to voice mail, which meant he had probably turned it off. Not helpful.

"He won't answer." I stuffed my phone back in my pocket.

"He gets like that."

"Like what?"

"Closed off. Moody. Angry."

"You think he's angry?" I said. "He was just doing his job, right? Isn't that what you were trying to convince me of back there? This is nothing personal, all in the name of duty?"

Shame drove for a bit, uncharacteristically quiet. "You know how everyone kept saying there was a war coming? That the Authority was falling apart, turning against itself, people taking sides?" He paused. "All the fights we've been in, all the hell we've been through, all the people we've lost—we've done it all to keep the Authority together. To uphold the rules, the things the Authority has always stood and fought for.

"But I don't know how much longer I'll stand on the side of an organization that tears down the people who were standing in the line of fire, and standing up for those ideals. I might not be able to play by their rules anymore."

"You sure you want to tell me this, Shame?" I asked. "They could drag it out of me with a Truth spell."

"What's a little treason between friends?" he said with a fast smile.

"Don't do it, Shame, whatever you have planned," I said. "I don't want you to be Closed too."

He shrugged. "What I do or don't isn't yours to worry about. And it's not even the point I was making. I was telling you this so you'd know that's the way I look at what's going on right now. We've been screwed. By our own people. And there is no way to correct that under Bartholomew's rules.

"But," Shame continued, "Zayvion isn't like that. He would never think the things I'm thinking and would certainly never act out on it. He won't break away from the Authority and its rules. He's a good soldier. I'm a good fuckup."

"Maybe you underestimate the both of you," I said.

"I think I have a pretty clean bead on this. You might want to decide what, exactly, you are," he said. "Because if you're going to stay in the Authority, in Bartholomew's Authority, you'd better be a lot more soldier and lot less so what."

"Maybe I'll just be me," I said.

"Don't know if Bartholomew has room in his Authority for someone like you, Allie."

We were at Zay's place. It had been a while since I'd been here—I liked my place and he seemed more than willing to hang out with me there.

"Want me to wait?" Shame asked.

"Just until he lets me in, okay?"

He nodded and pulled out a pack of cigarettes.

I pushed the door open, then leaned back into the car. "I love him, Shame," I said. "But I have spent my life not doing what I was ordered to do unless I thought it was the right thing."

"I know," he said. "It's one of the things I like about you, love. Go on, now. Go get your man."

I shut the door and walked quickly to the front steps of the building. It was dark now, the streetlights straight electric yellow, the closest spells attached to power boxes to deter criminals, and a very nice Flourish planted like a row of softly glowing red mushrooms in the shrubbery along the walkway to the door.

The smell of rotten meat was still on the air, but not as strong as when Collins had cast it. I resisted the urge to get down and sniff at the mushrooms and see if the very faint magic that supplied that spell also stank of the dead.

I climbed the few steps to the door and rang the bell. I could hear the rumble of Shame's car engine, and knew he was still waiting. But the way the building was situated off the road, he couldn't see me. I rang the bell again.

Just as I reached to hit the buzzer one last time, Zayvion answered.

"Yes?"

"It's Allie," I said. The silence went on so long, I almost pressed the buzzer to make sure we were still connected. Then the door made that sound that meant it was unlocked, and I opened it.

I pulled my phone out of my pocket and dialed Shame's number.

"Did he let you in?" he asked.

"Yes. Bye, Shame. See you tomorrow."

"Be careful, all right?" And then he hung up.

That was weird. He'd never told me to be careful around Zayvion before.

I climbed the stairwell—all concrete but well lit and so quiet I would have been able to hear a fly sneeze. At the top of the stairs, I looked through the window in the door, which showed the hallway beyond. No one there, lots of light, no problems.

Well, one problem. I didn't know what I was going to

say to Zay. I felt angry and betrayed that he'd Closed my friends—his friends. I'd always known his vows to do his duty and uphold whatever the Authority told him was right took precedence in his actions, but this?

This was criminal.

It changed how I looked at him. Made me wonder what else he might do just because the Authority told him to do it.

I headed down the hall to Zayvion's door, then knocked.

Again the long wait. I wondered if maybe he was in trouble. Maybe Bartholomew's men were in there with him, holding him captive or making him Close people or something.

Maybe he'd been Closed.

Hells.

I thought about pulling on magic, but passing out into someone's arms didn't really count as a surprise attack.

I so needed to get a nonmagical weapon.

The footsteps approaching from the other side of the door sounded like Zayvion's pace. He paused, threw the locks, and then broke the protective Ward on the door.

I held my breath, but not in time. The smell of rotten meat hit me.

What was it with magic and me lately?

The door opened.

Zay wasn't wearing a shirt. He had on his jeans, no shoes. His eyes were bloodshot and he smelled faintly of alcohol, scotch, I'd guess. Just like when I looked at him with Sight, he appeared taller. The silver glyphs of spells wrapped around his body and burned with black flame.

It was a weird, sort of double vision of him—I could see Zayvion as Zayvion, and I could see him as a tower of a man covered every inch in magic.

"What do you want, Allie?" he asked in a voice that sounded like it had been sanded down.

"For you to let me in."

He hesitated. Finally stepped back so I could walk through the door.

There were no lights on in his house. The only light came from outside the window, where the city chipped at the night like faraway stars. I could smell the booze a little stronger in here.

"What do you need?" He hadn't moved away from the door, though he'd shut it. Hadn't locked it, but the Ward triggered automatically and sealed the door magically.

"I need to talk to you," I said evenly. "Have you been sitting here in the dark all night?"

He didn't say anything.

"Davy's sick," I said.

Still nothing.

"Zay . . ." I took a step toward him. He didn't move. I stopped before touching him. What could I say? How could I tell him how angry I was? How could I tell him I needed him to be the man I loved? The one who didn't go around ripping out his friends' minds.

"I know what you did," I said. "I know that you Closed them. Maeve, Victor."

"It is my job and my duty," he said stiffly. "I have sworn. . . ." Here his voice faded.

"You know it's not right," I said.

We stood there, that truth between us.

"Doesn't matter what I know," he said. "I don't have a say in if it's right or not."

"You could have tried—"

"I tried," he said, cutting me off.

"You could have refused."

"And what?" he asked, his voice growing louder, "let one of Bartholomew's men cleaver through their brains? Just stand down and watch someone else do my job?"

"Would it have killed you?" I asked, a little more

heated than before. "Couldn't you have found a way to stop them? To stop Bartholomew?"

"He is my superior," Zayvion said.

"So was Victor until you tore his brain apart!"

He lifted his head as if I'd just slapped him and glowered down at me. But his voice was ice cold.

"Victor was relieved of his position before I Closed him. There wasn't a damn thing I could do about that either."

I took a couple of breaths to rein in my temper. Zayvion was obviously hurting from this, from what he had been ordered to do. And I was standing here angry at him, when I should be taking my frustration out on Bartholomew. "Victor would have wanted you to do . . . something," I said, much softer, but still unable to let it go.

"No," he said. "He wanted me to do my job. The job he trained me to do. That was what he was telling me at Chase's wake. To follow orders. To follow Bartholomew. No matter what Bartholomew ordered me to do. And I did exactly that."

His voice didn't rise, no room beneath that ice for emotion to lift it or drag it down. He was a statue of silver and black fire. It reminded me too much of when I'd found him in death, standing right in front of me, close enough that I could touch him, but was still unable to free him from the chains that bound him.

"I know," I admitted. I dragged my hand back through my hair, pulling it away from my face and then letting it go. I was frustrated. But I was fighting the wrong battle. Zayvion wasn't the only one at fault in this. He wasn't even the main person at fault. He may have been the weapon, but Bartholomew was the man who had told him to strike.

"Is that all?" he asked. Cold, shutting the conversation down. More than that. I couldn't feel him, couldn't hear his thoughts or feel his emotions even though we were standing near enough that I should have been able to. He had pulled so far back behind walls that I didn't know if he was furious, or sad, or just tired of talking about it. Or maybe just tired of me.

"No," I said. "That is not all."

I took the remaining three steps toward him and pressed my body against his, wrapping one hand up around the heat of his bare neck, sliding the other around his bare waist to hold him hard against me.

I kissed him.

He did not return my kiss, not for a long, long moment. Then it was as if a glacier had sheared apart under the heat of the sun.

His emotions whipped through me like a hot summer wind, and I had to lock my knees to stay on my feet.

Allie, he thought, asked, called. That one word filling me with his desire, filling me with his need.

I wanted him. Needed him. Needed to know he was still the same man I loved. Needed to know we were both still the same. That even this hadn't destroyed what we were together.

Too full with my own desire, I poured into his mind, his soul. There were no walls between us. No hiding. No doubt. No different. We were Soul Complements. One. As we chose to be.

His mouth moved against mine, hard, hungry, his arms holding me so tightly I almost couldn't breathe, but I wanted him to hold me even tighter. He pushed his hands under my coat, rubbing his palms up my back, then down the curve of my hips.

I knew what he wanted, could feel the hunger for it thrumming beneath my skin. And he knew what I wanted.

I savored the smoky whiskey of his mouth, savored his anger, his sorrow. Drank down the realness, the sameness of him. Heat and need trickled down my spine, licked between my legs and shockwaved upward.

I was not naked enough.

Neither was he.

He pushed my coat up, but that wasn't enough, so his hands tugged at my jeans, undoing the button and pulling down the zipper with two quick twists.

He slid his hand into my pants and gently stroked me there.

I took a hard breath.

Yes. My hands slid around his waist and unbuttoned his jeans.

There were too damn many layers of clothes between us.

I don't know if that was his thought or mine.

"Wait," I said, gasping for air. I took a step away from him, but he caught my wrist. His gaze was heavy-lidded, smoldering, as he pulled me back to him.

"Hold on, lover," I said. "I need naked, more naked."

He held my wrist, breathing hard, deciding, as I was trying to decide, if he, if we, could wait that long.

I lifted his fingers off my wrist but didn't step back. We were so close together, I could feel the heat radiating off him. I shivered under his exhales against my skin, heard the litany of thoughts running through his mind, things he wanted to do to me, things he wanted me to do to him, and had to bite my lip to keep from moaning. I did a little careful gymnastics not to knock into him with my elbows as I shucked my coat and then my sweater.

I kicked off my shoes and wriggled my jeans down over my hips.

That did it.

Zayvion wrapped his hands around my rib cage and lifted me. I am not a small girl, but he made it feel like I weighed nothing. He shifted his grip to cup both hands under my butt, and I wrapped my legs around his waist, dragging his mouth up to mine so I could taste him again.

We kissed, hard, his tongue laving stroke after stroke of pleasure that slid deeper, hotter, feeding the deliciously heavy hunger blooming between my legs. Lightning shot through my body, every nerve on fire. So hot. So good. I drew a shuddering breath, wanting to pull that fire into every inch of me. I bit Zay's lip, tugged, and he responded with a growl, a deep rumble of pleasure.

Love me, he said, I said, we thought as one.

My hip hit the doorway as he walked into the bedroom.

My foot knocked something over on his dresser. Then we were on the bed, and I made it my one and only goal to get Zayvion Jones out of his pants.

He pinned me down, pulling my bra up and over my head, then dipped down to kiss my breasts, each one slowly, his tongue sliding heat across my hard nipples, and leaving a cool wash of mint behind.

I dragged my fingers up through the tight black curls of his hair and arched against his mouth, wanting more. Wanting now.

"More," I breathed. His thought, my thought.

Yes.

I moaned.

Heat, pleasure, and pain wrapped me in a shock wave of sensations, of need and sorrow as his body joined with mine. Bodies followed souls, souls followed sensation, pleasure, love, lifting, pausing, only to lift again. No longer two people, no longer separate, no longer alone.

Sweet wings of pleasure rolled through me and I shivered beneath the heat of his body. Our bodies. We answered before the other asked, a tangle of thoughts, emotions, memories, hope, need, rising higher, higher, into a sweet single moment.

I wanted him to never let me go.

Never, he said, I said, we said, caught on the edge of ecstasy.

We surged over that edge. Broke. Fell together, still together. Always together. One. There was something dangerous about this. We knew it. Knew breathing as one, thinking as one, soul to soul, was wrong.

It didn't feel wrong.

But slowly, slowly, we drew apart, one last languid stroke, one last lingering touch, one last gentle kiss.

I was aware again of my fingers, clenched against his back, my nails digging too deep. I was aware of his teeth at the curve of my neck and the tender heat of a bruise there. Then finally, finally we pulled away.

He relaxed against me in increments, breathing hard, sweating, just as I was breathing hard and sweating. Each of us tried to sort which thought was our own, which body was our own.

I don't know how long we lay there, him on top of me, as I ran my fingers back through his hair, his head resting on my breast. But finally the cool air of the room was too cold and I shifted. He moved with me, lying beside me, and then pulling me tightly against him as he drew the covers up over us.

I curved into the familiar shape and feel of him, and took a deep breath. I was just me again. Mostly. There were still echoes of Zayvion within me. Echoes I hoped would never fade.

He was quiet and held me tightly as if he was afraid I'd leave.

"So not going anywhere," I said.

"Damn right," he whispered into my hair.

I waited for him to fall asleep, for his breathing to even out, for his heartbeat to slow. But even after what felt like a long time, he was still awake.

I, however, was fading fast. His warmth, his arms

around me, were enough to lull me, until I fell blissfully asleep.

I heard the phone ring at a distance, but I was too tired to go get it. Luckily, I didn't have to. Zayvion shifted, rolled away from me, and slipped out of bed. He made the phone stop ringing. I was pretty sure he said something, but sleep tugged on me, and I followed.

The next time I woke, I realized Zayvion had not slid back into bed with me.

The shower was running. The bed was empty. It was morning—or at least the clock on his bedside table said it was a little past eight o'clock. His windows were curtained so heavily, no light could shine through.

I rolled over onto my back and stared at the ceiling. If I had any say over what would happen today, it would involve coffee, Davy waking up and feeling fine, and Bartholomew deciding he had important business on the other side of the world.

One of those things I could absolutely guarantee: coffee.

I got out of bed and went looking for my clothes. Found them scattered like a trail leading out to the living room. I carefully plucked my sweater off Zay's bonsai tree and checked through my haul. What was I missing? Ah, yes, my bra.

I walked back to the bedroom. Zay was standing there, a towel wrapped around his waist, my bra dangling from one finger. "Looking for this?"

"Yes. And the bra too," I said with a grin.

He gave me that shy-boy smile that made my heart beat faster.

"So," I said walking over to him. "How was the shower?"

"Good. Not as good as last night." He held the bra out of my reach.

"Hey, now." I stretched, trying to grab it.

He put his other arm around me and pulled me in close.

"Need something?" he asked.

I was naked, except for the clothes currently clutched in my arms. Zay was naked except for the towel around his waist. It made for a very pleasant predicament indeed.

"Hmm. Bra or sex?" I mused. "I suppose it depends. You got any coffee in this house?"

"Yes," he said.

I grinned. "Mmm. Coffee sounds so good. Bra it is."

He chuckled. "You sure?" He leaned down, just a bit, since he and I were nearly the same height, and kissed me. He smelled of pine and soap, and tasted like mint toothpaste. Warm, slow, easy. Way better than coffee.

My phone rang. Since it was in my jeans pocket between us, it was pretty hard to ignore.

I pulled back.

Zayvion growled.

"It might be important," I said. "Just a sec." He released me and I fumbled with my clothes until I dug my phone out.

"Beckstrom," I said.

Zayvion leaned down and nibbled on my ear, then pressed a soft kiss on my neck over the sweet ache of the bite he had left there, and started working his way down along the marks of magic across my collarbone.

"Allie, this is Stotts. The lab has the results of the cause of death for Anthony Bell."

"Okay. What?"

The heat from Zay's mouth against my skin, against the magic that always flowed beneath those marks was making me a little dizzy in a hot and bothered kind of way.

"He was poisoned. By magic."

I stepped away from Zayvion and held my hand up. That was exactly what Collins had said about Davy.

"Someone cast a spell on him that poisoned him?" I asked.

"His toxicology report is off the chart," Stotts said. "He had more magic running through his veins than blood. It went gangrenous."

"Have you ever heard of that before?" I asked, searching my own memories—what I had of them— from college, from all I'd learned from the Authority of that ever happening.

Pretty much if someone cast magic at you that did a damaging thing, they had to bear an equal or similar damage. It was why people didn't kill people with magic. Death to someone else meant death to the caster.

And while I knew now that I was part of the Authority, that people could kill people with magic and do creative things with Offloads and Proxy costs so they didn't actually end up dead, most people did not know that.

"No, I haven't," Stotts said. "But he's not the only one."

"What?"

Zay dragged his fingertips down my arm, then walked over to his dresser for his clothes.

"There have been similar cases reported. The death count is rising."

"That's bad," I said. "What can I do to help?"

"I talked with his mother," he said.

"How is she?" I asked. I hadn't called her yet. Hadn't faced her.

"She's . . . coping. She has family in the area. They're caring for her."

"That's good," I said. I was glad she had someone to lean on.

"She wasn't able to give me much information about where Anthony was that night. Do you know where he was, who he might have been in contact with, anything he told you about the kinds of magic or spells he was using?"

"He was at the wake at the den—briefly. He left quickly after that. I last saw him walking up the street. That was before he bit Davy."

"Was he alone?"

"Yes."

"Was he doing a Hounding job?"

"No. Wait." I looked over at Zayvion.

Zay, who had done a pretty good job following the conversation, shrugged. "The Veiled?" he suggested quietly.

"He might have been looking for something. For someone," I said.

"Who?"

"Remember those ghost things that attacked you and me in the graveyard? They're called the Veiled. They're attracted to magic. It might be the Veiled he was looking for."

Stotts was silent, but I heard the squeak of his office chair and two soft clunks of his shoe heels resting up on his desk.

"Why do you think that?"

I rolled my eyes and walked back over to the bed, dropping my clothes there, and digging for my panties. "I saw a Veiled. Or I thought I did, while I was looking out on the street. I was worried it was, um . . . bothering someone."

"Bothering? How?"

I managed to get into my panties one-handed and picked up my jeans. "I don't know, maybe I'm remembering things wrong."

I most certainly was not remembering things wrong. But I didn't want to tell him the Veiled had been inside some man, then walked off, and how weird that was, and that I thought maybe Anthony had been bit by the Veiled. No, wait. Maybe I did want to tell him that.

"Do you think Anthony could have been bit by the Veiled?" I asked.

"Bit? The marks on Anthony weren't the same as the ones you and I got back in the graveyard by the . . . creature that attacked us then."

"True. So we can rule that out?"

"Mmm. Maybe not," he said. "Anything else you can remember about Anthony? Did he mention anything to you?"

"Other than getting his diploma, no, that pretty much sums up what I know."

The chair creaked again. "Okay. I'll keep you in the loop if I have any other information."

"Thanks," I said.

"Allie?"

"Yes?"

"How is Davy Silvers?"

"Still sick. Why?"

Stotts didn't say anything for a minute. I heard his chair creak again. "I have nothing to back this up," he said, "but if Anthony was sick, infected, it's possible he passed that infection on to Davy when he bit him. You should make sure he goes to a hospital to get checked out."

"I know," I said. "I've had a doctor look in on him. You said there have been a lot of people dying from this . . . from this magic poisoning?"

"Yes."

"What are their symptoms?" I asked.

"You watch the news lately?"

"Yes." A chill rolled down my spine. Don't say it, I thought. Please don't say it.

"Their symptoms are flulike."

Holy shit. The epidemic. Could it be a plague of people being bit by the Veiled?

"Well, hells," I said.

"Pretty much, yes," he said. "Gotta go, Allie. Stay in touch."

"Bye." I thumbed my phone off.

"Zay," I said, "I think we have a big problem on our hands."

"We always have big problems on our hands," he said as he tucked his shirt in. "What did Stotts want to know?"

I filled him in on the other side of the phone conversation.

Zay put on his shoes as I went over everything. "So you think the sickness sweeping the city is from the Veiled biting people?"

"I don't know," I said. "Yes? Maybe? I think it's something we should consider. We could at least see if Bartholomew is looking into it."

He went silent.

"What?" I asked. "You don't think he will look into it?"

"I don't think he'll want to share any information with us even if he does," Zay said. "He runs the Authority his way. Which appears to be through demands, orders, and his people to back him up with physical and magical consequences."

"You've seen him work before?"

"I've heard what other people have said about him. Victor, Maeve. Even your dad."

"Dad still doesn't like him."

Zay chuckled. "Well, that's an upgrade. They used to hate each other with a passion. Bartholomew was convinced that magic and technology should never be used in concert with each other. He was outvoted on a national level, mostly, some people say, because your dad had the funds to push his agenda and buy off other members of the Authority to see things his way."

"He bought votes?" I asked. Sounded like something Dad would do.

"It's rumored," Zay said. "Although as soon as the tech and magic devices were developed for use in health care, there wasn't anyone who thought mixing magic and technology was a bad thing."

Except maybe Bartholomew.

"He can't ignore what's going on, though," I said pulling one of Zayvion's sweatshirts over my T-shirt. "The Authority is all about keeping people safe from magic. And if the Veiled are why people are getting sick, that's a part of magic." I found my socks and put on my shoes.

"What was that other call earlier?" I asked.

"Terric. He wants to meet with us today. I told him he could find us at the den looking in on Davy."

"How'd you know that's where I was going this morning?"

Zayvion shrugged. "You're predictable. When someone's hurt, you immediately think you need to do something to fix them."

"That's not predictable. That's having a conscience. And besides, Davy was hurt because of a decision I made."

"I doubt Davy would see it that way," he said.

"Doesn't matter." I picked up my coat, looked around his living room to make sure I hadn't left anything else behind. "Still how I see it. You coming?"

Zayvion shrugged into his ratty blue ski coat and pulled on a brown beanie. "Let's go."

It didn't take us long to get to the parking garage below the building. We didn't say much. Zayvion was walking in front of me, and I could tell from his movements that he was worried, or angry. Probably both. Even the silver glyphs that superimposed his body flickered with a rise and fall of light that was similar to a heartbeat. Whatever was bothering him—and if I'd had to put money down I would've said it had everything to do with Bartholomew and the Closing he'd ordered Zayvion to do—was digging into him bone deep.

The glyphs of magic he had always worn as a badge of honor were chafing like chains.

We got in his car and I asked, "Get Mugged for coffee and quiche?"

"I thought you didn't like quiche." He smiled and I couldn't help but smile back. This felt like normal again, if we'd ever really had a normal.

"If there's cheese, I like quiche. If not, you know, other eggs are superior."

"I could use a cup of coffee," he said.

We drove to Get Mugged and parked around the back side of the buildings. It was early enough that the morning coffee crowd was still in full swing and street parking was scarce. That was okay with me. I wanted a walk in the cool air, in the sunlight. Even though the magic I could see everywhere was still pretty distracting.

"What are you doing?" Zayvion asked me as we passed by yet another window with an Unbreakable Ward so strong I could almost feel the prickly heat snapping off it.

"Walking?"

"Really?" He stopped and I stopped too. "I think that's called weaving."

"I'm not weaving."

"Yes, you are. I almost ran into you three times already."

"Well, then let me walk on the outside of the sidewalk." I stepped in front of him, but hadn't realized there was a Lure spell on a piece of statuary just ahead. As we headed that way, I corrected my course so as not to get caught by it.

"That," Zayvion said as I bumped into his arm.

"What that?"

He put his arm around me, and I could tell he wasn't

angry, just sort of frustrated and curious. "That drunken stagger you've got going."

I slapped his chest, which didn't do anything since I wasn't trying to hurt him, and his ski coat was too damn fluffy.

"I'm not staggering. Or drunk," I added.

"So?" he asked.

"I can see magic. Everywhere. All the time. It's just . . . distracting."

"Are you using Sight?"

Oh, right. I hadn't told Zayvion about this yet. "No. Ever since I tried to use magic, passed out, and gave myself a light concussion, I've been seeing magic. All the time."

Zayvion stopped again. We were on the corner now, the front door to the coffee shop in sight, just a few steps away.

"Coffee?" I pointed at the door.

Zay moved to stand in front of me and put both arms around my waist. "When," he asked quietly as if we were lovers sharing secrets, "did you pass out and get a concussion?"

Ah. Apparently I hadn't been doing a very good job keeping him in the loop. "Yesterday. After coming back from the meeting with Bartholomew. I saw a Veiled step out of a woman on the street. And when I tried to cast Hold so I could maybe get a better look at the Veiled, I passed out. I woke up to people calling 911, but told them I was fine. Jack Quinn took over from there."

"Do you think casting magic made you pass out or was it something else?"

"I don't know."

He got that look on his face that told me he'd made up both our minds. I hated that look.

Then he swung his arm around my waist and started us walking back the way we'd come.

"No," I whined. "Coffee was right there. I could smell it. Can't you smell it? C'mon, Jones. We'll do all the magic talking you want over coffee. Please?"

He didn't answer and didn't stop walking. The worry radiating from him was the only reason I didn't trip him so I could get my way. He rounded the corner to the back of the building and I sighed. So close to coffee, and yet so far. I pulled out of his arms.

"Just for that, you are paying for breakfast," I said.

"Cast magic," he said.

"No."

We stared at each other for a minute or so.

"I could order you," he said.

"Which would make me refuse to do it until they put me in the grave." Yes, I'm stubborn that way. Zay knew it.

"Allie, I need you to do this so I can watch and see if it's magic that's hurting you."

He put his arms around my waist. "I'll even catch you if you fall."

Sweet. But the idea of casting magic and having it hurt that much again made my hands sweat. That wouldn't keep me from doing it, though. Because he was right. We needed to know this. I needed to know this.

"For cripes' sake. Fine. Something small."

Light was one of the earliest spells I'd learned, and the easiest. I cleared my mind, and had to recite the Miss Mary Mack song to get my nerves settled enough so I could cast. When I was feeling calm, I set a Disbursement, not a headache—I'd had enough headache lately from the concussion. I went for muscle aches. I planned to make Zayvion give me shoulder rubs until they went away.

And then I cast the glyph for Light.

So far, so good. But I hadn't pulled any magic up into the glyph yet.

I hesitated, the glyph balanced on my fingertips.

"Allie?" he asked.

"Fine. I'm fine." I exhaled, and pulled magic up out of the ground, out of the pipes that networked the entire city of Portland, and drew that magic into me, like I always did, and directed that magic into the glyph, like I always did.

But before the glyph could so much as begin to glow, my vision started to dim. Magic burned, too hot. It bit my skin and tore across my nerves. I wanted to get away from it, get it away from me, cut a vein or do . . . something to purge it.

I tried to stay focused, even through the pain, tried to complete the spell because I'm a Hound, damn it, and I can deal with pain.

Zayvion's hand closed over mine, destroying the glyph, and probably giving himself a second-degree burn on his palm.

"Allie?" he said. His hand pressed on my forehead, then my cheek. "Allie?"

"I'm good." It was weird. With all the ringing in my ears and the need to throw up, my voice sounded really far away. "Barf," I added.

What did you know? Zay caught my subtle hint and helped me over to a patch of dirt where I could heave.

He even held my hair back. Aw. True love.

But since he had been the whole reason I was chucking up that which I hadn't even downed yet, I was not in a good mood.

It took a bit, but finally my stomach stopped cramping, my ears stopped ringing, and all the rest of me stopped hurting. I straightened and wiped the tears off my face. Zay handed me a fast-food napkin from out of his pocket, which I took and then blew my nose.

"Magic is making you sick," he said.

"Brilliant deduction, Holmes," I said.

"Magic didn't seem to be acting any different to me," he said. "I was watching with Sight."

Huh. I hadn't even seen him cast Sight. "Well, it's different for me," I said. "And now I think we've both proved our point and you owe me coffee and breakfast. Big time. And shoulder rubs."

I started off toward the sidewalk, trying not to inhale too deeply. It wasn't just using magic that was a pain. The stink of magic bothered me too. All those Lure and Attractions and safety Wards and other, long-term refresh spells just made the entire city stink like rotted meat.

This was getting old fast.

Zay caught my wrist, and I stopped to look at him.

"What?" I said.

"You're just going to walk off and get coffee? Even though we both know magic is making you sick?"

"Yes." At his frown, I said, "I don't know what else to do about it, Zay. Maybe being around Anthony and Davy, and them being infected by the Veiled did something to me."

I thought about it. No, back when Melissa had cast Truth on me, magic had made me sick and that was before I'd seen either Hound. I'd thought it was because she was making me Proxy the cost of the Truth spell— and maybe that was partly it—or maybe even then magic was starting to make me sick.

"But unlike Anthony and Davy, I'm fine if I just don't use magic."

"Are you?" he asked. "Fine?"

I held his concerned gaze. "Yes." Didn't have to lie because it was the truth. So far. "I'll be better when we figure out how the hell to stop the epidemic, and how to save Davy. But until then, I want coffee."

Zay nodded and walked beside me, between me and

the building, where most of the spells lingered, which was sweet of him, though I wasn't sure it was doing me any good.

Yes, I was a little cranky. Girl needed coffee, food, and to stay far away from magic.

Zayvion opened the door for me and I paused just inside it. I'd never really cast Sight to see what kind of spells Grant kept around the place. From how busy he was, I'd expect he had at least a Relax or maybe something to stimulate appetites.

But Get Mugged was bare. The only magic I saw in the place clung to the people themselves. Some little safety spells like Return and Lock on valuables like cell phones and purses, and of course, those who could afford the Proxy price or the pain, carried Enhancement spells to make their wrinkles disappear, noses straighten, and teeth whiten.

Other than that, the space was completely and blissfully empty of spells.

I strolled over to the counter, where Grant's employee Jula was working.

"Hey, Allie, Zayvion," she said, putting down the receipts she was sorting. She had dyed her hair black with orange stripes and little blond polka dots. It was cute. "What can I get you?"

"I'll take a coffee, black, and a cheddar quiche," I said.

"Same for me," Zayvion said.

Zay stepped up and pulled money out of his wallet. I looked at him and he raised his eyebrow. Well, at least he'd been listening when I told him he owed me coffee.

"Here or to go?" she asked.

"To go," I said.

"It'll be right up."

Zay and I stepped to one side to let the person behind us order, and I eyed the food behind the glass. Lots of scones, breakfast bars, and crumbles. Looked like Grant had doubled his menu.

I didn't see him in the dining area and figured he must be in the back cooking, or maybe he actually took a day off and was in his apartment below the shop.

Jula had our order done quick and Zay and I picked it up and started walking. I took a sip of the coffee—so good—and then we headed over to the den.

I did my best not to inhale the stink of magic. Keeping the coffee near my nose helped some. We took the stairs, and by the time we reached the den, I was really hungry.

"Morning," I called out as I walked in. The Hounds gathered were a mixed bunch. Most were the regulars, Sid and Bea and Jamar. But a couple of them were new faces to me. A tall, thin redheaded woman in black slacks and sweater, and a dark-haired bearded man who looked like he could use a bath, a meal, and a cardboard sign that said WILL HOUND FOR MONEY.

"Who are the new recruits?" I asked with my all-business-all-the-time voice.

"Allie," Sid said, "this is Toya. She's been working Vancouver for a couple years. Says she's Jack's friend."

"Nice to meet you," she said from across the room.

"And," Sid continued, "this is Karl. He's just back from Klamath Falls. We don't know him," he added.

"Hey," he said, with a nod. "Sorry about the clothes. And, I assume, the smell. It's been a long year."

I unpacked my breakfast and found a fork. Zay did the same. "What brings you both here?"

"I heard about this group you've started," Toya said. "Jack is a friend of mine, so I thought I'd come check it out. Maybe talk to you about starting something like this in my own neighborhood."

I took a bite of the quiche. Hot, melty, salty, delicious.

I wanted to stuff the entire thing in my mouth, but then there would've been no room for coffee.

"And you?" I asked Karl as I carried quiche and coffee over to my desk and settled in. Zay stayed put in the kitchen, where he could keep an eye on most of the room.

"I was just working my way north. Heard about this place from some Hounds on the street. I'd be grateful if the rumors about a complimentary shower were true."

"Right back there," I said. "Knock yourself out."

He smiled and headed back to the bathroom. I had set this place up to take in Hounds who needed a place to crash and recover from the pain the job put them through. We didn't get a lot of new people that often, since Hounds were suspicious loners by nature, but it was pretty clear Karl didn't have another door to knock on.

I wasn't running a full-time charity, though. He could stay here a night or two, but then he'd need to move on. This was a pit stop, not a home.

"I'd be happy to go over the details with you," I said to Toya. "Have a seat."

She did a not-very-subtle check to see what the body language and reaction from people around us was to that comment. Sensing there was no trap, because, duh, there wasn't, she sat in the chair across from my desk. If she was a Hound, she wasn't very good at it.

"So how do you fund this place?" she asked.

I liked a girl who could cut to the chase.

"I cover rent and utilities. Food is handled by each person. Linens are taken care of by a service that I also pay. And that's about it."

She nodded. "I'd hoped you tapped into some kind of federal or state funding that helped with this sort of thing."

"Nope. I was thinking of setting up a fee-based system. Haven't gotten around to it yet, though I've negoti-

ated with the police and other public officials to raise
the baseline Hounding rate for jobs hired. That's something."

"That's a lot," she agreed. "Did you have someone
inside any of the agencies you worked with? Someone I
could contact?"

I finished off the crust and took a drink of coffee.
Her question had suddenly gone from interested to
prying. She was digging for something. Maybe for
someone. Problem was, I didn't know who she was digging for.

"My business dealings are not up for public scrutiny,
but you can be assured that I contacted all the appropriate people and agencies before going forward with this
venture."

I could do business-speak "back-it-up-missy" like a pro.

She smiled with her mouth, but it didn't make it to
her eyes. "I wasn't trying to insinuate that you had done
anything illegal."

"Of course not," I said. "We also have some rules in
the house to keep things running smoothly. No drugs, no
weapons, no contraband. The house operates on an open
warrant for the police to search it at any given moment,
which makes people who have something they want to
hide stay away. It's worked so far."

"It seems that it has," she said with a laugh that would
have fooled me if I hadn't seen that hard spark in her
eyes. "So do you also decide who gets what jobs?"

"No. We're all responsible for finding our own business. So how long are you in town for?"

"Oh, just the day. I'm visiting some family in the
area."

That was a lie. I think the other Hounds were picking
up on it. The atmosphere in the room took a sudden,
tense dive.

"It was great meeting you," I said, not getting up. "I

have a lot of things to take care of today. I'm sure you can find your way out."

She stared at me a half second too long. And then she got up and, unconcerned about the sudden silence among the other Hounds, which should have been a dead giveaway that none of us trusted her, she left.

"Who told you she was a Hound?" I asked Sid.

"She did, when she walked in." He shook his head. "Posers gotta pose."

Zayvion walked very quietly over to the door and looked out. I didn't have to. I heard the elevator doors open, heard her heels as she stepped in, and that particular grind of the motor as the elevator went down, not up. Which meant she wasn't going upstairs to try to nose around Davy or Collins.

Not that the Hounds looking after him up there would let her in.

"Anyone have anything on her?" I asked.

Sid had his tablet out and was plugging in data. "Give me a sec. I'll see what I can find."

The shower turned off. I leaned back in my chair and gave Zayvion a small smile. We'd see who this Karl turned out to be before long too.

I could hear him towel off. Then he stopped moving. He must have noticed that none of us were talking. Good. Meant he was paying attention to his surroundings, and the people in it. A very Hound-like thing to do.

I felt a subtle pull on the magic network and smelled the faint stink of rotten meat. He had drawn a spell. I wondered if it was something to enhance his hearing. I thought maybe I should find out.

"Take your time," I whispered. "We're all still here."

"Didn't know if I'd interrupted a moment of silence or something," he said, loud enough to be heard through the walls with normal hearing. "Should I let myself out the window?"

I grinned. Overcautious, slightly suspicious. Definitely a Hound. Everyone went back to what they were doing and making noise. "No. There's coffee and food in the kitchen. You're welcome to it."

I stood. "Tell him the rules, Sid. He can stay the night if he needs a place, but nothing permanent."

"Got it, boss."

I strolled over to Zayvion. I felt better. A lot better. A little food and kicking someone out of my space somehow gave the whole day a little more shine. Maybe I'd stroll on up those stairs to Davy and tell him that he had to get better now because I said so. Not that it would work, but a girl could dream.

Chapter Thirteen

"Hey, you," I said to Zay as I walked across the room, "let's get moving."

"Lead the way."

I did. Right out the door to hall. I took a deep breath, didn't smell Toya, didn't hear her. "Terric stopping by?" I asked.

"He's down at Get Mugged now," Zay said, holding up his phone and the message there. "On his way up."

"Tell him we'll be on the third floor."

I started up and Zayvion texted, then followed.

I tried the door—it was unlocked but Jack was right on the other side.

"Beckstrom," he said. "Jones."

Zay nodded and I said, "Do you know a Toya, Jack? Tall, thin, good-looking red-haired thirtysomething woman who Hounds in Vancouver?"

Jack frowned. "I don't know any tall, thin, good-looking redheads from Vancouver. Any reason why you're asking?"

"She was here, downstairs. Saying she was a Hound and she was your friend. One of those things I know for a fact is not true. You could go get a sniff and see if you recognize her."

"Huh. I'll let you know."

"Give us a half hour or so, okay?" I said. "I want a private conversation with Mr. Collins here."

Jack looked at Collins, who was currently spread out in the easy chair, a book opened across his face, in what looked to be a sleeping pose except for the fact that he wasn't breathing evenly enough. Then Jack looked back at me and Zayvion. "All right. Don't have too much fun without me."

He left and I walked across the room, not trying to hide the sound of my footsteps across the old wood, though Zayvion behind me glided like a cat's ghost.

"So how's Davy?" I asked.

Collins pulled the book off his face and put the chair into a sitting position. He gave me a quick half smile, then stood and turned to face Zayvion.

"Mr. Zayvion Jones. So very good to see you again."

"Collins. Is there a reason you're still in town?"

"I live here."

"That's news to me."

"Perhaps you're a little behind on recent headlines." Zayvion approached him with that calm Zen-like manner. "Why don't you catch me up?"

"Allison has hired me to tend to her young friend here. Frankly, I don't know what you are doing here."

"He's here because I asked him to be," I said. Obviously they had history. And while I was curious about it, right now I wanted to know how Davy was doing. "Any change?"

Collins paused before turning his back on Zayvion. He tried to hide that it didn't bother him to have Zayvion behind him, but it was clear that he was very, very uncomfortable with that man of mine. Interesting.

"He hasn't gotten any worse that I can tell," he said as he took the few steps over to the side of Davy's bed. "He is resting comfortably even though I've reduced the amount of narcotics. The Syphon is still active and seems to be doing a fairly good job of keeping the magic from spreading."

From his tone, I knew he wasn't telling me the whole story. "But?" I asked.

He studied my face, his gaze lingering the longest on my mouth before he finally said, "I have been unable to find a way to stop the poison."

"Tell me what that means in very clear language," I said.

"Davy is dying. A much slower death than the people who are being tended by more . . . traditional medicines and procedures. But I haven't found a way to stop the spread of the poison. Soon it will reach his organs and shut down his vital functions."

I just stood there. I thought that kind of news would devastate me, but I'd known that's what we were dealing with since I'd seen Anthony's dead body in the alley.

"Blood transfusion?" I asked.

He shook his head. "It's magic. It won't drain out with blood just because blood is draining."

"Antidote?"

"Not of the magical nature. I'm using very slight magical spells on him, spells that do not radiate much magic at all. Like the Syphon. I'm concerned that any stronger magical intervention will just accelerate the speed of the poisoning."

I crossed my arms over my chest and stood there staring at Davy. He looked like he was running a fever—too pale, the scars he still carried on his face from Greyson's attack months ago pink against his parchment skin, his freckles too dark.

He didn't look well, but he didn't look like he was dying either.

"Which Syphon are you using?" Zayvion asked.

Collins looked over at him, then back at Davy. "Draw with an alternating second current."

"That's pretty gentle," Zay noted.

"Agreed. But when I cast Draw with a straight feed, his vitals were compromised."

Zay walked over to the table where Collins had laid out his supplies.

"These are new," he said.

"I have been kicked out of the Authority and Closed, Mr. Jones. I am not dead. And neither am I unable to follow through with my research."

"I thought we destroyed all your records."

He didn't look at Zay, but he smiled. "You did."

Dad in my head shifted slightly. Just enough that I knew he was uncomfortable with this conversation. Which meant he was probably a part of Collins' having new research.

"Even so, it would take a finer hand than mine to calibrate these spells and tech to do any greater good," Collins said.

"Then we need to find a finer hand," I said.

Collins glanced at me. "There isn't one, Allison. Not any longer. I am the expert in these sorts of things, or I used to be before the Authority made a butchery of my skills."

"You're saying there's no one better at this than you?"

He inhaled slightly, considering his response. "Not that I know of," he finally said.

Cody, Dad said.

I rubbed at my forehead. *Why are you so full of suggestions now?* I asked. *And do you really think Cody can help anybody with anything?*

Perhaps my . . . focus has shifted. It wasn't a full answer. Still, behind it I could sense his thoughts lingering on one thing. His newborn son.

I'd heard it could be like that. When men have sons, their perspective and priorities in life change.

Cody is a Savant, Dad said. *A great artist, even though his mind has been broken. His hands should remember.*

"What about Cody Miller?" I asked.

Collins turned toward me like I'd just declared there were ninjas coming out of his ears.

"Is he still alive?"

"Yes."

"If you can find him," he said doubtfully. "If he is . . . of sound mind, then yes, he might be very useful."

Well, I didn't know how sound of mind he was, but it was still worth a try.

I thumbed my phone on and dialed Nola. I also paced across the room because I really didn't want to have this conversation a few inches away from Collins.

Zayvion just stayed where he was, arms folded across his wide chest, watching Collins watch Davy. I wondered if they had worked together in the past. Or if maybe Zayvion had been the person who Collins said had made a butchery of his head. From Zay's reaction, I didn't think so. But then, I doubted any Closer would leave his victim with the memory of who had done the Closing.

"This is Nola," Nola answered.

"Hey, it's me," I said.

"Allie, I'm so glad you called. We'll be headed back to Burns in a couple days and I wanted some time to hang with you before we go."

"I'd really like that," I said, "but I kind of need to talk business first."

"Which business?"

"Hounding and magic."

"Okay. Want me to take notes?"

"No," I said, "this isn't one for the memory files. I need to know if you can bring Cody with you over to the den today."

"When today, and why?"

"Now, and because I need to ask him, and you, a favor."

"What aren't you telling me?" she asked.

"Davy's hurt. I'm worried. And probably a half dozen other things I should catch you up on since we last talked."

"I told you we need some girl time," she said. "All right. The den. That's next to Get Mugged, right?"

"Yes. And come on up to the third floor. I'll be here with Zayvion, Davy, and a doctor. Maybe a Hound or two."

There was a soft knock on the door and Zayvion walked over to open it. Terric strode in.

"So this is a serious visit?" Nola asked.

"Yes, it is."

She sighed and guilt flickered through me. I hadn't been much of a friend lately; too caught up in the Authority's business to really spend time with her, even though she had come to town to visit me. Well, me and her boyfriend, Detective Stotts. I wouldn't have blamed her if she'd just told me no.

"We'll be over," she said.

"Thank you, Nola." I wanted to say more, but not in front of Collins. "See you soon."

I hung up.

Terric wore a brown leather jacket and jeans. His silver hair was pulled back in a band that kept all but the bangs from falling across his face. He looked like he'd gotten some sleep, or at least a good dose of caffeine. But he did not look happy, or relaxed.

He greeted Zay, then noticed Collins.

"Hello," Terric said, testing the ground.

"Mr. Conley, it has been a long absence, hasn't it?"

Terric's eyebrows raised. "Yes, it has. I thought you moved overseas."

"I moved. The distance of my relocation may have been slightly exaggerated."

"Did you come into town with Mr. Wray?" Terric asked.

"No. I don't work for the Authority any longer. You know that. If I remember that much, you must remember more."

"It's possible," Terric said. "Not that I had any say over such things."

Great. More history I didn't know.

"Why did you want to see us, Terric?" I asked. "Did Bartholomew send you?"

He walked off to the kitchen and poured a cup of coffee from a pot that smelled like it had been cooking on the warmer for too long.

"This has nothing to do with my . . . official capacity." He took a drink, closed his eyes for a moment too long, then walked back into the spacious main room with us. "I wanted to check on you, both of you, and make sure you were okay. And Davy."

"What official capacity?" Collins said, ignoring everything else he had just said.

"He's the Voice of Faith magic for the Portland area," I said.

Collins, who as far as I could tell didn't get ruffled by anything, turned a shade of white most often seen in paper products.

"Is that so?" he asked with forced levity.

Well, I supposed if I was informed I was in a room with the head Closer in Portland, and also the Guardian of the gates, I'd break a sweat too.

"It is," Terric said with such calm authority that it was like looking at a younger, silver-haired Victor.

"Then I am not comfortable with you being here while I am tending my patient, Mr. Conley," he said.

"If you're uncomfortable around members of the Authority," Zayvion said, "then maybe you're the one who shouldn't be here, Mr. Collins."

Collins looked from Zay to Terric, and finally to me. I just gave him a steady look.

"I see." He seemed to come to a decision. "Well, so long as the paycheck clears the bank." He smiled and walked over to the window, putting as much space between himself and the other two men as he could.

Also interesting.

"If you want to know how we're doing," I said to Terric, "I don't know what to tell you. Davy's hurt—dying if we can't find a way to stop the magic spreading through him. I got a call from Stotts telling me he thinks the flu epidemic that the doctors can't seem to contain is somehow linked to how Anthony died—and Anthony probably died from fighting with a Veiled and definitely died from too much magic poisoning him.

"Since Anthony bit Davy, we're pretty sure he has the same infection, but whether it's the Veiled that are poisoned, or magic itself is poisoned, we don't know. And we don't really know how it's spreading so quickly, how other people are being infected. . . ."

Or did we? I'd seen two people start coughing after a Veiled stepped out of the same space they'd been inhabiting. Were the Veiled doing more than occupying the same space with the living? Were they somehow possessing them, if even only temporarily, to make them sick? If so, why? What did they get out of it?

"Something you'd like to share with the class, Allison, dear?" Collins asked.

Zay leveled him a dirty glare.

"I thought I saw a Veiled step out of a person on the street the other night," I said. "And yesterday I saw it again—different person, and I think a different Veiled. Do you think they might be possessing people?"

Zayvion shrugged. "It's not very likely. Let's say that they are. What danger would that present? They can't control a living body. The Veiled have no physical or magical mass in life."

Unless they had a disk stuck in their neck. That not

only gave them mass, it gave them life. For as long as the magic in the disk lasted.

I hadn't seen whether the Veiled on the street had a disk. So that wasn't helping much.

"Ideas, people?" I said.

Terric walked to the window that looked over Get Mugged. "Let me see if I have this straight. You think that magic is poisoned or that the Veiled themselves are poison and are somehow infecting people with magic?"

"I'm trying to find the connection," I said, "between the Veiled Anthony followed, Anthony dying of magic poisoning, him biting Davy, and Davy being infected with poisoned magic. Have there been cases of people transferring magical poisoning through bites?"

Terric looked out the window, thinking it over. Zay shook his head, his eyes on Davy. Even Collins nodded. "Not that I know of," Collins said.

"So somehow Anthony infected Davy with poisoned magic with a bite?" I said. "How?"

"Can you see any Veiled right now?" Zayvion asked me.

I looked around the room. Nothing. I walked over to the window and checked outside. Streets, buildings, spells, people. No Veiled. "Not right now."

"We could always have a volunteer put himself in the path of a Veiled and see if he is possessed," Collins said.

"No," Zayvion and Terric said at the same time.

"We could try to contain a Veiled and dissect it," he said.

"We'd have to hold it with magic," Terric said. "And dissecting through that wouldn't give clean results."

"Are you going to talk to Bartholomew about this, Terric?" I asked.

He shrugged. "I have no proof on anything yet. It's all hearsay at this point. And I don't think Mr. Wray is the kind of person who is interested in hearing theory or hearsay."

"Good," I said, and he glanced over at me, gave me a small smile.

"So here's what we're going to do," I started.

Shame strolled through the doors without knocking. "What are we going to do? Did I miss the fun?"

Terric went stock-still. I knew Shame knew Terric was in the room. He'd told me that they could practically close their eyes and know what the other one was doing.

Which suddenly made me realize that if Terric kissed a man, or Shame kissed a woman, they'd totally feel it through their connection.

Awkward.

But maybe even stranger was how very, very still Zayvion had become. He was watching Shame like a man watches a snake.

"Come on, now," Shame said, smiles for everyone except Zay. "Someone fill a man in. Are we hunting? Killing? Drinking? 'Cause any and all, or a mix of them, would do me fine."

"Shame," I said, "have you seen any of the Veiled possessing anyone?"

"Lately?" He made it look like he was thinking about it. "No."

"Okay, so what we're going to do is find out if there really is a connection between the epidemic and people being poisoned by the Veiled. Who wants to follow that up?"

Terric raised a finger. "I'll talk to some trusted members of the medical community."

Collins chuckled. "Trusted," he mumbled.

"Trusted," Terric said. "I should have an answer by the end of the night."

"Good," I said. "Call me when you have any information. Shame, do you think you could track down a few

Veiled and see if they are doing anything un-Veiled-like?"

"With those amazing specifics how could I fail?" he said.

"You know what I mean. See if they seem to be intentionally hunting and possessing people, or if they're just ghosting about the city like normal. Specific enough?"

"I'll manage."

"Someone should go with Shame," Terric said softly.

Shame turned toward him. Full eye contact, and not a small amount of anger.

"Don't think you can order people around, Terric. Just because that bastard told you you're above me doesn't make it so." Each word was bit off sharp, as if it took everything Shame had not to yell.

"Doesn't matter what title anyone's given me," Terric said. "It doesn't take a title to see that you shouldn't be hunting alone."

"Fuck you," Shame said.

"Shut up," I interrupted. "Fight on your own time. Shame, someone's going with you because nobody does anything alone until we figure this out. Zay?"

"I'm going where you're going."

There was no way Shame and Terric would work together. I didn't trust Collins enough to have him do anything more than care for Davy. We needed more people.

"Hey," Jack said as he walked into the room. "That's your half hour. Going to let me in on this little scuffle?"

And right behind him was Bea. "Hi, everyone," Bea said in her bouncy-happy voice. "I brought doughnuts. Who are we killing and how much does it pay?"

Okay, this had quickly gotten out of hand. I wasn't planning to involve the Hounds with Authority business.

It's not Authority business, Dad said. *It's your business.*

Huh. He was right.

Thanks, I said to him.

And since everyone was looking at me and waiting for a decision, I started deciding.

"No killing unless it's in self-defense, then knock yourself out and don't tell me where you hid the body."

Bea threw me a smile over her shoulder as she opened the box and walked to each person in the room, offering a doughnut. It was sort of funny. Here I was talking about murder and they were all picking out pastries.

"Can either of you see ghosts?" I asked.

Jack shook his head. Bea stopped in front of me with the doughnuts. I took an old-fashioned glazed buttermilk.

"I've seen things that might be ghosts," Bea said. "Maybe. But I just chalked it up to working the morgues so much. Active imagination." She ran her finger in a circle by her temple in the universal gesture for crazy.

"Here's the thing," I said. "There are ghosts—but it's a little more complicated. There are also echoes of past magic users who sort of walk around town. They tend to stay near networks because, like film recordings, they need a little bit of magic to power them."

"We're hunting ghosts?" Jack asked.

"No," I said, "we're hunting Veiled. Echoes of past magic users. People who were good at using magic. Really good."

"Did the ghosts—I mean Veiled—do something bad?" Bea asked. "Haunt someone? Leave goo behind?"

I sighed. "This isn't a joke. We think they might have somehow infected Anthony, who then bit Davy and landed him there." I pointed at the bed just in case either of them needed reminding that Davy was fighting for his life while we were eating doughnuts.

"Is there a mark on him?" Bea set the doughnuts down and walked over to Davy. Jack was already there.

"Cast Sight. You'll see it," I said. I also crossed the room so I didn't have to smell them working magic.

"Me," Bea said to Jack's look. She cast Sight, wide enough that Jack could look through it. These two had been practicing together. Good for them.

"Black lines of tar covering him," Jack said. "Son of a bitch."

I nodded. "That's what Anthony looked like too. Except worse. Covered in it. Smothered by it. Dead."

"So how do you see one of these Veiled?" Jack asked.

"You don't have to," I said to him. "You and Bea are backups. Shadows for the jobs Shame and Terric will be doing."

"I don't need a Hound following me," Terric and Shame said at exactly the same time.

Collins tipped his chin up at that. He peered through his glasses at Shame and Terric, who were scowling at each other. They were also breathing in the same rhythm, though I didn't think they knew it, and their hands were fisted at their sides, identically.

Collins looked at one, then the other, then the other again. Finally, his eyebrows went up. He must have still remembered something about Soul Complements too.

"I," Terric said, "refuse to have anyone go where I go, Allie. You know they can't follow me."

I thought about it. Terric would probably contact a doctor within the Authority to see what information he could find out about the epidemic. He might even contact Dr. Fisher. And there was no way she was going to be forthcoming with Jack or Bea in the room.

"I agree. Terric, since you are gathering information from people in the medical community, and not stalking down dark alleys, you can go alone."

"Thanks," he drawled. Yes, I was bossing him around. Deal.

"But, Shame, you need someone with you while you hunt Veiled."

"I don't need a babysitter."

"Hounds aren't babysitters," I said. "We're hunters. We're quiet, we have sharp eyes, damn sharp survival instincts, and God help us, we're loyal. At least to money. I am tired of people talking down about this business. You want a part of my team, you play by my rules, Flynn."

Shame's eyebrows had gone up with each declaration. He finally said with a dead blank expression. "I love it when you get sassy."

I did not dignify his comment with a reply, though if I had it would have been of the four-letter variety.

"So which of you wants to shadow me?" Shame asked, turning that Irish charm of his full tilt on Bea.

"I'll follow." Jack stepped in front of Bea and got in the way of Shame's smolder. "If we run into trouble I might even call 911 for you."

Shame wandered over to the doughnut box. "No officials. If we run into trouble you call the boss."

"Do you have the boss's number?" Jack asked.

Shame jerked a thumb my way. "Allie. The boss is Allie. You can't tell me you don't have her number." He plucked up a maple bar. "Later, lovelies. C'mon, Jack, my friend. Let's see what this city's made of. Bet it's whiskey." Then Shame was out the door, Jack following him.

I watched Zayvion's body language relax by a fraction. Why had he been worried about Shame? And then it hit me. Zay had Closed Shame's mother. Shame had been arguing with Terric, but he had also been completely ignoring Zay. They hadn't said one word to each other. That wasn't like them at all.

Great. Just what I needed. More problems between us.

"So Shame is going to track some Veiled," I said, "and see if they are behaving differently than normal. Terric, you're going to get information on the epidemic. That leaves you and me, Zayivon."

"And where do you think we're going?" he asked.

"To the cisterns."

"Lot of cisterns in a city this size," he noted.

"Are there ghosts in the cisterns?" Bea asked excitedly.

"I don't think so."

She deflated like a popped balloon.

"So why are you Hounding the cisterns?" she asked.

"Because they hold magic for the city. That's a large concentration of magic. I just want to check and make sure there aren't any Veiled messing with it."

Okay, that was only part of the truth. The rest of the truth was that I wanted to get to a source of magic—if not a well, then at least a holding and storage facility, so I could make sure that the contagion wasn't being transmitted by magic itself. Because if magic was tainted, poisoned, we were all dead and just didn't know it yet.

Chapter Fourteen

I was finishing off my second doughnut and checking my phone for messages from Nola when the elevator out in the hall dinged, soon followed by a soft knock on the door.

Nola and Cody.

I walked over and opened the door.

Nola wore a really cute red wool jacket, jeans, and boots. Her smile was like sunshine on a gloomy day.

"Hey, Nola." I gave her a hug and once again remembered how much smaller than me she was even though she was in heeled boots and I was in running shoes. "Missed you."

"Missed you too. I haven't been up here before. Is it yours?"

I stepped back so she could walk in. "I'm leasing it, along with the second floor, for the Hounds. Hey, Cody. How are you?"

Cody looked how he always looked. Fair-haired, blue-eyed, a little lost, but happy. Even though he had a childlike view of the world, he was in his early twenties. "Monster doesn't talk anymore."

I knew who Monster was. It was Stone. I hadn't seen Stone for days. "Have you seen Monster?"

Cody nodded. "He doesn't talk anymore."

"Where have you seen him, Cody?"

"Outside."

So not helpful.

"Maybe he'll talk again soon." Stone didn't talk. So all I could assume was that Stone wasn't making his cooing sounds. That was sort of odd.

"Come on in, Cody. This is one of my houses."

Nola gave me another smile and walked in, Cody right beside her.

"Nola, you know Terric and Zayvion," I said. "This is Beatrice Lufkin, and Eli Collins. And over there on the bed is Davy Silvers."

Nola stopped in her tracks, her smile faltering. "Is he sick?" she asked. Which probably meant she'd seen the newscasts and the warnings of the epidemic.

"He is," I said.

"Bad." Cody took a step forward. Nola reached out to catch his wrist and stop him from strolling over to Davy, but he pulled his arm out of her way, his one and only goal being Davy's bed.

"Hello, Cody," Collins said. "Do you remember me?"

Cody looked up as if seeing him for the first time.

"I do remember you," Cody said.

I totally couldn't read his tone of voice. Not exactly afraid, not angry, more like someone who had just opened the door to a salesman and was too polite to slam it in the salesman's face.

"Why is he hurt?" Cody asked.

Collins seemed to spring into motion. "I think magic is poisoning him, Cody. Can you look and see if magic is poisoning him?"

"No," Nola said. "Cody doesn't use magic. And people do not use him to do so. Allie?"

"I'm sorry—Nola, was it?" Collins said. "I didn't mean to overstep my bounds. But I believe that is what Allison brought Mr. Miller here to do."

Nola turned her accusing stare on me.

Great. Ass of a thing to do, Collins, I thought.

"Let me tell you what's going on," I started.

"I said no one can use Cody for their magical needs," Nola said. "You know that. It's the only way to make sure that he can live as normal a life as possible."

"I know. And if you decide you don't want him to help us in any way after I explain everything, I will not push it. You're his Guardian. What you say goes."

She held my gaze for a long moment. "You've changed, Allie. Do you even know that?"

It was like she had just slammed her fist in my stomach. I had changed. I'd been possessed by my father, joined the Authority, lived a secret life trying to keep the city safe from people who used magic in secret ways. I'd walked into death and back. Literally. And I'd tried to keep her safe from it all. Cody too. I was asking her to break her own rules, rules she put in place to try to keep Cody safe. Maybe this was all wrong. Maybe I was all wrong.

Be patient, Dad said. *Cody will come to no harm.*

Cody rubbed at the side of his head with his palm. "Hello?" he said.

That was weird.

"Yes," I said, to Nola, as steady as if I were sitting on a witness stand. "I have changed. But I'm still me. Please listen before you go."

She looked down, thinking.

"Hello?" Cody said again, looking up at the ceiling.

"I have doughnuts," I said.

"Doughnuts!" Cody said. "Please can I have one?"

"If Nola says you can."

She looked back up at me. Shook her head, but didn't look as angry. "Yes, Cody you can have a doughnut. One," she added.

"Okay, one," he said. He walked over to the box and studied the contents before choosing a jelly-filled.

"So what is the problem?" she asked.

"How about some coffee?" I walked with her to the kitchen area because I wanted space between us and everyone else in the room. Not that they wouldn't be able to hear us. Even though Bea was chatting with Collins, something about the most gruesome magic deaths they'd both witnessed—girl had a macabre sense of humor—there was no hiding our conversation in this echo chamber.

Still, I felt bad dragging Nola and Cody into this.

"You really are worried, aren't you?" she said.

"How could you tell?"

She pointed at the coffeepot. "A half-burnt pot of coffee on the burner? Blasphemy."

I laughed. "That, I can fix." I took the pot to the sink, filled it with fresh water, scooped fresh-ground coffee into the filter, and started the pot.

"Davy's been hurt by magic—poisoned, more specifically," I said. "Collins is caring for him medically and magically. That table full of gadgets is mostly magic and tech units doing what they can to slow the spread of magic in his body."

She glanced at the table, taking note of everything there. I had no doubt that she'd be able to recall every object if asked. Nola had a very sharp memory.

"Collins said he's fine-tuned the instruments to the best of his abilities, but we wondered if Cody could fine-tune them even more."

"With magic?" she asked.

"Not necessarily."

"I don't think he can use magic, Allie," she said. "He's not . . . up to that kind of thing."

She was right. Cody's mind was broken, Closed. And I doubted that he had enough mental stamina and concentration to actually be able to use magic. "If he could just look at the things Collins is using, maybe he can see something we can't."

"He won't use magic?"

"I don't think he'll have to."

She nodded. "We can try that." She walked over to Cody, who was shoving the last of the doughnut into his mouth, a little bit of red jelly on his bottom lip.

"Cody, Davy is sick," Nola said.

Cody looked over at Davy, then back at Nola. Waiting.

"Allie wanted to know if you could look at the magic things the doctor is using and see if you think they're good." She shot me a look and I nodded.

"Just the things on the table," I said. "Some of them have dials and stuff. We don't want you to touch them, but look at them."

"Like art?" he asked.

"Like looking at art, yes," I said.

Cody walked off to the sink and very meticulously washed his fingers, hands, and his arms halfway to his elbows.

When he turned around there was more focus than I usually saw in his eyes. "Let me see," he said.

I led him over to Davy's bed. "Those are the instruments there—they have magic in them too," I said.

Cody stepped over to the table and folded his hands behind his back, bending at the waist to take a closer look at the gadgets and their functions, but careful not to touch a single thing.

"These work now?" he asked.

Collins walked around the head of Davy's bed and stood next to the table. "Yes. Fully functional. I've followed through with the designs, made some improvements, that sort of thing."

"Have you two worked together before?" Nola asked.

Collins glanced at her. I noted his gaze did not wander all over her body. That must be something he saved just for me.

Special.

"Not really, no. But some of these designs are his. I worked for a business that he did some work for."

"Really?" Nola stepped up closer to the table. "Did you make some of these things, Cody?"

"Some of them," Cody said. He looked over at Davy, then back at the table.

"Can we make any of them work better, help Davy get better faster?" I asked.

Cody frowned. "I think that one." He pointed with one finger but didn't touch the machine.

"How so?" Collins asked.

Cody straightened and looked up at the rafters. He started rocking a little from foot to foot, maybe just agitated, but with his hands folded behind his back, he looked like he really was trying to figure out the problem.

We all waited patiently.

"I think something." Cody looked back at Collins. "That's the wrong magic." He pointed at the machine he'd been studying.

"What would be the right magic?" Collins asked.

Cody looked around the room as if he were about to reveal a big secret no one should know.

"You can whisper it in my ear if you want." Collins walked over to Cody and Cody leaned forward to say something.

I, and probably Bea, heard him clearly whisper, "Death." I was pretty sure no one else, like Nola, heard it.

"Ah. Well, I can certainly adjust that," Collins said. "Thank you, Cody. You may have done a lot of good today."

I was surprised at how kindly Collins was treating him. Cody practically beamed. "Can I help more?" he asked. "Can I do magic?"

"No," Nola said. "I think you've helped enough. Right, Mr. Collins?"

"Very much so."

Cody looked disappointed. "Okay," he said quietly. Then he walked over and sat in the chair next to Davy, staring at him. "Bad," he said.

"I think I'll be heading out," Terric said. "Good day, all."

"See you soon," Zay said.

Terric left and I took a deep breath. "Okay, so that's good," I said. "Nola, I do have some other things I need to take care of today. How long are you staying in town?"

"We're leaving day after tomorrow," she said. "Want to catch up tomorrow sometime?"

"Yes. I'll call."

"You better," she said with mock sternness. "Cody, it's time for us to go. Cody?"

I looked over at him. He had placed his hand on Davy's chest, delicately, so as not to disturb the magic or the leads that were connected there.

His eyes were closed and he was humming softly.

"Cody, don't," Nola said.

"Wait," I said. I could see magic. Could see the Syphon spell, and the hard ropes of magic that were slowly strangling Davy.

And I could see more.

Cody's hand, in the center of Davy's chest, glowed with a very soft pink light. And that light spread like slow water across Davy's chest, reaching out to the lines of black. Where the light touched the black, they muddied and diffused, creating a sort of bluish fog.

Davy took a deep, easy breath and exhaled. The tightness around his eyes and mouth softened, and a little color seemed to flood his cheeks.

"Cody," I said quietly, "what are you doing?"

Cody opened his eyes, and at the sight of everyone watching him, stopped humming and snatched his hand away. "I want to go now." He stood and walked stiffly away from Davy as if he'd been caught stealing cookies.

"It's okay, Cody," I said. "You're not in trouble. I think what you were doing was very nice."

"No," Cody said. "I want to go now." He walked over to the door and stood there facing it, not opening it, but not turning back to the room either.

"What did you see?" Nola asked.

"Nothing bad," I said. "I'm not sure it was magic. He just had his hand there and it seemed to help Davy some."

Collins frowned and cast a Sight spell that stank to high heaven.

Okay, whatever Cody had done couldn't have been magic—it didn't stink.

"Is he okay?" she asked.

I looked at Cody. "I don't think he's done anything wrong. I don't think he used magic. Is Davy all right?" I asked Collins.

He nodded. "He's perfectly fine."

I gave Nola a quick hug and walked with her to the door. "Whatever he did it wasn't a bad thing."

"Are you sure?"

"Positive."

She nodded. "You'll call tomorrow?"

"Yes," I said. Whatever we decide to do should have chocolate involved."

I opened the door for them, and Nola touched Cody's arm. "Now stop being sad," she said. "Everything is okay. I promise."

Cody nodded. "Everything is okay?"

"Yes."

"Monster isn't talking." He walked out in the hall beside Nola.

Just before I shut the door I heard Nola say, "That's okay with me. Monster is too noisy."

Cody laughed. "No, he isn't."

I turned back to the people in the room. Collins was carefully adjusting the dials on one of the machines.

"Did Cody do something?" I asked. Dumb question. I knew he did something. I just wondered if he made things worse.

"He did indeed," Collins said distractedly. "I don't know what, exactly, he did, but Davy is resting much more comfortably."

"Do you think he helped slow the poison somehow?"

"I'll run tests. I'll let you know."

I picked up my coat and shrugged into it. "Bea, can you see who's available to keep an eye on Davy and Collins while we're out?"

"How about me?" Sid said, walking into the room.

"I don't need a guard," Collins muttered.

"He's not a guard," I said. "He's my eyes and ears in case anything changes with Davy."

"Typical micromanagement," Collins muttered. I didn't care.

"Ready?" I said to Zay and Bea.

Bea bounced up like she had springs in her shoes. "This is going to be so much fun!"

I exchanged a glance with Zayvion. Tracking down magic to see if it had been contaminated or if the Veiled were messing with it somehow sounded like the same kind of fun as a root canal. Plus, if we found out magic had been poisoned, the next logical questions were: from what and by whom?

Usually those answers were found only on the other side of a heaping pile of pain.

"I'll drive," Zayvion said.

I zipped up my coat. "Good. Bea, I'd like you to take your car. Better we have options."

"Oh, I wouldn't want to get in the way of you two lovebirds," she cooed.

"Thanks," I said.

She giggled and headed out the door. If she did her job right I wouldn't see her again until this was done.

"We should have sent her with Shame," I grumbled.

Sid snorted.

Collins seemed to notice there were people in the room again. He looked over at me, then at Zayvion. We were just about to head to the door.

"Allison," he said, "I'd like a word with you. In private."

"This is as private as it's going to get," I said. "Talk."

"There is something I thought you might need." He walked over to the door and I followed him. Beneath his coat that was hung neatly on the coat hook on the wall was a black leather doctor's bag. I hadn't even noticed it.

He picked it up and opened the lock. No magic, but I believe some kind of high-tech scanner was involved. He pulled the handles apart and sorted through a few things on the inside, all muffled by cotton or cloth since they didn't make any sound against one another and didn't squeak or smell like plastic wrap either.

He withdrew two small bundles wrapped in cloth. The string tying them tight was certainly magic in some way. The strings seemed to be moving around the packages, like a slowly creeping snake, even though with normal sight they just looked like string.

"What are they?" I asked.

"Weapons," he said. "Of quite a fine design, actually. And useful even in the hands of someone who doesn't use magic."

I hesitated to take them.

"Come now," he said. "Faint heart never saved fair Davy."

"Faint heart never got her hands blown off by bombs in brown paper packages tied up in string."

"Cotton," Collins said. "And a fine cotton at that. But completely inappropriate for a bomb. A bomb I'd wrap in silk."

"Why?" I asked.

"Silk around a bomb? Irony."

"No, why this? Why now?"

"I made a promise to your father." He nodded. "Years ago. That if I was in the position to offer you assistance of this sort, I would."

Dad? I asked.

It's true, he said quietly.

I took both packages, expecting the string to hurt. It felt like string.

"Thanks," I said.

"Good hunting to you." He relocked the bag and Zay and I walked out the door.

"You going to open it?" Zay asked before we reached the stairs.

I was holding both packages at arm's length like I was balancing nitroglycerin. I wasn't quite sure what to do with something Collins thought my father would think would be helpful to me.

"I'm not going to carry it around without knowing what it is." I handed him the smaller package because it was making my hand itch. I tugged on the string on the larger bundle. A stinky snap of magic later and the package fell open.

"It's a gun," I said.

"So it is," Zay agreed.

We both just stared at it. "Bet I can guess what's in the other package," I said.

"Bullets," Zay said. "Mind?"

"What's mine is yours, baby." I handed him the gun. He picked it up like it wasn't going to turn into a monster and bite his eyes out. I watched him, watched how he tipped it sideways, inspecting various, uh . . . doodads on it, then turned toward the blank wall and sighted along it.

He grunted, tipped it again to look at some other thing, and spun part of it with another satisfied grunt.

He handed me the other package. I opened it. Stinky snap and, ta-da, bullets.

Correction, incredibly stinky bullets. "Whoa," I said. "Do these smell like shit to you?"

I held the box of bullets up to Zay's face and covered my nose with my left hand.

He jerked his head back, expecting a wave of stink, then stopped. His nostrils flared as he breathed in. "No. They smell like magic."

Right.

He traded me the gun for the bullets. A sweet deal since the gun didn't reek.

Zay plucked a bullet out of the box and turned it between his fingers. "These are forged with glyphs," he said with something almost like wonder. "Amazing work. I'm not sure. . . . yes, it's Impact." He dropped it back in the box. "Shoot someone with these and they will not be getting back up."

"Good to know. How do you shoot a gun?"

He held his breath and, mostly, his surprise. "Seriously?"

"Not everyone grew up ghetto," I said.

He gave me a warning look.

"Well, then. Let me run you through the basics, rich girl." He stepped next to me and named off the parts of the gun, how to hold it, how to aim it, how to fire it. "Chamber, trigger, sight and squeeze" was about all I remembered.

"Got that?" he asked.

"Totally."

He grinned. "You are such a liar. Since the bullets are magic, I think if you put the shooty end of the gun toward the bad guy"—he tapped on the tip of the barrel just in case I'd forgotten where the bullet exited— "and focus your mind on where you want it to hit, it won't disappoint."

"The shooty end?"

"That's ghetto for barrel."

I laughed. "Okay, fine. Where did you learn to use a gun?"

"Training for my job with the Authority."

"So, not ghetto."

"Not so much, no."

We started down the stairs and didn't say anything more. Hounds had big ears, and the building was full of them.

Outside, the day was promising to be warm and cloudless. The sort of day that made you want to skip work and drive over to the coast to walk the beaches. But the magic on the streets was still just as bright and distracting as before. I had to get used to it, get used to seeing magic so I could ignore seeing magic. Otherwise I'd be jumping at shadows—well, and lights and colors— that weren't really there.

We made it around the building and to Zay's car in good time. Once we were both in the car and Zayvion had pulled out onto the street, he asked me, "Which cistern?"

"Um."

Suggestions? I asked Dad.

The least-guarded cistern is under Forest Park.

"Dad thinks under Forest Park," I said. "Do you know where that cistern is?"

"Yes. Do you know how to load that gun?"

I sighed. "I think I can do it, yes."

"Try. I'll talk you through it if you get stuck. Remember, point the shooty end at the floor, but not at your feet."

I rolled my eyes. "Have I ever told you how helpful you are?"

"Never hurts to hear it one more time."

I took the unloaded gun out of my coat pocket and stared at it for a minute. "It's lighter than I expected."

"It's not made of metal," Zayvion said.

"Huh." I turned it to the light, but made sure the damn shooty end was still facing the floor. "You're right. Plastics of some kind?"

"Yes."

"So it could go through metal detectors, Wards, scanners, stuff like that?"

"What Mr. Collins gave you is a very wicked weapon, and easily concealed. Not one I've seen before. No actual spells on the gun itself, so it won't set off Wards guarding against magical intrusion. I know of a few people who spell their bullets, but not like that. Those bullets hold a spark of magic in them. A latent spell waiting to be triggered. It's a lot like your dad's disks."

"Probably a prototype," I said. "Do you trust him?"

"Your father?"

"Collins."

Zay drove for a bit, thinking that over. "I think he is doing exactly what you asked him to do—trying to find a way to keep Davy alive."

"But otherwise?"

"No. There was a reason he was Closed."

"Did you Close him?"

He shook his head. "Victor did."

I didn't know why that made me feel better, but it did. "Have you talked to Shame?" I loaded the first bullet into the chamber. The bullet stank of rotted meat with a slight gasoline overtone. The magic was so subtle, it just looked like a regular shiny bullet to me.

"No."

"I think you should."

Zay's voice was carefully neutral. "He knows I didn't want to Close Maeve. He knows I was as careful with her as I could be."

"I still think you should talk to him. He's furious about it."

"I know."

I finished chambering the bullets. "Is there anything else I should do?"

"Make sure the safety's on."

"Got it." Luckily, I remembered where it was. I tucked the gun in my pocket and it was strange to know it was there, strange to know I had something that I could kill someone with. I mean, yes, magic could kill people, but the price to pay for that was your own life, so it sort of cut down on the knee-jerk revenge magics.

I had killed people with a knife and sword, but that took time and effort and I had plenty of chances to decide to pull back if death wasn't the outcome I wanted. With the gun, it seemed like one ill-timed twitch of my finger, and people would die.

I didn't like the feeling.

"So, Shame?" I brought up again.

Zayvion sighed. "Is there an 'off' on your stubborn button?"

"No."

"Fine. Shame and I, we've talked this over. We knew it could happen, knew it years ago when I first took the job."

"And he's fine with it? Because he looked mad as hell to me."

"I know he's angry. But there wasn't anything else I

could do. The Guardian of the gates follows orders from the head of the Authority. Even if that's Sedra, even if that's Bartholomew."

"Duty unto death?" I said quietly.

"It's what I've vowed. It's what Victor taught me. It's what being Guardian of the gates stands for. Upholding the law of the Authority above all others. Friends, family, enemies."

"Even if it means you're doing the wrong thing?"

He was quiet, the muscle at his jaw tight as he clamped down on his molars. Probably to keep from yelling. I knew he wasn't happy about what he'd done. I knew it made him furious. What I still didn't understand was why he didn't fight it. Why he didn't stand up against Bartholomew's orders.

Maybe he was having a hard time convincing himself it had been the correct thing to do too.

"Zay . . . ," I started.

"Don't," Zay said. "Just don't talk about it."

I studied his profile, the anger radiating from him, the guilt. I didn't need to point out that he didn't agree with what he'd done, no matter what Victor had said, no matter how he had been trained.

The Authority came first. Before friends, family, enemies. And apparently even before self.

I wondered how long Zayvion would hold that line, wondered if anything could make him change his mind about blindly following what the Authority, what Bartholomew, told him to do.

I knew me making him more angry wasn't going to change what he'd done. Nothing I could say would change his vows.

I turned my head away and watched the city roll past.

Chapter Fifteen

I'd lived in the city most of my life and hadn't been to Forest Park more than maybe once. Okay, make that only once that I remembered.

Zayvion, however, seemed to know exactly where he was going.

He parked. "The cistern is up that path. We'll need to hike."

We got out of the car and I was glad I was wearing my coat. There was more shade here, the old fir and pine soaking up the day's sunlight and warmth and leaving nothing but cool breeze and shadows beneath them.

I heard a car approaching. Bea drove up, parked, and got out. "Hey, you two."

So much for us not seeing her until this was done.

"You're not following us up there," I said.

"Why not?"

Huh. Why not indeed? If all we were doing was looking to see if a concentrated storage point of magic was tainted or being messed with by the Veiled, there was no reason she couldn't come along.

How many people are guarding this cistern? I asked Dad.

None, last I knew, Dad said. *It's a very minor storage. If it fails there are other stronger cisterns that will automatically take on the load.*

If it's so unimportant, why was it built? I asked.

There was a time when I was going to run the network of magic lines through St Johns. He paused and I could tell he was sorting through how much of that he wanted to talk about. Finally, *This was support for that.*

He had plans to run magic through St. Johns? This was the first I'd heard of it.

Why didn't you? I pressed. He didn't answer.

Why didn't you run magic through St. Johns, Dad? I asked with a little more force.

It was a decision that seemed right at the time.

There was something melancholy in his thoughts. I wondered what he regretted about that decision.

"Um, Allie? Hello?" Bea said.

Right, just because I was having a conversation with a dead guy didn't mean everyone was in on it. What had we been talking about? If Bea could follow us?

"Sorry," I said. "Yes, fine. Follow us. All the standard rules apply."

She pulled out her cell phone. "I'll dial 911 if we run into any trouble."

"Not with the cell reception up here," Zayvion said.

Bea glanced at her phone. "Right. Forgot about that. If we run into any trouble, I'll drive into cell range and call 911 from there."

We headed off up the hill. Zayvion took the lead since he knew where the cistern was located. I walked right behind him and Bea stayed a respectable distance behind us. I'd expected her to chatter all the way there, but she was silent, observant and damned near invisible when I glanced back to see if she was following us.

The trail led up a ridge with sword ferns and moss-covered rocks scattered between the tall brush and taller trees. Forest Park was one of the largest urban forest reserves, about five thousand acres or so, with seventy miles of trails, just west of Portland. I was glad

Zayvion knew where we were going. Easy to get lost out here.

Birdsong filled the air and little things skittered in and out of the trees and layer of leaves and needles on the ground. I took a nice deep breath and realized I didn't smell the stink of magic at all.

Finally Zay stopped. "That's it."

I looked at the more level area we had arrived at, then at the trees, scrub brush, and the path that ambled off into the distance.

"What's it?"

"The cistern." He pointed.

"It's a tree?"

"It looks like a tree."

It really did. The level area was still covered in grass, some wild roses, and a few daisies and ferns. In this area were also trees, just like all around us were trees. And the one Zayvion pointed at looked like an old cedar.

"I thought they buried all the cisterns," I said, walking over to it.

"In the city, yes. Better way to keep vandals from tapping into them. But this was one of the early models. There was an idea, when your dad first came up with this stuff, that the cisterns could also be a sort of public art."

"An artist made this? Was it Cody?"

"This was made almost thirty years ago," Zay said.

Cody wasn't even born then.

I sniffed, trying to catch a whiff of the rotten smell. Nothing.

"It doesn't look magical. At all."

"It's not magical. It just contains magic. And it doesn't let magic leak." He strode right up to it and walked around the base, running his hand over the rough bark.

I followed him, noting that the grass hadn't been worn down. "Does anyone know this is here?"

"It's not a secret, but I don't think very many people

come up this way. Even if they did, they might look right past it."

True. It was realistic. Moss was even growing on it and the branches above looked alive. "So how do we tap into it and see if the magic is okay?"

"There should be a manual trip. Hold on." He circled the tree again, this time more slowly, his hands running up and down the bark, his fingers following cracks and ridges like he was reading braille.

He stopped on the other side of the tree from me, completely hidden. "This is it. You might want to take a couple steps back, Allie."

I did so.

Lines of magic shot up through the bark of the tree, looking like water flowing upward. For a second, it was just a white-gold light, and then the light darkened, a push of gray, green, and finally black, spreading up the tree like a bruise.

I put my hand over my nose. It stank like rotten flesh.

"Can you see that?" I asked Zay.

"Yes," Zay said. "You?"

The black flow of magic pulsed, and a Veiled stepped out of the cistern, pulling itself up out of the ground at the base of the tree like a man climbing out of a swamp.

"Veiled," I said calmly, "coming out of the ground."

Zayvion came around the tree to where I was standing. He held a very clear Sight in his hand that made me want to barf.

I went through the motions of drawing a glyph for Shield, but stopped halfway when pain stabbed my brain. I could not draw on magic and did not want to pass out. I pulled the gun out of my pocket instead.

"Will this work?" I asked.

"Might," he said.

The Veiled finally pulled all of itself out of the ground.

It took a step away from the cistern. The darkness drained away from it, and then it was just a pale water-color pastel reflection of a man, which is what the Veiled usually looked like. It walked straight toward Zayvion and me, shuffling slowly, not moving like I'd seen Veiled move, not running. Yet.

"Shield?" I suggested.

Zayvion had already dropped Sight and was casting something that made my eyes water from the stench.

Shield.

The Veiled continued shuffling our way. Once he reached the Shield, he ran his fingertips, then palms, over it. He pressed, as if expecting the Shield to let him in. When it didn't, he opened his mouth, revealing a set of serrated teeth I'd never seen on a Veiled before, and bit down into the Shield. Black lines, just like the black lines on Anthony's body, just like the black lines on Davy, snaked out from that bite, twisting and squirming over the spell like leeches.

"Holy shit," I said. "Can you can see that?"

"Yes." Zayvion began chanting, something soft and low, then raised his left hand. Magic wrapped around his fist like a silver gauntlet of fire. He broke the Shield, and threw the silver fire at the Veiled.

The Veiled writhed and screamed. It shriveled up like a piece of plastic catching on fire.

Just as the Veiled reduced down to nothing but a burnt smudge on the grass, another Veiled pulled up out of the cistern.

"I think," I said, pointing at the other Veiled, who was almost on her feet, "we can conclude that yes, something is wrong with magic. And something is horribly wrong with the Veiled."

Zayvion didn't screw around with Shield this time. He just did the chant and threw flaming silver magic at the thing. She caught fire, screamed. Zay strode over to the cistern, ignoring her as she melted, and made his way around to the back of it where he could undo whatever kind of opening he had just done.

"There's more coming up," I said.

He did something on the other side of the tree and all the black magic that was pulsing up through the trunk of the tree, up into the limbs, and stretching out into the tips and fan of needles, stopped pulsing.

About six Veiled stopped coming up through the ground, caught half in and half out and opening and closing their black hole mouths like fish biting air.

Zayvion calmly chanted and set each of them on fire, leaving scorched patches in the grass.

I tried to breathe air that didn't make me want to hurl but wasn't having much luck.

"Let's go," Zayvion said. "We've seen enough."

I put the gun back in my pocket, only then realizing that I hadn't even remembered to take the safety off.

"We've seen enough what? Magic tainting Veiled or Veiled tainting magic?"

"Magic tainting the Veiled."

"Are you sure?"

"Enough that I want people out here, scientists, magic users, investigating it before it spreads."

Zayvion pulled out his phone and dialed with his thumb. Interesting, it wasn't a number he had on speed dial. "Put me through to Bartholomew," he said.

I looked around for Bea, caught just a glimpse of her ahead of us. She might have seen most of that. Or if she wasn't casting Sight, she might have just seen us walking around the tree trunk.

No, she'd probably seen it. If I were shadowing this job, I would have had Sight ready to go the moment Zayvion started messing with the tree.

We had hiked halfway down the trail before Zayvion spoke again. Apparently his cell reception was good.

"The magic in the cistern isn't clean," Zay said. No preamble, no pleasantries, just straight to the point.

Because we were hiking and Zay was a good distance ahead of me, and the wind was making that ocean wave sound in the trees, I couldn't hear Bartholomew's response.

"Yes. I've gone to a cistern and seen it with my own eyes. I want a team at every cistern in the city checking this out." He paused. "Like hell we don't need any further investigation." Pause again. "The Veiled," he said just a little louder, then took his tone down, "crossed through the cistern, and the magic changed them. They were immune to my defensive spells." He waited as Bartholomew spoke.

Then, "No, it *is* a problem. If magic is poisoned, the poison may have spread from the holding tanks down the networked lines throughout the city. If there are any failures or leaks in those lines, then not only is the magic everyone pulls on going to make them sick, it's also going to draw the attention of the Veiled, who are attacking anyone who casts a spell."

Again the wait. We were almost back to the parking area. The wind had picked up some, cooling the sunlight.

"You are forgetting Sedra had been possessed by Isabelle for years," he said. "She had full access to the cisterns and the wells. There's no knowing what she might have had set up to trigger when she died. No, you're wrong. They both have done harm with magic—first they sent the Veiled with disks to kill us and then, over the Life well, they tried to join together—with magic—in one body.

"They broke magic's rules because they are Soul Complements." He paused again, but I could feel the anger building in him. Anger that had been building ever since Bartholomew had fired Victor.

"Guardian of the gates means I protect people, I

don't just stand by and watch them die. No, not even under orders." A longer pause this time—probably Bartholomew telling him exactly what he expected Zayvion to do. "My *duty* is to keep magic from killing people." Zayvion stopped so quickly I almost ran into his back. "Bullshit." Pause. "No. I absolutely refuse."

I could tell he had made a decision. His shoulders squared and his left hand curled into a fist. "Fuck that," he said. "You can find a new Guardian of the gates. I quit."

He thumbed his phone off and threw it into the forest, where it smashed against a tree.

He stood there, hands clenched into fists, chin high, looking like he wanted to beat the living hell out of something. I waited for him to calm down, waited for him to pull that cool Zen mask of his over the fury.

That didn't happen. He stormed down the last of the trail, and out into the parking lot. His anger hadn't eased even a notch by the time we reached the car. "Get in," he said. "We need to be out of here before they track my phone."

"Who?" I asked.

"Bartholomew's dogs."

Chapter Sixteen

"What just happened?" I asked as soon as we were in the car.

"Bartholomew will not listen to me. He doesn't give a flat damn about how many people are dying, doesn't believe magic is tainted, doesn't believe the Veiled are tainted, and doesn't want me, or anyone else, to do anything about it."

"So you quit?" I asked, feeling strangely dizzy from the suddenness of that decision.

He glared at me.

"Haven't you've been telling me you would never quit—that you had to uphold your vow and your duty?" I said. "You promised Victor you'd follow Bartholomew's orders. And now, when things are getting bad, you decide to just give up on being Guardian of the gate?"

Zayvion's breathing was pretty shallow, like there wasn't enough room in his lungs with all the anger crowding his chest. "Do not lecture me," he said tightly. "You don't understand this, Allie. You could never understand what I have done as Guardian. What I have had to do."

"Make me understand," I said. Yes, Zayvion's quitting the Authority was freaking me out way more than I'd expected. I hated that he'd Closed people I loved, but I'd found a way to accept it because he'd told me that duty would always come first for him and that was never going to change. But now he was changing his mind, changing the rules, changing who he was because this thing at the cistern hadn't gone the way he wanted it to.

"You Closed Victor and Maeve because you were ordered to, but when Bartholomew doesn't listen to your advice to scramble a team, you quit?" I asked.

"Do you think that's what this is about?" he said quietly. "Me wanting Bartholomew's respect? Is that who you think I am?"

"No." I looked away from his eyes that were burning gold. "I don't know. I don't understand the timing of this, Zay. You've always been the Authority's man. You've told me that will never change, and now it's changing. Why now? What happens to you if you quit? What are they going to do to you?"

I reached over and touched his arm.

A cavalcade of emotions crashed through me—Zayvion's emotions. Anger, frustration, and more than that, guilt, sorrow, loss. Zayvion hated the choice he was making. Hated being forced to decide if his life with the Authority—the only thing he had ever wanted to be or do—had become not only a mockery but also a tragedy under Bartholomew's reign.

And overriding those feelings was the single clear note of his conviction.

"Yes, I have Closed people. Yes, I have taken the memories away from magic users, from my teachers and my friends. But I will not stand idly by while innocent people are dying."

I couldn't look away from him, from the pain that had cornered him into this final moment, this final decision.

People who were a part of the Authority understood the risks they were taking with magic. They understood they could be Closed, or that magic could hurt them in ways the common magic user did not know. But the innocent, people who were not a part of the Authority, people who were not a part of the secrets and ancient dealings, did not know any of that. Zayvion had vowed to keep magic users safe, keep the innocent safe from the harm magic could cause. He was keeping that vow. Even if it meant he had to break his promise to the Authority.

I understood his decision now. "Victor wanted you—," I started.

"Victor wanted me to follow the rules and laws of the Authority," he said softly. "That's what I'm doing. Bartholomew isn't upholding the Authority's most basic tenet—to protect the innocent. He might say he's here to fix all our problems. But he doesn't have a clue, and he won't listen to what's really going on."

"They'll Close you," I said.

"They'll try."

I drew my hand away and the intensity of his feelings subsided. "Do you have a plan?" I asked.

"I don't need a plan." He started the car and began driving out of the park.

I sighed. "I do. What we need is some way to neutralize the poison in the cisterns and city system if it's gotten that far. We'd be able to help the most people that way, and maybe it will also help with the epidemic. Unless you think we should try to track down the Veiled first and try to stop them from spreading the poison. If that's what they're actually doing."

He shook his head. "That would take days, maybe months."

"How we can clean magic?"

"I don't know."

Dad, I thought. *Do you have any ideas on how to cleanse magic?*

It took him a moment or two before he finally answered. *I don't know if it's fully possible to cleanse magic.*

You don't know what the toxin is, or where it's stemming from.

Here's how this is going to work, I thought to him. *You are going to tell me everything you know about the cisterns and magic storage and containment in this city. Then you're going to tell me the best way to cleanse the poison from the magic flowing through the city.* The one good thing about sharing a brain with someone was you could tell when they were very, very serious.

I was very, very serious.

There are ... filters built into each cistern, Dad said. *Placed there in case of an emergency such as this. They can be triggered, and they should purify magic, or at least most of it. If the poison is naturally occurring, if it's still pouring into the cisterns and lines and network in a passive manner, even the filters might not be enough to neutralize it. I might be able to think of something else if we have more data.*

I don't think we have time for data, I said. *This is a good start. Thank you.*

"Dad says there are filters on the cisterns," I said. "We can trigger them, and they might cleanse magic or slow the spread of the poison."

"Does he know how to trigger the filters?"

Dad? I asked.

It was set as an emergency procedure that would be enacted by five members of the Authority—each working one of the five disciplines of magic.

"We need five people who can work the disciplines," I said. "I can't cast, so I'm out. You can handle Faith magic, Shame would probably do Death for us. We need Blood, Flux, and Life magic."

My mind was spinning, but I couldn't think of magic users who could handle each of those disciplines and who would be willing to go in direct conflict with Bartholomew's orders to help us. Not to mention that if we were caught doing it, I was pretty sure Closing wouldn't be the worst of our punishment.

"We need more people," I said. "Who do you trust in the Authority who might go along with this?"

"Shame, Terric, Hayden, Kevin." And then, quieter, "Victor and Maeve if they had their memories."

"You think Kevin would help us?" I asked.

"Not as long as Violet is a part of the Authority. He won't put her in jeopardy like that."

That was true. He had started out as her bodyguard, and I was pretty sure had fallen in love with her. He might be on our side but he wouldn't risk her safety.

There was one fairly straightforward option. I knew it. Zayvion knew it. But if we did it, there would be no going back. His career with the Authority would be over for good.

"Can Victor and Maeve cast magic well enough even without the memories you took away?" I asked.

Zayvion didn't say anything for a while. I knew he was working out the repercussions of what I was really asking: would he be willing to Unclose them? I didn't push. This was something only he could decide.

We were almost back in the downtown area when he spoke.

"They can cast magic, but not at a high level," Zayvion said. "That was part of the Closing required for those levels—some of their memories, and instincts for certain of the more advanced spells, remain inaccessible."

I still didn't comment.

Finally, "Victor. I'll start with Victor. It will take the longest to Unclose him. Then I'll try Maeve."

"Are you sure you want to do this?" I asked.

"I know what my job is. And," he added, "I made up my mind. This is our best chance to turn this disaster around."

"How long will it take?"

"For Victor, maybe an hour or more. Maeve, less."

"Okay. I want you to drop me off at the police department," I said.

"Like hell."

"I'm going to talk to Stotts. He's already suspicious about the epidemic. Seems open to the idea that the Veiled are involved. And if we're working some kind of magic to trigger all of the cisterns in the city, or filter them, he's going to see the spike on the grid."

"I don't care."

"If he can see it, the Authority can certainly see it."

He scowled. "Still don't give a damn. Let them see it."

"And then they send out Bartholomew's dogs and every other magic user in their employ. Hundreds of people, Zayvion. And some of them will be more than happy to use magic, guns, or anything else to stop a mutiny."

The lightbulb still wasn't flickering.

I tried it another way. "Stotts can cover our tracks, cover any flares, cover the spike so even the Authority can't see it. He has the equipment, he's just never known there was an Authority to hide things from."

That, finally, got through. "He's a civilian."

"Maybe," I said. "But he's been Closed because he helped save me and you when we walked through the gates of death. And he's been attacked by the Veiled. I think he deserves to know what's going on in the town he's trying to keep safe, and then he can make his own decisions about helping us."

"Dragging the law into this—"

"If you're not a part of the Authority anymore, then you are no longer required to cover up for them. Let the chips fall, Zayvion. Bartholomew can try to pick them up."

"You seem awfully comfortable with this kind of thing."

"What kind of thing?"

"Rebellion."

"It gets easier with practice," I said with a smile.

Zay took a tight U-turn and headed toward the police station.

"We'll need a meeting place," I said. "Somewhere the Authority doesn't know about."

"There isn't any crack or crevice in this city the Authority doesn't know about."

"Grant's," I said.

"No. Everyone knows Get Mugged."

"Not Get Mugged. His place, his apartment under the shop. He said he has access to the Shanghai tunnels." The tunnels were built over a hundred years ago as a way for tavern owners to smuggle drunks out of the city and into forced servitude on ships headed to China. I'd always heard that most of the tunnels had been closed off. Hopefully, that's what the Authority had heard too.

Zay nodded. "The Authority doesn't really monitor the tunnels."

"Good. We'll meet there, and decide which cistern filter to trigger first, and how. Can you stop the car for a minute?"

Zay pulled over into an alley and Bea's car rolled past us and parked along the street. I got out.

"Allie—"

"A minute. I'll be back."

I jogged over to Bea's car and knocked on the passenger-side window, which she powered down.

"Way to blow my cover, Beckstrom," she said. "Want to get in? I have cookies."

"For a sec. Can I borrow your phone?"

"Sure."

She unlocked the door and I got in. Her car smelled of strawberries and she had a little teddy bear hugging a stuffed alligator on her dash. The toys bore an amazing resemblance to her and Jack.

She handed me her phone. "What trouble are you getting me into?"

"I'm calling Detective Stotts so I can meet with him. I think my phone's being tracked."

"Nice."

I dialed his number, got him on the first ring. "Detective Stotts," he said.

"This is Allie. I need to see you now. I know what's going on and I know what to do to fix it."

"Where are you?" he asked over a creaking sound in the background.

"I'll come to you. Bye." I thumbed it off, handed it back to Bea.

"Gonna let me in on the secret?" she asked.

"Not yet. If I need help, yes. But do me a favor. I need you to go back to the den and tell Collins to take Davy somewhere safe. Anyplace that he knows no one in an authority position would find him. And be sure to say it like that."

"The whole thing?"

"Just that he needs to find a place where people in an authority position won't find him."

"Got it, authority position. Be careful," she said.

I got out of the car, pulled my phone. I erased all numbers and messages and removed the battery. Just for good measure, I threw it into the garbage Dumpster.

Then I got back in with Zay. The whole thing had taken maybe two minutes.

"What was that?" He drove down the alley and back onto the street.

"I needed to call Stotts, so I used Bea's phone. Also I dumped mine. I told Bea to go tell Collins to take Davy somewhere safe." My stomach clenched a little at that. I was trusting Davy's life to a man I'd barely met. A man who had come highly recommended by my father, of all people.

"I should have taken Davy to the hospital," I said.

"No," Zay said. "If he were there, he'd be under the Authority's watch. Too easy to use him as a bargaining chip."

"I don't bargain."

"If Davy's life was on the table?"

"Shit."

"I'll contact Hayden after I've taken care of Victor," he said. "Are you sure your dad knows how to neutralize the poison?"

Dad?

It's what I would try first, he said.

"He just said this is the first thing he'd try."

"Hell." He sighed.

That pretty much summed up my reaction too. But we were out of options here, and frankly, Dad had been really helpful lately. He felt trustworthy to me.

"If that doesn't work" I said, "we'll try something else. Pull over here. This is good. You don't want to be spotted by the cameras."

Zay slowed the car and turned down a side street. He stopped the car. I unfastened my seat belt.

"See you soon."

I put my fingers around the door handle.

Zay reached over and caught my arms. His hands were warm and strong as he dragged me to him.

He didn't have to drag. I went willingly.

I glanced at his eyes, burning with anger and the gold of magic, then at his mouth, turned down in a frown. He kissed me, hard. And I kissed him back.

Short, hot, needful. His anger and love pulsed through me like a burning, cleansing wave and I wanted to wrap myself in it forever.

But all too soon, he pulled back. He gently let go of my arms as if surprised he'd been holding me so tightly.

"Be safe," he said.

"You too."

I got out of the car and headed down the street to the police station. Yes, there were cameras, which meant Bartholomew's men might have the police station under surveillance. I didn't think they'd expect to find me here. I didn't think they'd expect me to walk in through the front doors either.

But that's what I did. In the front, where the length of the room ended with glass doors, behind which I could see a few police officers working. Detective MacKanie Love was there, working three phones at once, while typing on a computer. I didn't see his partner, the slim, quiet Mia Payne. I hoped she was okay. She and Love were two police officers who dealt with magical crime. I didn't take the time to go talk to him. Headed instead down one set of stairs and down another to Detective Stott's office. I was pretty sure that was where he'd be. I had heard his chair creak when I was on Bea's phone.

I knocked on the door.

The chair let out a screech, then there were footsteps. The door opened.

"Allie," Stotts said. "Are you alone?"

"Yes. We need to talk and I don't have much time."

He motioned me in, looked up and down the hall, then shut the door and cast a very nice Trip spell—something that would literally trip up the first person who tried to walk over that threshold.

"What's wrong?" he asked.

"There's a lot, but I'm going to give you the basics. We think magic has been poisoned. Zayvion and I went out to one of the cisterns. I could see the black taint in the magic. I think the taint in the magic is what's been making people sick. But there's something more. When the Veiled come in contact with magic, the magic changes them. It's like it poisons them too and they want to bite and feed on magic. I think the Veiled are spreading tainted magic through the city."

Stott's office was pretty small, most of it taken up by shelves of files. It had enough room for his desk, a small refrigerator, and a couch with a coffee table in front of it.

I was pacing between the coffee table and the couch, about three steps by three steps, gesturing with my hands, thinking fast. "I think a Veiled stepped into and possessed Anthony, and that's why he's dead. I know that sounds kind of crazy, but I saw a Veiled step out of someone, or out of the same space they were both occupying, and it looked like the person was hurt by it. Possessed. Anthony bit Davy, so that might be why Davy isn't dead yet—a bite is less potent than a full possession. I don't know how to stop the Veiled, so we need to neutralize the poison in the networks so we can stop the spread of the contagion."

Stotts inhaled, exhaled. "That's a lot to take in, Allie. Have you brought this to the attention of the agencies responsible for the maintenance of magic, the cisterns and networks?"

"I brought it to the attention of people in a position to do something about it. They didn't believe me."

"There are proper channels you should follow for this," he said. "Proof that will need to be gathered, tests that need to be run. I can get you in touch with the proper authorities."

"They won't listen."

"Oh? Why do you think that?" he asked.

I stopped pacing. Stotts was a nice man, a good cop, and as far as I could tell, good for Nola. Revealing the secret of the Authority could get him killed.

Not telling him might just do the same.

"There is a group of magic users who have infiltrated every layer of society," I said. "They know spells and disciplines of magic that no one else knows. Powerful things. Things that magic should not be able to do. They monitor how people use magic, and allow only certain advances and knowledge to be released to the general public. They have established themselves in every decision-making position in our government, our business, and our social communities. That's who I went to. That's who told me they didn't care that magic might be poisoned, didn't care if people were dying from magic."

He gave me a long look, gauging if I was telling the truth or had just gone conspiracy theory in the head.

"The things in this city that don't make sense?" I said. "The things that you've seen magic do that you can't explain? They're behind that. All of that."

Stotts finally paced over to his desk, and leaned back on the edge of it. "Let's say you're telling the truth and there is a vigilante group of magic users. Why wouldn't they want magic clean? If it's tainted, it will be tainted for them too."

"I don't know," I answered. "There's been a... change in leadership. And I don't know what agenda this new person has."

"How do you know about all this, Allie?"

"My dad was a part of the group. It was why he was murdered. It was why a lot of weird things have happened here. I only found out about the group after Dad died."

"Are you working for them?" he asked.

"Not anymore. At first, yes. I did a few jobs." Let him assume they were Hounding jobs. He understood that Hounds contract out for anyone who signs a paycheck. "But not anymore. I can't work for someone who turns a blind eye and lets this epidemic spread."

"I'm going to want names," he said.

"I'll give them to you. But I need something from you first."

He folded his arms over his chest and nodded for me to continue.

"I need you to cover my tracks."

When he didn't immediately say no, I continued. "My dad had filters for magic set up when he built the cisterns. People don't know about these filters because they can only be activated with the right spells, and most of those spells haven't been released to the public. I can trigger the filters with the right spells. And that's going to spike on the monitors—your monitors and monitors for the people who don't want me to be doing this. I want you to mitigate the spike through the lines so it isn't as severe. You can do that, right?"

He didn't say anything. Didn't move. What I had told him could just as easily be a cover-up for something else I wanted to do with the cistern. Like maybe I had bombs set up in the cisterns and wanted him to cover up the spike while I blew the town off its foundations.

"Allie," he started, resigned, "I can't just trust your word on this. I can't trust that your father had some kind of filtration system set up that no one would have discovered and used by now. I can't trust that what you are doing won't make matters worse, make magic worse. Possibly kill people. Even if magic is infected, and I'm not the one to say it isn't, you are not an expert. You're just a Hound. I'm sorry."

I'll admit it, I was surprised. I always thought Stotts would be on my side, would believe me if I told him everything. If I just told him what was really going on. But he was right. There was no evidence in my favor. And I supposed if I did my job right, there never would be.

"If you can bring me proof," he said, "hard evidence, Allie, then I will do everything in my power to bring this organization down. But I have to have more than just your word to go on. Get me more. Get me something solid. Does your dad have records?"

"I can look," I said. "I'll do what I can to get proof. Thanks for listening."

"Wait, where are you going?"

"I'm not going to tell you that."

He held my gaze for a long minute. "All right. Can you give me names? I can start looking into things on this side."

I knew he wouldn't find anything out of the ordinary with anyone in the Authority. Sid always did background checks and he'd told me everyone involved in the Authority came up smelling like roses.

But there was one person Sid had not checked into. A man I very much hoped had a shady enough past to bring him down. "I'd start with a man named Jingo Jingo."

He nodded. "And?"

"And I'll get you a list of other people tomorrow," I said. "Right now I have an appointment I'm late for."

"Don't do this, Allie," he said.

"I'm not going to do anything," I said in probably the most convincing lie I'd ever told. "I'm going to follow up on the filter idea by talking to a few more people who might be in a position to look into it and I'm going to go through some of my dad's old files. I won't touch the cisterns. I just, you know, thought if I talked to you, we could help stop this epidemic. But you're right. It's bigger than the two of us."

"I'm not saying I won't look into your claims," he said.

I nodded. "Thanks. Oh, and I heard that Nola's heading home in a couple days. Thought I'd meet up with her sometime tomorrow for a little girl time."

"She'd like that," he said.

"Great, it's all settled then. I'll call her later. Bye, Stotts." I paused at the door. "Did you put something here?" I asked. I didn't have to ask. I could see the spell: a swirling ball of strings and smaller balls that I knew would break apart and trip whoever touched it.

He nodded. Walked to the door, broke the spell there. Smelled like someone with a mouth full of rotten teeth had just exhaled. I didn't let on how much it stank.

"Be careful, Allie," he said.

I walked through the door and up the stairs, leaving Stotts, and our chance of any kind of backup, behind me.

Okay, fine. He wasn't on my side yet, and I didn't have time to give him hard evidence. Hells, I didn't even know what kind of hard evidence would convince him to believe me.

But that wouldn't stop me from trying to filter magic. Surprisingly, I didn't feel guilty about lying to him. I'd done my best to let him know what was really going on, and I'd promised to rat out some of the Authority members, which I planned to follow through with because I was just that pissed off about the whole thing.

He was sure to see the spike in magic, though. Once we activated those spells, he'd know I had lied about not touching the cisterns. I had, essentially, just made myself culpable to the crime. If activating filters on the city's cisterns was a crime.

Hopefully it was only a misdemeanor—something along the lines of drawing mustaches on political posters.

I got up the first flight of stairs and the second with nothing but my breathing and shoes sending echoes against the bare walls. Then I pushed out into the main lobby.

Two goons in dark suits were right across the room. Not the charmers I'd seen with Bartholomew but obviously part of the same boxed set.

Unless I was incredibly lucky, they had to be here looking for me.

I was never incredibly lucky.

I didn't panic, didn't make eye contact, didn't walk fast. Just took a nice, easy stroll toward the doors, glad that I was wearing tennis shoes that didn't clack against the marble floor and draw attention my way.

I could feel them following me. They were at a distance, but they had definitely spotted me. Suddenly the gun in my pocket felt too heavy, too big, like everyone could see it and at any moment I'd be tackled from behind and put up on charges for going into the police department intending to shoot someone.

I couldn't use magic. Until this moment, I hadn't realized just how much I relied on it to keep me safe. How was I going to get out of this?

Think, Beckstrom, think.

Too late to go back to Stotts. No cell phone because I threw the damn thing away. No one around to come to my rescue if I yelled for help, and even if I did, that would bring all the focus on me. The police would get involved, which might be good.

Except the Authority would just take over. Then I'd be jailed. Closed. Killed.

Which would be bad.

The best I could do was run. Hide.

I hated running for my life.

I hated dying more.

So I walked out the doors, then ran. They ran after me, two sets of feet. After a few minutes, I heard another set of feet join them. Hells.

I bolted down the closest side street, looking for an alley, a pocket, a stairway, an open door—anything, any-place I could hide—my heart beating hard and the strangling tickle of fear clogging up my throat.

Ahead was an open garage attached to a hardware

store. I dashed through it and tried the door to the warehouse. Unlocked. Hello, luck. Where have you been all my life?

I ducked into the warehouse and hid behind a stack of boxes, listening for the goons behind me. I didn't have to listen. They were throwing Track spells. I could smell the foul egg stink of their magic getting stronger as they came nearer.

No place to hide here either—or at least not enough that tracking spells would miss me.

Out, then. Out the front. Out fast.

I jogged through the warehouse, looking for the exit. Found it and hit it at a dead run.

Heard the goons' boots slapping concrete behind me. Couldn't hear the third man. Didn't know where he'd gone. Probably for a car.

Shit. Shit. Shit.

Faster. I put my stride into it, my legs into it, my fear into it, and ran. Down one block, a side street, an alley. Run. Run. Run.

My breath burned in my lungs—I'm in good shape but I'd traded daily workouts for recovering from death, magical battles, Leander yanking me out of my body, and now, magic making me sick.

Not that I was complaining. I just very aware I was not at my prime.

Which made me pay damn close attention to how I was running and where. I needed to find a place to hide—to really hide—soon. Because my stamina was shot.

Hedges, walls, gated stairways, not a lot of help.

Holy shit, my chest hurt. I couldn't run forever.

I'd made my way down toward the river, down toward the train tracks and under bridges and through construction. You'd think someone would leave a frickin' manhole open or something.

Nothing.

Okay, so they were going to catch me. That meant I needed to put my back against a wall and see if my shooting skills were good enough to stop those two assholes.

And look at that. An abandoned brick building just half a block down the tracks. That ought to do.

I jogged across the weeds and chunks of concrete and around the corner of the building where a car could not follow since there was a concrete barrier lining the side and back of the building. I put my shoulder against the building, fumbled in my pocket, pulled out the gun, thumbed off the safety.

The area between the wall and the brick building was tight. As tight as an elevator. I felt my pulse rising, my heart thudding heavy and thick, for another reason. I felt trapped, boxed in, smothered.

My hands were shaking. I knew I had to hold them steady to shoot the gun. I wanted to hold them steady. But I could not make them stop shaking.

I held my breath and listened. The goons were picking their way across the weeds. Still just two sets of footsteps, and one rotten-smelling Track spell.

Okay, Beckstrom, you can do this. Do what Zayvion told you to do: aim the shooty end, squeeze the trigger.

I heard a scuffling of rocks behind me. Looked like third goon decided to go the opposite way around the back of the building so they could trap me in the middle. I stepped away from the corner enough that I would not be in range if they decided to rush. Then I crouched down. Most people aimed for the chest or face. If they were coming up for me, they'd be expecting someone six feet tall, not four feet tall.

Plus this put the shooty end of the gun just below belt level.

Might not kill them, but it sure would shut them down.

I pivoted on the balls of my feet, ready to shoot to either side.

Scuffles behind me came closer. Sounded like he found a buddy. I could make out two sets of footsteps.

But something wasn't right with those sounds behind me. The footsteps were in lockstep, like the goons were walking in perfect rhythm. Or like they were four-footed.

I shifted and lifted the gun, shooty end out.

The goon was not one goon. He was not two goons. About the size of a St. Bernard, made out of rock and magic with wings, Stone stood there. He pulled back his lips and gurgled like someone had just run their fingers through marbles. It was a very quiet sound, a lot wheezier than normal. And he looked darker than when I'd last seen him, like the concrete gray of him had gone slate. But he was definitely my buddy gargoyle.

I was so glad he'd found me. That meant I only had two goons somewhere out there toward the front of the building trying to kill me.

Neat.

"Stone!" I whispered. "Good boy. That way. Get the men, Stoney. Attack."

I stood up and somehow Stone squeezed past me and I managed not to scream from claustrophobia. I wasn't sure if he understood what I wanted him to do. But it didn't matter. Stone could be damn intimidating, and certainly distracting, no matter what he was doing.

"Fine," I called out. "I surrender. I'm coming out peacefully."

Stone's ears laid flat against his skull, and his ruff was hunched up. He crouched, ready to spring.

"Go," I whispered. "Attack."

Stone jumped on the side of the warehouse, making it ring out like a wrecking ball had just hit it, and started climbing. He was on the roof so quick, he was a blur.

And then he was on the goons.

I could tell, because I heard the screaming.

I glanced out around the corner, my back still tight against the building. Stone had landed on top of one of the men, who now looked unconscious. He had probably hit his head, or Stone had hit it for him.

The other guy was chanting, getting ready to cast a spell that looked like a huge Venus flytrap but with massive teeth.

I opened my mouth to warn Stone, but didn't have to. Stone snarled, quiet and wheezy like a rusted pipe organ, and then leaped, his wings pumping hard.

You'd think a man in the employ of Bartholomew Wray would be able to keep his concentration on that spell he was weaving while half a ton of gargoyle, fangs, and claw was falling on him.

Nope.

The man yelled out and threw the incomplete spell, which just tattered apart in the wind. Stone opened his huge maw and clamped down on the man's neck. He unfurled his wings and pumped upward, the man's neck still in his jaws. He flew up ten feet, twenty. He shook his head like he was shaking off water. Then he opened his mouth.

The man fell, twisted, hit the ground. Hard. And was still.

Stone landed beside him and snarled. He looked like he wasn't done hurting him yet.

"Stone?" I said.

Stone turned toward me. For the briefest moment, I saw a spark of green in his eyes, the same green I'd seen in the Veiled. Then it faded and it was just Stone's eyes looking back at me. Happy eyes. Happy Stone. His ears perked up and he tipped his head to one side.

Okay, that was a little worrisome. The last thing I needed was for magic to taint Stone.

"Good boy," I said. "Let's go. Come on, Stoney, we need to go."

Stone trotted over to me and wrapped his wing up around my back, the prehensile tip holding tight to the collar of my coat. He didn't smell like bad magic, didn't smell like the Veiled. He seemed just like his normal self now.

I dropped my hand down on his head and petted him as we walked—quickly—away from the scene. This was a pretty deserted part of town, but people still came down here. The police came down here.

I didn't want to be around when they started asking questions.

Chapter Seventeen

Here's the thing. When you're on the run, every shadow looks like a goon, every person looks like a member of the Authority you might have once seen, and every street is so covered in magic that you wonder if you would even notice a person hiding behind it if you tried.

And here's the other thing. None of that was going to stop me from finding my way to Grant's apartment under Get Mugged.

I stuck to the shadows and least-used streets and alleys, but that wouldn't get me to the coffee shop. Lots of open, well-traveled streets between here and there. And I couldn't just go strolling down the street with Stone beside me. People would see him.

"You need to go, Stone," I said. "Go play." I pointed to the top of a building. He sniffed at my finger, gurgled at it.

"Go," I tried again. "Before someone sees you. Hide."

I don't know when "hide" had entered his vocabulary, but I was glad he finally seemed to get what I was saying. He tipped a look up at the building next to us, then trotted back the way we'd come. He wiggled his rump and jumped, catching the fire escape with his front hands, then nimbly clattering up to the rooftop.

Good enough.

But since I couldn't fly from rooftop to rooftop, my

best chance of disappearing was to blend into a crowd out in the open.

I took off my coat and emptied my pockets. I stuck the gun down the back of my pants, dropping my sweater over the top of it. My journal didn't fit in my jeans pocket, so I'd have to carry that. There was no way I'd leave it behind.

My wallet was small enough to shove in my pocket.

I folded up my jacket and left it in the alley. It was cold without my coat, and I wanted a coat and hat so I could cover up anything the goons had seen me in and maybe reported to other goons. I ducked into a second-hand store and went straight for the coats, finding a wool beast of a thing that was two sizes too large and sported a plaid in shades of pea soup and muddy berries.

Not pretty. Not even close to what I'd usually wear. Perfect.

I also grabbed a black slouchy beanie that looked like it had been hand-crocheted. It had taken me less than a minute to shop.

I walked over to the counter.

"You're ready?" a girl called out from somewhere behind the racks of shoes. "Be right there."

I tried not to look nervous or in a hurry as she came over. "Hi there," she said.

"Hi." I made a big show of being busy pulling out my wallet so I could avoid eye contact while she rang up the items. Handed her my card and still didn't look up.

Dumb, dumb mistake. My name was on that card. The Authority could track that card. Hell, the police could track it.

"Um," I said, glancing up. "Can I have that back? I'd rather pay in cash."

"Oh, sorry," she said, her hand hovering with the card over the reader. "I already ran it." She frowned. "Funny, it's not working. Hold on. Oh. It says you don't have sufficient funds." She continued reading something on the computer screen. Then she went dead silent and flushed red. She licked her lips, sweat peppering her forehead.

"I'm sure it's going to be fine, um . . . Ms. Beckstrom," she said. "Would you like me to try it again, or do you want to use another card?"

Shit. They must have frozen my bank account.

"I'll just do cash," I repeated. I dug in my wallet. Three dollars. Not enough for the coat. "I guess I'll only take the hat." I handed her two bucks. She nodded, but her fingers were cold and she was trembling as she took the money and gave me back my card.

"Sure," she said. "Sure."

I didn't think a secondhand store had a silent alarm, but that didn't mean that she wouldn't call the cops. Crap. She'd tell them I had the hat on too. So much for the disguise idea.

She rang up the purchase. "Do you want a bag?"

"No," I said with the best smile I could manage. "But thanks."

I picked up the hat and headed out. No money meant no cab. I had to get across town and the longer I was on foot, the bigger the chance they'd find me. But what other choice did I have?

I'd been Hounding the streets of this city for a long time. I knew where the security cameras were set up. I knew which roads the police cruisers didn't ever patrol. I could see the magic spells dripping all over everything. There was a chance, a very thin chance, that I could get to Grant's without being seen. If luck stayed with me.

I started walking. Not too fast, didn't want to draw attention. Not too slow either.

It was nerve-racking. I hated being out in the open like this with nothing for safety but the gun rubbing a bruise into the base of my spine.

I hated not having magic.

I'd probably gone about two miles when a man stepped out of a bar doorway, his back toward me as he fumbled in his shirt pocket for a smoke.

That was not just a man. That was a Hound. Jack Quinn.

"Car's this way," he said as he lit a cigarette and walked off. I followed, trying to keep it casual. Thank you, Pike, for making it a rule that no Hound goes out on a job alone.

I had no idea how long Jack had been following me. Couldn't have been for very long because I would have seen or heard him. But I was so grateful he was here, and had a car, I almost wanted to hug the man.

Jack's car was up two blocks. We both got in.

"Thank you," I said.

"For what?" he asked, easing out into traffic.

"For following me."

He shrugged. "Bea said she was worried and made me come out looking. You can thank her."

I nodded. I planned to do just that. Give her a raise maybe.

"So why'd you do it?" he asked.

"You're going to have to be a hell of a lot more specific than that," I said. "Why'd I do what? You are headed back to the den, right?"

"Yes. Why'd you steal from your own company?"

"What?"

"Embezzlement. Why did you drain the corporate bank accounts and piss off all the stockholders?"

"I didn't," I said, sort of dazed. "Who said I did that?"

"Every news channel in the Northwest." He glanced over at me. I knew he was deciding whether I was lying. Since I was pretty much in shock over what he'd just said, he should deduce this came as a bit of a surprise to me.

"What are they saying?" I asked. "I don't . . . I haven't even been in to the offices for a week or more."

"They are saying they found your backpack with a thumb drive with all the account information," he said. "They are saying they caught you on the surveillance cameras going into the offices day before yesterday. They are saying you gutted Beckstrom Enterprises because you are jealous of Violet Beckstrom's control and share of the company, and also angry that her son is likely to inherit everything your father disowned you of.

"They also say you're armed and dangerous and probably on your way out of the country."

I licked my lips and tasted the salt of my sweat. "My backpack. Someone punched me in the stomach and stole it from me a couple days ago. It just had my gym clothes in it, so I didn't even report it to the police. Oh, fuck me. I'm being framed."

"If you say so," he said.

"I say so." It had to be Bartholomew behind it. He knew Zayvion and I were together. Zayvion had just quit. Violently. Bartholomew probably thought Zay would go to me for money and resources.

Either that, or it was Violet. Bartholomew might have convinced her that this was the best thing. For me, for her, and for the Authority.

Damn it to hell. I was sure Bartholomew had looked into our files. I was sure this had to be his doing.

Dad, in my head, shifted. He was angry, and that anger confirmed my suspicions.

Is he the kind of man to play hardball like this? I asked.

Bartholomew Wray, my dad said, *will do anything to get his way. Including destroying my company.*

And your family? I said. *Hello, I could be put into prison for this. Violet could lose her livelihood.*

Of course and my family, Dad growled. Then he did the mental version of slamming a door in my face. I could tell he was still angry. It felt like a headache.

"Ever been a fugitive before?" Jack asked.

"Not like this."

"Want any advice?"

"Probably not. Just take me to the den and drop me off. Then don't look for me, okay, Jack? Tell all the Hounds not to look for me. I'm going to do what I can to figure this out and to clear my name. I do not want to drag any of you down with me. As a matter of fact, I want you to vacate the den, scatter. Don't get caught and don't get questioned."

"For someone who hasn't been chased by the law before, you're doing pretty good so far."

He handed me a small package of wet wipes—the antibacterial kind. "Keep one of these in your palm when you touch things like door handles. Won't leave fingerprints, won't leave your scent behind. Don't cast magic. Don't use your cell phone. Don't use your credit cards."

"I thought I wasn't asking for your advice," I said, taking the wipes and putting one in the palm of my hand.

"I don't care. And we've already cleaned the den. No magic, no traces, no scents. But we aren't going to leave you behind. You're one of us."

I opened my mouth but he kept talking.

"I understand you're hot property right now. We'll give you room and we'll be careful. But we'll be in touch."

I nodded. No sense trying to talk logic with a Hound. Like I said, we're the loyal type. "I'll get in touch with you," I said. "When I can."

"Or if you need us," he replied. "For anything." He stopped in front of Get Mugged. "Good luck, Beckstrom," he said.

"You too, Quinn. See you soon." I got out of the car and he drove away.

I walked into Get Mugged. I didn't know what time it

was, maybe dinnertime. The place was almost empty, five people sitting at separate tables. None of them were Authority that I knew or remembered.

Grant was working behind the counter. I didn't see Jula or the other employee, Ryan, anywhere.

I walked over to Grant. "Hey," I said. "Large coffee, please, room for cream."

"Hey yourself," he said. Grant smiled, but he was not his normal happy self. Tense was a better description. "For here or to go?" he asked.

"To go," I said. I didn't know if any of the others had contacted him, and I hadn't had a chance to ask if we could get to the tunnels through his apartment.

"Can I—?" I started.

"—use the bathroom?" he asked. "Sure. It's down the hall, to the left. Use the stairs."

The bathroom was not to the left and down the stairs. It was at the end of the hall. The directions he had given me would take me to his apartment.

"Thank you," I said.

He held my gaze, and nodded. He knew I wasn't thanking him for the coffee, I was thanking him for letting us use his house, the tunnels, and his business as a cover.

"Anytime, girlfriend," he said.

I walked down the hall, which had both the middle and last lights burned out, conveniently throwing the door to Grant's apartment into darkness.

I tried the handle to his door, the sanitized wipe in my hand. The door was unlocked. I stepped through and closed it behind me.

I took the stairway down. Sure, Grant lived under an old brick building. But the man had a taste for expensive and fashionable and knew how to put old together with new to make the place more of a home than any of my apartments I'd ever had.

"Anyone home?" I asked quietly.

I heard footsteps, soft. Then Zayvion emerged from the shadows on the far side of the room. "This way," he said.

A rush of relief washed over me, but I didn't have time to think about it, didn't have time to give in to it, even though a whole lot of me wanted to run over and put my arms around him. "Good to see you, babe," I said.

"You too. Everything okay?" He pushed a wall panel aside, revealing a door. He opened it with a normal, non-magical key.

"Yes," I said. "Stotts doesn't believe me. So he's out."

Zay nodded. "Everyone's back here."

"What is this, a storage room?" There were boxes stacked and neatly labeled and a few pieces of furniture shrouded in dust covers, along with several framed paintings tucked on shelves and along the wall. A fixture in the ceiling—very industrial Art Deco—gave off enough light to see there was a low brick arch at the end of the room.

"Grant uses it for storage," Zay said. "It connects to the tunnels."

"How far?"

"He said he doesn't know and hasn't had time to fully explore it, though he did give me a map he's been working on over the years."

"All the tunnels lead to the shipyards, right?" I said. "I'm not sure how much getting to the river will help us."

"All the tunnels that the public knows about ran to the shipyards," he agreed. "The others were put in place by the Authority before Portland was even incorporated."

It figured the Authority even had their hands in the building of secret smuggler tunnels. "I don't suppose you have the Authority's map of that?" I asked.

He gave a frustrated sigh. "I do not. To the left."

I ducked under the archway and took the left branch of the tunnel. It was lit by the one bulb behind us. Zay clicked a flashlight and handed it to me.

A lot of dust. A lot of dirt. A lot of bricks and a tiny enclosed area. My own perfect little hell.

I worked on breathing evenly. It was going to be okay, the tunnels weren't going to collapse, weren't going to close in and trap me forever. I had lots of space, enough that I could put my arms out to either side if I wanted to and still not touch both walls.

One good thing—there wasn't a single flicker of magic down here so at least it didn't smell like rot. But this claustrophobia was going to undo me.

"Watch your step," Zay said softly. "It goes up, then takes a tight right."

Tight. Just what I wanted to hear.

I followed those directions and after the turn, which was more like a wall of stone that I had to squeeze around while not screaming, I was in an open living room–sized space lit by several lanterns.

Air. There was actually air.

Leaning against the walls or sitting on the floor were the people I'd come to love and trust. Victor, Maeve, Hayden, Shame. They had their weapons next to them.

I wondered why Terric wasn't here.

"Where's Terric?" I asked.

Shame rolled his eyes. "Not even a hello? Not even a hey, how about I split the money I embezzled with you?"

"I didn't embezzle any money," I said. "And hello."

I really wished I'd brought my coffee down here with me. It was cold, I didn't have my coat. I did recall I had a black beanie still in my hand, so I put that on.

"How is everyone?" I asked.

Victor was leaning against the stone wall farthest from me. Even in the low light of the lantern, I could tell how angry he was. He drummed his fingers on the arm of his dark coat and stared into one of the lanterns as if trying to focus on fleeting images. He was stiff-shouldered and furious.

I understood exactly how he felt. Losing memories was infuriating, and always left me feeling twitchy and vulnerable.

He also smelled like pain. I don't think Closing so recently, and Unclosing him so soon, had been done without him enduring some hurt.

Maeve sat on an old wooden milk crate pushed up against the wall. She had her eyes closed. From the flush of red across her cheeks, and the paleness of her skin, I knew she'd recently been in a lot of pain too.

Hayden sat next to her, his arm around her, watching Zay like he wanted to break the man.

Unclosing someone did not seem to be a gentle process.

"We're just dandy—can't you tell?" Shame finally said.

"Do we have a plan?" I asked. I looked at Victor, who rolled his head to one side and looked over at me like he had just noticed I'd walked in.

"Plan? No. We do not."

Whoa. Okay, he wasn't angry. He was scorching mad. But his anger didn't seem aimed at Zayvion. That was something at least.

There was no time to be guessing about who had hurt feelings about whom. Someone needed to call some shots. Looked like that someone was me.

"We need to trigger the filters on the cisterns," I said in full lecture mode that sounded so much like my father it made me want to gargle and spit. "Grant has a map of some of the tunnels. Does anyone know if any of the tunnels come out near a cistern?"

Nothing. Maeve shook her head.

I have a map of all the tunnels, Dad said. *And I know where all the cisterns are built. I can lead you to them.*

"Well, Dad says he knows all the tunnels and where the cisterns are."

Again the nods. I had never seen any of them so silent.

We'd been through battles, betrayals, death. We could get through this too.

"Can everyone use magic?" I asked.

"Yes," Zayvion said. "Except you."

"Right, so I'm not going to be any good to us during the actual work. Dad said it takes one user from each discipline to trigger the filters. Shame, you'll be Death magic, Maeve, Blood. Zay, Victor, Hayden, which of you wants to take Faith, Life, and Flux?"

They were all Closers, and Faith magic would be their strength. I was just hoping they had done some cross-training in the other disciplines.

Victor cleared his throat. "I can handle Life. Zayvion, you should take Faith. You'll have a steadier hand than me right now. And Hayden, you can cast Flux, can't you?"

"It's been a few years, but yes," the big man said. "What spells are we using and where?"

"Good question," I said. "We can't hit every cistern. We'll have to hit the one that will do the most good. And quickly. Bartholomew is already looking for us—well, for me. Thoughts?"

"Why don't you ask your da?" Shame said. "I'm sure the old bastard has plenty of good ideas."

"There has to be a central cistern that can affect the largest area of the city," I said. Then, *Dad? Any ideas?*

He was quick to answer. *The mid cistern holds nearly half of all the magic used in Portland.*

Can we get there through the tunnels? I asked.

He paused a moment, calculating. *Yes. To the right at the next junction.*

"Dad said the mid cistern holds half the magic in the city. We can get to it through the tunnels."

I grabbed one of the lanterns and started walking.

I heard them all get to their feet. Then the swing of lantern light against the walls and ceiling told me they were following. Good.

"So," Shame said, coming up beside me. "Losing all your money puts you in a bossy mood, doesn't it?"

"People dying puts me in a bossy mood," I said.

"Do you know where we're going?"

I shook my head. "Dad knows. He thinks the mid cistern will do the most good."

"Sure, but that's miles from here." He lowered his voice. "Don't know how well Mum will hold up on a hike. Victor either, since the Unclosing."

"I could tell them to stay behind," I said.

"They wouldn't listen," he said.

We were quiet for a bit, only the sound of our muffled footsteps interrupting the silence. Even though we were under the city, I didn't hear any city noise at all.

"So did your da tell you anything else about the filters?" Shame asked.

"No."

"Maybe you should ask him what spells we'll have to work."

Dad? I asked.

He pressed at my lips and it felt like a person putting their finger on my mouth as if to hush me. Weird. But I knew what he was asking. To let him use my mouth to speak.

No, I said. *You tell me, I'll tell them.*

I was so not going to let him use my body if I could help it.

Something as intricate as the filtering system can't just be explained in a single sentence.

But instead of going over it word by word, he sort of opened his memory for me. The knowledge of what the filters were made out of, the tests that had been run, the failures, the adjustments and redesigns until he had incorporated the correct material and spells to hold magic latent, but fresh for the using—it all flooded through me.

"It's kind of complicated," I said, sorting the information. "The trigger actually sets off receptive spells in the other cisterns, so triggering one should trigger the others. All the receptive spells are worked in the lead, glass, and iron of the lines. The magic in those spells is latent, like the disks. I think triggering the filter is a one-shot thing."

It is. Unless someone knows how to recharge the spells, Dad said.

"Spells are Unlock, Cleanse, Element, Ground, and Flow." I thought about it. I only knew half of those. "Does everyone know those spells?"

"Say them again," Zayvion said from the farthest back in the tunnel.

I repeated the list.

"We know them," Hayden said.

I took the right, and another left. We'd been walking maybe fifteen minutes.

"So why isn't Terric here?" I asked Shame.

"We couldn't contact him," he said.

"What do you mean?"

"He's not dead," Shame said, even though that wasn't what I had assumed. "I'd know. He's either gone turncoat and is Bartholomew's boot licker, or he's . . . unconscious."

"Can you feel him?" I asked.

He was quiet for a little while. "Only that he's not dead. Maybe he took off. Left town. I'd do it if I were in his shoes."

This is it, Dad said. *Allie, stop.*

I stopped. The tunnel opened up a little to maybe half again as wide. It felt like I could breathe here, which was a nice change.

There's a Gate spell in the ceiling, Dad said.

I looked up. "Holy shit."

Everyone held up their lanterns, and simultaneously pulled on their favorite spells and weapons.

In the wash of lantern light, the brick walls arched up into a grayish ceiling. Carved into that stone was a glyph.

"Gate," Zayvion said, coming to look more closely at it. "But it's not finished. There." He pointed at a line on the outside curve that looked like someone had cut it in half.

"Will it work?" I asked.

Zayvion shook his head. "Hell if I know."

Victor walked over to it, and so did Hayden. I stepped back and let the experts get a good look. Didn't look like any of the experts had ever seen something like this.

You carved a Gate into the Shanghai tunnels? I asked Dad.

Yes.

Does it work? How does it work? Where does it go?

Yes. Blood magic. To the cistern.

"It takes Blood magic," I said.

"Let me see." Maeve walked over, her limp still fairly pronounced, but not as bad as I had feared. She walked directly under the spell, then turned a circle.

"Blood magic will seal the glyph, pull the magic from the networks into it, and open the gate," she said. "Do you know where it leads, Allie?"

"Dad says it leads to the cistern."

Zay nodded. "It's in the correct alignment."

"Can you open it, Zay?" I asked.

He nodded again. He pulled a knife out of his belt and opened his left hand.

It has to be your blood, Allison, Dad said.

"Wait," I said. "Why?"

"Why what?" Zayvion asked.

"Sorry. It gets confusing whether I should be talking

to Dad or talking out loud. He said it has to be my blood."

Because I coded it with my blood, he said. *It has to be Beckstrom blood that triggers it, or it won't work.*

"Beckstrom blood," I said, walking forward and offering my left hand.

Zayvion studied my face. "Are you sure?" he asked so quietly I didn't even think the others could hear him.

I nodded. "Let's get this done."

Zayvion put his left arm around my waist, maybe so he could hold me up if I decided to pass out from magic being used with my blood.

Dad shifted in my head, curious, and wanting a front-row seat to see exactly what would happen.

I braced my feet and hips so if I did fall, it would be into Zay. "Do it," I said.

Zay's knife was small and razor sharp. The pain was quick, hot, and then only a sweet aching focus of sensation remained. Zayvion chanted, catching up my blood and balancing it in the grooves of the knife blade as he carved out the glyph for opening the Gate.

The sweet, sweet smell of cherries filled my nose, my mouth, my throat as Zayvion's voice poured into me, thrumming. My blood warmed and raced a hot pulse, faster and faster until I was hot, dizzy. I was stretched, caught, drawn out. My nerves followed every stroke, every word, every line of magic Zayvion drew with the point of the knife. And when he set magic free to pour through the glyph, I followed with it.

Everything went white . . . and then the darkness crashed down around me like a wave.

Chapter Eighteen

"**A**llie?" Zay called. I opened my eyes.

"Stay with me." His eyes were pure gold, the pupil gone bronze. He held me tightly against him, both arms wrapped around me to keep me on my feet. I was so hypersensitive to magic, I could feel the drops of blood, my blood, falling off the knife he still had clenched in his hand against the small of my back where the gun was safely tucked in my pants.

The cut Zayvion had left on my hand echoed sweet discomfort with each pulse of my heart and a deep, primal part of me wanted him to do it again. There was a reason Blood magic was addictive.

"I'm here." I smiled, or tried to. "Still here. Did we make it?"

He nodded and released me carefully as if expecting I'd fall if he weren't touching some part of me.

But I was good with pain. I knew how to compartmentalize it, knew how to deal with it. Only after Zay let me go did I realize it wasn't just me hurting. He was hurting too.

And I knew why. Since he was no longer a part of the Authority, he had to Proxy his own pain when he used magic. Oh, I suppose he could still Proxy the price of using magic, but Bartholomew was smart enough to have some sort of trace that could track that price back to Zay.

And since Zayvion was a deserter who had very much gone against orders, that meant we were all on our own as far as casting magic. As much pain as we each could endure would be as much magic as we could use.

Fair enough. That's how Hounds used magic every day.

I took stock of our surroundings. We were in a warehouse with hard electric light pouring down from the tall ceiling. It was so well lit, it took me a second to figure out that we were still underground. And in the center of the room was the cistern.

It didn't look like a tree. It looked like a huge ball, about one story tall and wide, with carvings worked in iron and lead and glass surrounding it to create a truly stunning piece of art. Spinning from the top of it in an almost joyous arc of metal were glyphwork pipes—very similar to the Beckstrom storm rods. These pipes fitted into the walls and ceiling, and the light caught against them in corners and edges, sparking metallic tones like beveled jewels.

It was beautiful.

I felt like I was standing in the middle of a sculptor's lifetime masterpiece.

Thank you, Dad said quietly in my mind.

So how do we do this? I asked.

Allison, he began as if knowing I would not want to hear what he was going to say. *It would be easiest if you let me speak through you. I could give the information once, and it would be done.*

"Well, Beckstrom?" Shame asked. "What's the plan?"

"I'm going to let Dad tell you."

Dad moved forward and took what felt like the passenger's side of my brain. Even though he had enough reach to speak, I could still talk if I wanted to. It was strange. But kind of nice compared to most of the other times I'd willingly shared my body with him.

"You will all need to stand a safe distance away.

Here." He nudged me and I pointed to a metal platform that was about ten steps off the ground and to our left. "The pipes run through every inch of this room, and I do not know when they were last tested for weaknesses. The platform is Warded and set as a null. It is the safest place in the room to use magic."

Everyone walked over to the platform and took the steps up to it.

I followed and stood behind them. There was room for twenty or more people on the platform.

"The filter shouldn't be difficult to trigger," he continued. "You can stand a distance from each other, and cast your spell: Unlock, Cleanse, Element, Ground, and Flow. As each of those spells is cast and maintained, the cistern will open and reveal a control panel. Once that happens, Allison will be able to manually trigger the filters."

"What?" I said. "Wait. It's me, Allie. So there's a switch that has to be flipped by hand? That's it?"

"What did you expect?" he answered through my mouth. "Magic?"

Okay, I was not going to get into an argument with my own mouth.

"Where's the switch?" Zayvion asked.

"On the cistern," he answered. "At the base. Allison will be able to see it clearly."

"No," Zay said. "I'll do it. You—she won't stay conscious with that much magic being used."

"Yes," I said. "Hold on, it's me, Allie, again. I'll be fine, Zay. If the cistern is working right, the only magic I'll feel is the spells you each cast, and mostly I'll just smell them unless you throw them at me. The cistern holds magic, it isn't made of magic."

"And how are you going to fight off the Veiled if they come crawling up out of it?" he asked.

Oh. I hadn't thought of that.

"What do the Veiled have to do with this?" Victor asked.

"The tainted magic drew them up through the other cistern," Zayvion said. "We trigger the cistern and it's very likely we'll have a room full of mutated Veiled who soak up defensive spells."

"We can do this fast," I said. "Out at the other cistern you were trying to open it up to look at the magic it contained. All we're doing here is opening the control panel, not opening the actual cistern."

"So," Shame said, "your da didn't think maybe a key or a code would have been enough to get into this thing? He had to have five different magic users with five different spells to open up a fuse box? Overkill much?"

"The control panel does more than just trigger the filters," Dad said. "It is how any and all changes to the system are made. Each cistern has such a device, and there is a master. They all take the same five disciplines to open. It is a way of limiting who and how the magic throughout the entire city can be accessed."

"All right, fine," Shame said. "Enough with the history lesson. Let's get this shit done." He dug a cigarette out of his pocket and lit it.

Dad rankled at that. He very much did not like being told what to do by Shame. I was pretty sure Shame knew that.

"This is Allie," I said, trying to head off a fight between Dad and Shame. "Everyone know what to do?" They nodded and stepped apart far enough that each of them had room to cast without their spells colliding.

"Then let's begin," I said.

There was a moment of silence as they each cleared their mind of distraction. For the first time since I'd been in the Authority, I watched them all draw a Disbursement for pain. All of them except Shame chose a long, slow burn of pain instead of the short, fast, hard pain I always opted for. Slow burn didn't work for Hounds. You'd forget how many types of pain you were enduring over the months, take pain meds to cut the worst of it, and pretty soon you'd cast one spell too many, take one pill too many and you'd be dead.

And then they cast.

It was beautiful.

Hayden sliced lines through the air with the edge of his hand, sending out a mercury symbol that pulsed with sparks of gold. Maeve drew just a drop of blood from her pinky, and even though her hand trembled, her casting was strong and true, spooling magic and blood.

Victor, who was one of the most precise magic casters I'd ever seen, fumbled with the spell, canceled it, and cast again, his face a mask of concentration, his hands moving as if he expected magic to burn. But his spell was true, and magic flooded the glyph, liquid, strong.

Shame sucked the heat out of his cigarette, drawing the energy from the burning tobacco, and poured that energy into the first knotted ropes of his spell. He exhaled smoke, and drew the smoke in with his fingers toward his heart, toward the crystal embedded in his chest, and withdrew the soft pink-white energy from the crystal outward, binding, wrapping, and cinching the spell tight.

Zayvion burned with silver and black fire as he worked magic, calm, confident. He cut a spell into the air, and magic leaped at his command to fill it.

Lines, ribbons, fire, smoke, light, and ebony darkness formed from the fingertips of each user and twisted into a stunning expression of art and power. Each spell reached out, growing until it wrapped around the cistern. The metal and glass storage and pipes hummed like plucked strings, creating one harmonic chord.

I only wished it smelled as nice as it looked.

Now, Allison, Dad said. *The control panel.*

I jogged to the cistern. The control panel seemed to appear in front of it. I knew it hadn't appeared, but the five spells had somehow uncloaked it. Impressive since I hadn't even seen the cloaking spell.

No buttons, no switches. There were finely wrought glyphs worked in lead, iron, and glass. I'd never seen any of those glyphs in my life.

"Which one?" I asked, probably out loud, though I couldn't hear my voice over the sustained note that filled the room and seemed to be growing larger and larger as Zay and the others directed more and more magic into their spells. There was no way this was going to go unnoticed.

There are Mute spells in the walls, floor, and ceiling around us, Dad said. *But there are also sensors on each cistern that will trigger this event. Quickly.*

Dad showed me which three I'd need to press, all at the same time.

I pressed them.

And was blown back off my feet. I hit something solid with my back and screamed, then threw my arms in front of my face to ward off the blast of light.

No, not light. Magic.

Magic gushed out of the cistern like a broken fire hydrant, flying in all directions, cutting, burning, burrowing into walls and ceiling with squid-like tendrils.

And inside all that magic were the Veiled. Caught in a trance, drunk on power, the Veiled rose by the dozens, wide mouths open, gulping down magic and becoming more and more solid.

Shit.

I got to my feet, yelling at the pain that shattered through my spine as I did.

"What happened?" I yelled at Dad as I limped over to the platform.

He hesitated just half a second. But in the half second

I could see the thousands of possibilities that rolled through his mind. *The master control panel,* he said. *Someone wired it to open the cistern if it were accessed. Someone sabotaged my technology.* Dad was raging.

"Who?" I yelled. The Veiled hadn't noticed me yet. I couldn't see Zay or anyone else on the platform. They were trapped behind a protection wall of a spell that looked like it'd been built to withstand the apocalypse.

Good thing too.

Dad bit off the name like it was a curse: *Bartholomew Wray.*

It made sense that the head of the Authority would have access to the master control panels of the cisterns in the city. But Wray couldn't have approved this. Releasing the Veiled, pouring this much poisoned magic unchecked into the city would kill so many people. This had to be an inside job. Someone angry enough at Bartholomew to want him to fail.

Just a couple hours ago, I was on that list. Might still be, but I'd never do this.

"I have to stop it," I said. "Can I override the break here? Can I shut this cistern down?"

Not if it's been opened at the master control. It has to be shut down there first.

"Where? Where's the master?"

Not here. Too far to get to in time. That protection around the platform won't hold for long.

Which was a problem. Already the Veiled were turning my way, as if noticing a nice dessert to top off their feast. Other Veiled were starting toward the platform, clawing at walls, heading toward the tunnels. They were very soon to be a shuffling, hungry mass of bitty poison loose on the streets.

Holy shit.

We have to stop it, close it. Now.

Dad ran through possibilities again, and I was almost

drowned in the flood of options he sorted. I didn't know why he was suddenly so open to me, but I didn't care. I just hoped he had an idea that would work.

There is a disk, an old prototype, he said in a rush. *I set it as a monitor. For fluctuations in the crossover flow and ebb from the wells to the networks. If it hasn't been tampered with it's on the north wall.* And behind that was his anger and righteous indignation that anyone would massacre his inventions.

Which way is north? I asked.

That way. He nudged the back of my eyes, which felt really weird. Behind the platform, away from the cistern and Veiled.

Good enough.

I ran. *Where?* I thought. *Up, down? I could really use a hot/cold right about now.*

I didn't have to ask. It was hanging at about head level, a beautifully wrought iron, lead, and glass frame plate thing with two double crystals in opposite corners. The crystals were pinkish blue, just like the one I'd found on the shelf in his office back in his labs, the one that was now currently in Shame's chest.

I tugged it off the wall, distantly registering the ridiculousness of it being hung up by nothing more than a nail and some wire.

Now what? I asked him.

Remove the bottom crystal. There is a button you can push.

I did so and the bottom crystal fell into my hand.

Put that in your pocket, you'll need it for your return.

Return? I thought this was going to close the cistern, I said.

This is tied to the master control. It will take you there, and you can shut this down. You'll need to trigger it much like the disks. It is crude, far less refined than the disks since it's an earlier version and may be . . . uncomfortable.

Don't care. What spell do I use?

Light.

Okay, that didn't make any damn sense, but I wasn't going to argue.

I dropped the extra crystal in my pocket and pulled out the gun, taking the safety off. I didn't know what kind of situation I'd be dropping into at the master control. Better to go shooty end out.

I hugged the framed crystal to my chest.

Let me draw the glyph, Dad said. *There's a better chance that my using magic won't knock you unconscious.* Then, gently, *Please.*

Yes, I said. *Do it.*

He pushed forward in my mind and motioned me back. I didn't like being that far out of control of my body, but I understood he was trying to put distance between me and the magic. I could still see out of my eyes, but I couldn't feel my body, my arms, or any of the rest of me.

Dad drew the glyph with the point of the gun, and magic rushed into it like water following a streambed.

What did you know? He did draw Light.

A thunderclap shattered the world. I felt something heavy wrap around me like a thick blanket between me and the spell. It was Dad. My dad, protecting me from the backlash of magic.

And then I was standing in an office. An office I recognized, facing a familiar desk with a familiar man behind it.

Bartholomew Wray.

"Hello, Daniel," he said. "I was wondering when you'd answer my calling card."

Chapter Nineteen

Dad immediately fell back from the control of my body. He'd taken the brunt of the pain. I hadn't expected him to do that, to jump between me and magic, to keep me safe. Although I stung from head to foot like I had the worst sunburn ever, I was clear-minded, and not at all sick.

"Where's the master control for the cisterns?" I asked, ignoring his comment.

"Why?"

"The cisterns have been booby-trapped," I said. "Magic and the Veiled—both tainted—are gushing out of the cisterns and will hit the streets any minute. You don't even need to get anyone together to investigate it. All you have to do is look out that window. People are dying and more are going to die. The Veiled are going to bite them, infect them, possess them. And if we don't use the master control to shut down the filters and close the cistern, you're going to be blamed for Portland tuning into a hellscape."

He glanced from my face down to the gun in my hand and gave me a very thin smile.

"I think you can put that down now, Ms. Beckstrom. You're not going to use it. We both know that."

I lifted it. "No. We both don't know that. Where are the controls?"

"Why don't you ask your father?" He smiled when I

didn't say anything. "Or don't the two of you talk anymore? He never was fond of you, Allie. Not since you almost got him killed.

"I can still see it. Him standing there, you all but dead, bleeding in his arms. You were so small. And he was so very, very desperate. He made me promises, Allison. Promises that he would not continue to develop technology and magic and bring his advances to the notice of the Authority. Promises that he would side with me and stand against the Authority approving of the masses 'discovering' magic. Promises that would have made me head of the Authority. Promises he did not keep."

My dad betraying someone was not news to me. But I had no idea what he was saying about me being hurt when I was little. When had that happened? And why had Dad gone to Bartholomew? What could Wray have done to help me that my dad couldn't do?

All questions that needed answers. But not now. Not yet.

"I don't give a damn about what he promised you years ago. People are dying. Right now. Where are the controls?"

"Over there." He gestured to one side of the room.

The controls may have been there once. Now there was a podium that looked a lot like the control panel back at the cistern. But it was burned down to slag, like a very small, very precise bomb had gone off in the middle of it.

"You see," Bartholomew said, "I believe there should be a full and total changeover in the Authority. And not just Portland's Authority. In how the organization is run worldwide. I believe the best way to begin that is to kick the support out from under the people in power, so we can start fresh."

"You can't do this," I said with a lot more calm than the horror that was creeping down my spine. "You can't let hundreds of men, women, and children die. If we don't stop the Veiled, and the poisoned magic pouring through every network and line and storm rod out there, you will have the deaths of thousands on your hands."

"My hands? No. Not at all." He leaned back in his chair, a thoughtful frown on his face, as if we were discussing the state of the weather.

"It is Daniel Beckstrom's cistern designs that have failed. It is Daniel Beckstrom's network of lines and conduits that have failed. It is his technology that has failed. And these deaths, tragic though they are"—he shook his head with mock gravity—"will be the beginning of the real change. Magic will be outlawed. It will be deemed too dangerous for any to use. And then it will be back in our hands. My hands. The hands of the Authority. That has always been the right way, the true way."

Dad had gone so angry, he was silent. The kind of silence I'd experienced from him only a couple times in my life. Usually right before he destroyed someone.

The horror that had crept over me while he was talking was fading, leaving behind nothing but hatred.

"Ah, perhaps you are beginning to understand what your betrayal has cost you, Daniel," he went on. "I have everything you love. Your business, which I have torn apart from the inside out. Your daughter here, alone and I believe wanted by the law, and your beautiful young wife and her technology. In time, I may raise your son. Boy needs a father."

Dad lashed out in my mind. But there was nothing he could do. No way he could harm Bartholomew or make him stop what he had already done.

"I even have your city," Bartholomew said. "I am the head of the Authority, not you. Your bid for that position was destroyed all those years ago. When your unexpected and unwanted daughter forced you to make deals. Deals that strangled your plans, your power.

"Such a funny thing, fate. You are dead, killed by Sedra and her men, and I have made my *damned*—" He seemed to catch himself on that outburst and tugged a smile into place instead, his voice lowering. "—damned slow rise to the top. To a position of power. Real power. I am above you, Daniel Beckstrom. I am the one who will decide who will have magic and how it will be used. And if this entire city falls for my need to prove that I am right, so be it. It is just one town."

I raised the gun. Aimed at his head. "Tell me you're going to do something to stop the massacre out there."

"Why would I do that? Their deaths serve my purpose and the greater purpose of the Authority."

For a moment, everything seemed perfectly clear to me. He was killing innocent civilians. He was killing Davy. He was killing Zayvion, Shame, Maeve, Victor, and Hayden. That had been his plan all along. Destroy the Authority, destroy the technology, destroy Portland. So he could have power over us all. Power over magic. Power to decide who could and couldn't live. Power to rebuild the Authority in his image.

"Allison, put the gun down. I've read your files," he said softly. "I know you're not a killer."

He was right. I wasn't a killer, though I'd ended two other men's lives—Lon Tragger for killing Pike, and the convict, Jakob Single. But I'd fought them, magic-to-magic, blade-to-blade. They'd had a chance to defend themselves. I didn't think I could squeeze the trigger while staring into the eyes of another human being.

Dad? I asked.

This is your choice, Allie, he said with a gentleness I did not expect. *Your life and your decision. I'll stand with you no matter what you do.*

I wasn't a killer. But Bartholomew was. He was killing my friends. Killing hundreds of people. Killing everyone in Portland, if that's what it took. The police didn't believe me. The other members of the Authority didn't believe me. There was no one to stop him. Except me.

"It's not in your makeup to kill," Bartholomew said.

Maybe it wasn't. Or maybe he was wrong about me.

"People change."

I pulled the trigger.

The gun had a hell of a kick, much more than I'd expected. The bullet left streamers of magic behind as it raced to his head.

Hit him in the middle of his forehead. Right above his shocked expression. His neck snapped back and his body filled with a dark red flash of light. The spell on the bullet burned him from the inside out.

Then he wasn't smiling anymore. He wasn't talking anymore. He wasn't breathing anymore.

A small part of me was screaming, terrified by what I'd just done, the decision I'd just made. Too bad. I closed those emotions away behind a thick wall. I would deal with them later. What mattered now was shutting down that cistern.

I walked over to the master control. It was destroyed.

Bartholomew's men would be here any minute. I was surprised they hadn't already burst through the door.

Do you have another option? I asked Dad.

Dad was quiet. Surprised.

I grabbed hold of him in my head and squeezed until he noticed. Then a little harder until he knew I was not fucking around.

Is there any other thing here that will close the damn cisterns?

Dad stepped forward in my head and looked around the office. *Take the box on the bottom shelf.*

I jogged to that side of the room and picked up the little metal box. Felt like it was made of lead.

What is it?

But Dad didn't have a chance to answer. The door

burst open and two of Bartholomew's goons stood there, spells at the ready.

Magic is fast. Bullets are faster.

I fired off two shots, missed.

The goons ducked behind either side of the door. They'd throw magic any minute.

The crystal, Dad said. *Put it in the frame.*

I crouched down behind the desk and the burnt husk of Bartholomew's body. My hands were steady as I tugged the crystal out of my pocket and snapped it into the bottom of the frame. The top crystal was blackened and shattered. Must be good for only one trip.

The window behind me banged open.

I pivoted with the gun.

Stone stuck his head into the room, ears back, teeth bared. Angry gargoyle.

What the hell was he doing here climbing on this building?

"Go," I said. "Go home."

Stone dropped down next to me and took a step toward the door and the goons. They'd kill him and grind him into gravel.

Fuck this. I caught his back leg and held on.

Cast, I ordered Dad. *Now.*

I stepped back, he stepped forward. He cast Light.

Thunderclap. Pain. Light.

And I was crouched near the platform by the cistern. There were hundreds of Veiled now. So many, they filled the room. Claustrophobia clotted in my throat and I gasped to get a breath down. Zayvion, Shame, and the others were no longer trapped on the platform. They were on the floor, doing battle, killing Veiled, but not as quickly as they rose out of the cistern.

They couldn't hold out much longer. I could feel Zayvion's exhaustion and pain roll through me like an undertow, pulling at my strength. His movements were still strong, his spells hard and fast, but he couldn't do this forever.

Hayden was in the thick of it with Zayvion, wielding a broadsword and chanting. His voice bellowed a deep bass over the screams of the Veiled he set on fire with every slice of his blade.

Maeve was standing with her back to a wall, bleeding from both hands and cutting down the Veiled with magic in one hand and her whip in the other.

Victor was beside her, lightning shattering off his katana as he killed Veiled after Veiled, clean, concise. He was covered in sweat, and his arms shook.

Shame was swearing. Every spell he drew, every glyph he set loose upon the Veiled pounded like a hammer of his anger and hatred. The crystal burned black and hot from the center of his chest, and his eyes burned dark with death.

The control panel, Dad said.

Stone snarled and tore into the Veiled that rushed me. They struck him like a swarm of bees, sucking at the magic that powered him. Stone slashed with claws, fangs, and wings, shredding them into blackened ribbons of magic that fell to scorch the floor. But with each kill he was moving slower. The Veiled were draining him. And soon he'd be nothing but a statue.

I ran to the control panel.

I thought you said it couldn't be shut down here, I said to Dad.

We're going to override it. With force. There. He indicated the far right glyph. *Shoot it.*

I took aim. Fired. Missed. Heard Shamus yell. Didn't risk looking over at him.

Deep breath. Concentrate on where I needed the bullet to hit. Fired again. Hit it this time.

A flash of red—the same flash of red that had devoured Bartholomew—flooded the room.

Veiled screamed and burned and were gone. The gout of magic pouring out of the cistern slowed to a thin stream, then stopped completely, as if a door had been slammed against it. Red magic fell to the floor like ruby hail.

The cistern looked like a piece of art again, metal and glass, angle and curve. No magic.

It was suddenly very, very quiet in the room, except for the sound of our breathing.

I turned away from the control panel. Everyone was looking at me.

Stone paced over and stood beside me, his wing caught up on my shoulder, his ears still pitched back as if he expected a fight.

Zayvion wiped the sweat off his face with the sleeve of his coat. I noticed his nose was bleeding. "What did you do?" he asked. "Where did you go?"

"I went to the master control and tried to shut the cistern down there, but I couldn't. So I came back here and overrode the controls with my gun."

There was so much more. So much more that I had done. Let my father use magic and my body. Followed his plan, his advice. Made up my own mind and killed Bartholomew in cold blood. But I didn't say any of it. Because none of that mattered.

I was on borrowed time. Wanted for embezzling from Beckstrom Enterprises. Soon I'd be up on charges of murder. Those goons back at Bartholomew's office weren't dead. They'd seen me there. They'd likely seen what was left of their boss too.

I was a dead woman walking.

"Here's what we're going to do," I said. "We are going to go streetside and see what kind of damage that flood of magic has done."

"What about the filters?" Maeve asked, wiping her blood blade on her slacks.

"I don't think filters are going to take care of this

problem now. It's too late. The entire city has been infected. What we can do now is let the civilians know that they can't use magic. And trace the poison back to the source. I'm thinking the wells might be where the poison began, but I'm open to ideas."

"Why the wells?" Hayden asked.

"Natural source of magic," I answered. "Lots of shit happening around them lately. Veiled rising out of the Death well, Veiled rising out of the Blood well, Leander and Isabelle doing their sacrifices over the Life well."

Something niggled at the back of my mind. A memory. Strangely, it was Dad who caught it like a thread in his fingers and reeled it in for me.

Leander and Isabelle had done more than sacrifice people over the Life well. They'd done something right at the end of our battle with them—thrown some kind of spell at the well. I'd seen it; I just didn't know what it had meant at the time.

"They poisoned it," I said.

Shame was trying to light a cigarette with shaking hands. "Who poisoned what?"

"Leander and Isabelle," I said. "When we were fighting them. At the end." I tried to dredge up the memory. I had been pulled out of my body and was in a world of pain. Maybe I hadn't seen it right. "Did anyone else see them cast magic at the well before they disappeared?"

Victor and Maeve and Hayden all looked at Zay, Shame, and me. The three of us were the only ones who had been there.

"I wasn't conscious of anything but pain," Shame said. "Z?"

Zayvion's gaze held mine. His eyes were gold, hot, with fractured lines of black. He ached from head to foot, but didn't let it show on the outside. And he was worried for me. Maybe even frightened of me. He didn't let that show either. But he didn't have to.

"I saw them throw a spell. I don't know if it was at the well. Allie—"

"It's something to start with," I said, cutting him off. "Let's get the hell out of here before someone comes to investigate the breach." I strode off toward the tunnel, Stone beside me.

After an extended pause, I heard footsteps follow.

What's the fastest way to the surface? I asked Dad.

Stairs at the left of this tunnel. Elevator if you'd rather.

I nodded, even though Dad couldn't see me nod. I felt like I was strangely out of body and at the same time rooted in deep. After what I'd done today, being afraid of an elevator seemed really trivial.

The elevator was right where he said it would be. I keyed in the combination Dad told me, and the heavy steel doors slid open. I stepped in, distantly noting that it was a small elevator and the seven of us were going to have a tight squeeze, especially with Stone.

Everyone stepped in. No one said anything. The scent of pain and rotted magic was thick in the tight space. I tried not to care about any of it.

Shame hit the button, and I watched the door close.

Chapter Twenty

The elevator opened in a parking garage that must have been near a restaurant. I smelled the thick beef broth of onion soup.

We all filed out, looking like refugees of a war zone.

I was the last to leave the elevator. Stone was waiting for me. "You, go home. Go find Cody. Go fade into bricks," I said.

He cooed at me, ears pricked up. He sounded worried. Stupid gargoyle.

"Hide."

That, he seemed to understand. He pushed his head against my thigh, hard enough I almost lost my balance, then trotted off, slipping between cars like a concrete shadow.

"Allie," Zay said.

"We'll need to take a look at magic in the city," I said, purposely walking away from his reach. "We might need more weapons."

"Weapons?" Victor asked. "Why?"

"I killed Bartholomew."

No one said anything. The silence settled between us, heavy, thick. I waited for their judgment. Not that it would change anything I'd done.

"Well, that's the best damn news I've had all day,"

Shame announced. "Gonna tell us the why and the how of it? Spare no detail."

"He told me he wanted to destroy the Authority. He told me he broke open the cisterns so that the tainted magic could kill people, so that the technology would be deemed unsafe and magic would be restricted. He said that's what he intended all along. To become head of the Authority here in Portland, to destroy my father's company and technology by any means possible, and to secure a position of power."

"Do you have proof of that?" Victor asked quietly.

"No."

All I had was a gun, a lead box, and a death sentence on my head. "His men should have discovered the body by now. I'm assuming they'll be sending people out to hunt us. Hunt me."

"Did anyone see you?" Zayvion asked.

I nodded. "It might be in each of your best interests not to be anywhere near me."

"That's not going to happen," Victor said. "We have all broken with the Authority. We are all fugitives. We do this together."

"Do what, exactly?" Hayden asked.

"Cleanse magic," I said, "and make it safe for the common user. Kill the Veiled so they aren't spreading the poison."

Hayden studied me a minute. Then he nodded. "All things I'd stand behind. But let me offer another option: leave this city while we still can."

"Won't matter where we go," I said. "They'll find us. And there isn't any other person in the world trying to fix this."

"Six of us against at least a couple thousand?" Shame said. "Sounds like fun." Then he spun and looked behind him. At the man walking our way.

"Seven of us," Terric said. He pointed to a van. "I don't know what you've been doing, but every member of the Authority is out looking for you."

"Including you?" I asked.

"Yes. But I'm on your side." He walked closer, and stopped. I could see Shame's shoulders relax. I could see the energy from Terric pouring clean and strong into Shame. Terric being close to him gave him strength. Even the crystal in his chest seemed to stop burning as hot.

"I have an unmarked van," Terric said.

I nodded. We couldn't jog this city for the rest of the night. Especially not Maeve, she was already leaning heavily on Hayden's arm just to stay standing.

"That works," I said. I started off toward the van and everyone fell into step. Terric walked next to Shame, and I noticed he put his hand on Shame's shoulder—a buddy-buddy kind of touch. Shame did not shrug him away.

Zay walked beside me, very careful not to touch me, just looking straight ahead. I suddenly craved his touch. Wanted his arms around me, wanted him to tell me everything was going to be okay.

But those words would just be pretty lies. And I had too much ugly reality to deal with right now.

"Anyone have a stash of weapons we can raid?" I asked.

"I might have a few things tucked away," Shame said. Why was I not surprised?

"Somewhere the Authority won't look?" I asked.

"Probably," he said. "But I've been thinking. That gun of yours is more than decent, and it's untraceable."

He didn't say any more. Didn't have to. I knew right where he was going with this. Eli Collins. He had tech and a ready hatred of the Authority. He might be someone we wanted on our side.

"Terric, do they know you've defected?" I asked.

"I didn't see any reason to inform anyone," he said. "Besides, things are in a bit of an . . . upheaval."

I supposed they were. I wondered who would pull rank and take over the Authority. Jingo Jingo maybe?

"Can I borrow your phone?" I asked.

He stepped up and gave it to me, then opened the van for us. Hayden took the front seat. I waited as everyone else got settled in the back.

Zay waited too.

I dialed Bea's number.

"Bea Lufkin," she answered.

"This is Allie. Just tell me where Collins took Davy."

Hounds have sensitive ears. She would've known if it was someone faking my voice.

"He's below the water tower on the east side. Good to hear from you. There's a price on your head. Police."

"How much?"

"Not enough any of us would turn you in for it."

"Thanks," I said, and I meant it. "Stay safe. I'll contact you soon."

"You'd better. Luck." She hung up.

I deleted the call from Terric's record.

Zayvion had been standing there listening to the conversation.

"Getting in?" I asked.

He wrapped his arms around me and I caught my breath at how hard he held me. I tucked my face into his shoulder and for a moment I was home, safe, whole again.

Then I pushed away. "We need to find weapons," I said.

"Yes," he said, gently tucking my hair behind my ear. "*We* do. *Together*," he emphasized.

"For as long as we can be," I said.

"Forever." Flat. Uncompromising.

I held on to that promise, and gave it back to him. "Forever."

And then I climbed into the van. Zayvion stepped in behind me. I took his hand, sliding my fingers between his, and did not let go.

Read on for an exciting excerpt from Devon Monk's next Allie Beckstrom novel,

MAGIC WITHOUT MERCY

Coming in April 2012 from Roc

I had a headache. That headache's name was Shamus Flynn.

"Allie, my love," he said, earning a quick glare from Zayvion, who was sitting cross-legged on the floor in front of the fireplace, dragging a whetstone along the edge of his katana. "I'm telling you, you're best off with a projectile weapon. You can't use magic anymore, so you'll have to keep a certain distance from the fight. Get in too close, and magic will eat you alive. Then it will eat you dead just for good measure."

"I don't want a gun," I repeated.

"Come, now," he coaxed. "Look at all the pretty options."

Options was an understatement. When Shame had told us he had a small stash of weapons that the Authority didn't know about, his only omission was how damn many blades, cudgels, whips, sticks, pointed things, explosive devices, and guns he had squirreled away in the rickety three-story townhouse bolted into the cliffside.

Seriously. I flinched every time he lit a cigarette.

"Shamus," his mother, Maeve, said from where she was resting on the couch in what might have been a comfortable modern living room before Shame covered the walls, bookshelves, and entertainment center with both magical and nonmagical killing devices. "If she doesn't want a gun, don't trouble her so about it. What weapon would you rather carry, Allison?" she asked.

I glanced over at Maeve. She was drinking a cup of tea, her bare feet up on an overturned crate that said EXPLOSIVES on the side. She looked a little more rested after her short nap. Shame had had the sense to keep most of the house in working order. There were beds, a surprisingly nice kitchen, and a fairly well-stocked pantry.

I rubbed my palms down the sides of my jeans, wiping away sweat. Staring at the guns Shame had laid out on the coffee table made my skin crawl. I wasn't sure I could touch a gun, much less use one.

I didn't want to kill again. Not like that.

Bartholomew gave you little choice, my dad, who was still dead and still possessing a corner of my brain, said quietly. *Whatever advantage we have now, it is because of you. Of what you did to him.*

It was strange to hear my father talk about us—me, Zayvion, Shame, Terric, Hayden, Maeve, and Victor—like he was a part of our group, wanting the same things we wanted, fighting for the same things we were fighting for. Or maybe it wasn't so strange anymore. He'd helped us, helped me, more in the past few days than in my entire life.

And now that we had mutinied from the Authority, gone against Authority law—and, oh, yeah; did I mention I shot the man who had assigned himself as head of Portland's Authority?—we needed all the help we could get.

Even if that meant listening to the dead guy.

"I don't know," I said, answering Maeve's question. "Maybe I'll stick to a blade."

"Don't want to shoot a man, nice and clean," Shame said, "but you're more than happy to carve him up? You sure about that? Swords can be messy business."

"It's all messy business," I said. "And the only thing

I'm sure about is that I'm not going to decide this right now."

"Better sooner than later," Shame said.

"I'll do it in the morning."

Zay stopped running his thumb along the edge of his katana and sheathed it. He gave me a steady look. The same kind of measuring look that Victor, who I had thought was half asleep in the easy chair, and Terric, who was digging through the things on Shame's shelf, were giving me.

"What?" I asked.

"It is morning," Shame said. "Has been for hours now."

I closed my eyes and tipped my face up to the ceiling. Hells, I was tired. I didn't remember the last time I'd slept, didn't remember the last time I'd eaten. I smelled like old magic, death, and blood. And I was not going to pick up a gun, make another decision, or do another damn thing until I got clean and fed.

"Someone make breakfast, okay?" I looked back down from the ceiling. "I'm going to take a shower."

I strode down the hall, past the open kitchen area, where Hayden was already rummaging through cupboards, past the two guest bedrooms, where everyone had slept—except me. I'd spent my downtime sweating off nightmares and staring at the darkness while listening to make sure whoever was on watch was still awake and watching.

The last door on the right was the guest bathroom. I walked in and flicked on the lights.

I didn't know why Shamus had decided to buy a house. When we'd asked, he'd used his big innocent eyes on his mother and told her he hadn't bought it; he'd won it in a poker game.

More likely, he'd stolen it.

Whoever had built the thing was either a genius or a madman. It really was bolted into the cliff, the roofline beneath the road above that snaked the hill in hairpin curves; the hill was covered in sword fern and vine maple among the fir trees. If you weren't trying really hard to look for it, you wouldn't see the house at all. Not because of magic. No, nothing other than a perverse sense of architectural humor kept it hidden.

But for all that, it was decorated in a clean, modern style, with just enough nice touches to show that whoever had live here liked luxury and knew which luxuries mattered most.

And one of those luxuries was the shower. The thing took up half of the huge bathroom and had more sprays, mists, and other watery onslaughts than a November storm front. Dark marble and chrome hinted toward a man's aesthetic but didn't make the room feel cold.

I shucked out of every stitch I had on, hoped that Dad would do me the favor of not paying attention to me for the next twenty minutes or so, and turned on the shower.

The entire ceiling above the shower sprayed water like someone had nailed a rain cloud to the rafters. I stepped into that steady stream and closed my eyes, letting the water sluice away my pain.

But when I closed my eyes, all I saw were images of the Veiled—the ghosts of dead magic users—far too strong now, and growing stronger. The Veiled had always wandered the city—not that most people believed in them.

It didn't used to be a problem to share the city with dead magic users. But something had gone wrong with the Veiled. Worse, something had gone wrong with magic itself. Somehow, magic had been poisoned. The Veiled were carriers of that poison, biting, possessing, and killing people.

People such as my friend, Davy Silvers, who was infected by the Veiled; people such as Anthony Bell, who was dead.

The news outlets reported it as a fast-spreading virus. Nothing magical. But we knew different. And the one person who had been in a position to stop the spread of sickness and death was Bartholomew Wray.

He hadn't wanted to stop it. He'd wanted the disaster to reach massive proportions. That way the technology my father had invented to make magic accessible for the common magic user would be seen as unsafe. Deadly. Once it was destroyed, outlawed, magic would once again be under the singular control of the Authority.

Not that his hatred of my dad had helped much. He had planned to destroy more than just my dad's technology. He'd wanted to ruin his business, his wife, and me.

And he hadn't cared how many deaths it took for him to get his way. All of Portland could have fallen, and he wouldn't have cared.

So I'd shot him.

My thoughts skittered away from that—away from his death—and the back of my throat tasted sour. I'd stared him straight in the eyes and pulled the trigger.

I wasn't a killer.

No, that was a lie now.

I'd changed. I had killed. More than once. I didn't know what I was anymore.

Alive, Dad whispered from the back of my mind. Then, *Strong.*

Nothing like a dead man talking in my head while I was taking a shower to remind me that I had plenty of current problems that needed taking care of. One thing was for sure: I didn't want to talk morality with my father, of all people. I ignored him and got busy with the shampoo and soap and used a scrubby cloth over every inch of my skin.

Dad gave me the decency of privacy, or at least the

sense of it, since he didn't say anything more, and pulled far enough away in my mind that I couldn't feel him.

Problems. I had them. It was time to make a list:

One, I didn't know what was going to happen to the Authority now that Bartholomew was dead. Two, we had to find a way to cleanse magic, stop the Veiled, and get a cure to end the epidemic. Maybe that was really two through four. So five, I needed to find a way to cure Davy. And six, we were running out of options and allies.

In short, we were screwed.

I reached out to turn off the shower. Before my hands touched the handle, a flash of light filled the room, bringing with it the stink of hot copper and concrete. I squinted against the glare and pressed my back against the wall, tracing Block before I remembered I couldn't use magic without barfing.

Shit.

I shook the spell free, breaking it, then pushed off the wall and opened the shower door.

The flash of light was now a concentrated bolt of magic frozen midstrike at a ragged angle from the ceiling to the floor.

In the three seconds it took for that to register, I knew what the spell was.

Gate.

Something, or someone, was about to join me in the bathroom.

And here I was, all naked.

Go, me.

The lightning bolt burned black, then split in half, opening wide enough that I could see the arc of a distant blue sky against the ceiling lamps.

A man stepped through the Gate.

Tall, rugged, world worn, Roman Grimshaw, the ex-con, ex–Guardian of the gates, strode into the room. Ashes of the already-dying spell, the closing Gate, clung to his long leather jacket as the bolt of lightning faded to an afterimage in the steamy room.

For a moment there was no sound other than our breathing and water raining against tiles.

Roman held very still, his hands away from his body, no magic other than the ashes from the Gate on him. His frown slowly shifted to a look of surprise as he focused on the slightly damp, exceedingly naked me standing in front of him with my hands on my hips.

"You going to hand me a towel or what?" I asked.

That seemed to snap him out of his shock. He quickly turned and picked up the towel folded on the edge of the sink.

The bathroom door burst open.

Hey, just what I needed. More people in the bathroom with me and my birthday suit.

Roman spun to face Zayvion, who had a fistful of wicked Impact spell that snapped like a ball of red fire, and his blood dagger in the other hand already halfway through a Cleave spell.

"Peace," Roman said, with the slightest hint of his Scottish accent. He threw his hands out to the side, dropping my towel on the floor.

Neat.

Zay stopped drawing the Cleave and flicked a gaze at me. I gave him what I hoped to be a bored look and he went back to glaring at the ex–Guardian of the gates. He did not, I noted, drop the Impact spell.

While they were sizing up each other and the situation, all the warm copper-tasting steam was cooling on my bare skin. I shivered and turned off the water. Then I bent and got my own damn towel, shaking it once before wrapping it tightly around me.

No one said anything. No one moved.

Until Shame strode up to the door, a mug of coffee in his hand. "For Christ's sake, Grimshaw, use the frickin' front door. Is it some kind of requirement that all Guardians of the gates have to do that creepy stalker thing?"

"What are you doing here?" Zayvion asked.

"I have been hunting Leander and Isabelle," Roman said.

Straight to the point. I liked a man who didn't pre-amble.

"And?" Zay asked.

"They are no longer in Portland."

"Super interesting," I interrupted. "Really, just. But I'd rather hear it clothed. Take it outside, gentlemen."

"You're naked?" Shame said, trying to get a better look around Zayvion and Roman.

Zayvion canceled the Impact spell and motioned Grimshaw out into the hall with his blood blade.

"She's naked?" Shame asked again as Zayvion shoved his shoulder to make him turn around.

Zay closed the door so that only he could see into the room. "Are you all right?"

"Peachy. I don't think he expected to show up in a bathroom. It's hard to predict where gates will open, right?"

Zay paused. "For normal people. Roman can open a gate on the head of a pin." He gave me a look and shut the door behind him.

Fantastic. So Roman had intended to show up in the bathroom, alone, with me. Or maybe he just wanted to show up in the bathroom. I wondered how he even knew there would be a room here. He'd been in jail for years before Shame had wheedled his way into homeowner-ship.

More questions that needed answers. And how he knew we'd be here was just the beginning of them.

Devon Monk

The Allie Beckstrom Novels

*Using magic means it uses you back, and every spell
exacts a price from its user. But some people get out
of it by Offloading the cost of magic onto an innocent.
Then it's Allison Beckstrom's job to identify
the spell-caster...*

ALSO AVAILABLE IN THE SERIES

MAGIC TO THE BONE
MAGIC IN THE BLOOD
MAGIC IN THE SHADOWS
MAGIC ON THE STORM
MAGIC AT THE GATE
MAGIC ON THE HUNT

Learn more at
devonmonk.com

Available wherever books are sold or at
penguin.com